GENEROSITY

Richard Powers is the author of nine novels. *The Echo Maker* won the National Book Award and was a finalist for the Pulitzer Prize. Powers has received a MacArthur Fellowship, the Lannan Literary Award and the James Fenimore Cooper Prize for Historical Fiction. He lives in Illinois.

Also by Richard Powers:

The Echo Maker
The Time of Our Singing
Three Farmers on Their Way to a Dance
The Gold Bug Variations
Operation Wandering Soul
Galatea 2.2
Gain
Plowing the Dark

GENEROSITY

RICHARD POWERS

Atlantic Books
London

First published in the United States of America in 2009 by
Farrar, Straus & Giroux.

First published in Great Britain in hardback and export and airside trade
paperback in 2010 by Atlantic Books, an imprint of Atlantic Books Ltd.

This paperback edition published in Great Britain in 2011 by
Atlantic Books.

10 9 8 7 6 5 4 3 2 1

A CIP catalogue record for this book is available from the British Library.

ISBN: 978 1 84887 127 4

Printed in Great Britain by CPI Bookmarque, Croydon

Atlantic Books
An imprint of Atlantic Books Ltd
Ormond House
26–27 Boswell Street
London WC1N 3JZ

www.atlantic-books.co.uk

GENEROSITY

For JTK—

La vraie générosité envers l'avenir consiste à tout donner au présent.

—Camus

PART ONE

OF STRANGE LANDS AND PEOPLE

Exuberance carries us places we would not otherwise go—across the savannah, to the moon, into the imagination—and if we ourselves are not so exuberant we will, caught up by the contagious joy of those who are, be inclined collectively to go yonder.

—Kay Redfield Jamison, *Exuberance*

A man rides backward in a packed subway car. This must be almost fall, the season of revision. I picture him in the thick of bequest, tunneling beneath the *I Will* City, the world's twenty-fifth biggest urban sprawl, one wedged in the population charts between Tianjin and Lima. He hums some calming mantra to himself, a song with the name *Chicago* in it, but the train drowns out the tune.

He's just thirty-two, I know, although he seems much older. I can't see him well, at first. But that's my fault, not his. I'm years away, in another country, and the El car is so full tonight that everyone's near invisible.

Look again: the whole point of heading out anywhere tonight. The blank page is patient, and meaning can wait. I watch until he solidifies. He cowers in the scoop seat, knees tight and elbows hauled in. He's dressed for being overlooked, in rust jeans, maroon work shirt, and blue windbreaker with broken zipper: the camouflage of the non-aligned, circa last year. He's as white as anyone on this subway gets. His own height surprises him. His partless hair waits for a reprimand and his eyes halt midway between hazel and brown. His face is about six centuries out of date. He would make a great Franciscan novice in one of those mysteries set in a medieval monastery.

He cups a bag of ratty books on his lap. No; look harder: a ruggedized plastic sack inscribed with bright harvest cornucopia that issues the trademarked slogan, *Total Satisfaction . . . plus so much more!*

His spine curls in subway contrition, and his shoulders apologize for taking up any public space at all. His chin tests the air for the inevitable attack that might come from any direction. I'd say he's

3

headed to his next last chance. He tries to give his seat to a young Latina in a nurse's uniform. She just smirks and waves him back down.

Early evening, four dozen feet below the City on the Make: every minute, the train tunnels underneath more humans than would fit in a fundamentalist's heaven. Aboveground, it must be rainy and already dark. The train stops and more homebound workers press in, trickling September drizzle. This is the fifth year since the number of people living in cities outstripped those who don't.

I watch him balance a yellow legal pad on his toppling book sack. He checks through the pages, curling each back over the top of the pad. The sheets fill with blocks of trim handwriting. Red and green arrows, nervous maneuvers and counter-maneuvers, swarm over the text.

A forest of straphangers hems him in. Many are wired for sound. A damp man next to him drips on his shoes. Humanity engulfs him: phone receptionists for Big Four accounting firms. Board of Trade pit bulls, burned out by twenty-eight. Market researchers who've spent days polling focus groups on the next generation of portable deionizers. Purveyors and contractors, drug dealers, number crunchers, busboys, grant writers. Just brushing against them in memory makes me panic.

Advertisements crown the car's walls: *Outpsych your tyke. Want to know what makes the planet tick? Make your life just a little perfecter.* Every few minutes, a voice calls over the speakers: "If you observe any suspicious behavior or unattended packages . . ."

I force my eyes back down over the scribbler's left shoulder, spying on his notes. The secret of all imagination: theft. I stare at his yellow legal pages until they resolve. They're full of lesson plans.

I know this man. He's been fished from the city's adjunct-teacher pool, an eleventh-hour hire, still working on his first night's class even as the train barrels toward his South Loop station. The evidence is as clear as his all-caps printing: ethics has wrecked his life, and this fluke part-time night job is his last hope for rehabilitation. He never expected to land such a plum again. Death and resurrection: I know this story, like I wrote it myself.

The train wags, he pitches in his seat, and I don't know anything. I stop deciding and return to looking. A heading on the top of his pad's first page reads: Creative Nonfiction 14, Sect. RS: Journal and Journey.

A heavy teen in a flak jacket bumps him. He squeezes out a retreating smile. Then he resumes drawing red arrows, even now, two subway stops from his first night's class. As I always say: It's never too late to overprepare. His pen freezes in midair; he looks up. I glance away, caught spying. But his hand just hovers. When I look back, he's the one who's spying on someone else.

He's watching a dark-haired boy across the aisle, a boy with a secret quickening in his hands. Something yellow floats on the back of the boy's curled fist. His two knuckles pin a goldfinch by the ankles. The boy quiets the bird, caressing in a foreign tongue.

My adjunct's hand holds still, afraid that his smallest motion will scatter this scene. The boy sees him looking, and he hurries the bird back into a bamboo cylinder. My spy flushes crimson and returns to his notes.

I watch him shuffle pages, searching for a passage in green highlighter that reads *First Assignment*. The words have been well worked over. He strikes them out once more and writes: *Find one thing in the last day worth telling a total stranger.*

∞

Clearly he's terrified there may be no such thing. I see it in his spine: he'll bother no one with his day's prize, least of all a total stranger.

It's up to me to write his assignment for him. To describe the thing that this day will bring, the one that will turn life stranger than total.

∞

He gets out at Roosevelt, the Wabash side. He struggles up the stairs against the evening human waterfall. Remnants of the day shift still pour underground, keen on getting home tonight at a reasonable hour. Home before the early autumn rains wash away their subdivision. Home before Nikkei derivatives trigger a Frankfurt DAX panic. Before a rogue state sails a quick-breeding bioweapon through the St. Lawrence Seaway into Lake Michigan.

At street level, my adjunct is hit by the downtown's stagecraft. The granite gorges, the glass towers with their semaphores of light he's too close to read. To the northeast, the skyline mounts up in stunning ziggurats. His heart pumps at the blazing panorama, as it did when he was a boy gazing at World's Fair futures he would inhabit, any year now. Someone in the crowd clips his back, and he moves on.

Down a canyon to the east, he glimpses a sliver of lakefront: the strip of perfected coast that passes for *Chicago*. He has stood on the steps of the fabulous nineteenth-century Palace of Taxidermy and gazed north up the sheer city face—the boats in the marina, the emerald park, the epic cliff of skyscrapers curling into the two blues—and felt, despite everything, this place pushing toward something sublime.

Off to his left, dumpsters the size of sperm whales swarm a block-long abyss, each overflowing with last century's smashed masonry. One more angel giant rises from the pit, its girders taking on a sapphire skin. Luxury skybox living: late throes of a South Loop renaissance. Last year's homeless are all hidden away in shelters on the city's perimeter. Chicago hasn't looked better since the fire. The place is after something, a finish line beyond any inhabitant's ability to see, let alone afford.

He wants to fetch his legal pad from his sack and make some notes. *Rule one: Get it down before it goes.* He'd like to get this down—something about the furnace of renewal, the fall and rise of any given block on the way to this city's obscure goal. But he keeps to the stream of rush-hour foot traffic, afraid of getting arrested for suspicious activity. He pulls up at the entrance of Mesquakie College of Art, a steel-framed limestone temple from back in the age when skyscrapers topped out at a dozen stories.

∞

No, you're right: those streets don't really run that way. That neighborhood is a little off. The college isn't quite there; it's not *that* college.

This place is some other Second City. This Chicago is Chicago's in vitro daughter, genetically modified for more flexibility. And these words are not journalism. Only journey.

∞

His name is Russell Stone, or so he tells the security guard in the Mesquakie lobby. The guard asks to see a college ID; Russell Stone has none. He tries to explain his last-minute hiring. The guard can't find Russell on a printout. He makes several calls, repeating the name with increasing suspicion until Russell Stone is ready to apologize for believing that the job might ever have been his.

At last the guard hangs up. He explains with simple scorn that Stone missed the cutoff date. Against his better judgment, he issues Stone a security badge, shaking his head all the while.

By the time Russell finds his room, his eight students are already encamped around its oval table, deep in a dozen discussions. He grasps at once how badly he has mis-prepped. He fingers his carefully selected textbook through the thick plastic sack—Frederick P. Harmon's *Make Your Writing Come Alive*. Too late, he sees: the book's a ridiculous blunder. This group will mock it into the hereafter.

I should feel sorry for the man. But what in the name of second chances was he thinking?

In the doorway, he tries a feeble smile; no one looks up. He makes his way, head bobbing, to the gap in the student oval. To hide his shaking hands and call the group to attention, he dumps the sack out on the table. He lifts up Harmon, cocks an eyebrow at the group. The copy in his hands flaps open to a highlighted page:

Convincing characters perform differently for different audiences, in different flavors of crisis. We know them by their changing strategies, often better than they know themselves.

"Everyone find a copy?"

No one says anything.

"Right. Ahhh . . ." He flips through his legal pad. "Let's . . . see . . . Don't tell me!" One or two students chuckle deniably. "Oh, yeah. Roll call. How about a name, biographical tidbit, and life philosophy? I'll start. Russell Stone. By day, mild-mannered editor with a local magazine. Life philosophy . . ."

For convenience, I give him mine.

"When you're sure of what you're looking at, look harder."

He glances at the woman to his left, all purple and steel. "So who are *you*, when you're not at home?"

∞

I wish I could make out Stone's students better. I can see how they disturb him. But I just can't see *them* in any detail. They're hiding in the sullen, shiny performance of youth.

The circle starts with Sue Weston, a small, hard woman who must run with both wolves and scissors. She has recently been pierced in all her few soft spots. She looks at the world slant, from underneath a lopsided pageboy she cuts herself. Public judgment excites her so much it's scary. She gives her life philosophy: "The shittiest five-second advertising jingle is superior to any symphony, if more people hum it."

A big, bleached, omnivorous woman to Sue's right barrels her way through the ritual intro. Charlotte Hullinger has lived at thirteen addresses in twenty-two years. Dozens of sketches on rag paper tumble out of her overstuffed backpack. The left side of her mouth pulls back in permanent skepticism. She scares me, shrugging off her credo: "I'll try anything once. Twice, if it's nice."

Cowboys crawl across Adam Tovar's shirt and zoo animals parade around his baggy trousers. It's his universal outfit, from rooftop croquet games to his forebears' funerals. He says, "My great-grandfather was a miner so that my grandfather could be an engineer so that my father could be a poet so that I could be a goofball." The others give him the laugh that's all he really wants in life. He tells of being on a cruise ship last summer that was taken over by Somali pirates, one of whom he's still in e-mail touch with. "The only thing I know for sure is you can never be too misinformed."

Roberto Muñoz—long, gaunt, head shaved, and haunted—never stops checking the exit. He should see a doctor about those skin lesions. I picture his parents walking into the country across the Chihuahuan desert, at night, though that's my own clichéd noise. For the last four years, painting has kept him off crystal meth. "Play the hand you're dealt," he insists. "Everybody's got to play their own deal."

The cowering figure next to Roberto whispers, "Kiyoshi Sims." He disappears behind the bridge of his black glasses, as if the group will forget him if he holds still long enough. Machines are his people; among them, he's widely and well loved. He could make $100 million by accident on a world-changing digital patent and not be able to figure out how to buy a condo with it. "I'm not sure about life philosophy," he stammers. "I haven't given it much thought."

"Mason Mason," Mason Mason announces. Worked briefly loading luggage at O'Hare, until they discovered he'd lied on his application. Worked briefly as a youth counselor, until someone heard what he was counseling the youth. He scratches his ear and announces, "More people probably want you dead than want you alive."

Next to last comes John Thornell, a massive, impassive monolith. People bother him less than snow bothers a mountain. He tells the class about his current project, a series of 365 pen-and-ink drawings, each one meticulously re-creating a different product logo he uses in daily life. His philosophy comes out robotic: "The supreme human emotion has to be boredom."

Stone's students perform themselves, each a work in progress. Their eyes fill with the designs they'll draw, the clips they'll shoot, the hypermedia they'll conjure. Russell Stone remembers them all from ten years ago, when he was one of them. He already pities their descent into noncreative nonfiction.

Introductions come full circle, to the slight, short, ethnically ambiguous woman to his left. She's clothed in bleach-streaked jeans and a canary tunic, silver bracelets up both auburn forearms, and a scarf in bright Mediterranean spirals over her shoulders. Her curly, dark hair is pulled back in a profuse ponytail. She waits her turn in a blush of listening.

She, I can see in detail.

"Let me guess," Russell Stone says. "Amzwar?" The last name remaining on his list.

She smiles at his foolishness. "Yes! Amzwar. Thassadit Amzwar." Her accent is unplaceable. She says she's a Berber Algerian, from *Kabylie*, via Algiers, via Paris, via Montreal. Her eyes are claret. She sits inside her nimbus, chatting with ease. He thinks he hears her say she fled from the Algerian civil war. He wants to ask her to repeat herself. Instead he panics and prompts her for her life philosophy.

"Life is too good for philosophies," she tells them. "I try my best to decide no more than God."

∞

My eyes adjust: dark, cracked linoleum and broken-sashed windows. Fluorescent lights humming like a prop plane hang low over a circle of students filled with that first-day mix of nerves and thrill, as if anything might still happen, even this late in history, even in Chicago.

The first class goes so well it scares Russell Stone. The students pretty much hijack the syllabus. Each of them is starved for *fresh*.

Even the older ones still believe in a destiny sure to reveal itself, any semester now. Three of them admit they're here because Journal and Journey is the easiest way for visual majors to complete the writing requirement. Words are not the shape their desperation takes; sentences can't hope to survive the flood of images. But who knows? Even a journal entry might someday become a short video.

Mason Mason asks the obvious. "Why don't we write online? Aren't journals just dead blogs?"

Russell has prepped three days for this question. He defends private writing against writing for any stranger with a search engine. "I want you to think and feel, not sell. Your writing should be an intimate meal, not dinner theater."

They shrug at his nostalgia. They'll take a spin in the Wayback Machine, just for the sheer novelty.

Sue Weston details her current artwork. "It's called 'Magpie.' I stand in Daley Plaza, jotting down the things people say into their cells. Then I post it on a tumblelog. Amazing, what people will tell a street full of strangers."

Roberto Muñoz whispers, "I'm amazed you think that's ethical." A hoot comes from the group, and soon it's an art-student free-for-all. Russell Stone watches his lesson plan vanish.

Adam Tovar describes his automatic spirit writing. "I just let it come." After a roll-call vote, the class decides that ghosts do indeed exist and are the soul's upload to virtual storage.

"Writing always comes from beyond the grave, anyway," John Thornell says. "I mean, either the author or audience is already dead, or will be soon."

The Algerian watches fascinated, like a child fresh from months in the sick bay, at a tennis match under a spotless sky. The others ignore her, with pretend nonchalance. But when Thassadit does raise her finger, the room freezes. "In my country? During the Time of Horrors . . . ?"

Russell loses her words. Something about her father being shot for writing a letter, but she speaks so serenely it must be a metaphor. Stone knows nothing about Algeria except that it's a former French colony with an astronomically impossible flag. Their civil war is news to him. The whole world is news to him.

The Berber's ready grin unnerves the Americans, who return to the ethics of eavesdropping. She resumes watching them, hands peaceful on the table, centered in herself, smiling through the discussion as if it's the most entertaining feature film.

This first night's class runs overtime before Russell can get through a quarter of his notes. He assigns them twenty pages from *Make Your Writing Come Alive*, half apologizing for the text, as if someone else chose it. He gives them their first journal assignment, the one about rescuing one fragment from their last day worth telling a perfect stranger. They'll read their entries out loud together, two nights from now. "Have fun," he tells them, avoiding the eyes of the Algerian. "Surprise me."

Then he stumbles back out through Building Security into the September night. The Loop has quieted. Its 3-D lattice of light now looks like the twitch-grid computer games his brother is addicted to. Nine million lives from here out to the horizon, and God only knows how many art schools calling it quits for the night. Night classes in Lima will follow in an hour. Day classes in Tianjin are already under way.

It strikes me that my adjunct has never heard of Tianjin. He boards the northbound Red Line at Roosevelt, avoiding the sparsely populated cars. The train emerges from its grotto into a canyon flanked by the backsides of brick apartments scaffolded in wooden fire escapes. Tonight's glow turns tenements into upscale condos. He's elated by how well his first class has gone. He spends the subway ride scribbling an account of the last two hours into his own journal. He describes his students' willful naïveté and fearless self-invention. *What would life be like,* he writes, *if art students finally had their revolution?*

Russell Stone doesn't answer his own question. I watch him trying to decide no more than God.

In his studio apartment in Logan Square, he makes himself a one-hand sandwich of wilted veg and cheese, from which he scrapes a thin skin of mold. Then he sits down to find *Kabylie*. He wants to see it on a printed page, not online. He finds it in the atlas. In the Atlas Mountains. The place is a rugged hideaway, a separatist hot spot full of goats and olive trees, a land graced by all accounts with the most aromatic and beautiful spring known on earth.

He lies in his dark bed, replaying the night's conversation. Creative nonfiction runs through his head. He needs to be up in four hours, for the long ride back to his daytime editing shift. After forty minutes of mimicking sleep, he rolls over and turns on the light. His journal still waits on the nightstand. Beneath his keyed-up subway entry, he adds: *She must be the world's most blissful refugee.*

∞

I give myself a first assignment: Russell Stone in one hundred and fifty words.

Start with this: His earliest crime involved a book about a boy whose marvelous scribbling comes alive. He wrecked every page with crayon, aping the trick. His mother never really forgave him.

He hates books with teacher protagonists. He avoids stories set in any school. He can't think of a single bildungsroman that seems useful anymore, or beautiful, or even merely true.

Taped to the inside of the desk he inherited from his grandfather, he keeps the Schiller quote found in Melville's desk after his death: "Keep true to the dreams of thy youth." His forgotten note awaits the discovery of death's garage sale.

He dreads the question *What music do you listen to?*

He'd be pleased to know that in my mind, he's still mostly white space.

Once, out of character, he scrawled on the bathroom stall at the magazine where he edits, "Manuscripts don't burn."

∞

Stone hasn't kept a journal for years. He shed the personal memoir right around the time that the MyBits Age took off. Self-examination leaves him seasick.

Once he kept florid diaries. From sixteen to twenty-four, he couldn't see, hear, smell, or taste anything without polishing it into a perfect paragraph. He hoarded great descriptions to spend later, as needed. Before his private wipeout, he filled a whole shelf with spiral notebooks. He has tried to destroy them, but is too cowardly. They're in his mother's crawl space, awaiting discovery by a future stranger.

But even as he shrinks from it, the world graduates to runaway first person. Blogs, mashups, reality programming, court TV, chat shows, chat rooms, chat cafés, capital campaigns, catalog copy, even war-zone journalism all turn confessional. Feelings are the new facts. Memoir is the new history. Tell-alls are the new news.

He looks up his students online. All but two have flourishing personal pages. They reel off more intimate specifics than Stone has the courage to read: favorite music, favored drugs, preferred sexual practices, hated movies, crimes they've committed, appetites they've fed, celebrities they would kill or do or be if they weren't themselves . . .

Why this is happening Russell Stone can't say. He himself gave up journals when he realized his life story held no interest even for himself. *No: I'm deciding too much, again.* He gave them up overnight, shortly after tasting his first public success, in his fourth year in Tucson, just after completing his master of fine arts.

In the course of a dozen dizzy weeks, three leading magazines took his pieces for publication. His work was that contradiction in terms: *creative nonfiction*. Back then, people still called them *personal essays*. Russell Stone wrote them to amuse Grace Cozma, the rising star of the Arizona writing program, winner of the coveted Avignon residency, and—still bewildering—ten-time visitor of Russell Stone's own bed. Grace had told him, with an electrifying squeeze of the ribs on her way out the door to France, that letters during her year abroad would not be unwelcome, providing they amused her. So he wrote her long rambles, as if they were life itself.

He described his run-ins with Southwestern drifters. He told her about the old desert rat who ran a collapsing gem-and-mineral shop not far from Saguaro West. The man claimed to have once done some "groundbreaking work in geology," swearing to Stone that he was just $10 million short of producing a working prototype of a lightning farm that would "shoehorn the Wahhabis out of the West Wing once and for all."

Russell polished up the mordant letter to Grace and mailed it to a famous glossy, on a long-shot lark. When—craziest of fantasies—the magazine took the story, Stone went back to his letters to Grace and polished up another.

In his second piece, he recounted his fast-food-lunch conversation with a Tohono O'odham former EMT who'd just received a two-year suspended sentence for being up on the roof of a clinic with four buddies, a couple of pairs of defibrillator paddles, and a box of 200-gram tubes of paddle gel. "We weren't doing anything, really." The second reputable magazine Stone sent it to jumped on it.

The third essay transcribed Stone's meeting with a narrow-eyed vagrant outside El Con Mall who wanted Stone's opinion on nerve regeneration, water-powered cars, and the Pseudo-Baldwin. The man warned Russell not to cross him: "I can put the word out to a continent-wide street-person network that'll make your life hell from Miami to Vancouver . . . We've even got contacts in the European Union." At Grace's urging, Russell submitted the piece to the Valhalla of New York literary weeklies. The day the impossible acceptance letter arrived, he called Grace in France. They giggled at each other for half an hour.

The secret of these pieces lay in the hapless narrator: bewildered victim of the world's wackiness. "I seem to be the kind of flavorless, neutral guy whom the truly hard-core outsiders in this life claim for one of their undiscovered own." The reporter was exactly that goggle-eyed Midwestern rube ripe for conversion whom Grace always found so unwittingly hilarious.

Overnight, these three pieces changed Russell Stone's life. The magazine payments let him quit his desperate community newspaper job and write essays full-time. Agents called, wanting to represent him. An editor at a major New York house wrote to ask if he had enough pieces for a book.

Public radio commissioned him to write a piece for an omnibus program broadcast on 350 local stations. He wrote and performed a brief burlesque about trying to understand the musings of his Hindu dermatologist, whose sentences began in the *Physicians' Desk Reference* and ended in *The Ramayana*. The producer declared him as droll a voice actor as he was a writer, and offered another ten-minute spot whenever Stone wanted.

"Bravo," Grace wrote. "How much did they pay you? Enough for a transatlantic ticket and a week of B and B's?"

Then a letter came, nestled in a batch of reader mail:

Dear Mr. Russell Stone,

The Tohono O'odham Nation faces many challenges. You have just added to them. Charlie Melendez is a decent young man who got in trouble. You've profited by mocking both him and our people.

I hope your writing will be less destructive in the future.
Sincerely,

Phyllis Manuel, San Xavier District

Stone agonized for several days over an apology, which he mailed out just before the fan-mail bag delivered a new land mine:

14

Mr. Stone,

    I'm not sure why anyone would laugh at a man who is mentally ill. But I'm willing to forgive you, if you can help me find my father, Stan Newstetter, the man you call "Stan Newton" in your story, "Ear to the Network . . ."

Stone had to confess to Mr. Newstetter's daughter that he hadn't really met the man outside El Con, but in a strip mall somewhere in the vast retail wastelands along Speedway, the precise coordinates of which he'd failed to write down. When Julie Newstetter wrote back and asked why he'd said El Con, he had no answer except the name's comical sound.

A month later, Charlie Melendez tried unsuccessfully to take his own life.

∞

So you know this story: *Lord Jim*, or a plot to that effect. Not that Stone collapsed all at once. I see him shriveling gradually, over many years. He never told anyone about the letters—not his mother, not his brother, not Grace. He wrote another radio piece, this one about his Jack Russell terrier's misadventures in obedience school. The producer found it less biting than the first. Stone set to work on a fantasia on his phobia of Adam's apples—about his recurring fear that they were subcutaneous creatures trying to escape. Grace loved it; pure Stone, she decided. But he couldn't bring himself to publish the essay. It just seemed so pointlessly, weirdly *personal*.

He started a wry, detailed description of his mother's obsession with food supplements. He lingered over her enthusiasm for DHEA, with which she pared herself down to four hours of sleep a night. He described how kavalactones got her elected to the school board. But four thousand words into the portrait, he realized he couldn't possibly publish it, let alone mail it to Grace. He couldn't imagine what he'd been thinking, ridiculing his own flesh and blood for anyone to read.

He wrote an account of Pima County estate auctions. Every magazine he sent it to rejected it as polite and lifeless. He composed several short nature features involving no people at all. When even the nature magazines asked him to liven up his accounts with a little quirky presence, he lost heart.

Grace, back from France, called him from New York. She was

having trouble finishing her novel. Come out, she begged. Just for an escapade. Or at least send something fresh to read. "Something to unfreeze me. You know: the stuff you do. The wicked stuff. The grotesques. Everybody I'm reading is a patronizing bore."

He closed his eyes, gripped the phone, and laid out his sins for her, like a literary prize. He told her about Stan Newstetter. She laughed at him, harder than she'd ever laughed at his stories. Book-club moms were podcasting their teenage daughters' first sexual forays, and he was beating himself up for misrepresenting street people? He was crazy. Worse: he was threatening to become tedious.

He told her about Charlie Melendez. She couldn't understand. "You didn't make that man hurt himself. He volunteered everything."

He confessed that he hadn't run the piece past Charlie before publication.

They argued. She hung up on him. He vowed he wouldn't pick up for her the next couple of times she called. She never gave him the chance. Eighteen months later, her novel was published. It included a hilarious portrait of a small-town reporter terrified that his human interest stories were returning to haunt him.

He went back to his community newspaper job. But his interview subjects no longer opened up to him. After half a year, he lost all ability to put together a basic lifestyle feature. He considered returning to grad school, to train as a political correspondent or economics reporter.

He could no longer read anything even vaguely confessional. Intimate revelations or domestic disclosures creeped him out. He dosed himself with popular science and commodity histories—how the spice trade or the cultivation of the bee set mankind on an unforeseen destiny.

Best of all, he liked the white space, the virgin territory bordering a page. All his life he used to ink up that space, fill it with passionate editorial: *Couldn't have said it better myself* or *Stop this argument before it kills again!* Now he no longer wrote in books. In fact, he started making the rounds of Bookman's stores, buying up the best impersonal books faster than he could read them, just to save them from scribblers.

∞

He left Tucson. He returned to Aurora, to live with his mother in his boyhood home in the Fox Valley. His brother was still there, working for a satellite-dish company. Russell got a job in construction. The clean, repetitive tasks were best. He loved to staple insulation, to cut and nail large square pieces of Sheetrock to freshly plumbed studs. When he was in the flow, even his boss's hate-mongering talk radio didn't bother him.

He installed things for his mother: new kitchen cabinets, which she loved; oak bookshelves, which she couldn't fill. He dated some-times—kind women who were after exactly nothing. Many nights, he and his brother played long matches of deferential Ping-Pong in the basement on the warped table of their childhood. He read himself to sleep on *Silkworms and Civilization* and *A Small Guide to the Big Bang*.

He went to his ten-year high-school reunion. The prospect held no more dread than any working day. He didn't mind listening to his successful classmates' achievements. He almost enjoyed telling his own riches-to-rags story. Confession was his only penance.

A former buddy from the sophomore year 4 × 100 relay was intrigued. "You're a published writer?"

Was, Russell corrected.

The buddy—accomplished deadbeat throughout his youth—had hit on a publishing scheme that threatened to turn him into a philan-thropist. He'd founded a self-improvement magazine called *Becoming You*. Foods, workouts, lifestyles, finance: one of thousands, yes. But *Becoming You* had a twist: all the copy was subscriber-generated. And all subscriber-contributors were paid in quantities of advertisers' goods. Write a feature on how micronutrients reversed your declining memory, and you won a year's supply of Pom-a-Grenade antioxidant cocktail. Advertising exposure, underwritten costs, deeply involved subscribers, and the wisdom of crowds combined to leverage the zeit-geist.

Come to Chicago, the buddy told Russell Stone. Become a part of *Becoming You*.

Russell demurred: he no longer wrote for publication. But the buddy didn't need Stone's writing. He needed Stone to turn scores of semiliterate, fervent testimonials into something readable.

The offer felt oddly appealing. True, the pieces would be *personal* in the worst way. But the person in question wouldn't be Russell Stone. Ghosting for amateurs was the perfect contrition.

Russell worked the job as if volunteering for a humanitarian

NGO. With his new income, he found a Logan Square studio and decorated it with dozens of pastel scenes that he drew, now that Ping-Pong no longer filled his evenings. The ten-by-ten-inch pictures showed bright, fluid human figures caught in the process of becoming lakes, clouds, or trees.

Say he eventually fell in with Marie White, a giving soul who loved to come over and read in bed next to Russell while he edited. They never chafed over anything, except his paintings. Marie thought he had a gift, and people with gifts were morally obligated to develop them. Russell just laughed at her, which stung Marie into silence.

After fourteen months, Marie wrote him a full-page note on Matisse stationery saying she was afraid that Russell might be melancholic, which kind of made her love him, but she couldn't afford to sacrifice her life to his disease. She had to get on with making her own future, and she hoped that Russell would do the same. She was thinking of starting to see someone—a kind gallery owner, in fact. And if Russell ever finally realized how nice his paintings were, she could put him in touch . . .

Becoming You took up the slack. Editing gave the same pleasure as hanging Sheetrock. He fixed predications, aligned parallel structures, undangled participles, unmixed metaphors, and collared runaway modifiers. He ran a comb through the tangled thickets of prose until they almost shone. He went into the River North office three days a week, and he worked three more out of his apartment. Consummate tedium became his art. For two years, he kept to his verbal trade, hoping to sink without a ripple beneath the earth's crust. He could edit *Becoming You* for the rest of his life, provided he died in early middle age.

He edited a piece written by an administrative secretary at Mesquakie College about how to fight depression by feeding squirrels. The grateful woman alerted him to an emergency hiring in the Writing Department. A memoirist who taught the Journal and Journey course had taken unpaid leave after a bad episode with mood enhancers that made him travel to San Francisco and assault a blogger who'd insulted one of his published reminiscences about his father.

To Russell Stone's astonishment, he met the job's prerequisites. He had the degree and prestigious publications, albeit none for eight years. With just a month to staff the course, the college was ready to take anyone. The interview felt weirdly furtive, as if Russell were defrauding a credit union.

He got the job and crammed for three weeks, prep that the opening night's class scattered to the winds. But that night goes so well that now, for the first time in years, he imagines himself, with something like shock, becoming someone quite different again, by this time next semester.

∞

From where I sit, the whole human race did something stupid when young—pulled some playful stunt that damaged someone. The secret of survival is forgetting. If evolution favored conscience, everything with a backbone would have hanged itself from the ceiling fan eons ago, and invertebrates would once again be running the place.

∞

"The Genie and the Genome"—final cut—opens with that relentless, digital techno-throb that stands for *coming soon.* Out of the pulsing blackness emerges a face Donatello might have cast, successfully refuting middle age. The eyebrows arch. The mouth twitches shyly and confides:

> Enhancement. Why shouldn't we make ourselves better
> than we are now? We're incomplete. Why leave some-
> thing as fabulous as life up to chance?

The impish face turns golden and explodes. Each shiny shard tumbles away into more throbbing blackness.

Another face fades in from the void, a big, gruff, empirical Friar Tuck.

> Insane? No, I wouldn't say Thomas Kurton is insane. I
> might say profoundly nutty. But Darwin was nuts too,
> right?

Tuck shrugs, and his shoulder ripple starts a whirlpool that washes him away. The smiling Donatello rises from the flood.

A lot of people think this is all science fiction. But then, we live in a country where 68 percent of folks don't believe in evolution . . .

His face tears in two and rolls up into a double helix. Out of that spiral appears a woman with straight brown hair and eyes as sad as a bloodhound's. In a clipped Midlands accent, she declares:

One-fifth of human genes have already been patented. You have to pay a license fee just to look at them. People like Thomas Kurton buy and sell genetic material like it's movie rights . . .

She turns into a sand painting that the wind scatters. Next comes a quick, cross-fade cavalcade of talking heads:

He plays at life like it's a German board game . . .
The man made two fortunes by the age of thirty-five . . .
It's not really about profit, for Thomas. It's about ingenuity . . .
This is not your grandfather's scientific method . . .

The British bloodhound returns to declare:

He's driven by a massively dangerous altruism.

Kurton fades back, his face morphing into other instances of itself:

Superdrugs, smart drugs. Healthier people. Stronger people. Smarter people . . .

He turns into a watercolor, whose brushstrokes reassemble into Friar Tuck:

You do know that Thomas is going to live forever?

Thomas Kurton swims up again from the abyss:

The first person to live to one hundred and fifty has already been born.

The British bloodhound pushes back a limp hank of hair from her weary face.

> I don't want to live in his world. I do not look forward to the day when people will have to pay a royalty to have a child.

Her pall gives way again to Donatello's daybreak.

> We're heading toward something glorious. Something better than anyone alive can imagine.

The close-ups relax into expansive midrange. A tall, bright woman in surgical scrubs strolls through a clean room at a biotech facility. She turns, removes her sterile cap, and shakes out a mass of flaxen hair.

> Is Thomas Kurton the villain in a morality fable gone terribly wrong? Or is he the hero of a noble experiment that's just about to pay off? No matter how the future judges him, he's already helping the present to spin . . .
> *Over the Limit.*

As the host's Mid-Atlantic accent shapes these three last words, they animate, strobing in dozens of languages, spinning off mathematical proofs, chemical symbols, and physical equations until the entire laboratory is buried in bits of self-replicating information.

∞

Establishing shot: a crazy-cantilevered, glass-skinned building near Kendall Square, Cambridge, one of those prestige-designer palaces that look like the solution to a logic puzzle.

Interior: the big-windowed corner office reserved for high-volume grant winners. Ambient sounds of wind and trickling water fill the room. On a five-foot-wide LCD panel across one wall, wild landscapes cross-fade into one another.

Close-up: Thomas Kurton seated behind a swept-wing desk that looks invisible to radar. A complex pneumatic chair props up his spine whi..

hands work with the detachment of someone throwing the I Ching. More screens dot the glass desktop. He speaks into one, brushes two fingers across another, dragging data in changing formation across the parade ground.

Voice-over, the cool voice of Tonia Schiff, the video journalist who hosts this world:

> Thomas Kurton made his first splash at twenty-eight, when his PhD research helped lead to the creation of transgenic cows that produced disease-curing proteins in their milk. He formed his first biotech company soon after he got his first academic job. At Harvard, he plowed his pharmaceutical farming profits back into the search for a bacterial catalyst for fermenting bio-butanol from sugar beets. He spun off this search, too, into a success-ful venture . . .

The ginger-headed figure dispatches brisk communiqués. Between commands, he leans over to his desk's long glass return, and from a stash of hundreds of capsules and tablets, he selects two dozen rust-colored supplements, washing them down with a large bottle of Swiss spring water.

> At the Wyde Institute, Kurton helped to develop a tech-nique called rapid gene signature reading. Using it, he has produced three landmark association studies, isolat-ing complexes of genes correlated with susceptibility to anxiety, childhood hyperactivity, and depression . . .

The ginger man waves a matchbook-sized device in the air. The room dims into a hushed dusk. He spins to face the picture win-dow behind him, gazing out on a cluster of glass buildings oozing venture capital. He tips up in the chair, closes his eyes, and starts to meditate.

> He has founded seven companies and advises fifteen more. He serves on the editorial board of six scientific journals while holding positions with three different uni-

versities. He races in triathlons and breeds exhibition-quality zebra finches. In his spare time, he writes ecstatic pieces about the coming transhuman age that electrify hundreds of thousands of readers . . .

Close-up of his right wrist: a red medical-alert bracelet instructs the finders of his dead body to act quickly, administer calcium blockers and blood thinner, pack his corpse in ice water, balance its pH, and call the 800 number of a firm that will helicopter in paramedics to begin cryonic suspension.

The view out the window darkens and the sound of electronic surf starts up again. He swings back around to the circle of screens and resumes conducting a symphony of scientific management. In a sound bridge, his cheerful voice says:

I don't see why, given enough time and creativity, we humans can't make ourselves over into anything we want.

A jump cut, and Tonia Schiff, the amused show host, is sitting in a rocker in a flagstone-and-cedar cabin. Her clothes are a little young for her—a gypsy shirt and knit gilet with pleated floaty skirt. She's a parody of genetic fitness as it approaches forty. Her lips curl as the scientist finishes his thought.

Now when you say "anything . . ."

A reverse shot reveals Kurton—in moth-eaten flannel—grinning and tipping his chin up and down.

Well, look: we've been remaking ourselves for ten thousand years. Every moment of our lives, we do something that some previous incarnation of humanity would consider godly. We simply can't know our upper limits. All we can do is keep exploring them.

He reaches into the vest pocket of his ratty jacket and pulls out a Moleskine. He opens the soft notebook and hands it to her.

I carry this around with me. My mantra.

The shot reverses are clean and crisp. Tonia Schiff takes the notebook and reads:

> *"Our duty, as men and women, is to proceed as if limits to*
> *our ability did not exist. We are collaborators in creation.*
> Teilhard de Chardin." Wasn't he a Christian mystic?

Kurton grins.

> Nothing mystical about deep genomic understanding!
> It's just good science.

∞

Stone is more solid to me the second night of class. A breeze off the lake slows him as he walks from the Roosevelt stop to Mesquakie. He waits at a vendor window for a veggie wrap and green tea. Someone presses a flyer into his hand: *Did We Cause Darfur?* He mumbles a thank-you and pretends to read. Walking while sipping, he passes a clothing boutique—turbaned women in paramilitary jumpsuits. Two stores down is Prosthetechs: *1,000+ mobile, wearable, portable, and sportable electronic devices!* He lifts his head: three miles of this, from here through the Gold Coast. The city wants to burn him for fuel, and he's fine with that. Anything to be useful.

Surly art students fill the college lobby in nervous knots, planning the world's next essential, interactive, networked-art trend, one that will change the way the race sees itself. They remind him how it feels, to imagine you have the right to excite another human. He skirts past them tonight, careful to make no more than accidental eye contact.

Up on floor seven, in the dingy, fluorescent-humming nest, he comes on Mason, Charlotte, and Adam debating the merits of garage bands he's never heard of. He was an avid fan once, but these names sound like complex synthetic chemicals or villages scattered across Kyrgyzstan. "Are they running out of available garage band names?" he asks. The students laugh, at least. "Aren't they running out of garages, by now?"

The Kabyle woman isn't there. Russell Stone wilts, sure that he said something last time to make her drop the course. She has disappeared, like a nighttime life-changing insight he has forgotten to jot down. Confidence failing, Stone asks for volunteers to read their first entry. One thing worth telling a total stranger. Adam Tovar demurs. "Mine isn't ready yet. The story part is done; I just have to go back and put in the symbols." John Thornell launches into a clinical account of two policemen chasing a screaming teenager into the courtyard of John's apartment building. The tasers are just coming out when Thassa Amzwar appears in the doorway.

She's shorter than Stone thought. She's wearing a kind of needlework, coral-colored shift. She could be from southern Italy. But her round face shines with precisely the light he remembers, the flushed look announcing that the most remarkable thing has happened to her, just now, down this hall, outside this building, on the streets of this improbable city. A thing that redeems everyone, for years to come. No apology in her eyes for being late; just a rash smile for her assembled, long-lost friends. She takes a seat, her silver-bangled wrist grazing Sue's shoulder, her lilac fingernails curling around Charlotte's elbow in greeting.

All eight of them grow an inch more alert. John stumbles through another half a sentence then backs off, claiming the rest of the entry is too rough to share. "Roughness is the only thing *worth* sharing," Russell claims. The others flip through their pages, eyes down, stripped of their art-student élan.

No volunteers. Maybe it's suburban diffidence, the Islands of the Blessed deferring to the edge of the scorched Sahara. Or maybe they're just soaking in the glow of this woman, her eerie contentment. They shuffle their journals, glancing sidelong, checking to see if they've made her up.

"We're reading out loud?" Thassa asks. Her glee confers with everyone. "May I go next?"

Before Stone can wonder how she learned her modal verbs better than the native speakers, she starts her entry. Her voice is one of those mountain flutes, somehow able to weave a second melody around the one it plays. Russell misses the gist of the words, he's so wrapped up in the cadence of the sentences. It's something out of the dawn of myth, set in a Chicago all but animist. One thing worth telling a total stranger, and the thing is this: an ancient woman, hoisting her aluminum walker up the Grand Staircase of the Cultural Center at the rate of one step a minute.

The ascent is glacial, the staircase infinite, the climber a Wednesday-afternoon Sisyphus mounting toward the world's largest Tiffany dome. The worn marble steps droop like cloth under the feet of a century of ghosts. But every word of Thassa's description lifts the climber toward the light. By the third step, Russell realizes he's never looked hard at anyone. By the top of the stairs, a sharp blue filament of need makes him want to see what will happen to the species, long after he's dead.

"Shit," Sue Weston says, when Thassa is done. "Girlfriend? You expect me to read mine, after that?"

They all laugh, and laughing, Russell remembers to breathe. Roberto Muñoz shudders in his loose flak jacket, rubs his shaved, plum-colored head with one cupped palm. "Thank you for that," he murmurs. "Serious thanks. Makes me look forward to getting decrepit." He shoots Thassa a look. "How old are you, anyway?"

She's twenty-three, it turns out, give or take an era.

The others read, while the air is still jazzed with the colors of that ascent. They compete for approval, each of them fueled by Thassa's encouraging nods. Affection threatens to replace all other texts. Algeria is nowhere, and Chicago a place just now become visible.

The night ends before they get a chance to take a look at the assignment from *Make Your Writing Come Alive*. Russell scrambles to summarize Frederick P. Harmon's thesis:

> Unless you care for the people in your story the way you want your reader to, all the description in the world will arrive still-born.

Nobody cares. They're all too busy grooming and teasing one another. As the group packs up, Mason assigns them all nicknames. Kiyoshi becomes Invisiboy. There's Artgrrl Weston and Princess Heavy Hullinger. John Thornell makes a born Spock. Adam becomes the Joker and Roberto, the Thief. Mason christens himself Counterstrike and declares that Russell Stone will hereafter be known as Teacherman. Only Thassadit gives him pause. He studies her, timid in her amused return gaze. "Hello, *Dalai*!" Then he corrects himself: "No, no. I know who you are. Miss Generosity."

Teacherman has to wave the grade book to get their attention.

"Remember to e-mail your new pieces by midnight tomorrow." The Joker and Artgrrl moan like cartoon characters caught in an ambush. Russell assigns the next topic as if he hasn't been thinking about it for the last twenty-four hours, arranging and rearranging the words like a carpet of forest leaves hiding a pit trap. *Convince someone that they wouldn't want to grow up in your hometown.*

∞

Des Plaines, Terre Haute, Buffalo Grove: the perils of home are many, and the rewards slim. Stone reads all about the top hazards, tedium chief among them. "If Wheaton were a reality show," says Mason's piece, "the sponsors would have crashed it halfway through the pilot." Close behind come isolation, bigotry, aimlessness, crushing homogeny, commercial blight, crimes against every known aesthetic, and the terminal malaise of abundance. Charlotte Hullinger writes, "I spent my childhood simmering in a satellite dish." You know the place. A hometown now opening in a development near you.

Now come by train, a five-year-old from Sétif, into the swarming Agha Station, Algiers. Grow up in a sprawling suburban maze uphill from the port, in the sun-disintegrating, low-bid, postwar high-rises of that repeatedly despoiled recumbent odalisque, *Alger la blanche*. Postwar? Prewar. Midwar, now and always. Holy war. *La sale guerre.* Half a century of war that has emptied the country of a third of its people. The zeal of recent independence has turned on itself, and the state manufactures new enemies everywhere. The Islamic backlash against kleptocrat tyrants escalates into a mass movement. The separatist Berber Spring comes and goes, not so much suppressed as deferred into a simmering Berber Summer. *Reculer pour mieux sauter . . .*

The world's most promising new state has gone stillborn. The girl knows the problem. Her parents map it out, every night, in hushed voices over dinner. A century and a half of the colonized mind has spewed out tribalism with a vengeance, but without any noble cause this time. Dress, words, facial hair: every trait declares allegiance, intended or not. A generation into the country's third major linguectomy, words are again a capital offense. When her father slips into French while lecturing to his university engineering students—*et donc, voilà*—he's publicly censured. Her mother, a document translator for the national oil company Sonatrach, gets hissed at one afternoon by a small chorus on a Bab el-Oued bus for her neckline and bare hair, and when she complains to a patrolling policeman, he fines her for rabble-rousing.

Yes, the girl has her music lessons, her family seaside picnics, even her horse riding on holidays with cousins in Little Kabylia. Some days, the city still rises up like a dream of jumbled white from the azure Mediterranean. But destiny runs mostly backward, in Algiers. Birth rates soar and housing collapses. Corruption outpaces every industry; just walking down the street requires a payoff. Education starts to gutter, and as the girl enters second grade, the entire cobbled-up system reaches the brink. The Islamic Salvation Front threatens to sweep into power. Then the *Pouvoir* cancels all elections.

Real darkness settles in, a decade of it. Her mother instructs the girl and her brother never to sit next to each other on the bus or walk through the market together. Many of the nightly massacres occur in mountain villages, remote and unregistered. But murder—nameless, ecumenical—makes itself at home even in the capital, strolling downhill from the Casbah, spreading through the French quarter, wandering impudently all the way up to the grim joke of the Martyrs Monument.

The killers are many and generous. They massacre for any reason, even on one another's behalf. The Islamic Salvation Front, the Islamic Salvation Army, the Armed Islamic Group, the Islamic Armed Movement, the National Democratic Rally, the Salafist Group for Preaching and Combat: new charters by the week. Devout versus secular, traditionalist versus Western, Arab versus Kabyle . . . Whole villages disappear under cover of dark. Neighbors kill neighbors over old scores, then trick out the corpse to make it look political. A corpse can be ordered for a handful of dinars.

The elites flee the country for Casablanca, Tunis, or Marseilles. Thassa's mother's brother escapes to the vast minimum-security wastelands of the Parisian banlieue, where he finds a job with Public Assistance. He phones his Algiers kin with magical accounts of buying bread in a boulangerie without fear of retribution. The girl's father's sister gives up her prosperous dental clinic to become a groundskeeper in the Montreal botanical gardens. The girl's own parents— the last cosmopolitan Algerians not on a boat somewhere—resolve to leave when the death toll reaches eighty thousand. Then they say ninety. Then one hundred. They're still there when the deaths hit one thousand a week. They are the victims of congenital hope. They can't break themselves of that old habit, faith. Not religious faith, which they long ago consigned to the realm of vicious myth. Faith in their friends and neighbors. Belief in the average human.

The girl enters secondary school. Her world shrinks down to her classroom and her home. But the world of books opens to her, without borders. She, her brother, and her mother travel together to Dib's Tlemcen, Yacine's Bône, even Duras's Saigon. The three of them perform amateur re-creations for her father's entertainment. The crudest imaginary venue is a respite from Algiers.

Her engineer father waits for humanity's return to reason. He makes guarded, deniable appeals to his lecture classes, slipped in between load calculations and stress analysis. He cheers the amnesty programs and the gradual surrender of the guerrillas. He quietly champions the new elections. His innate optimism begins to pay off. He pictures the end of the endless war.

Then the Kabyle singer Lounès Matoub is killed. The country spirals into new violence, and Thassa's father suffers a conversion.

He writes a letter to the editor of *El Watan*: real democracy demands official status for Berber. Tamazight must be taught in public schools. All the deaths of the last decade will mean nothing without a return of that first tongue.

His stand is moderate enough, given recent years. But two weeks after the letter appears in print, students find Thassa's father at his university desk, facedown on a pile of fluid dynamics exams, two holes the size of finches' eyes high up in the back of his skull.

Thassa's mother collapses. She's two months recovering. When she can function again, Zamra Amzwar packs and takes her two teenage children to her brother's in Paris. She finds work in a community health clinic: light clerical. Just until. She's still working there over a year later, when the gendarmes near Tizi Ouzou, back home, kill a nineteen-year-old named Guermouh Massinissa. During the ten days of riots that follow, mother and children tune in nightly to accounts relayed from Radio Algerienne as scores of protesting Kabyle teens are gunned down.

Four months later, a doctor at the clinic notices Zamra Amzwar's jaundice and discovers her distended gallbladder. A six-centimeter pancreatic tumor has already spread cells through every system in Thassa's mother's body. Seventeen weeks later she dies, listening to her daughter read aloud the news from Algiers.

The Berber student fits all this into three pages of eerily idiomatic English. Her second journal assignment: why you might not want to grow up in my hometown. *But still*, she writes, *it is so beautiful there. I wish you could see it, up close, from the harbor. It would fill your heart. So crazy with life*, chez nous.

∞

True, then: both of Thassa Amzwar's parents are dead. Dead of identity and too much hope. And the daughter is either on newly discovered antidepressants or so permanently traumatized she's giddy. Her writing has that open confidence of a child who might still become an astronaut when she grows up. All her sounds ring, all colors shine. Crippling colonial inheritance, religious psychosis, nighttime raids: she's swept along by the stream, marveling. Her words are naked. Her clauses sprout whatever comes just before wings.

Stone's hands shake as he inks up her assignment. He uses a green marker to highlight great phrases. (*Never red*, the pedagogical texts insist.) By the end, her paper is streaked over in ghostly emerald. Even my photocopy looks like a kelp farm.

When he finishes, he tries to return to his delinquent work on *Becoming You*. These last two years he's become an editing machine — tea in, grammar out. But now he can't concentrate for more than a paragraph, he's so keyed up about that evening's class. After his fourth evasive visit in forty minutes to the Algerian Crisis Explained website, he decides that a walk might do him a world of good.

The walk from Logan Square to the South Loop takes hours. He's healthy, and the hike should be effortless. But he's winded by Bucktown. On foot, Milwaukee Avenue is another country. He knows nothing about the place where he lives. By Wicker Park, he's overheard six languages. And all the more recent ethnic groups supposedly live on the other side of town.

Frederick P. Harmon devotes a whole chapter of *Make Your Writing Come Alive* to place. Stone has the topic on his syllabus, for mid-October. Place, Harmon says, is as much a protagonist as any character. But place is in danger, Harmon claims. Our sense of *here* is rapidly disappearing in the globalizing, virtual onslaught.

By Greek Town, Russell decides that Frederick P. needs to get out more often.

Stone has a mental map of the city's neighborhoods, color-coded: do not enter unaccompanied, or after dark, or ever. He's never come close to those spots of true underbelly, the pockets of no-man's-land that even the police refuse to visit. He's seen the projects from the expressway, high-rise concentrations of pain on par with any of the earth's doomed places. But Chicago's grimmest threats seem laughable, after Algiers.

He's never once feared for his life here. He's always felt *safe*, that lazy delusion. Now, walking down Milwaukee, he sees armed youths waving their Scorpios from town-house windows. FIS and GIA spotters signal from the street corners. A rebel pipe bomb blows out the picture window of a used-record shop. The street fills with oily smoke. Black-hooded paramilitary ninjas on motorcycles sweep up and down Division Street, commandos working for God knows whom, pulling random people out of cars and beating them senseless in hidden warehouse interrogation chambers on the edge of Oak Park.

By the time Russell reaches the Mesquakie lobby, he's quivering. All the bitchy, nail-biting, tattooed, fashionably depressive art students that so terrified him last week now seem like guardian angels. He wants to hug these harmless ingenues, gods of health and childlike benevolence. Meeting his group again is like the summer's last poolside party.

∞

The Americans read their entries aloud. In a voice so self-effacing it's almost mute, Invisiboy Kiyoshi Sims describes getting paid to stay up all night on Provigil and exercise online wizard and warrior characters for busy professionals in his Geneva neighborhood. The Joker Tovar inducts them all into the perils of Wilmette: "My mother was once busted on Christmas Eve for letting more than half of her sidewalk luminaria candles blow out."

Then Thassa. She reads her words like she's just discovered them. Her voice brings Algiers—dry, white, and merciless—into the fluorescent classroom. She reads about herself as a young girl, pausing her game of kickball under the back-alley clotheslines to watch three men put a fourth into the trunk of a beige Peugeot. She recounts her father's death, almost poetry. When she gets to her mother's "wistful sickness," she stops for a long time. Her face is flushed and her eyes run, but she lifts her head and looks around the room gamely. No American can meet her gaze.

She returns to her words and finishes, back in that sunlit upland where she started. Algiers is once again a stack of sugar cubes rising from the Mediterranean. Maybe it's distance or time, American sanctuary, or a refugee's anesthesia, but she's good, everything that happened to her family is good, as are all things still to come. She radiates awe at ever having survived adolescence. Her brows relax and her eyes spark, ready for any scenario life might bring.

"What do you think?" she asks her peers. She shakes her head at the standing brutality of her birthright. "Can you imagine such a mad place?"

Princess Heavy Hullinger breaks the silence. "Could I see that for one second?" She snatches the pages out of the smiling woman's hands. Studying Thassa's sentences, Charlotte shakes her head and chants, "Damn, damn, damn."

The others melt into questions. Thassa answers with more stories. She tells them about the Islamists' futile attempts to save the faithful from exposure to Southern European reality television. She describes her family running the finger of her father's corpse over the fingerprint reader of his computer, to unlock the machine again after his death. She tells about her brother Mohand's ill-fated turn as Cheb Tony in a *Raï* adaptation of *West Side Story*.

She laughs as she talks, as if she hadn't just treated them all to a misery that would have broken saints. A few more anecdotes and she hooks even Spock Thornell. They all chatter at once, competing for Miss Generosity's nod. Before Teacherman can pay lip service to the evening's reading assignment from *Make Your Writing Come Alive*, their two shared hours end.

But no one quite wants to leave. They're addicted to the woman's elation. Charlotte—Princess Heavy—takes charge. "Okay, people: we're going to the Beanery right now and continue this." She points a threatening finger at Russell: "*All* of us."

And so Russell Stone rolls down Roosevelt with a pack of art students on their way to a coffee shop on a warm September night. He takes up the rear with an embarrassed Kiyoshi Sims, toward whom Thassa, from her circle of admirers, keeps turning and shooting warm looks. It thrills Russell: she could have any one of them, and she likes the geek.

The front ranks luxuriate down the vacated street, as thick and slow as the moment's pleasure, hanging on each other's shoulders, pulling at each other's arms, loud and here and full of eyes, under the best of the city's light shows, laughing and strolling, tuned to one another, embracing the spectacle of night all around them and feeding on the Algerian girl's standing enchantment. Rising together on a heart—how can I say it?—too soon made glad.

∞

Years ago, on a night much warmer, Stone walked with his own glad pack, equally free. I picture his band wandering with this same slow sweep, through the streets of Tucson's vanished Presidio, under a desert sky that between them, they owned. They sauntered together, the week before thesis deposit, on their way to their shared inheritance, planning the history of their unstoppable literary gang. Theirs was one of those great movie plots, where a handful of specialists come together to pull off an impossible caper: the classicist, the prince of the streets, the brainy one, the buckshot comic, the lyric queen of dialogue. They would change the way that writing worked, break the tyranny of convention, and reenchant the tired reading public with a runaway playfulness that not even the dead could resist.

Six months later, their movement collapsed. Ground down by realism, the gang scattered. Two of them bailed into office jobs. One became a dedicated drunk. One of them builds houses up in the Pacific Northwest and claims to be writing a three-hundred-thousand-word novel, one hundred words a week. Only one of them—Russell's Grace—proved merciless and mean enough for real creativity.

And one of that once invulnerable group can no longer even imagine his byline on any printed piece without succumbing to a profound death wish. That one tags along tonight on the streets of Chicago, ten steps behind another invincible pack, this one in orbit around a woman who might have walked out of a story he once dreamed of writing.

∞

Has he ever fallen in love with a fictional character? I might as well ask: Is the man alive? He's just a few genes away from those famous rhesus monkeys, clinging to their terry-cloth mothers as if life depended on it. The trait has all kinds of value: the ability to get warm from the mere symbol of smoke.

But which fictional loves? Okay: an early, inchoate lust for Jo March. He burned with the need to befriend Emma Woodhouse, to pass her funny notes in the mind's eternal freshman biology class. With Dorothea Brooke, he took long rambles through the country-side, camping out with her under the stars and never touching anything but her lips. Much later, Odette was great fun, until she wasn't. He tried to protect Daisy Miller, and failed miserably. He tried to desire Daisy Buchanan, but failed to do much more than shake her till she whimpered.

Emma Bovary scared the crap out of him, and he blanched in the corner with illicit craving every time they were in the same room. His time with Anna Arkadyevna was full of insane letters and rash, stolen meetings; she came to him in full sun, standing up, to excess, and right at the perfect moment in his own too-prosaic life. Lily Bart appalled him on two continents, but by the end, he would have done anything for her, had she but asked. Like the authors of the world canon, Russell Stone had a disproportionate fondness for pretty sui-cides.

There were scores of others: blind dates, admirations from afar, one-night stands, happy domesticities ending in no-fault divorces. He fell madly, licentiously, guiltily, and often, always without sense or purpose. And each time out, the woman on the page reduced all actual women to pale, insufficient reminders of the full-throated real.

But here's the thing about this man: a few months after he read any book, its plot twists faded into fuzzy sepia and he could deny, bald-faced, even to himself, that any leading woman had ever had his whole soul under her pretty thumb. That, too, seems to be an end-lessly useful and preserved trait: the ability to revise at will.

"All writing is rewriting," he tells the class, three times in the next two sessions.

They stare at him as if he's speaking Russian.

∞

Russell Stone used to watch three hours of tube a night, all he was good for after a day of repairing other people's words. He'd lie in bed marveling at the perfection of nightly network fiction, the best writing by committee since the King James Bible. He expected to hate the shows, all the proliferating private traumas and tiny triumphs. But they sucker punched him every time. Five minutes to the hour, his throat would seize and his chest heave, and by the denouement, he'd be wrung out yet again by one more perfectly timed self-acceptance or reconciliation, one more flawed human managing to be, for a few seconds, something better than he was. And in between episodes, Russell found himself yearning to be with all his old fictional friends again.

These nights he has no time for any fiction. He has a project, his first since collecting every mention of Grace Cozma in print. Whatever hours remain, after his two jobs, he invests in a crash course on the Maghreb. He searches through online Berber manifestos: twenty-five million people scattered over a dozen countries, and until this month, he's never heard of them.

"Careful saying Berber," Thassa teases him, the sixth night of class. "Berber means barbarian. Say *Amazigh*. That means free people."

With a single-volume French-English dictionary near his keyboard, he puzzles his way through *Le Matin* and *El Watan*—old newspaper accounts of the escalating violence that drags Abdelaziz Bouteflika's illicit government down into places too dark for prime-time fiction.

Late into the nights when he doesn't teach, Russell descends that spiral. He takes strange comfort, sitting at his maple writing desk under the knockoff Milton Avery seashore, in confirming the worst about Thassa Amzwar's country. He jots down notes, as if to quiz the girl on Algeria's grimmest particulars. Ten years of organized blood-bath have reduced a country the size of western Europe to a walking corpse. And Thassa has emerged from that land glowing like a blissed-out mystic.

He writes in his journal: *She takes intense pleasure in autumn.* Simply writing that makes him feel like Homeland Security.

When the weather turns foul, her pleasure just swells. She comes to class in a chill downpour, her smock and slacks soaked, her chocolate hair hanging in strings on her shoulders. *She stands in the door-way*, he writes, *laughing like she's just been to Disneyland. "It's ridiculous out there! Fantastic!"*

She tells the class about last night's party—three hours of tea and cookies with five strangers including her UPS man and a Ukrainian

35

woman who camps out at Thassa's bus stop and speaks no English. "Nice people, Chicago people. So friendly."

She sits dripping contentment as Artgrrl reads a journal entry about how America's real divide is not conservative versus liberal, rich versus poor, or rationalists versus Christians, but people with passports versus people without. At every third turn of phrase, Thassa smacks both cheeks and says, "Yes, yes—perfect!" And the object of her praise starts to levitate.

Their ninth night together, she brings a Tupperware wheel of pastry to class: honey-soaked clouds of semolina with a name— *timchepoucht*—the others can't even repeat after her. "What you can't find in life," she tells them, "you have to make yourself!" The rest of them eat freely, hoping that whatever chronic, viral euphoria infects her has also contaminated her kitchen.

∞

That night, the group—so protective of one another when reading aloud their raw journal entries—has its first fight. It starts with the evening's assignment from *Make Your Writing Come Alive*: Frederick P. Harmon's smug insistence that everything ever written derives from one of only twenty-four possible plots.

"I have a little theory about that theory," Counterstrike Mason announces. "I'm thinking that's what you might call a fucking brain fart."

Russell says nothing. He has preached freedom for weeks; he can't police them now.

Spock Thornell does the calculus. "Disagree. If anything, the man's being generous. I'd put it at half that number. A dozen story lines, tops."

"You're shitting me!" Counterstrike bangs the oval table. "It's billions. As many stories as there are—"

"Everyone's a major motion picture," Princess Heavy sneers. "Every life, based on a true story."

"Listen . . ." Counterstrike sounds desperate. "I'm not saying everybody is interesting. I'm just saying that no two . . . This whole mathematical permutation thing is bullshit."

Artgrrl raises her fist. "Exactly! How many times have you seen this story? Nine people argue about how many plots there are. One of them gets up and throws herself out the window, just to prove—"

"That's Harmon number twelve." Spock holds up the page. "Personal Sacrifice for Moral Belief."

"Or, or, or . . ." Roberto stresses his way down the list of possibilities. "Or number seventeen: Passion Disrupts Judgment."

Princess Heavy oozes mock approval. "Or number twenty: Audacious Experiment. Choose your own adventure!"

Lumpers and splitters square off, as if victory here will decide things out in the unplotted world. They nibble at Thassa's *timchepoucht*, which tastes of ancient oases.

Kiyoshi, the Invisiboy, sets down his pen and looks up. He's the last person Russell expects to wander into the crossfire. "There's something I don't get about this class. I mean, are we supposed to be making up stories, with a plot and everything? Or are we just supposed to put down what actually happens?"

The others go on arguing, as if Invisiboy's confusion is just one more available story line.

"When you really stop and think about it," the Joker concludes, "there have to be something like . . . three? I mean: happy ending, miserable ending, and 'Watch me get all arty.' "

It's two, Russell thinks, though no one bothers to ask him. It's the old, elemental two, the only two that anyone will read: the future arrives to smack around the past, or the past reaches out to strangle the future. Hero goes on journey; stranger comes to town.

Here in front of him, at any event, is one plot no one will ever bother writing down: *A happy girl passes through the world's wretchedness and stays happy.* The hung jury turns to Miss Generosity, who hugs herself against their combined outrage. By tacit agreement, Thassa's vote is now worth any three of theirs.

"Yo, Genie!" Charlotte corners her. "What do you think? Lots of stories, or not?"

Her radiant face insists, *This one is easy.* "No hurry!" she tells them. "The time to choose *that* is after we're dead."

∞

I search for Russell Stone all over. I read the almanac for that year. I read his class textbook, of course. I read back issues of his magazine. I even loot those hall-of-mirrors avant-garde novels whose characters try to escape their authors, the kind he once loved, the kind he thought he'd write one day, before he gave up fiction.

He's nowhere, except in his work. On the day shift, in between classes, he puts in his stints on *Becoming You*. He sits motionless in his shared cubicle in the refurbished River North warehouse, pruning effusion back to the root.

According to many of the two thousand new self-help titles that appear every year, once a person rises above poverty, income influences well-being only slightly, and social class affects it just a little more. Marriage counts for a bit, and volunteering works wonders. But nothing short of pharmaceuticals can help sustain contentment as much as a satisfying job.

What pleasure does he get from his selfless editing? Stone strikes me as the kind of guy who might not know what his pleasures *are*. He's not alone. No one does: the happiness books are adamant on this. We're shaped to think the things we want will make us happy. But shaped to take only the briefest thrill in getting. *Wanting* is what *having* wants to recover.

∞

Russell phones his brother—the first call he's made from work since the half-minute dinner negotiations he used to make with Marie. He reaches Robert's cell; it still amazes Stone that his own flesh and blood even *has* a cell. All the remaining hunter-gatherers on Papua New Guinea will be packing loaded smartphones before Russell goes mobile. Mobile is the last thing in existence he wants to be. His every original thought is already being interrupted by real time.

His brother is camped on some stranger's pitched roof in Oak Brook. It's what he does—crawl around on strangers' roofs, installing satellite receivers. He tells people he's in the throughput business. It troubles Robert that a lot of the general public is still getting only a few dozen stories an hour. His company can get anyone up to a couple hundred plus. And then there's retrieval and on-demand and downloading. As he often tries explaining to Russell, it's all about shifting. Time shifting and place shifting. Taste shifting and mood shifting. And if you get the throughput up high enough, it's like nobody's even *telling* you stories anymore; it's like you're making them up yourself.

"You busy?" Russell asks. "Got a minute?"

"No problem," his brother tells him. "Parallel is more efficient than serial."

For some reason, Robert always has time for Stone. He still thinks that Russell is going to be famous someday: a famous writer, whose hilarious stories will pour through the pipes of all the need-shifting, narrative-addicted strangers in the country.

"Bro?" Robert prompts, when Russell says nothing. "'Sup?"

When white guys walking on strangers' roofs in Oak Brook start using any given street argot, it's time to seal the word up in the dictionary mausoleum.

"You know that stuff you're taking?" Russell asks.

"What, the fulvic acid?"

"No. The emotion stuff."

"The selective serotonin reuptake inhibitor? Not to worry. I got the kinks out. It's working fine now."

"Can it make you . . . I don't know . . . *euphoric*?"

Robert makes the sound of a laugh. "I told you. All it does is let me talk to strangers without wigging. Makes me feel a little bigger than I am. Like I've got something to give other people."

A shudder crests across Russell's skull. The drug makes his brother more *generous*.

"Pretty subtle effect," Robert insists. "Really: once you get over the slight depersonalization, it's no biggie."

"Sure, but do you think that other people who take it might get more—"

"Little brother wants euphoria? Huh. I'd have to shop around."

"It's not . . . I'm not looking for, for myself . . . It's about that class I'm teaching."

"I got ya," Robert says, not convinced that Russell is teaching anything.

Russell pictures his brother micropositioning a dish with one hand, C-clamping the cell to his face with the other. It doesn't matter. You never have anyone's full attention anymore, anyway. Focus has gone the way of other flightless birds. "There's a girl in the class . . . a woman, and I just wanted to know if—"

"You want *Rohypnol*? Date rape? Don't do it, man; you can go to prison. Like for*ever*."

Russell says nothing. Prison would simplify many things.

"Look," Robert says, concerned. "Little bro. I've known you, like, always, right? Euphoria is not for you. You used to sit in front of the Saturday-morning cartoons like you were studying for a final exam. You're the kind of guy who needs his pleasures in very modest dosages. Have you thought about maybe a multivitamin?"

"I'll try that," Russell tells his brother.

Robert chuckles at whatever truculent antenna he is trying to hogtie. "Roscoe, let's face facts. We're depressives. It's in the Stone gene pool. Embrace it. It wouldn't have hung around for so many generations if it wasn't essential."

∞

Thomas Kurton has never doubted that happiness is chemical. Meaningless to call it anything else. Like a third of the country, he's tried mood brighteners. They did indeed brighten him, a little. But they also smeared him. They took away a little of that fighter-pilot clarity. So he ditched the brighteners; if he had to choose, he'd rather be keen than bright.

But he has never accepted that people should have to choose.

He talks often about the massive structural flaw in the way the brain processes delight. The machinery of gladness that *Homo sapiens* evolved over millions of years in the bush is an evolutionary hangover in the world that *Homo sapiens* has built. Back on the savannah, stress kept us alive. Natural selection shaped us for productive discontent, with glimmers of heavenly mirage to keep us going. As Kurton puts it in his article "Stairway to Paradise":

> A mix of nasty neurochemical pathways, built, doubtless, by a small set of legacy genes, now plagues us with negative feedback loops and illusory come-ons. What passes for everyday consciousness feels to me increasingly like borderline psychosis. Depression had its uses once, when mankind was on the run. But now that we're somewhat safe, it's time to free the subjugated populace and show what the race can do, armed with sustainable satisfaction at last.

∞

His sister had a chemistry set: Kurton's life follows from that. He was eight, Patty ten. Up until then, he had been the better magician. He

40

could make a coin look like he was bending it over his thumb. Now, overnight, Patty could combine two perfectly clear liquids and turn them a shocking pink. There was no contest. Her magic blew his out of the water, and consumed him with jealousy.

He took to theft: no other choice. He tinkered in the darkness of her closet while Patty was out of the house. he worked with tiny bits of chemical, so she would never know that anything was missing. Somehow, she always knew, and she'd explode with all the violence that the chemical safety manual warned about.

The fourth time his sister caught him sneaking experiments behind her back, she gave him the set. Truth was, she couldn't stand the smells. Patty had been born with the wrong alleles. Even ammonium chloride turned her stomach, and after her first few excursions, she couldn't bring herself to open the vials.

Three months into his sole proprietorship of the chemicals, young Tom completed all 150 experiments in the printed booklet and began inventing his own. His alarmed parents bought him a grandiose expansion for Christmas, although such gear was beyond the budget of a Detroit assembly lineman with five children. Armed with "forty-nine solvents, catalysts, and reagents . . . one thousand hours of pure chemistry!" the boy never really broke stride in his life again.

Even without that proximal cause, he might have landed someplace nearby. From early childhood, he showed all the signs: the model rocketry, the ham radios, the long afternoons gazing into tidal pools, the complete Herbert S. Zim Golden Guides, and later, the expanding universe of cheap science-fiction paperbacks, those lyric hymns to alien life-forms with the surreal cover art where you couldn't tell buildings from geographical features from living things.

Eighth-grade frog dissection revealed how nearby species were already more alien than any fiction. His first microscope opened his eyes to life's true measurements. Diatoms everywhere, whose biomass dwarfed those mutant giants too large to see the real scale of living. In high school, he discovered the Haldane quote about God's inordinate fondness for beetles. The year Kurton came through puberty, God disappeared altogether, replaced by deeper wonder.

In senior year, he read *Microbe Hunters*. He turned his bedroom into a shrine to de Kruif's heroic microbiologists. He painted the names Pasteur, Koch, Reed, and Ehrlich on his ceiling, the last thing he saw at night and the first thing he opened his eyes on in the morning. His mother couldn't object; he was heading to Cornell on full scholarship in the fall.

In short: Kurton's genes might have led him to genomics, no matter what environment threw at him. But environment pulled all the right triggers, at just the right times. All the right teachers, the right toys, the right texts in the right order. In the first month of college, he came across the most beautiful concluding sentence in world lit, words that gave him far more epiphany than any novel. The book itself was a long, hard slog, but oh, that arrival!

> There is grandeur in this view of life, with its several powers, having been originally breathed by the Creator into a few forms or into one; and that, whilst this planet has gone cycling on according to the fixed law of gravity, from so simple a beginning endless forms most beautiful and most wonderful have been, and are being, evolved.

By sophomore year, he was spending long hours in the lab, in his private chapel with its very own fume hood. *Do not put your nose over the unknown; waft the air of the unknown to your nose.* In his third year, he earned a key to the storeroom, where all the supplies were lined up in orderly glorious ranges on the shelves. Sometimes he would simply stand among them, as if on the podium in front of an orchestra, listening.

In graduate school at Stanford he made his first real discovery—a gene-promoter mechanism that no one on earth knew about. The find infused him with terrible urgency, a hurry to discover something else, now, before all the discoveries were made. And when, in his late twenties, his research team assayed the milk of their transgenic cows and confirmed the presence of a protein they themselves had placed there alongside all of nature's own tangled enzymes, he felt for two months that he could die satisfied.

Then the two months ended, two months during which he had done absolutely nothing new for the world. Frantic again, he returned to the lab, to learn something about real work.

He and his girlfriend—a sociologist who studied the power of crowds—got married. They had two children, one of each. He and his wife raised the kids somehow, between them. It crushed Thomas to discover his daughter could not abide the smell of life science. It hurt him worse to discover that his son preferred making money to making discoveries. He released the children into the laboratories of their own lives. He got divorced. He wished his ex-wife all the world's fresh horizons. Later, he had affairs, when there was time. But the love he really lived for was *knowing*.

That thrill of first discovery returned a handful of times over the next twenty years, in diminished forms. He pushed himself forward on the pleasure of *first*: first place, first to lay eyes on, first in the hearts of his peer reviewers. But he wanted more than simple primacy. *First* was just a sporting bagatelle. To look on a thing that had been true since the start of creation but never grasped until *you* made it so: no euphoria available to the human brain could match it. Cleaner than drugs, broader and more powerful than sex—Huxley's "divine dipsomania." Anyone who tasted it once would spend the rest of his life trying for more.

Science fit the very folds of Tom Kurton's brain. Its exuberance tempered the tedium of daily lab work, kept him alert, overrode fatigue, and rendered risks trivial. And the goal of scientific exuberance, like the goal of life, which it helped to propel, was to replicate itself.

And so his life, from the simplest of beginnings, has spun out endless living forms, not all of them viable, not all of them pretty, not all of them sane or even wise, but each a turbulent attempt to lay bare the order in things, and all of them variations most wonderful.

∞

Russell Stone lies in bed at night, reading about Algeria and its victims until he can't breathe. He reads about a "vast national passion for reticence." He reads about a culture struggling to emerge from feudal female sequestering and subservience. He can't connect these accounts to his student's existence. Even her years in Canada don't explain such a leap.

When the Algeria books threaten to suck him under, he switches to a layperson's handbook on happiness that he's checked out from the public library. He flips around in it, buffet style, hoping that some paragraph somewhere might explain *something*, or at least lull him to sleep.

Sleep is not an option. He reads on, squinting at the clinical studies. One study claims that the most satisfied people are also those who can list the most peak experiences in sixty seconds. He sits up in bed with his yellow legal tablet and tries to write down the happiest moments in his life. The first one he remembers stops him cold.

He's tried to kill it, over the years: the three-day escape with Grace Cozma to Flagstaff that frosty March, in their last spring in the writing program. Her idea: *Come up with me to see the canyon. I have to see the damn Grand Canyon before I escape this place.* Until then, the farthest they'd gone was her ordering him to lick Mexican beer off her fingers one crazed happy hour after workshop.

They rented a car—midsized luxury sedan, when they couldn't afford economy—and drove up. But until they were standing at the reception desk in the ponderosa-pine lodge in Flagstaff, he had no idea whether Grace would ask for one room or two.

She asked for one. One of everything, for the next three days. *Come up with me.* Come hike with me, eat with me, bathe with me. Come learn how to want something more than you want to write. Their first night, after burritos in a dusty dive, they holed up in their chilly room. He looked to her to set the pace. Her pace was geological. She wanted him naked under the covers with her, knees up, reading, as if their thirtieth anniversary came before their honeymoon. He was reading *The Varieties of Religious Experience*. She was deep into *Far Tortuga*. He loved when she wore her glasses, which she hated to put on. She curled over her book like in prayer, the back of her hand distractedly grazing his thigh. He did not know a body could pound like that. Reading lasted maybe forty minutes, until she turned to him, slipped one leg over his, and asked, "How's the book?" They read no more that night.

In the morning, after gorging on complimentary breakfast, they stood on the South Rim giggling like maniacs at the bizarre optical effects: near, middle, and distant cross sections of the earth sliding decoupled against one another like bad back projection in a forties movie. He could not accept the colors, the rose irons and coppery greens. They climbed down Bright Angel into the chasm on foot, she singing Ferde Grofé's clumping mule theme, he wanting to take her into the thickets of tamarisk and do her like deer. She was insane, insisting that they descend to the Inner Gorge, all the way down to the Vishnu Schist. They made it as far as Plateau Point and barely dragged themselves back up to the rim by nightfall. That night, as if they weren't dead with fatigue, they skipped the studying and went right to the exam.

He never imagined that Grace might feel any less than he did. Just hearing her hum contentedly under her breath as she drove home was like returning to a country he didn't even know he'd been banished from. But back in Tucson, they didn't move in together, didn't join futures, didn't even change their old routine except for sleeping together eight increasingly tense times before her departure to France that May.

As she left the country, she goosed his ribs and said she expected great things from him. To date, his greatest achievement has been his appearance as a most convincing character in Grace's deeply convincing first novel.

He writes down *Grand Canyon w/ G*, and in that instant, the one-minute timer starts beeping.

∞

Other things his happiness encyclopedia says:

Well-being is not one thing. It surprises Stone to read that optimism, satisfaction, capacity for happiness, and capacity for unhappiness are all independent. He puts his average across the four at about .235, or just shy of respectable for the North American league. Nor is he much of a long-ball hitter.

Happy people have stronger social relationships, more friends, better jobs, higher salaries, and stronger marriages. They are more creative, more altruistic, calmer, healthier, and longer lived. Russell skips the self-scoring checklist.

Happy people know that they're happy and don't need to read happiness books to determine how happy they are. Russell's book doesn't actually say this. It's what psychologists call inferred knowledge.

People in positive moods are more biased, less logical, and less reliable than people in negative moods. Score one for what the book calls "depressive realism."

The prefrontal cortex of happy people lights up more on the left, while the brains of the congenitally dour favor the right. This seems to Russell either profound or meaningless.

Happiness is probably the most highly heritable component of personality. From 50 to 80 percent of the variation in people's average happiness may be accounted for by genes. People display an affective set point in infancy that doesn't change much over a lifetime. For true contentment, the trick is to choose your parents wisely. No argument at the Stone household.

Yet the conflicted book insists on a role for nurture. Joyousness, it says, is like perfect pitch: a little early training in elation can bring out a trait that might otherwise wither.

Stone assumes that Algeria's Time of Horrors is not exactly the early training of choice.

∞

Late one class, as Thassa is leaving, he works up the courage to ask her how she's surviving the local Arabophobia. She just grins. "But I'm not an Arab! I'm Kabyle. You might be more Arab than I am. *Stone*: that's *Hajarī*. That's a good Arab name. Hey! Are you planning any terror, Mister?"

His terror is all unplanned.

He's like a man who has just seen some mythic creature fly past the window—teal and ruby against the concrete neighboring high-rise, a species blown a continent off course, not listed in any of the books he now spreads along the windowsill in the hopes of making an ID. A thing of complete unlikelihood. Game for anything. And anything's game.

∞

Stone shares an office with two other adjuncts—a converted smoking lounge on the sixth floor. There he holds his first student conferences. The half-hour sessions feel more like counseling jags than writing tutorials.

Joker Tovar drums on his thigh with a chewed-up uni-ball, his knee pounding like a woodpecker spattering a concrete phone pole. "Digital media is over," he tells Russell. "Played out. Nobody's done anything fresh for three months. The whole scene is *Night of the Living Dead*. And no one has a clue what to do next."

Roberto the Thief sits forward on the hot seat, his soul stretched as taut as shrink-wrap. In a soft voice, he announces, "I go to the edge of the abyss every other night. Sometimes I look over."

Russell asks, "Would it help you to talk to someone?"

Roberto just cocks his head. "I'm sorry . . . Help *what*?"

Charlotte, intrepid Princess Heavy, shows Russell her portfolio—charcoal vortices of human bodies that look like the Venus of Willendorf, which is to say, a little like Princess Heavy. She works snippets of journal entry around each image. One sketch, more sinewy than the rest, jumps out at Russell. He doesn't even need the hand-scrawled accompanying passage: *It's like she's glowing. Like she knows something. Makes me want to be a refugee.*

Maybe it's just a fragment of indie-song lyric. He flips to the next image, but not fast enough to evade Charlotte. "So what do you make of her?"

He flips back, holds up the sketch, lifts an eyebrow. He's remarkably good at being the one thing his father taught him never to be: a fake.

Charlotte tsks. "I don't mean the sketch. Is there something broken with her? Or something really . . . fixed?"

"I don't know," he mumbles. "I've never met an Algerian before. I . . . probably shouldn't be discussing—"

"No, of course not." Charlotte retrieves her drawings and slips them into her portfolio. "Wouldn't be caught dead discussing real life."

∞

When Thassa is five minutes late for her appointment, Russell unravels. The Islamic Salvation Front has sent a death squad after her. Or the America First people. Her total lack of depressive realism leaves her a walking target.

At eight minutes after the hour, she sticks her face around the doorjamb, puckered with sweet shame. He's so relieved to see her that he stands up. He's shocked all over again at just how short she is: the crown of her curly hair reaches no higher than his collarbone.

"I'm sorry to be so tardy," she says. "I was talking to the security guard downstairs."

Just the sound of her voice is like a governor's pardon. Her accent has drifted: too much time in North America. He wants to stop the sound from drifting any further.

"He has a fascinating story," she says, touching Stone's wrist and making him sit. She sits just next to him. "He's a Bosnian Muslim. Imagine: he taught himself English when he moved here, and now he's writing a book!"

Russell treads water. "Do you know him?"

"I do now! He's a beautiful man."

The adjective stabs him. He'll never be able to protect her from her own promiscuous warmth. "A Muslim," he says, brain-dead. "Like you?"

"*Me?*" She laughs. "I'm no believer. I'm some kind of half-Christian atheist. My mother's family have been Catholic for generations. Hey!" She shakes his arm. "Don't look so surprised! You know that Saint Augustine was *Berbère?*"

Russell didn't know. His ignorance is more or less complete.

"From Annaba. A Kabyle even more famous than Zidane. But my father was so disgusted with religion that he wouldn't let it in our house. I don't know, myself. If there is God, he is just laughing at every religion we invent!"

He's stunned silent: faith is not the author of her bliss. Blessed are those who do not believe, and yet see.

She carries on amusing herself. "You know, maybe those jihad suicide people will really get their seventy-two virgins in heaven — except they will be seventy-two American Christian virgins, saving themselves for their Baptist husbands!"

Her glee is a dance. Stone seizes up even worse than he does in front of the class. He stutters his way through a few gibberish clauses. He's stunted by this thing she owns, the thing that beautiful people seem to possess but never really do. If only she were merely beautiful . . .

Her face is small but ursine. Her nose veers hard to the right, and her eyes are slightly askew. She shouldn't even be pretty, except for the conspiracy of delight rounding her cheeks. A rill of melted skin runs up the outside of her left arm from elbow to shoulder. How could he have missed it until now? She must think the scar too banal to mention in her journal.

He says some generic pedantries about her entries for class. She nods and scribbles into her notebook, which she safeguards up near her narrow chest. He tries to say things that won't look ludicrous, copied down. A few more of his clumsy maxims stolen from Harmon, a little more of her laughter and scribbling, and she turns the page to show him: not notes, but a felt-tip cartoon caricature of him, perfect down to his squint of bewilderment. She draws like she breathes — a gull enjoying a gust.

Happy people must *know something* that no one else does. Some key to being alive, obscure and hard-won, almost out of reach. Otherwise, he would have met a truly happy person or two, long before her.

"What made you apply to this place?" he asks. "How did you choose Chicago?"

She declares Mesquakie a great college for her major: film arts, the documentary concentration. "I fell in love with films, in high school, in Montreal. I was making little movies for my brother, to make him feel less, um . . . country sick? Homesick. Come on, Thassa! *Homesick.* I made him funny clips, to get him to laugh. Then, I started . . . splicing? I love film; I just *love* it. I love putting the shots together. I love dubbing the sounds. Anything! I could play with the editing softwares all day long."

He's so nonplussed he can't even nod.

"What I would really love—more than anything?—is to get very skilled, then to go home and make beautiful films, *chez nous.*"

"Of course!" At last it clicks: witness and voice, in the world's most powerful medium. "Like Pontecorvo . . . Has anyone done something like that for the civil war?"

She smiles confidentially and touches his wrist. Her skin shocks him. "Not politics! Politics and film?" She tsks and waves her index finger like a windshield wiper. "That's not my glass of tea. No, I just want to shoot—you know! *Kabylie.* The mountains. The coast. Those peoples. That sky."

"Nature?" He can't keep the bafflement out of his voice. A child of death who's thrilled about the future. An Algerian who shuns politics. A film lover who chooses the banality of mountains.

She shakes her head again and pulls a tiny media player out of her rainbow bag. Before he can decode, she shows him her work in progress. A Thassa the size of his fingernail grins at him from inside the matchbox screen. She's in front of a large fish tank at what must be the Shedd Aquarium. Spots of bioluminescence in the fish blink on and off. Then the glowing spots animate, spelling out the words: *Secret Chicagos. A Film by Generosity.*

Then they're in Grant Park, at the foot of Buckingham Fountain, the spouting green sea horses. It's a sunny day; people of all stripes stroll around the basin. A mixed-race couple goes by arm in arm. A woman in full hijab tries to rein in two little girls, both in their own white headscarves. A sizable Japanese tour group makes a collective, rising glissando of appreciation at the words of their guide. But the camera settles on an ancient bald man sitting on the edge of the fountain. He's talking to himself, except that the camera hears.

> I can't really say I miss it. Italy? God! That's over sixty years ago. But I like to come down here anyway, because it feels like something . . . back then. You know what I'm saying?

A voice from behind the camera says, "I know."

> Maybe I'm finally getting senile. But you know what would be great? If all this water just—if it all just kept flowing . . . Venice!

With the sweep of his illustrating hand, the water spills over the fountain rim and streams its way up Congress. It doesn't look like real computer graphics. It looks like a living watercolor, splashes of primaries better than life, and much more generous.

> Russell jerks up, searching her face for clues.
> She giggles. "Compositing," she explains, freehanding in the air.
He nods like an idiot and looks back.

Boats appear on the watery Congress Parkway. Gondolas paddle upstream, underneath the old post office. San Marco's materializes alongside the old Illinois Central tracks. The camera swings back, cutting up State Street at high speed. It ducks down into the subway, settles on a dark, middle-aged man standing on the platform waiting for his train.

> I'm from Eastern Turkey, Cappadocia. Every time I come down here, I think of the caves. They should have cities down here, right? They stick all those people up in the air; they can put some underground. Am I right?

The tube of tunnel stone behind him begins to seethe with hand-drawn passageways. Doorways and windows open in the walls. The camera pops into one of them, then pops out again on a tree-lined street of brick bungalows somewhere in Bronzeville. A young man in leather jacket and felt porkpie studies the lens:

> My kinda town? Sister, you could take a weekend out of the war budget and turn this whole neighborhood into Heaven South. Homes for the homeless. Music falling out of the sky!

He has only to speak it, and a third-story paradise of visible melody springs up all around him, at tree level.

So it goes for a handful more shots: Kraków spilling out of a cathedral in West Town, Cinco de Mayo flowing down the Back of the Yards, the Bahai Temple turning into Isfahan, the Devon corridor releasing a desi incense procession.

"Who made all this?" Russell croaks.

She dives into her bag and retrieves a Handycam the size of a newborn schnauzer. She's seen more of this city in a year and a half than he has in his life. He looks at that face, its invincible grin. She's fearless, ready to travel into any neighborhood. All he can think is: It's not safe out there. Happiness is a death sentence.

She squeezes the camera trigger and starts filming him. He grimaces, trying to smile. "But this isn't really . . . a documentary, is it?"

She stops filming. Even her frown is delighted. "It isn't? What is it, then? It's all perfectly true. Maybe this is your creative nonfiction!"

"But is there any market for that kind of film?" He can't help himself. The orphan girl's self-appointed uncle. "Can you make a living, after school?"

She waves her hand and scowls. "Pff. Livings are easy. My father was an engineer. He always liked the English expression: There's no free lunch. That's crazy! There is *only* free lunch. We should all be nothing but clouds of frozen dust. This is what science says. All lunch is free. My father was a scientist, but he never understood this one simple scientific fact, poor man." She shakes her head at the man's perversity.

So she didn't get the bliss from her father, either.

They talk beyond the allotted half hour. She's in no hurry to go. Russell realizes that he has saved her appointment for last, just in case it runs overtime. Finally, he can keep her no longer. She stands up to go, scooping her possessions back into the rainbow bag. She turns to him, her brightness challenging.

"You know, Mister? You are a very unfair teacher. You make us all read from our journals. But you never read to us from yours!"

∞

His details are coming to me now, more easily than I care to admit.

∞

He watches for a long time at the plate-glass window after she leaves, gazing six stories straight down onto the building's entrance. She takes forever. She's talking to the Bosnian security-guard novelist again, or to some new newly met, soon-to-be bosom buddy. His chest clutches when she does appear. She takes a few steps south, then slows, distracted by something across the street. She starts up again, then greets a woman walking toward her. She spins around as the woman passes, turns like a planet in an orrery, and calls out. When the woman looks back, Thassa taps her own bare head and laughs something: *I like your hat*. The stranger's delight is visible from six floors up.

Thassa walks down the street as if through a spice bazaar. She takes all of five minutes to go a block. From high up in his spy's nest, Russell imagines the composited, hand-drawn documentary she's seeing at all times, while everyone else drags their way through the depressing, psychological realist version: Wabash, blooming into a Casbah watercolor.

He lifts his eyes to the building across the street—an astonishing, ceramic-clad, honeycomb lattice far beyond anything the present could afford to build. He's never noticed it before. He glances back down just in time to see the Kabyle girl duck into a building two blocks south: one of the college's two dormitories. He knows where she lives.

He grabs his valise, skips down six flights of stairs, bursts out to the street, and follows her south. The air is weirdly ionized; the lake smells like ocean. He's never noticed, but each shoulder-rubbing façade in this police lineup of buildings is a different color. Marble, sandstone, granite: Paris on the Prairie.

He stands across the street from her dormitory, scouring the window grid. He can't see anything, and he's just about to skulk away when she appears in a fourth-story window on the right, looking down on the Wabash pageant. She's smiling at the possibilities beneath her, sizing up the adventure. She sees him; she doesn't see him. She lifts one hand. The hand holds a leather-bound book. She cradles the small volume from beneath and spreads it face-open against the window. The alien gesture freezes him.

He ducks into the doorway behind him, heart pounding. A musical-instrument store. He pretends to shop for acoustic guitars. He might, in fact, be interested in guitars. He hasn't touched one since moving back from Tucson.

He leaves the shop ten minutes later, empty-handed. He walks from campus up to the river, just to clear his head. He feels vaguely criminal. He *is* vaguely criminal.

Home again, he sits on his back deck next to the fire escape, trying to capture in his journal what happened that afternoon. He writes under the yellow deck light as darkness falls, unable to shake her image.

He writes: *She pressed the pages to the glass, as if for someone with a powerful telescope on another planet.*

He looks up. The night is clear and the wind comes off the moon and literature has just been invented.

PART TWO

WALK ON AIR

True happiness, we are told, consists in getting out of one's self; but the point is not only to get out—you must stay out; and to stay out, you must have some absorbing errand.

—Henry James, *Roderick Hudson*

The British ethicist with the bloodhound eyes returns to the screen. She's seated in the library of Magdalen College, Oxford. Her face is lined by a lifetime spent gate-guarding science's worst excesses. An *Over the Limit* caption identifies her: Anne Harter, Author, *Designs on Humanity*. She says:

> More expensive, high-tech antiaging breakthroughs will just produce even more horrendous differences between the haves and have-nots. If we really want to extend the average human life span, then let's supply clean drinking water to the majority of the planet that doesn't have it.

Cutaway, and the caption reads: *University of Tokyo conference, "The Future of Aging."* Thomas Kurton stands behind a podium, covered in hazelnut curls, fifty-seven going on thirty-two, a Sarastro of the cult of antioxidants. He speaks from the hip:

> The script that has kept us in gloom and dread is about to be rewritten. Labs across the globe are closing in on those ridiculous genetic errors that cause life to suicide. Aging is not just a disease; it's the mother of all maladies. And humankind may finally have a shot at curing it.

Cut back to Oxford: Professor Harter questions the scientific basis to Kurton's optimism. Back in Todai, Kurton cites the discovery of a single gene mutation that more than doubles the life span of *Caenorhabditis elegans*.

Oxford:

> Aging is not the enemy; the enemy is despair.

Tokyo:

> Cure age, and you beat a dozen ailments at once. You might even help depression.

The camera turns the scientist and ethicist into a bickering couple, airing their grievances in front of friends.

A quick jump to Maine, where keen Tonia Schiff asks Kurton:

> What about those people who say society can't survive more old people than it already has?

He can't ratchet down that boyish smile.

> Naysayers have always been around to challenge any human dream. And that's good! But that objection just doesn't make sense to me. I'm talking about a future where the aged aren't *old*.

Back to Anne Harter, in Oxford:

> Dr. Kurton might want to fund an association study for the wishful-thinking gene.

The match is as unfair as genetics. The scientist is brighter, more informed, and more relaxed. All Harter can do is sink her teeth into his ankle and hang on.

Kurton, back in the Maine cabin:

> People want to live longer *and* better. When they can do both, they will. Ethics is just going to have to catch up.

Tonia Schiff sits, her knee to his, enjoying the ride:

How do you think the market will price the fountain of youth?

He does this funny little head-bow of concentration, like he's never been asked this question and he wants to think about it, for the sheer pleasure of thought.

Well, the market seems to price food and water fairly effectively. It could use a little help pricing medications, I suppose.

Schiff, in something like awe at the man's ingenuousness:

Do you really mean to live forever?

He rocks good-naturedly and squeezes the back of his neck.

We'll see how far I get. I'm on calorie restriction, daily workout, and a few supplements, especially megadoses of resveratrol. If I can keep myself healthy for another twenty years, at our present rate of discovery . . .

The techno beat starts up again. Cross-fade to a slowly focusing midrange shot, and the genomicist floats twenty stories in the air over the apocalyptic dreamscape of Hachikō Crossing, Shibuya, Tokyo. Below him spreads Times Square squared—spectral neon blazes fringing a bank of LCD screens each several stories high, towering over seven major thoroughfares that converge in the world's largest pedestrian scramble, which, from twenty stories up, looks like mitosis under the microscope. Multilevel train station, bass-thumping department stores, costume outlets, twisting warrens of mirror-lined game arcades . . . The streetlights stop all traffic, and the accumulated mounds of crowd disgorge into one another, massing into the intersection from all sides in an orderly, omnidirectional tsunami.

Thomas Kurton gazes down on this orgy of the urban dispossessed. The camera follows his gaze: kids as bowerbirds; kids as noble savages; kids as Kogal Californians; kids from the outer reaches of galaxies far, far away; kids as baggy, knee-socked, schoolgirl-sailor prostitutes; kids as mutants—cosplay, Catgirl, GothLoli, maid-nurse-bunny—all in a gentle, frenzied, nightly theatrical performance of rebellion that will wander home at four in the morning to broom-closet apartments and wake up two hours later to head to classes or clerical jobs.

The scientist looks down into the costumed mass and smiles.

> We're trapped in a faulty design, stuck in a bad plot. We want to become something else. It's what we've wanted since the story started. And now we can have it.

The camera follows him into a glass elevator and plunges down into the maelstrom. The transparent capsule opens, and Thomas Kurton disappears into the carnival of midnight Shibuya.

∞

Tonia Schiff appears briefly out of character at the seven-minute mark in "The Genie and the Genome." She's seated near the front of that University of Tokyo auditorium, looking nothing like the show host who scampers through the interview segments. Her alert amusement disappears. For two seconds, her aura teeters, scared by the show onstage. Then the camera dives back into the sea of eager faces behind her in the auditorium.

She surfaces again ten seconds later, in the milling crowd. Even the way she stands and chats feels somehow experimental. Something in her hand movements hints at her childhood in New York and Washington, her adolescence in Brussels and Bonn. She speaks to one scientist in flowing German, but stops for a moment to greet a passing acquaintance with a few snippets of Japanese.

She turns to a couple next to her and says something that makes them bloom. She learned the trick from her father, a career diplomat: how to make everyone she meets feel like a conversational genius. From her mother, a medical policy adviser for international relief agencies, she's learned how to turn a person's worst impulses to good use. That is the secret of her edutainment fame: assure us all that we might still become the authors of our own lives. She'll use the skill again, later, on a New York soundstage, filming the lead-in to this show's segment. A flash of cosmopolitan charm undercut by a sardonic grin: "My kind of future would probably ask, 'If I let you have your way with me tonight, will you still respect me in the morning?' "

∞

From childhood through the age of twenty, Tonia Schiff nurtured the belief (acquired in a series of elite international schools) that the deepest satisfaction available to anyone lay in those cultural works that survive the test of Long Time. But a collision with postcolonialism in her second semester studying art history at Brown shook her faith in masterpieces. A course in the Marxist interpretation of the Italian Renaissance left her furious. For a little while longer she soldiered on, fighting the good fight for artistic transcendence, until she realized that all the commanding officers had already negotiated safe passage away from the rout.

In her junior year, vulnerable now to the world's corruption, she belatedly discovered (blindingly obvious to everyone else alive) the lock on human consciousness enjoyed by the medium that her parents always treated as a lethal pandemic that would one day be successfully eradicated. At the age of twenty, Tonia Schiff, fair-haired, blue-eyed heir of dying high culture, at last got roughed up by television, and loved every minute of it.

In short order, she discovered:

Broadcast was what Grimm's fairy tales wanted to be when they grew up
Broadcast was an eight-lane autobahn into the amygdala
Broadcast was the only addiction that left you *more* socially functional
Broadcast was what *Homo ergaster* daydreamed about, on the shores of Lake Turkana, between meals

One semester of Modern Visual Media Studies taught her that she didn't want to analyze the stuff; she wanted to *make* it. After graduation, she talked her way into a Manhattan production studio, reassuring them that the Ivy liberal-arts degree could be overcome. She served time as a fact-checker for local news, where she learned, to her astonishment, what her country really looked like. From there, she worked her way onto a team specializing in archival footage for the Hitler Channel.

She realized, early on, how fast broadcast was becoming narrow-cast, and she signed on with a boutique production outfit to work for a consumer-electronics tech showcase that the whole crew called *Geek of the Week*. She graduated to assistant producer and executed her responsibilities meticulously until someone had the brilliant idea to let her try hosting. The camera loved her, and so did the week's geeks. In front of the lens, her old Brahmin insouciance combined with a sexy bewilderment to turn her into everybody's favorite new toy with a new toy. Her arched-eyebrow amusement at the constant torrents of techno-novelty made *Over the Limit*, in the words of *Entertainment Weekly*, "science like you wished it had been, back in high school."

Each week, the show delivers another round of *Scientific American* meets *Götterdämmerung*. In the months just before "The Genie and the Genome," they do:

off-the-shelf electronic surveillance
drugs that eliminate the need for sleep
geisha bots
thought-reading fMRI
Augmented Cognition weapons systems
runaway nano-replicators
radio frequency skimming
untraceable performance enhancers
remotely implantable human ID chips
viral terrorism
Frankenfoods
neural marketing
smart, networked commodities

The show taps into the oldest campfire secret: in terror begins possibility. A sizable slice of the viewing public has unlimited appetite for all the latest ways that godly gadgets will destroy their lives. Schiff measures the success of each segment by the number of illegal clips floating around the Internet the next day. Even the occasional Photoshopped nude of her seems a testimonial.

It's beyond lucky, getting to spend all her hours in the company of ingenious people. Her interviews have led to a few intense adventures with amusingly driven men. But even the ones who know how to entertain themselves need far more approval than she can deliver without irony. The best of these intervals are bittersweet, like Mahler by candlelight. In between, she's content with her circuit through the exercise rooms of three-star hotels, listening to podcasts of technology-show competitors while on the elliptical cross-trainer. Lately, she has begun to bid in online auction houses on the letters of famous inventors. She imagines giving the whole collection to the smartest of her nieces, when she graduates from high school.

Meanwhile, Tonia enjoys the admiration of everyone she knows except her humanitarian mother. Sigrid Schiff-Bordet watches the program now and then, when she's not in Afghanistan or Mali. Tonia's mother long ago adjusted to the world's basic schizophrenia. She thinks nothing about passing from climate-controlled concourses studded with free drinking fountains into armed outposts where mortars battle over a few potable liters. But she can't adjust to *Over the Limit*.

"I'm too old for your stories," Sigrid tells Tonia. "I've voided my citizenship in that kind of future. You have to let me die a functional illiterate."

Once, in the closest thing to a compliment she could muster, Dr. Schiff-Bordet told her daughter, "Your show is probably good for me. It sickens me to watch, but it's powerful medicine. Like chemotherapy for the naïve soul."

∞

As for Tonia's father, Gilbert Schiff died three years before "The Genie and the Genome," at age sixty-nine, of a massive heart attack in the consulate in Tyumen. Two weeks before his death, in one of their biweekly phone calls, his daughter had the gall—or call it the enduring filial pride—to ask him when he was going to write his long-postponed diplomatic memoirs. The former young cultural attaché under Camelot had managed to survive in the State Department all the way through Bush the Second, battered up to the rank of vice-consul, still trying to convince the six billion neighbors that America had gentle, nuanced, humble, and diverse insights to offer the world conversation. Tonia had grown up on his increasingly embattled accounts, a foreign policy hiding inside the official foreign policy, a beautiful losing proposition that only a handful of lifers kept alive.

Her father answered her challenge in his best stentorian white-tie voice. "No one wants to read my autobiography. Story of my life." She foolishly pressed him, hinting at the ticking clock, until he released his last, jagged barb. "I'll make you a deal. I'll write my memoirs as soon as you give up the technology ringmaster act and write that history of interwar regionalist realism you once promised me."

The rebuke stung; she knew how deeply she'd failed the man. Both Vice-consul Schiff and his beloved doctor wife felt something hopelessly magnificent about the human adventure, its ability to channel the brute instinct of a few hard-pressed hunter-gatherers into creating Athens, Byzantium, Florence, Isfahan. But in Gilbert Schiff's considered opinion, the project had been running in reverse for more than a century; the beasts of unlimited appetite were loose and weren't going back into the kennel anytime soon. Every individual being with any skill had to fight the fatuous, disposable present with everything of worth. Instead, his daughter—his polyglot, caryatid, harpist daughter, National Merit Finalist, queen of the debating society, captain of the chess club, choral society soloist—was partying with the barbarians.

She knew how much she'd once pleased him. On the morning of her first communion, he told her she was closer to perfection than any father could have asked. In her first year of college, during their long Christmas-vacation discussions of late Reginald Marsh and early Stuart Davis, she even detected a little hangdog adoration in his glance, a self-policing cringe ready to punish himself for imagining the full range of her lucky gifts.

The summer that she told him she'd switched to media studies, he was stationed in Oslo. She called him from Providence; the announcement merited more than a letter. He laughed from the gut at the send-up, until he realized it wasn't one. He regrouped gracefully and told her that he and her mother would back her in anything she chose to study. When she got her first television job, he resigned himself to noble stoicism over her late-onset disease. But he'd have given anything for her cure, if any medicine offered one.

In time, he shifted his hopes from his daughter to her genes. Throughout her twenties, he treated every man she introduced to him with polite reserve. *Fun, maybe, for a weekend* or *Settling a little quickly, aren't you?* In her thirties, he began praising even the bottom-dwellers. *So he has a record; half the justices on the D.C. circuit have a criminal sheet. The question is, where does he come down on the Pampers Size Six controversy?* Once, he even pronounced the abomination "speed dating." Both he and Tonia's mother were too well-bred to come out and tell her, *Breed, damn you!* But that was all she could do for them, finally.

Tonia never confessed to her parents a genetic defect even more lethal than susceptibility to broadcast. But by thirty-three, the syndrome was undeniable: she possessed no maternal desire whatsoever. One glance at the only available planetary future made having children at best benighted and at worst depraved. Nulliparity—human build-down—was a moral imperative.

But Tonia never made that point to Gilbert Schiff. Even when she was still single at thirty-six, her father held out the same forsaken hope for her as he did for making the case for America abroad under Bush II. "I wouldn't even insist on a monograph," he told her, during that wretched phone call just before his death. "I'd be happy with a modest little coauthored study . . ."

"Someday," she teased him. "When someone as good as Daddy comes along." But she was already a member of the Voluntary Human Extinction Movement, even if she could not quite bring herself to qualify for their Golden Snip Award.

The old diplomat went to his grave nineteen days after that phone call, as defeated by his daughter's choices as he was by his innocent, beginner country's embrace of extraordinary rendition. After her father's death and her mother's subsequent expatriation, Tonia threw herself into a brief period of purposeful mate-seeking. But the thing about ghosts is that they outlast their own hopes. A dead father is forever beyond placating.

Now she concentrates on appeasing one million total strangers. Each forty-two-minute segment is an exercise in insouciance, taking her sixty hours to perfect. The goal is to compile an accurate map of the present at the scale of one to one, a massive mosaic of thumbnails of the blinding future.

For four decades, Tonia Schiff's parents kept a pact. However busy they were, whatever remote outpost each of them found themselves in, they always managed to meet every two months for a private dinner. And at that dinner, one of them would argue a fiercely prepared debating motion. Resolved: the human race would have been better off if the agricultural revolution had never happened. Resolved: the government should cap the salaries of professional athletes. Resolved: Bach's Passions should be banned from concert halls for anti-Semitism. And the other delivered the fiercest possible rebuttal. In this way Gilbert and Sigrid preserved the fires of argument that had supplied such heat to their love.

Now, a decade past the age her parents were when they birthed her, Tonia revives the ritual, with the only difference being that she meets for a new topic twenty times a year with no fixed opponent. Resolved: the human race will not survive its own ingenuity. Resolved: the cure for our chronic despair is just around the corner. And no matter whom she spars with on any given occasion, Tonia Schiff can make the most cataclysmic debate almost as entertaining as reality itself.

∞

Stone sits at his desk with tea and a slice of Dutch rusk, ignoring his stack of delinquent manuscripts. Instead, he reads yet another happiness book checked out from the library. This book stands apart from all the others—the bad seed. The book says happiness is a moving target, a trick of evolution, a bait and switch to keep us running. The doses must keep increasing, just to break even. True contentment demands that we wean ourselves from all desire. The pursuit of happiness will make us miserable. Our only hope is to break the habit.

He lifts his eyes from the page to wonder whether the Algerian woman might be experiencing massive anesthesia from post-traumatic stress disorder. Maybe her free-floating ecstasy might signal a coming collapse. But in all the hours he's spent in her presence over recent weeks, the lowest she's ever descended to is mild amusement. She will sit in class from beginning to end, whatever the tempers erupting around her, basking in light and loving her flailing peers. Russell has watched her all class long out of the corner of his eye, levitating in the middle of the fray, shining like some giant horse chestnut in full sun.

Does the woman feel real elation, or does she just imagine it? He runs the meaningless question into the ground.

He launches his slow Internet connection, then stares at the search-engine box, wondering how to initiate a search for unreasonable delight.

He taps in *euphoria*, and erases it. He taps in *manic depression*, and deletes that, too. He taps in *extreme well-being*. And right away, he's swamped. In the world of free information, the journey of a single step begins in a thousand microcommunities. Inconceivable hours of global manpower have already trampled all over every thought he might have and run it to earth with boundless ingenuity. Even *that* thought, a digitally proliferating cliché . . .

In less time than it would take to comb through the global auction houses for a favorite childhood toy, he discovers the positive-psychology movement. One more massive development he's never heard of. An empirical science of happiness—why not? And an international phenomenon—but what isn't, these days? After centuries of studying all the ways the mind goes wrong, psychology has finally gotten around to studying how it might go right.

The whole field seems to have kick-started around the year 2000, just as the world began to descend into a new round of collective misery. And already the discipline is overflowing with enough articles, books, and conferences to make a casual lurker like Russell Stone overdose.

Results 1 through 10 of about 9,300,000. He feels that vertigo he gets from going out to the end of Navy Pier and glancing back at the hundred-story, steel-and-glass towers spinning out their million innovations per cubic meter per minute. He scrolls through the matches, this network of seething bits at last made visible to anyone with a browser. The vision is almost bracing, the feeling Russell had as a boy of ten, when he and his brother, Robert, stood in the mist at Table Rock, Niagara Falls, shouting in the murderous cascade. The sheer scale absolves him. The world falls at too many buckets per second for him to rescue anyone.

He clicks on link after link, diving down into the maelstrom of discovery, not sure what he is looking for, but finding no end of things he isn't.

∞

Russell finds what he's after at last, not online but in archaic print. He sees it in a sidebar in his latest bedside happiness manual, a tinted box with the heading "The Better Without the Bitter?"

Have you ever come across someone with an oversized appetite for life? Someone who seems to feel nothing but major keys, resiliently joyous, impervious to distress? Some people are simply the big winners in genetics' happiness roulette. They live every day bathed in renewable elation, enjoying a constant mania without the depression, ecstasy

67

without the cyclic despair. These people (and they are very rare) may possess a trait called hyperthymia . . .

He hasn't made it up. It's biological. Researchers study it. It has a Greek name.

But don't be fooled: people who are exhilarated, inspired, and full of vibrant life may actually suffer from hypomania, a condition associated with full-fledged bipolar disorder. Hyperthymia is a durable trait; hypomania is a cyclical state. The first can be life-enhancing, the second, deadly. As usual, it's best to leave a full diagnosis to the professionals.

The thought creeps up on him, as unreal as that euphoric refugee. The woman has something that should be looked at. He, Russell Stone, in deeply over his head, needs to consult a real professional about Thassa Amzwar.

∞

He tries the Mesquakie home portal. The college must have shrinks, or whatever the latest euphemism calls them. With little effort, he finds it: Psychological Services Center. On the screen, it looks just like a brokerage. The counselors each have their own page for potential student clients to scan.

He searches their images, feeling no more than a twinge of shame. He has used website photographs to pick a dentist. He has checked out the Facebook mugs of the amateur authors he edits. It doesn't feel creepy anymore. It feels like self-defense. If his grandchildren ever read the journal entry where he considers the ethics of "face peeping," they'll just laugh. If he doesn't burn his journals first. If he ever has grandchildren. Maybe his grandchildren will post his journals on whatever replaces the Internet, alongside every embarrassing photo of him ever taken. It won't even be *posting* anymore. Shared will be the default condition.

Face peeping does for Russell what selective serotonin reuptake inhibitors do for his brother. It allows him to cope with a torrent of strangers, without wigging.

The first psychologist looks like a ridiculously benign Realtor. The second looks like somebody's fervently maiden aunt. The third would eat him for breakfast with just a squirt of no-cholesterol spread. The fourth stops him dead.

She's Grace's clone.

Only older, he thinks. Then he remembers: Grace is older now, too. Candace Weld, Licensed Clinical Psychologist, looks so much like Grace Cozma that Russell goes tachycardic. He sees the differences, but none is big enough for his gut to give a damn. It's Grace, give or take; the spray of fight-or-flight hormones cascading through his limbs proves it.

He folds his shaking hands behind his neck. He feels himself plummeting into paranormal genre fiction. *Know* this story? He *wrote* it. He should close his browser, flush his history, delete all his cookies, and run.

The words on the profile page swim into focus:

Candace Weld works with students who are coping with stress, anxiety, low self-esteem, burnout, and difficult relationships. She also specializes in eating disorders and questions of body image. Candace helps students understand that feeling good about themselves is more important than being "perfect . . ."

He rereads, reeling, wondering how Grace could have come to *this.* He stares at the picture of the counselor; the resemblance weakens, but not the recognition. All his pictures of Grace went long ago to the flame, so he has nothing to compare this woman to. After another few minutes of paralyzed staring, what's left of Grace Cozma's face blends into this one.

Someone else dials the center, gives his Mesquakie ID number, and asks for an appointment. He hears that someone say *No, not urgent* and *Nothing really wrong with me.* An appointments secretary who has heard that particular danger signal once too often slips him in for early next week.

∞

I bring him back his old obsession—at least her face. It isn't my idea. This twist has been lying in wait for him. For years now, Russell Stone has bunkered down against the memory of a woman he doesn't even like. He's written his own ghost story, in advance.

I never seek out uncanny plots. I find them way too cheaply grati-fying. I stay away from books with inexplicable coincidences, pro-phetic events, or eerie parallels. But they seem to find me anyway. And when I do read them, however conventional, they rip me open and turn me into someone else.

This is what the Algerian tells me: live first, decide later. Love the genre that you most suspect. Good judgment will spare you nothing, least of all your life. Flow, words: there's only one story, and it's filled with doubles. The time for deciding how much you like it is after you're dead.

∞

Candace Weld's picture, vita, and life philosophy sit online in the Mesquakie directory for any spammer or sicko to find. Any nut with a keyboard could stalk her. Russell could probably get her credit history without too much trouble. In fact, the lightest digging reveals that she's got a ten-year-old boy with a photo-filled page on a kids' social networking site. It took the species millions of years to climb down out of the trees, and only ten years more to jump into the fishbowl.

∞

Five afternoons later he's up in the counseling center, trying to keep his limbs from shaking free of his body. The reception area is cheerful and fabric-oriented. Two female students sit nearby, each texting into their laps. In the stack of magazines spread around for waiting clients, he finds, to his horror, a copy of *Becoming You* with his fingerprints all over the text.

They call him in by anonymous number. He's a wreck by the time he reaches the office. Candace Weld, LPC, rises from an L-shaped desk in the corner to shake his hand. She introduces herself, but he knows her already. She holds herself nothing like Grace: a cardinal in place of a scarlet tanager. She regards him, her face tipped in a tenta-tive smile. She's maybe thirty-eight, six years older than she should be. But the puzzled eyes, the brave cheeks, and the childish pug nose combine to slam his chest.

"Please sit," she says, and waves at a stuffed chair. She sits in another, angled toward him. A shaded reading lamp stands between them. A half-height bookshelf hugs the wall behind her, filled with books on healthy living. He recognizes one of the happiness encyclopedias he's been poring over these last weeks. On the wall above the bookshelf hangs the azure dream of Hopper's *Lee Shore*. The room is an aggressively cozy corner of a furniture showroom. They sit together, home again after a long day, trying to decide on pizza versus sushi. Grace, wild Grace, domestically tranquil at last.

"How can I help you?" she asks, her face a cheerful blank. It's no one he's ever met.

He tilts his head and grimaces as warmly as he can. "I'm not here for myself, really. I'm concerned about one of my students."

She recoils an inch. For just an instant, he's unreadable. Like he's grabbed her by the elbow and started cackling. Then she smiles and says, "That's fine. Tell me."

∞

Weld thought: *This man has recently been shocked to discover that he still has a future.* He sat in her stuffed chair, his eyes panning like a security camera, his chest so cupped that she twitched a little when he claimed to have come about someone else.

Four weeks earlier, yet another besieged student had erupted and shot up yet another school, this one in Wisconsin, only three hundred miles away. It happened every other semester, like some natural cycle, and every time, in the wake of the tragedy, a wave of concerned Mesquakie instructors flooded the counseling center. When those waves hit, the counselors were cautioned to work doubly hard at treating each case as if it were unique.

Candace Weld started the consultation with all the set protocols: Has the student made any direct or implied threats? Does the student display violent, erratic, or aggressive behavior? The questions just baffled the visiting instructor. Does the student display behavior that might require immediate medical attention? His each *no* was increasingly agitated.

Early on in every consultation, Weld liked to give her clients vivid shorthand names. She often tagged her art students after artists— *Munch*, a photography MFA candidate badly in need of lorazepam. *Botero*, a pale girl who planned to eat her way into her mother's heart. *Morandi*, a sandy glass-bottle freshman reconciled to his gray still life. But Russell Stone was a writer, or, as he explained, "At least I play one in the classroom." *Fyodor*, she decided, penning the name at the upper right of her fresh spiral pad: Fyodor, feverish with beliefs.

In what way did he find the student's behavior troubling?

He laid out the whole story, which Candace Weld noted in detail. *Document everything.* The stranger the tale, the more important the paper trail. She leaned forward into his accounts, as if some scrap might otherwise fall between them. As he launched into his exposition—Algeria, murder, exile—she had to remind herself to stop listening and keep writing.

He wandered deep into backstory. She tried to guide him, but he seemed trapped inside a thick volume, and all the pace and cadence of her profession were powerless to extract him.

She asked: Are you worried Ms. Amzwar might be suffering some kind of breakdown?

Her transcript has him answering: "I'm worried that she is excessively happy, in a way that can't possibly be right."

Why not?

"Because she's an Algerian civil war orphan refugee."

Why couldn't an Algerian refugee be happy?

But at that question, Fyodor just slumped and shrugged.

She asked if he'd consulted with anyone at the college—any of Ms. Amzwar's other teachers.

"One or two of the other students . . ."

Seeking another opinion had clearly never occurred to him.

Had Ms. Amzwar ever approached him in distress?

Fyodor: "I'm not sure she's capable of distress."

Then why, exactly, was he so concerned?

"From what I understand, if she's truly hyperthymic, then she doesn't need anything from anyone. But if she has hypomania, she's in trouble. All that elation is just waiting to crash."

She breathed in and transcribed his words, not for the first time in her counseling career silently cursing Wikipedia. Out loud, she said, "She'd have to make an appointment for me to do a complete assessment."

He shut his eyes, then opened them. "Of course. I just don't know how I can ask her to do that without . . ."

"Without asking her to see a psychological counselor?"

He nodded, defeated.

"I understand," she said. "Tough to tell someone, 'Get help. You're too happy.' "

He nodded again, his lip half curling. *Fyodor smiled.*

"You should consult with her other instructors. See if any of them are also concerned."

"Okay," he said, not even pretending that he might.

Obeying the protocols, Candace Weld bit down and started again. Would he say that Thassadit Amzwar was sociable?

The question amused him. "Every single person she meets is a long-lost friend."

Did Thassadit race or free-associate when she talked?

"Just the opposite. She brings everyone back down to a reasonable pace."

Did she fidget or jiggle or bite her nails?

"She sits beaming for the whole class period."

Did she ever seem cryptic or allusive or grandiose?

"My God, no."

Was she ever edgy or aggressive?

He twisted his lips and shook his head, the question too ludicrous to humor.

What did she eat? How much did she sleep? He answered the best he could. Something heartbreakingly amateur clung to him. But *he* wasn't the subject of the consultation.

The psychologist set down her pen. She steepled her fingers to her lips. "Maybe someone should get a urine sample from this woman?"

He took his time answering. She admired that.

"If I knew a drug that produced sustained, intense, level, loving well-being without any trace of stupor or edge, I'd take it myself."

She cocked her head and twisted her lips. "You'd have to. Everyone else would already be on it."

He laughed then, a sharp little bark of alarm. She caught her hand smoothing her cheek and dropped it into her lap. "You've never seen her get irritable?"

He waited a beat, but only out of respect. "I've watched her for almost two months, and I've never seen her even grimace."

She flipped through her notes for a hidden explanation. "Obviously, I can't say anything without seeing her in person. This isn't a diagnosis. I'd never say you have no cause for concern. But . . . you aren't really describing mania, from what I can tell."

He couldn't even pretend composure. She liked that in him. "What *am* I describing?"

"We can talk more, if you'd like. About why she disturbs you. You could make another appointment."

For a moment, Fyodor fumbled. Then all the visiting instructor wanted was to get away.

For her doctoral thesis, Candace Weld had studied 480 cases and analyzed the various ways that clients ended their treatments. Some reached a satisfying stopping place. Some terminated prematurely, when they were almost home. Others spent years going nowhere before finally throwing in the towel. This one, she knew from the moment he walked into her office, was destined to terminate before therapy even began.

But waiting was her art, and her medium, the blind confusion of others. "Come talk whenever you like," she told him. "I'm here, if anything changes."

∞

She sits in the chair next to him, Grace poised on the South Rim. He fights to keep from lapsing into old, private patois. He answers her professional questions, hearing himself stutter as if on tape delay. She gives him nothing but her guarded opinion that Thassa is probably not about to hurt herself. He's come to the wrong place. This woman is a licensed counselor. He needs a positive psychologist. He wants to apologize for wasting her time. He's long ago written off his own.

They stand and shake hands. She starts to speak, but something stops her. He has the weirdest sense that she recognizes him. She almost remembers that they, in another life, were lovers.

"Wait a moment," Candace Weld tells him. She crosses to her desk. She walks the way Grace would have, if Grace had been the person he thought she was. She riffles through a drawer and retrieves a small white rectangle. She writes something on it, then holds it out to Russell at arm's length.

The gesture freezes him. The outthrust arm, the cradling grasp: it's Thassa, pressing her book against the plate-glass window. He shrinks from the offering. But she holds it steady, reeling him back in.

It's only her business card. He takes it like it's an archaeological artifact. The college logo, a counseling center address, her name and title, phone and e-mail, and another phone number scribbled in ink. "That's my direct line."

In tiny italic font, centered beneath the words "Licensed Clinical Psychologist," he reads:

You have cause — so have we all — of joy.

He's sixteen, and seated in a metal lawn chair in the backyard of his childhood home, struggling through a mildewed Shakespeare, with the dictionary and encyclopedia on a drinks table beside him. July of his junior year in high school, and for months, he's felt an overwhelming premonition that he'll be a playwright when he grows up.

The premonition was a lie. He never quite grasped drama, never got the hang of how people really talk, never mastered human psychology. The best he managed was a scene or two of clumsy imitation vérité.

He lifts his head, again fighting the sense of being scripted. He searches for any hint that she's running him through an elaborate psychological experiment. But her face is frank and open in a way Grace's never was.

"For our escape is much beyond our loss." He doesn't mean to speak out loud.

She stares at him. "Oh! The quote. I do like that one. The students usually do, too."

"Is this . . . the only card you use?"

"Yes. Why do you ask?"

No reason. Less than no reason.

Back outside, on the street below, whiplash settles in. The appointment has done nothing but fill him with shame. Who is he to police someone else's well-being? A cold wind slices down from Milwaukee. A week ago, the city was a blast kiln. The temperature has dropped from ninety to sixty in four days. Seasonal affective disorder: the entire spinning planet must be bipolar.

∞

Seven things worth journaling about Candace Weld:

Boston accent, not yet obliterated by the Midwest.
She used to be religious; now she's empirical.

She's never been without some calling. For the last twelve
    years, it has been reminding people that they're free.
Her office walls have three pictures of sisters and two of girl-
    friends. Five of her little boy. None of the boy's father.
She has twice taken herself off cases after developing compro-
    mising emotional attachments.
Most of her clients love her. The few that hate her need her
    love.
She wakes up every morning feeling almost criminal that she
    can make a living doing exactly what she was born to do.

Three things Russell Stone actually writes about her in his journal
that evening:

She's a middle child, a helper. She doesn't know how obvious
    this is.
She'd be the best kind of person to have in your court.
The gaps between her keyboard keys are filled with cookie
    crumbs.

∞

The class grows closer, reluctant to let the holidays split them. They
open up their unedited notebooks to one another. Journal and Journey turns into group therapy by another name. They swap all their
hidden hostages now, when they trade their nightly writing. They
travel together, down into one another's darkest places and up to their
wind-whipped peaks. For one last moment, the eight of them share
something better than a story.

They take on Roberto's nineteen months of annihilation by meth,
the weekend-long punding sprees, taking apart and reassembling an
old pendulum clock six times in a row. They join Charlotte's permanent guerrilla campaign against her father after the baffled automotive
executive punches daddy's little girl in the mouth, then spends the
next three years begging for forgiveness. They cheer Kiyoshi's provi-
sional victory over agoraphobia the day he summons up the courage
to order a fish sandwich in a McDonald's.

And they share Thassa's bewildered glimpses of the United
States—waiting to get a license at the DMV, trying to recycle batteries

at a behemoth box store, witnessing her first televised megachurch evangelical service. Her journal knocks them back down into immigrant senses. Their country goes wilderness again, through her eyes. Her words make it okay to find pleasure in nothing at all—trading folk songs with the mailman or mapping the trees of the near South Side. Joker Tovar cuts his ADD engines and listens, one hand cupped over his eyes. Even Artgrrl Weston drops the groomed irony and nods, like she, too, wants to be Thassa when she grows up.

Suppose that panic or even pointlessness can't touch us. Say that nothing can touch us, but what we say.

∞

There's the scene where Stone asks Thassa to stay after class. As if he wants to talk to her about her course writing. The others, on their way to their traditional post-class jamboree, beg him not to monopolize their ringleader for too long.

He's practiced this speech for so long that he almost gets the question out without bobbling. "There's something I'd like to talk about. Would you have a minute? We could grab something downstairs . . ."

"Hey!" the Algerian asks. "Are you trying to date me?"

He steps back, slapped. "No! I just thought we could sit for a minute and discuss—"

Thassa laughs and shakes his elbow. "*Yes*, Mister Stone. It's fine. I'm joking!"

They descend to the makeshift café, off the main-floor lobby. They hit the self-serve tea station and take their paper cups to a tiny steel-mesh table. Stone chatters nervously about the recently discovered miraculous benefits of tea polyphenols. Thassa waves him off. "Kabyle grannies knew about that, long before chemicals!"

Stone asks about Thassa's surviving family. Thassa pulls pictures from her shoulder bag. She shows off her brother, Mohand, who has dropped out of community college and returned to Algiers, where he makes a living hiring himself out to stand endlessly in line for people mired in the bureaucratic state services. She passes him a shot of her aunt Ruza, the former dentist, tending the water lilies surrounding the chinoiserie pavilion in the Montreal botanical gardens. "A funny city," the Kabyle says, shaking her head. "But it's home now."

Seeing his chance, Stone blurts out, "Do you miss it?"

"Sure! I miss every place I've ever lived."

"Do you ever find yourself a little low? A little gray, down here, in this place?"

She tips her head, trying to figure out what kind of scene they're writing. "Of course! I think you can imagine. How else to feel, so far from everything?"

"And . . . does that ever frighten you?"

She sighs and looks skyward. Anyone who didn't know her might say she's exasperated. "You think I'm too happy, don't you? The whole world thinks I'm too happy! Isn't this America? No such thing as too much?"

His pulse spikes, and he looks around to flee. "I'm sorry. I don't think that. I was just concerned that sometimes—"

She reaches across the table and flicks the back of his hand with her fingernails. "What do you *think*? I'm not strange. I feel everything you do. Can't you tell that from my journals?"

He catches her eye; she must be joking again. At worst, her journal entries admit to tiny flecks of brown—small craft scattered across an open, golden sea. Everything that he feels? Maybe, if you invert all the doses.

"The problem is really my name." She's frowning, or at least it looks like a frown.

Stone shakes his head.

"*Thassadit*. This name means *liver*. I'm stuck with this prophecy. I can't help it!"

Stone just looks at her, worse than worthless.

"Well, liver is the Tamazight for *heart*. You know! *Joie*. Expansion. Big feeling?"

She won't say the word. "Generosity?"

"You see? I was doomed from birth." She looks down, embarrassed. "Russell? The others are waiting at the bistro. Why don't you join us?"

His heart tries to kickbox its way through his sternum. "I don't think so."

"Just ten minutes? You like these people. They like you."

"I still have some work tonight." Manuscripts to mark up; enthusiasm to edit back down into harmlessness.

"Please don't worry about me," she says. She stands and hugs him.

She's halfway through the emptied lobby before he can say, "No, of course not."

He goes home and binges all weekend on nineteenth-century Russian short stories. Just this once, fiction.

∞

I need a *genealogy* for the word. It comes through the loins of that giant Latin *gens*, the one that so liberally shares its family name, family property, family ties, and family plot. The original root of the thing has spread its genes into an absurd number of offspring: genial, genital, genre, gentle, general, generic, germane, germinate, engine, generate, ginger, genius, jaunty, gendarme, genocide, and indigenous, while scattering cousins as far afield as cognate, connate, nascent, native, nation, children, kind. Generous to a fault. Too many progeny for any paternity test.

A heterogeneous word, but how benign? Does *generous* include all those who are by nature genuine, generative, anyone pregnant with connections, keen to make more kin?

Or is generosity a question of having the right blood, the innate germ of the genteel gentry?

It strikes me that genomicists will soon be able to trace a full lineage for any person with more journalistic precision than the dying race of philologists have ever been able to trace a given word's more recent journey.

∞

Forgive one more massive jump cut. This next frame doesn't start until two years on. It's the simplest of predictions to make. Tonia Schiff will find herself on a warehouse-sized plane flying east above the Arctic Circle, unsure what she is hoping to come across at the end of the ride.

She'll be on a flight to Paris, economy this time, where she will catch a connecting flight to North Africa. A packed plane, 550 passengers: elder hostel groups, college kids with Eurail plans and *Rough Guides*, middle-class French couples—instant aristocrats of the plunging dollar on their way back from overnight shopping in New York—commuter businessmen with their spreadsheets full of pharmaceutical sales or financial services. And on this flight, she will try several times to watch the episode again, "The Genie and the Genome," that segment of *Over the Limit* she filmed two years ago. Armed with a notebook computer, several disks from the archives, and dozens of hours of raw clips, she intends to weave a sequel that might somehow redeem her.

The third time through the episode, she'll get as far as the bit where Kurton starts in on our being "collaborators in creation" when she'll have to shut off the computer and put it back in her carry-on. She'll look up through the rows of her fellow passengers, smothered by the coming world. And she'll think how the species almost completed one magnificent act of self-understanding before it snuffed itself out.

I have her flip up her window slide and look out the plastic portal. Far below, at a distance she won't be able to calculate, something the size of a continent will slip away west. The endless surface, a sheet of unbroken white just a few years ago, will be speckled all over and shot through with blue.

∞

Tonia Schiff will sit for seven hours in the melee of the concourse at Orly Sud waiting for her connection to Tunis. Say it has happened already, just the way it will. Her flight is delayed and reposted half a dozen times. Reading becomes impossible, in the seething free-for-all of the gate. Continuous PA announcements shred all thought, and the age of talking to strangers in transit ended long ago.

To pass the time, she scans the crowd for cognitive biases. It's a nasty little hobby, one that has driven away several boyfriends, including a trophy congressman whom she almost considered marrying. But the habit is too consoling to break.

All the flavors of bad science are out in force. Several twitchy passengers bandwagon around a sealed jet bridge for no good reason except that others are standing there. A red-faced Russian, sick with information bias, accosts a beleaguered ticket agent, who indulges a little skilled *déformation professionnelle* of her own. A pretty young couple hold hands and together influence the departure monitor by staring at it. And a loud compatriot of Schiff's complains to no one about the loss of an upgraded seat that was never really his.

Here in the portal to the northernmost South, the glottal cadences of Arabic already immerse Schiff. The sounds of the crowd broaden and deepen into rhythms she no longer recognizes. A three-generation clan sits next to her, decked out in holiday-finest tunics and scarves among ziggurats of cardboard boxes lashed up with string—presents from France for an entire village, once they get *home*.

The father of this family in transit could almost be that mythic fair-haired, blue-eyed, Afro-Eurasian Kabyle that so obsessed nineteenth-century Europeans. Then again, they could all be Schiff's own distant cousins, differing from her by only a handful of alleles.

She thinks: *Look at me—as Islamophobic as anyone.* Phobic of contemporary Muslims, anyway. For Golden Age Muslims, she feels the respect most people save for dead patriots. Alhazen, Avicenna, Averroës: advancing science when Europe was still waist-deep in angels and devils. Then something happened. Exploration stopped, replaced by received wisdom. Observation, washed away by certainty.

Much the same is happening again, this time on Schiff's branch of the family tree. Her own government has long crusaded against all kinds of science, secure in the revealed knowledge they needed. Now Schiff herself wades into the middle of a fray that might just turn the moderate American citizen against any more discovery.

Once she assumed that it was just a matter of time before humanity mastered its own destiny. Now she knows that only the past is inevitable. Reason could break down at any moment. Look at Orly Sud.

Enough philosophy; she has sworn off it. Philosophy never consoled anyone. Tonia Schiff finds an outlet and flips on her notebook again. She cues up her rough clips and searches for a way to splice their cataclysms into a future worth birthing.

∞

Then comes the next classroom scene. From Friday to Monday, ten suicides have succeeded in metropolitan Chicago, six of them the result of mood disorders, the second-leading medical killer of people Stone's age. From the time he says goodbye to Thassa in the college cafeteria until he sees her again in next week's classroom, 287 people nationwide take their own lives. It's number three in Harmon's list of most frequently used plots.

Stone holds forth to the class, clunking his way through Harmon's chapter on focalization:

The world has *seconds* and *minutes* and *hours* and *years* and *centuries*, but only the mind has *long* and *short*. The world has *inches* and *yards* and *miles*, but only the mind can turn *near* into *far* . . .

"Grandpa Fred has finally lost it," Princess Heavy says. "He's starting to drool."

"Totally," Spock agrees. "The man is whack. Fascinating."

The rest of the class piles on, and pretty soon, Frederick Harmon is left in a quivering, bloody pulp in the center of their encounter group. Russell loses his losers and abandons the lecture in favor of more journal read-alouds.

He conducts the group feedback the same way he always does. But Thassa, who grazed his shoulder on her way in, just sits in the oval in a bubble of contentment. He tries to draw her into the discussion, but she hovers alongside it, soaking the words in. To receive may now be more generous than to give.

Invisiboy apologizes to everyone. "I'm sorry you all have to listen to my lameness. Twenty-five new blog posts every second, and every one of them is more entertaining than my entry."

Charlotte berates him. "You shouldn't worry about entertaining anyone." Before Russell has a chance to shout *Yes!* she adds, "Nothing really matters except entertaining yourself."

Russell moves the group on to John Thornell's excerpt. Spock reads a piece about playing paintball up in Wisconsin with a dozen strangers for thirty-six hours without sleeping. When he's done, Russell can do nothing but sit, his face yipping, unable to sink the putt of appropriate response.

He tries, ever so gently, to suggest room for improvement. He cloaks the suggestion in a general observation. "As I always say, all the best writing is rewriting." The circle just blinks at him. No way they're buying perpetual revision. Half of them don't even believe in the Shift key.

Counterstrike dismisses Teacherman. It's his God-given constitutional right. He gives Spock's entry his highest praise: "Perfect the way it is, boo. Don't change a word. The thing flows like manga."

They have to explain to Russell what manga is.

"Comic books?" Teacherman pleads. "Do we really have to go there?" His eyes latch onto Roberto, usually reliable in bringing the group back to sense.

But even Muñoz turns on him. "Well," the Thief whispers, his hands like balls of bailing wire, "the best comics must be better than any print-only book. It kind of follows: pictures plus words gives you more to work with than just words alone."

"What about interiority?" Russell challenges. "Complex levels of concealed thought? Things that aren't material or visible. What about getting deep inside people's heads?"

"I hate books that tell me what people think," Princess Heavy says.

"Exactly," Counterstrike agrees. "That Henry James guy? He is right at the top of my bitch-slap list."

Russell snaps. "Fine. Let's all just drown in shiny consumer shit." He hears the word too late, garbling himself only at syllable's end, like a television censor asleep at the bleep switch.

Even Thassa is stunned. They all sit frozen, until the Joker says, "Only the mind can turn shit into shiny."

Stone apologizes to everyone, twice. He's so ashamed he can't even restart the conversation. He lets them go early. He's ready to resign. Mesquakie was crazy to hire him.

The Berber woman stays after class. It's all he can do to meet her eye. "Are you ill?" she asks.

Of course he's ill; he's alive, isn't he?

She puts the back of her hand to his forehead. "Mmm. Yes. Warm. You need poly-pheelys, I think."

They take the elevator down together. She studies him, shyly, but shows no need to ask about his meltdown. She just wants him to be well. Same as she wants from any stranger she passes on the street. She just needs him to delight in the world's obvious inconsequence. It's all she's ever needed from anyone, in any country.

The elevator opens into the main lobby. Three night students straggle in, grinning knowingly as they exit. Thassa stops. Her olive skin blushes russet. "Maybe your problem is that you believe too much in words."

He can't even reply *maybe*. All he can do is stand wincing at everything in this life that ever made him happy. She takes his elbow and steers him toward the corner café. He follows her to the tea canteen, then freezes, dead. Seated at one of the tiny mesh tables is Grace's double, the psychologist, Candace Weld.

∞

Weeks later, Candace Weld would try to decide if she'd deliberately ambushed them. She'd been working late, catching up on session annotation. Between a sick soul and the healthy law, nothing mattered more than a good document trail. She was adding a closing appraisal to Russell Stone's interview when she noticed in her notes that his evening class was just about to let out. Gabe was at his father's; nothing waited back at her apartment except dirty dishes. She still had a good three hours of work. She put in one more, then went downstairs and sat for a moment on the edge of the café. She wasn't even sure she could pick out an Algerian from the mix of evening students. But a potentially hypomanic one she might just notice.

They came from the elevators arm in arm. Candace couldn't control her face, and Fyodor certainly saw her fail to. He shook his arm free fast enough to startle the girl. That's when Candace Weld wondered what exactly she'd come for, sitting idly in the college lobby, when she should have been heading home.

Weld told her clients that if she ever saw them in public, she would never acknowledge them unless they initiated. She got so practiced at that professionalism that she sometimes failed to acknowledge simple friends. Russell Stone was not a client, of course; he had come to her in consultation only. Had he come out of the elevators alone, she probably would have said hello. But not like this.

She didn't have to. Fast enough to surprise all three of them, the adjunct steered the girl toward the counselor's table and made introductions. He didn't say *friend*. He didn't say *psychologist*. He didn't say *student*. He just gave names and let the roles fend for themselves. She did admire that.

The girl was no girl. Twenty-three, but the radiance made her seem younger. People, like paintings, usually darkened with age.

"You *know* this man?" the Algerian asked. "That's perfect! May we join . . . ?"

Without Stone's prior account, Weld might have thought she had just come from a concert or film, some exhilarating work of art that made life, for a moment, seem kind and solvable.

"I was just leaving," Weld said.

"Five minutes?" The student grabbed her instructor's wrist and shook it. "You know this man. You have to explain him to me."

As Candace Weld did whenever she was lost, she grinned broadly.

And in that moment of her confusion, the pair sat down. The younger woman could not stop beaming at Weld, her eyes all speculation. As soon as she hit the chair, she rose again. "I'll make the tea. What do you take? I know already what this man drinks."

As soon as the student wandered away to the self-serve station, the teacher started up, in that male shorthand that needs each word to do twelve things. "I'm sorry."

Weld donned her counselor's mask. "For what?"

"She's trying to cheer me up."

"Why is that?"

"I lost my temper in class."

The man was artless, whatever else he was. But before Candace Weld could press deeper, Thassadit Amzwar returned with three hot drinks. She handed them out, saying, "*Saha, saha.*" Weld put hers to her lips and set it down, just to be doing something.

Thassadit asked, "So did you know this man when he was young?"

"No," Weld said, stupidly adding, "not really."

"This is a shame, because I need to know—"

"Ms. Weld is a college counselor," Stone blurted. "I just met her recently."

Weld's face went hot at the man's scrupulousness. But the news electrified the younger woman. "Serious? *Une psychologue?* Then I really must ask you some things!"

Counselor and teacher both froze.

"Do you think it's possible for people to change their own story?"

Candace Weld had planned to down half the tea and bolt. But that question was her drug, her hottest hot button, her hobby and her calling. She could no more refrain from weighing in on it than a gambling addict could keep from testing out a new pair of dice. Before she could stop herself, Candace was holding forth about the untapped ability of any human temperament to recompose itself. Everyone could be redeemed, given the right combination of behavioral adjustment, medical intervention, and talk. And of these three, the foremost was talk.

And as they talked, the counselor's words turned playful, to match the immigrant's. Something contagious about the Algerian. Her delight was irresistible: like being seven, and ten hours away from turning eight. Like being eighteen, out on the highway when a tune with a hook like resurrection came on the radio for the first time. Like being twenty-nine, and having the doctor tell you that company was coming.

Candace Weld could count on her two elbows the number of people in life who always made her feel lighter than she was. She'd met both of those people before she'd turned this woman's age. And yet here was this knocked-about refugee putting her, within twenty minutes, high up on a thermal, reluctant to do anything but circle and enjoy the view.

They followed a bread-crumb trail of topics: How long therapy takes and when you know it's done. Whether some cultures were healthier than others. Why America was terrified of every country that the Ottomans had ever ruled. Weld trotted out the twelve words left from her two years of college French; her pronunciation paralyzed Thassa with mirth. A week or two would turn them into big and little sister.

The secret of happiness suddenly seemed absurdly simple: surround yourself with someone who was already happy. Weld caught Stone's eye and screwed up her face: *You're right; she's unnerving.* Fyodor barely acknowledged her, as if his job in this scene—*the three principals meet for tea*—was to sit stock-still and regret the development he'd set in motion.

Thassa, finally, broke things up. "Hey! Some people have homework to do, if they want to succeed in life."

The three of them rose and stepped outside into a late-October night still warm enough to walk without hunching forward. The wind came in crisp off the lake, and in twos and threes, the leaves of the caged city trees made their apricot escape. Thassa walked backward for a few steps, looking at the couple through a director's shot box she made with her thumbs and index fingers, pleased by whatever she saw inside the frame. Then she smiled at the future, waved goodbye, turned, and vanished.

Candace Weld felt a twinge she couldn't quite identify. She turned to face Russell Stone, warming to all the bewilderment that the man had nowhere to put. He looked back, but couldn't quite hold her eye. He wanted to insist that he'd initiated nothing. She dismissed his apologies with one raised eyebrow.

"That isn't mania," she told him, even as doubt spread across his face. It was, in fact, something much weirder. "That's what we in the mental health business call peak experience. And you're saying she's like that *all the time?*"

∞

She offers him her hand good night. The hand is polished driftwood. He takes it and feels something awful and instant. One of them squeezes, then the other, and they tumble too quickly into mutual knowledge.

He knows this story. *You* know this story: Thassa will be taken away from him. Other interests will lay claim. His charge will become public property. He might have kept quiet and learned from her, captured her in his journal, shared a few words at the end of his allotted four months, then returned to real life, slightly changed. A vaguely midlist literary story. But he's doomed himself by calling in the expert. It's his own fault, for thinking that Thassa's joy must mean something, for imagining that such a plot has to go somewhere, that something has to *happen.*

I know exactly how he feels.

∞

The "Genome" caption reads: Geoffrey Tomkin, Author, *Tomorrow's Child: The Science and Fiction Behind Germline Engineering.* The image says: dead of coronary heart disease in two years.

TOMKIN:
If you want to issue a blanket pardon for every social crime we commit against one another, you just have to convince the public that destiny is in our genes.

SCHIFF:
You're saying that it would be bad for social justice if Thomas Kurton is right?

TOMKIN:
I'm saying, the minute you claim, "My genes made me do it," accountability disappears. And the minute you tell prospective parents, "We'll give your child the traits you want and get rid of the ones you don't," you turn humanity into a fast-food franchise.

87

SCHIFF:
It would be bad if he's right, but the evidence doesn't necessarily prove he's wrong?

TOMKIN:
Genomics says there are no genetic contributions without countless environmental ones.

SCHIFF:
Is it too late for me to get taller and prettier?

TOMKIN [*glaring*]:
These transhumanists are really big on making people taller. But taller than what? When Kurton's company starts selling parents the genes for a seven-foot son, someone else is going to bring out an eight-foot model.

SCHIFF:
Is it too late for me to become an eight-foot model?

∞

Weld calls Stone three days later, to postmortem the meeting. He's in his other life, at *Becoming You*. She's the first person from the college to use this listed contact number. It's Halloween, and he's dressed up as himself.

"I've been thinking a lot about Thassadit," the counselor says.

Russell suppresses a grunt. The lamb has crossed the lion's mind. But there's something in her voice, some professional reticence that worries him. "You think there's reason for concern?"

"No. I wouldn't say concern. But I'd like to talk to you about some possibilities."

He says, "What kind of possibilities?"

She's silent one beat too long. "I think someone should work her up. Take a good look. She seems immune to anxiety. Her positive energy is amazing. She maintains a continuous state of flow. Maybe she's benefited from some kind of post-traumatic growth."

A sick feeling comes over him. "It sounds like you've already worked her up."

"Well, she did stick her head in the counseling center over lunch. Just to say hello."

"And stayed for a chat?"

"We talked a little."

"And now you're her new best friend."

"Russell, I think she should be explored."

He catches himself gouging the margins of the manuscript in front of him with red pen. "You've seen her. You said she's okay."

"I mean really looked at, under controlled conditions. There's a research group over at Northwestern . . ."

She trails off when he says nothing.

"Russell?"

He no longer thinks anyone needs to test anything but Thassa's journal entries. "You said this isn't hypomania."

"It isn't. I would bet my career."

"Do you think it's hyperthymia?" The better without the bitter.

Her silence oozes dislike for the term. "I think a professional researcher should look at her."

"She likes you," he says.

"I like *her*. Anyone would."

This woman is not Grace. Grace always thought he was attacking when he was making nice. Constance Weld thinks he's making nice when he's attacking.

"Why are you asking my permission?"

"Well, I'm not, really. But I am asking your feeling."

Testing is an excuse. The psychologist just wants to spend more time around the Berber woman, like everyone else.

"You asked her already? About Northwestern?"

"I mentioned the possibility."

"And she said that sounded like more fun than a roadside explosive."

"You don't have to be like this," the counselor says.

He watches himself regress. "No? What *do* I have to be like?"

"All right. Let's not talk about this right now."

He's pathetic. Worse than a prepubescent. "I'm sorry," he says. "I'm out of line."

"No," the psychologist replies. "I understand entirely."

Cold, wet leeches attach to his brain, the way they did when his

89

first writing successes turned into nightmare. "Look," he tries. "I don't mean to . . . Maybe you and I could talk about this sometime. Coffee or lunch, or something."

He means fake lunch. Purely symbolic hostage swap. Nothing she might take him up on.

Luckily, her acceptance is as hypothetical as his offer. "Sure," she says, her voice weird. "I think I'm . . . Are you free Saturday?"

For want of anything more appropriate, he says, "Saturday's good."

"Good," she says, meaning nothing. They make plans, plans the Kabyle might just as well have written for them. Candace Weld names a place dangerously close to Water Tower, a nice Moroccan restaurant. "That's next to Algeria, right?"

"Streeterville, I think."

She waits just a beat, her silence wicked. "Am I supposed to laugh at that?"

∞

Candace ran her own experiment once, three years earlier. The packet sat for at least a day, in plain sight, in her mail slot at the counseling center. The creamy envelope with the coneflower painted on the bottom right corner must have been handled by at least two of the center's clerical staff. The nub was small and folded into thick paper, but still it amazed Candace that the bulge had alarmed no one.

The letter was unsigned and handwritten, its fat, loopy script with balloon i-dots the graphological equivalent of that coneflower stationery. It read:

Don't judge the ride till you tried!!!

And nestling happily in the top crease of the unfolded page was a flat, bright-yellow pill stamped, absurdly, with the universal smiley-face icon.

Weld knew at once who had mailed the pill. It came from a free-spirit painting major Weld called Frankenthaler, who had all sorts of complications, including ritual praying to the spirit of anorexia: *O goddess Ana, in your depravity* . . . She had told Weld all about an amazing series of expeditions on threshold doses of so-called X: *Everything just perks up, and you wonder who killed the big bad wolf.*

Weld had given Frankenthaler the usual literature, with its well-researched warnings. And Frankenthaler, feeling judged, had sent her this tiny yellow sun. The pill could not be cheap, on a student budget, and for any twenty-year-old to care about the empathic education of any adult was almost touching. Weld should have turned it in immediately to the center for analysis. Instead, she slipped it into her purse until she had a chance to think.

Carrying around a Schedule I drug as she walked through the university building to the street altered her awareness all by itself. She'd read about the substance over the years, and three of her friends had described it in detail. She knew of at least one psychologist who'd used MDMA in his practice, before it was banned. Her husband, Martin, had tried it before their marriage, and he called it one of the most meaningful experiences of his life.

Now, just having the stuff in her purse gave Candace sympathetic symptoms. She felt the unbearable dearness of the faces coming downstream in the rush-hour foot torrent along Adams. She could talk to them without talking. She could see with ridiculous clarity all of the needs lining their faces. She felt the full, desperate desires of a populace 58 percent of whom needed some kind of chemical intervention just to manage. All this from a little pill sitting in the bottom of her purse.

This was in her last few months together with Marty. She thought: Just go home, put it on your tongue, talk with the man like a little child for the next four hours, rediscover the world with him as if it were freshly invented. Save your relationship. Bend a little. Put your family back together. Just try it, in the interest of science.

She stood in line at the car park, clutching her magnetic-strip card as if it were her lottery ticket out of Purgatory. Even the man in the cashier cage seemed Shakespearean. On Lake Shore Drive North, she remembered Frankenthaler's awed description of how she'd sat in her kitchen, looking at a box of Mister Salty pretzels, feeling gratitude and wonder for everything in the solar system: *I was afraid to look out of the window on the park across the way. Scared it would be more than I could take. But I looked, and I was astounded. Peace just overpowered me. I'd spent my whole life coming here, and now I was home. Everyone alive deserves to feel that way once.*

For a day after her mistake Weld felt depressed, a depression as strong as the residual effect of any phenethylamine. Hers was an intense sadness at the thought that some brain-chemical look-alike could simulate for an hour any human emotional state in the spectrum. Not just simulate: duplicate. Produce for real.

In their next session together, Frankenthaler asked if Weld had gotten any recent presents in the mail. Candace said she had. An excited Frankenthaler asked, "*And?*"

Weld just smiled wistfully. "I flushed it down the sink, I'm afraid."

∞

So there's a scene where adjunct and counselor meet for another consultation, this time over *bisteeya*. Weld shows up looking like another person: flannel slacks and a funky hand-knit sweater. She catches him eyeing it. "Knitting is supposed to be the best relaxation. You can see the rows where it worked and the rows where . . . not so much."

"You *made* this?" He tries to gauge how much surprise is flattering.

She nods, beaming. "I started taking knitting lessons right around the time that I began studying how to read Mayan glyphs. Now I can kind of do both!"

He's braced for an ordeal, so he's off balance all lunch long when talk is nothing but pleasant. She's not without her own anxieties about handing Thassa over to the positive-psychology labs. She's exploratory and knowledgeable and open to negotiation. She genuinely wants to know what Stone thinks.

He thinks science can turn up nothing that he didn't already intuit, the first night of class.

She nods at his objections. She has no idea she's attractive, and probably doesn't care. The anti-Grace. It strikes him that she may not even like the way she looks. A wave of lust courses through him, which he rides out.

They talk about work histories, life at Mesquakie, near north neighborhoods, the industrial fear state. Over date pudding, she tells him about negativity bias. I'm not really sure if she tells him this over date pudding, of course, or even if she tells him at this lunch at all. But she tells him, at some point, early on. That much is nonfiction: no creation necessary.

She tells him to imagine he's in a deserted parking lot and a twenty-dollar bill blows right in front of him. There's no one in sight he can return it to.

"How do you feel?"

"Good," he admits.

"Right. A nice meal or a CD just dropped out of the sky."

A book, he thinks. *Nedjma*, by Kateb Yacine. The book Thassa described in her latest journal entry. A dream of escape from the colonized mind.

"Now imagine you're in a store. You approach the cash register with a purchase, reach inside your pocket for the twenty, and find it's missing. You accidentally threw it away when disposing of a crumpled tissue."

He feels the difference, before she has to explain. The freebie was fun; the loss panics him, like he has just let terrorists into his apartment. The bad is crazily out of proportion to the good, and it's the same twenty bucks.

"I see. I'm a nut job."

She smiles with disturbing gusto, reaches across the table, and shakes his fingers. "So's everyone! I'm right there with you, and I've *studied* this stuff. We remember a compliment for about three and a half days, but we hold on to a criticism for months. We think unpleasant events last about sixty percent longer than same-length pleasant ones. Threatening images get our attention faster, and we have to fight harder to look away. We need about five positive events to compensate for one comparable negative one. If you hurt a friend, you have to do five nice things to offset the damage."

"We're broken," he intones.

"Not at all."

"Five to one! We're completely incapable of balanced judgment."

She pulls her hair into a ponytail. She's warm and clinical, at once. "Actually, if anything, the bias is accurate. There's a solid reason for it. Think back to the Serengeti."

"Ah, yes. I remember it well."

She sticks her tongue out at him, then pretends she didn't. "If you're scouting and find food, that's dandy. But if a pride of lions discovers your hidey-hole while you're sleeping: Game Over. The bad can hurt you much more than the good can help. So nature selects for pessimists."

He catches himself twirling his spoon between his fingers. He's been doing it for minutes. He drops his hands into his lap, like stones. "So how did *she* slip through?"

The counselor's face is novice bewilderment. It's like they're discussing their daughter's just-discovered eating disorder. "That's why I thought someone might want . . ."

But Candace doesn't push it. She doesn't push anything. It's almost relaxing, and Russell Stone wonders just where this woman's clinical interests start and stop.

They split the check down the middle. Then they walk back out into the outrageously gorgeous day. The sky is a Chagall deep cobalt, and the buildings are etched against it with a fine ink liner. Even the surly pedestrians pressing past them seem like friends. The psychologist sighs. "Just look at this beautiful place!" Grace's good twin twists her face up at him, and he has to look away.

He closes his eyes and inhales. He's deeply depressed by the thought: true happiness may depend on the weather. And in the next breath, he's depressed that it might not. One of his happiness manuals claims that weather and mood strongly correlate, but only until people are cued to notice it . . .

"So why should autumn make people feel so good?"

She smiles secretly. "I don't know the precise chemistry. I'm sure it's been studied."

It's the perfect day to play the tourist in one's own life. They walk three blocks, into the shopping crowds surging up and down the Magnificent Mile, hunting for a cure to their misery that has not yet hit the market. She cranes her neck up at the Hancock. "When was the last time you went up?"

He squints at the calculation. "Sixteen years ago?"

Her eyes are aghast, delighted. "Come on. You can see four states from up there. And a good seventy-five percent of them aren't ours!"

∞

In my country, a new work of fiction is published every thirty minutes. That's 17,530 new volumes annually, not including Web publication. Even assuming a tenth of the U.S. rate in other parts of the world, the total figure may be something like 50,000 invented worlds in this year alone.

Say the infant novel was born four centuries ago and grew at the rate of 100 titles a year for its first several decades. Say the curve shoots up sometime in the last century. I don't know: a million total novels seems a plausible worldwide guess. You know what the next decade will bring. Beyond that, imagining is beyond imagining.

I try to calculate how many of those million-and-growing volumes are saddled with a romance—bright or doomed, healthy or diseased. I can't do the math. Surely it must be most of them.

Sexual selection, the surest and most venerable form of eugenics, has molded us into the fiction-needing readers we are today. Part of me would love to belong to a species free, now and then, to read about something other than its own imprisonment. The rest of me knows that the novel will always be a kind of Stockholm syndrome—love letters to the urge that has abducted us.

∞

They stand at the glass wall, elbow to elbow, watching crowds flow through the gorges below them. The city turns into a techno-opera, a glorious nanotechnological enterprise beyond the power of any coordinated forces to engineer. They find their neighborhoods, the college, six universities, a dozen museums and monuments, the dead stockyards and living stadiums, churches and commodities exchanges, the river-reversing channel, the four-mile-wide particle accelerator off in the distance. Their city is a staging ground too huge and hungry to dope out, lying like a scale maquette at their feet.

"Gabe loves it up here," Candace says. She keeps her eyes earthward. "My son. Anything complicated and blinking, from high up. Ten years old, and he already has a résumé on file with NASA."

"High up or deep down." Stone talks to the glass, remembering. "Or far away, in some parallel universe. A thousand years before or after, anywhere but now."

"That's right!" She smiles at him, surprised. "How do you know my little guy?"

He shrugs: met him way back. "So tell me where that comes from. Infinite hunger for the unreal. Why should that be useful, in little boys?"

She gazes back down at the microbe races. He watches her trying to take in the panorama. Puzzled, vulnerable, hand-knit: she will not look like this again, the next time he sees her.

"I wish I knew."

Numbing to the aerial view, they return to ground. The elevator drops so fast his ears hurt. This scene ends with Candace Weld studying him in return, in the tower lobby.

"So. Mr. Stone. I'm sorry to say, but I've enjoyed this. We should do it again somewhere else, sometime."

He wonders if she means the Sears Skydeck.

Though he stays silent, she doesn't wither. "I'm all about gathering more data. We in the social sciences like to avoid the small-N problem."

"I . . . sure. That sounds like fun."

I watch him twist, the way he did so often in real life. *Sounds like fun.* A little of her poise, and he'd admit: *Fun isn't something I do very well.* A little of her candor, and he'd ask: *Is this about me or my student?*

"And we can wait and see, about taking Thassa to visit the group at Northwestern. No hurry, obviously."

They stand there awkwardly, two more victims of natural selection, caught between negativity bias and the eternal belief that the future will be slightly better than the present. In possession of all the data she's going to get, Candace Weld smiles and waves and weaves her way across the homicidal traffic of Michigan Avenue.

He's still awake the next morning at three thirty, doing the math, wondering how a thirty-two-year-old editor is going to take care of a ten-year-old son who works for NASA, let alone a twenty-three-year-old daughter who's still in college.

∞

Interior: a lab at Truecyte, one of Thomas Kurton's many experimental spin-offs. A long room with eight rows of fifteen-foot workbenches, half of them capped by chemical fume hoods. Glassware and reagents spread a chaos across shelves and countertops, although the gloved, safety-goggled lab workers know exactly where everything is.

Some of the profuse gear could be straight out of labs two centuries old: pipettes and flasks, burners and retorts. But the crucial new gear has all gone digital: inscrutable black boxes covered in LEDs, sealed microelectronic sarcophagi that swallow up samples and report the relevant chemistry in clean columns on bright monitors; devices the size of bread machines that accept matchbox cartridges filled with tens of thousands of biological macromolecules suspended in arrays; sensors that read millions of data points in minutes, that make errors only once every few million reads, and that spit out answers to questions three billion years in the making.

The whole room is charged and alert, perched on the threshold of the next liberation.

Thomas Kurton's close-up fills the video frame, a koala with a shy smile. He could fund-raise for some endangered wildlife fund. At fifty-seven, the man looks like he's just been awarded a Presidential Junior Investigators grant to visit the National Institutes of Health over summer vacation.

> TONIA SCHIFF:
> You sure you don't have a painting tucked away in the attic somewhere, taking the hits for you?

> KURTON [*deadpan*]:
> Actually, all you need is a high-resolution JPEG, these days.

He's befriending the camera—slipping it a rum candy out on the far edges of the playground, while the proctor is distracted by more hardened delinquents. It's just fun for him, however many times he's done this, and fun for the casual viewer, stumbling onto *Over the Limit* after the sudden-death quarterfinal rounds of *Be America's Next UN Ambassador*.

> KURTON:
> Oddly enough, it's much easier to repair genes in egg cells than it is to do somatic gene therapy in a living person. And the beauty of germline engineering is that the fixes are inheritable! In a few decades, we're going to be doing everything that way . . .

Crosscut to Tonia Schiff. She's in a distressed-denim skirt and embroidered vest. She tried once to lose the boho chic, to adopt a wool-suit gravitas for a segment on how easy it would be for anyone to introduce neurotoxins into the air systems of a large office building. But the focus groups weren't having it. Schiff-hip was essential to the show's sangfroid. *Over the Limit* is Tonia, and Tonia is the girl whose hands-in-the-air, wry bewilderment could make anyone's heart skip a beat, just before the real bedlam hits.

> SCHIFF [*waving her legal pad*]:
> Okay, let's just talk about that "inheritable" for a sec. I mean, *forever* is a long time, right? Suppose the gene doctors decide that they've made a mistake with my mail-order kid . . .

Kurton laughs from the belly. He loves Schiff as much as the next viewer. *America's most irreverent science television journalist.*

> KURTON:
> Well, that's where the artificial chromosome pairs come in. We can insert them, right alongside the regular set, and load them up with useful genes, as we discover them. And we can flick these genes off and on as desired, without interfering with other gene regulation.

> SCHIFF:
> Plug-and-play chromosomes. Why didn't I think of that?

> KURTON:
> Offspring wouldn't inherit the artificial chromosome cartridge, of course. But they could get an upgraded version, with all the advances in genetic knowledge since their parents were born.

> SCHIFF:
> Kind of like downloading a patch to your computer operating system.

> KURTON:
> Exactly!

> SCHIFF [*looking around the lab for a SWAT team*]:
> Ri-ight. And would Microsoft be involved in any of these upgrades?

A cutaway animation sequence follows, base pairs assembling into genes and genes flying in and out of rotating chromosomes, spinning out kinky proteins that bind and catalyze stray chemicals like some sorcerer's apprentice part-stamping factory. The chemicals swarm into a face, at which the screen splits repeatedly, filling up with patent lawyers, philosophers, a clergyman, a science writer, a senator-judge, and several geneticist-businessmen—those who need to safeguard innovation and those who need to save us from it. Each face gets five words, then ten, the words overlapping, finally all surging together in one mighty Stockhausen tone cluster.

Then, in a wash of time-lapse shots backed by looping, stacked ghetto-house tracks, there comes a collage of courtroom dramas and judicial mind-benders, divorced couples suing each other over frozen embryos, companies making fortunes on cancer screens derived from the genetic material of uncompensated subjects, companies suppressing patented genetic tests that reveal the effectiveness of their patented medications.

Over the Limit: That the show has avoided extinction for four years is already freakish. That each episode passes for compelling television is a miracle of protective coloration. The fight for eyeballs is as merciless as any in nature.

"The Genie" returns to archaic talk. Schiff steers Kurton away from his enhancement fantasies toward practical business, but he keeps sailing out into waters that teem with more astonishing life. And every time, like a lithe pilot fish, Schiff follows him.

She can't help herself. Her heart, too, beats to something transhuman. You can see it in her face: she's already working on whole new segments to follow this one. You can see it in the way she tilts in her chair. She's ready to enhance herself. So are 78 percent of the show's demographic. Her job is to erase all trace of the thousands of staff hours of research and make every twist of this script sound freshly improvised. *Fresh*: the core engine of the information economy. Every idea spontaneous, every argument off the cuff. Every word to be consumed before expiration date.

SCHIFF:
I understand you recently became a technology consultant for a start-up venture that specializes in pet cloning.

KURTON:
Regenovia creates delayed identical twins of animals who played important roles in their owners' lives. For some people, it's a chance to reexperience all the qualities they loved in their companions.

SCHIFF:
Is it true that a California woman has mortgaged her house to raise the $50,000 needed to bring her dog back from the dead?

KURTON:
A lot of us might be willing to pay as much, for meaningful connection with another living thing.

∞

Kurton's smart house in Maine does not quite read poetry to him, but it does almost everything else. It darkens and lightens windows, detects motion and shuts off extraneous appliances. The cottage is a monster hybrid, a family summer cabin from the twenties where, just behind the cedar wainscoting, just inside the retrofitted beaded ceiling, cables course and signals seethe in all flavors and protocols. Despite the tangled network of digital devices, Post-it notes cover every surface, like mating butterflies massing in a hidden glade. Thomas sits among them in his rocking chair, with the spray of the Atlantic surf visible outside his smart window, chatting about drugs tailored to fit the individual genome.

Jump to that haunted Cassandra, Anne Harter, in her Oxford warren, her eyes darting everywhere but into the lens:

These people want royalties for tests that used to be free. They're prosecuting others for mentioning patented scientific discoveries in public. They own entire organisms.

They own natural fact. What about a few billion years of prior art?

Back on the shores of Boothbay, Thomas Kurton watches the same clip of Harter on a seven-inch screen in his lap while he rocks in his wooden rocker. He nods in sympathy.

> I agree; no patent should be allowed to prevent progress. The only thing profit is good for is reinvesting in research. I want a world where the one source of real wealth—genetic possibility—is common knowledge and accessible to everyone.

He talks about the companies he has formed: one synthesizing biofuels, one dedicated to rapid sequencing, one set up to perform genetic screens . . . Bayh-Dole has given public science a way to turn itself to the quickest practical use. And so he creates private ventures, releases them into the world like new experiments, creatures compelled to live or die by the same rules of fitness that govern all creation.

> What we want is a rich ecosystem: lots of ways of doing business. Lots of ways of doing science. The point is to find out where collective wisdom wants to go . . .

I want the story to stay there, to develop this conflicted, tragically flawed character: *collective wisdom*. Instead, "The Genie and the Genome" squids off into a wholly unnecessary subplot concerning a healthy middle-class Chicago suburban couple who used preimplantation genetic diagnosis to keep their daughter from inheriting the colon cancer that has ravaged her father's family. The couple simply had their embryos screened, then implanted one that didn't contain the lethal mutation. All the others were tucked away in deep freeze, joining the burgeoning population of embryos that float in dreamless suspended animation complete with legal status.

And no group wisdom can possibly condemn these parents for plotting their daughter's lucky escape.

∞

Tonia Schiff will scour these clips years later on the flight down to Tunis, studying the sardonic show host for signs of herself as the Airbus glides over the black Mediterranean. She'll freeze-frame through *Over the Limit* segments, examining the interviews for any hint of what she herself felt about the future of life, before it caught up with her present. Eventually, the battery on her notebook will give out, somewhere over southernmost Sicily. The future Schiff will study the past one for answers, but telegenic to the last, America's most irreverent science journalist stays hidden in questions.

∞

The group wants to see what the Bliss Chick is like when she's tipsy. They take Miss Generosity to an Irish bar on North Wells where the bouncers don't throw you out until you mess all over the floor. Someone *should* throw them out, just for ordering appletinis. They feed Thassa the first two mixed drinks she's ever had and won't let her eat anything. "In the interest of science," the Joker says.

Everyone's there except Kiyoshi, who mastered his agoraphobia as far as the bus stop before beelining home. Even Roberto sits in, trying not to spoil the fun. The result of the experiment is that the appletinis leave Thassa exactly like she is when sober, only less steady on her pins.

"You know what she's like?" Adam says. "Every day, 24-7. She's like being on a perpetual hit of E."

"She's nothing like that," Roberto hisses. The two battle over the precise effects of 120 milligrams of 3,4-methylenedioxy-N-methylamphetamine. The girls look on as all four boys thrash out the matter, which is halfway to a shoving match when Thassa chides them. She channels them back into a group sing-along. She gets them all clapping a backbeat and singing a Berber folk song, like a circle of Kabyle women at a wedding. Strangers at other tables graduate from glaring to joining in.

They play pool. She shows them how much more fun the game is if you're allowed to nurse the balls a little bit by hand, after hitting them with the stick. She helps everyone get the hang.

They talk about their teacher. Spock declares him as monumentally, magnificently tedious as a John Cage piece. Charlotte and Sue settle on the word *hapless*. Thassa asks for a definition, then fiercely disagrees. "I think he knows something big. I love him."

"Umm . . ." Sue giggles. "Define your terms?"

"I simply love him!"

They settle back into their corner booth, their heads on each other's shoulders—even brittle Sue Weston—reciting poetry. Thassa has them beat in every language. They don't even care that they can't understand four-fifths of her recitation.

"Do you know this Irish man Heaney? 'Walk on air against your better judgment.' He deserves immortality, just for that line!"

This line, they understand. The ceiling of the bar vanishes onto the open night, and all parties finally see that there's no reason on earth why people can't be one another's eternal comfort.

But poems end and the night goes on. The group breaks up, scattering to three compass points. John, Charlotte, and Mason follow Thassa south. They want to take the train, but she refuses. "You can walk anywhere in this city. Nothing is so far as you think." They stroll down glittering Wells, linking arms and harmonizing early Beatles songs, accusing each other of stealing one another's parts. Thassa is ravenous and stops for kebab, which she makes all three of them taste.

Charlotte and Mason peel off at the Metra station. Mountainous Spock Thornell walks Thassa as far as her dorm. Then Maghreb hospitality, appletinis, American freedom, or hyperthymic naïveté kicks in. She asks him up to her tiny efficiency to see the volume of Tamazight poetry she quoted from tonight, the only possession that has accompanied her everywhere in her long upheaval from Algiers to Paris to Montreal to the world's erstwhile hog butcher.

Her room is a tiny tent in the desert. Spock barely feels her sit him down, hand him hot hibiscus tea, place the book in his lap, and turn the pages. Deep inside his tangled passageways, he's already breaking free. Art is whatever you make. Walk on air. No one gets hurt by any true invention. She's showing him the foreign pages, and the words are all in a Martian alphabet no human being could possibly read. The writing is chaos, the coldest thrill, the best drug of all.

He is slow in all things, monosyllabic, a great believer in the irrelevance of any emotion. But even for Thornell, the night is still magical. He has never been so close to a foreign country. He has never been outside the Midwest, except for the wild expanses of the Web. He's waking up, after years of the grid system, to a life beyond containing.

What does he want? He wants what anyone wants. He wants this thing he can never have, this effortless glow, the one that's so exhilarating just to sit this close to. He wants a release from his relentless *his-ness*—just for a minute, a little of her spark, her art of pulling a story out of annihilation. He wants to eat her flame.

Or he wants to pinch the wick. To snuff her into nothing. To leave her as terrified as anyone.

"Strip," he says, and pulls at her blouse.

She clasps both hands to her breasts and laughs. "John! Quit. You're mad!"

Her fear thrills him. "Off. Come on. Let's go."

"No! You're nuts! You've lost your mind."

And he's loose in total liberty. Walking in the vacuum of outer space. He stands and starts tearing. He's burned alive, refined inside the thing he needs.

She falls backward, but there's no place to land. She grabs his wrists, but that's worse than pointless. He's twice her size, a crushing dimorphism. It thrills him to see the happiness vanish at last. She can do nothing, and that is more moving than any art.

All impediments tear loose. They are together, skin to skin. He looks down at the helpless brown thing between his legs. It hasn't gone feral. It's speaking, still her. She's saying, "John, not this." She's terrified, but not for herself. She says, "John, this kills you."

He slows to figure what she can possibly mean.

And slams back into the trap of thought. He rears up, rolls off her like she's burning. She calls out, "Spock?" and the word scalds him. He curls up into a fetus on her carpet, moaning like a thing trying to be unborn.

∞

Mid-November, the semester's home stretch, and the city drops into real chill. The sky molds over, and even the two-block walk from the El to the college cracks Russell Stone's skin. Now the lake effect begins to work against this place, and the vanished autumn is just a tease that he should have known better than to trust.

The security guard stops him in the lobby, flanked by two policemen. Someone has invented the scene just to create rising action. Harmon: story starts when a character's core value no longer suffices to stabilize his world.

Stone is ready to confess, even before he hears the charges. They take him into a first-floor conference room to talk about two of his students. There's been an incident. The officers are vague, cagey. Law and procedure everywhere. It seems that John Thornell—Mr. Spock, the icy conceptual artist whose most emotional journal entries read like commuter-train schedules—has attempted to force himself on . . .

Stone already knows the victim. He's known since before he heard the crime. It's Generosity, who escaped the maiming of Algeria in order to be raped in the States. The moment he laid eyes on the Kabyle woman he knew someone would need to violate her.

Russell sits still and listens to the officers. Thornell has turned himself in. Wandered in a daze into the station on South State and demanded to be put away. By his own account, the American got the Algerian to let him up to her room on false pretenses, then sexually assaulted her. But when the police talked to the alleged victim . . .

Stone knows this already, too, without hearing. When the police went to question Thassadit Amzwar, she denied that anything like rape took place. Yes, she invited Thornell up to her room after an evening out with the other students from their Journal and Journey class. Yes, he did become inappropriately excited. He did tear her skirt and blouse. But that's where things ended. By her account, she talked the man down without much effort at all. Thornell was crying by the time he left. She was afraid to let him go, afraid he might hurt himself. She was relieved to hear that he'd arrived safely at the police station.

The lead cop can't figure it. "She knows this case had no bearing on her student visa. She knows she'll have the full protection of the law if she takes action. But she refuses to file charges."

The second cop is as mystified as the first. "She actually apologized for giving us unnecessary trouble."

The police ask Stone if there's anything important they should know before they release Thornell over his own protests. They grill him about sexual tension, aggressive statements, any part of the classroom dynamic worth reporting. Do the man's journal entries suggest anything unusual?

They are filled with art at its most inexplicable. Plans for mailing Christmas cards to total strangers, to see how many baffled receivers reciprocate. Plans for selling tickets to the next rain shower, with a stiff surcharge for the good seats. Hand-drawn re-creations of bar codes. Long poems composed of song lines sampled at random intervals off

Internet radio. Powerless art in a confidential medium offered up in complete trust to a supportive community. By a would-be rapist.

An image of the man's cock between Thassa's thighs cuts through Russell, and he shudders. The man should rot in prison, raped by others. "No," he whispers. "I wouldn't say anything unusual."

And the woman: Any anxious behavior? Any reason why she might be afraid of pressing charges?

They've met her. They've talked to her. Surely they must have seen. "No," he tells them. "No reason."

"We're afraid this may be some kind of Muslim cultural thing. Many Muslim families will disown a rape victim."

Christian families, too. "She's not Muslim," Russell tells them.

"Arab, then. You know: where the woman gets punished if—"

"She's not . . ."

The cops perk up. "Not what?"

"Nothing," Russell says. She wants her assailant free.

Now the police are all attention. They ask if there's anything about the woman—any health conditions, behavioral quirks—anything that he should mention.

Well, there's a set of careful notes sitting in a psychologist's office just a few floors up. There's a telephone call—perhaps recorded by conscientious antiterrorist agents listening for references to students of Algerian origin—where a psychologist says that the woman should be studied in a lab.

Stone doesn't know what is confidential anymore and what the state owns. He hasn't a clue what he owes to professional discretion, what to justice, what to Candace Weld, what to Thassa Amzwar, and what to basic truth. But it's pointless to hide from the Informational Oversoul. Everything in the full digital record will be discovered. An hour of digging in the likeliest place and they will find him out.

"It's possible she might be hyperthymic." And to their inevitable, blank stares, he explains: "Excessively happy."

He only answers what the law asks. The policeman with the notebook asks him how to spell the word.

∞

Then he's supposed to teach the class. He's known from the start that he'd never get through the semester without disaster. He climbs the seven flights, buying time. He's buried deep in the Vishnu Schist, forcing his way back up to the present, and every ten steps is a mass extinction.

He hears the group pleasure, from down the hall. Thassa's voice weaves some goofy solo, and the rest of them laugh in adoring chorus. He rounds the doorway, his anemic frame coiled for pain. They're all there, huddled in the dingy room, listening to her read from her journal. All except the animal, still in police custody. She's told no one.

Thassa breaks off in midsentence. The group looks up, caught red-handed in enjoyment. Stone's eyes search the Berber's. For an instant, she's ready to minister to whatever tragedy has hit him. Then she remembers: *she's* the injured party. Their faces rewrite each other twice before anyone else in the room realizes anything's wrong.

And just as quickly, Thassa returns to the clause where she broke off. Russell Stone stumbles toward the mocking oval, book bag to his chest. Soon everyone is chuckling again at her story, about an Algerian and an Indonesian in a Chicago Mexican grocery, neither able to understand two consecutive words of the other's English. And all the while that her pliant face encourages her audience's laughs, she's coaxing the mute teacher, begging him to be okay, as okay as she is. In the sparkle of her glance, she reassures him: *John couldn't help himself, you know. The problem was inside him. The man just couldn't help.*

∞

Back in her snug, cinnamon, Edgewater apartment after nine and a half hours in the counseling center, Weld began her real day's work. First came forty-five minutes in which her son, Gabriel, gleefully destroyed her at every known flavor of computer game—battles of skill and strategy all rigged to favor the ten-year-olds whose thumbs had already inherited the earth.

Then she conscripted him into fifteen minutes of light housework. After that, she parked the boy in front of the plasma screen as she fixed dinner. She rationed him to an hour of fiction a day, but allowed all the informational programs he could stomach. Recently, the boy had discovered that the early *Chicago StreetSharp News* was almost as diverting as the average role-playing game. *Four stars, Mom; highly entertaining.*

As Candace pulled ingredients from the refrigerator, the boy sat cackling at amateur camcorder video of an escaped six-foot pet iguana scrambling across a busy North Side intersection as hulking SUVs veered all over, trying to avoid the reptile. Gabriel hadn't laughed so hard since the story, a month ago, when two rival architectural tour boats rammed each other in the Chicago River, throwing six culture tourists into the water.

Slicing her son's grilled chicken into strips—*fingers, Mom, always*—she heard the sweet news reader (whose glossy friendliness seemed to fill the boy with an inchoate longing he ordinarily reserved for Best Buy gift certificates) announce one of those stories that cause a community to transcend itself and knit together in shared awe.

Two area college students are in the news tonight . . .

Candace Weld oiled her skillet and smiled at the growing commonplace: newsworthy because in the news.

. . . after turning himself in to the city police and demanding . . .

She let the pan heat and prepped the broccoli. She could get the boy to eat small amounts if she pureed it with butter and a splash of maple syrup.

. . . a twenty-three-year-old Arab woman in the country on a student visa. The victim of the assault apparently not only persuaded her would-be assailant . . .

As Gabe called, "Mom, what's a *saylent?*" her cortex caught up with her limbic system. In three quick steps, she stood in front of the set, curling her boy's head gently away from the next words.

. . . close to the woman suggests that she may have hyperthiam . . . hyperthymia, a rare condition that programs a person for unusual levels of elation. It's not known how the condition contributed either to . . .

"Shit," the psychologist said.

"Mom! Five bucks, Mom." The delighted boy leaped up and beelined for her purse on the dining-room hutch.

"Fuck."

Her son beamed. "Ten more!"

The police have released the self-confessed alleged suspect, despite his demand that they . . .

Candace Weld's field of vision shrank and grayed. Reflux came up her throat. Self-confessed alleged. She lowered herself to the carpet and sat.

The boy set her purse down and crossed back to her. He shook her shoulder, blanching. "Mom? Mom. Never mind. You can keep the money. I don't need it."

∞

I see them clearly now: Thassadit Amzwar and her two self-appointed foster guardians, on the verge of that Chicago winter. I assemble the missing bits from out of the reticent archive. I'd dearly love to keep all three tucked away safely in exposition. But they've broken out now, despite me, into rising action.

∞

Weld called Stone four times that night. First his line was busy. Then he wouldn't pick up. She fired off a terse e-mail: *I had to learn about this on the news?* She redrafted the note three times, blunting her fury at his public diagnosis, that ridiculous little pseudoscientific tag. She focused on the attempted rape. The damage of public airing.

∞

He shoots a message back at five the next morning. It's frightened and sick with explanations. *I was answering under fire, complying with a police investigation. I gave them everything that might possibly have any bearing on the case. I assumed what I said was for the police only.*

They need two more e-mails and a jagged phone call before each settles down.

Weld asks if Thassa is all right. He tells her about the confused exchange he had with the Berber after class, in hushed and painful code, Thassa reassuring *him* that John Thornell's bungled assault could never have harmed her.

"You didn't call her last night? After the story ran?"

"I wanted to let her breathe." After a beat, he adds, "Cowardice."

Twice, she tells him that he did his best. But they both know: there would have been no *Chicago StreetSharp News* story without *hyperthymia*. "How can they possibly have used that word on television? Ridiculous."

"I'm sorry. I never dreamed the police would sell it to TV." But of course, television didn't have to buy it. The media simply exercised eminent domain. *Reality* has become *programming's* wholly owned subsidiary.

However the word got out, Thassadit Amzwar is an instant creative-nonfiction commodity. Harmon number nine: Harm Averted by Surprising Source. You know this story. Everyone knows this story but her. The Berber wouldn't know how to read this story for the life of her. No doubt she thinks it's Harmon number two: Group Misunderstands the Needs of an Outcast.

"The rape is my fault," Stone tells Candace.

"Of course it is," she agrees. Two handshakes, half of one ambiguous date, and they've been married for years. "This is all about you. You must have planted the idea in the man's head."

"If I'd been paying attention . . . She's a walking target. I should have warned her . . ."

"Are you serious? Criminal sexual abuse. A class-four felony. And she leaves her attacker so shaken he wants to be sent to jail for a decade. She doesn't need your protection. You need hers."

∞

The price of information is falling to zero. You can now have almost all of it, anytime, anywhere, for next to nothing. The great majority of data can't even be given away.

But meaning is like land: no one is making any more of it. With demand rising and supply stagnant, soon only the dead will be able to afford anything more than the smallest gist.

Minutes after the story airs, the Kabyle woman starts traveling abroad.

Your Day's Dose of Truly Fresh Weirdness in Pincer Movement 3 hours ago, *Influence*: 3.7

One happy victim, one hapless perp in <u>Closely watched change</u> 9 hours ago, *Influence*: 5.0

Hype, or hypertimin'? in <u>Shattered Visage</u> 12 hours ago, *Influence*: 7.8

bust me god dammit, im serious in <u>weasel while you work</u> 1 day ago, *Influence*: 2.4

Chic a Chicago in <u>Fuming Gaulois</u> 2 days ago, *Influence*: 2.6

When Goodness Wins in <u>Things That Lift Me</u> 2 days ago, *Influence*: 6.1

Search for: <u>Arab student rape Chicago</u> Results: 1–10 of about 312

But for a little while longer, the woman is still as meaningless as any local noise. She stays safely hidden in the million global narrowcast microcommunity headlines hatched every second. Bandwidth itself does not threaten her. Information may travel at light speed. But meaning spreads at the speed of dark.

∞

Hidden in the public static are three items of firsthand knowledge. Charlotte Hullinger adds a comment to *StreetSharp*'s feedback section, correcting some background data. Roberto Muñoz buries an agonized confession of complicity in a ghostly blog visited by three people a month. "I was there when they were getting her drunk." And Sue Weston posts an almost reverent appraisal on a college discussion forum: "He never had a chance of breaking her. She just blissed that creep away."

∞

The scene loops through Russell Stone's head, impossible to edit. It plays against the ceiling of the El train as he slumps in his seat, riding in for the public facedown. He watches his two students, the pleasure of their companionship crossing into animal violence. The scene, in his imagination, stays broad-brushed and dim. Always his downfall in writing: a complete lack of visual resolution. But he needs no great detail to be there. Thornell, the plodding minimalist, as depressed as anyone, electrified by the flash of something godly in the woman. Of course the man tried to force her. Ram himself home. It's coded into the deep program: fuse your sick genes to whatever looks healthiest. Feel the glow for fifteen seconds, even by killing it . . .

The guard scowls at Russell as the transient adjunct passes through security. Upstairs, in class, to Stone's relief, Thassa isn't there. The six surviving students fall silent when he enters the room. Neither respectful nor rebellious: just holding still for the sham of schooling.

They know everything now. They've passed around copies of the televised clip, downloaded onto their portable players. All but one were there that night, near accessories. Yet their faces interrogate *him*.

He should say something, anything. Clumsy or impotent, it doesn't matter. He owes her that much. Instead, he directs them to the chapter reserved for the end of the syllabus: "Bringing It All Back Home." "*Remember*," he reads aloud from Harmon's hectoring text, "denouement *doesn't mean tying up all your loose ends. Quite literally, it's French for untying.*"

They don't even bother to sneer. They will leave him to rot in the desert of pedagogy. Discussion dies on the vine. He asks for a volunteer for a first journal extract. Not even the Joker Tovar, in his silk-screened T-shirt—*Dada: It's not just for umbrellas anymore*—takes the bait. Russell waits. He's perfectly willing now to stand them off, to sit in silence for the rest of the evening and all that's left of the semester.

Deliverance comes from the doorway. "Hey, everyone."

Russell jerks around, between relieved and appalled. She's dressed in a Thinsulate vest over a hoodie and capris, this winter's worldwide youth uniform. She is as sober as anyone has ever seen her. But they all sense it, in her encompassing glance: whatever sadness she feels is just empathy for them.

She holds three fingers in the air in front of her, a scout's salute, which she draws to her pursed lips. "Um, may I just say . . . ?"

She drags her backpack to her traditional seat but does not sit.

"Maybe some of you saw the story on the news? It's just not true. It's not like that. We all know John."

None of them knows John. No one in this room knows the least thing about who they're sitting next to. They've traded nothing but the thinnest poses. They should have known as much, as early as the chapters back in week three. *Character is a performance born in a core desire that even the performer may not understand.*

"That isn't John, what the news said. John is someone with a great deal of . . . weight? He never hurt me. Okay: he tried for sex by force, but eventually, he knew this was a bad idea."

No one can look at her or stand another word. No one tells her to stop.

"I probably just confused him. He isn't the first person . . . he's not the first man I have ever confused!"

The circle of art students keep faces blanked, all of them would-be molesters.

"Please," she says. "You know what this is. It's nothing. It's just . . . desire. This doesn't damage me at all. I'm telling you, this isn't a trauma. I've written about this experience. May I just . . . ?" She pulls her notebook out of her backpack.

And with the steadfast failure of nerve that has penned his whole life, Russell says, "Maybe not right now?"

She looks at him as if he has just hurt her more than her assailant did. And she's sorrier for him than she is for John.

The others, too, appraise him. At last they understand his ultimate lesson: *Do as I say, not as I do.* He's failed them; he never really believed in journal or in journey. Story can save exactly no one. The only one in this room who knows anything of use is Thassa.

Sue Weston's face sickens over with tics: *How far did he get?* Mason twitches on his chair's edge, his fingers rapping out: *You stopped him with* what? Roberto hangs back, hurt that the Algerian isn't crushed, that she needs them all less than ever.

Only sphinxlike Kiyoshi Sims speaks. "We all knew there was something about you. But I never thought your whole mood thing is like . . . a *disease?*"

Thassa shakes her head, smiling sadly at Invisiboy, daring him to remember, to step out from this fiction back into the real. "Life is the disease. And believe me: you do not want the cure!"

She is again untouchable. Thornell must have foreseen this, even as he forced himself on her. Rape as surrender. Self-annihilation. The man knew she would destroy him.

∞

It stuns Russell the next morning to discover: her disease is still contagious. Life-threatening but not serious. He wakes up ravenous. He can't remember the last time that breakfast seemed such a brilliant plot twist. The winter air through the wall cracks braces him, and the table spreads itself. The boiling teapot sings like a boy soprano. The raisin muffin crisping in the toaster smells like muscatel. He's on a houseboat, moored on one of those mythical rivers that Information has not yet reached. That's how surely this mood has come on.

How rigorously drab his life has been. He's worked so hard at his own refugee status, piling up his Red Cross blankets into a tiny bunker. But all protection is powerless against this morning's brisk breeze—*this one*. He's only thirty-two, and more such mornings will keep arriving, despite his strongest resolve. What does he have to resent? Resentment is the coward's retreat from possibility. He could resent the night sky, for thrilling him.

The teaching job was his just by accident; he might never have met her. And tomorrow night, he'll have another two hours in the presence of joy. No one can punish him for that.

He grabs the newspaper from the landing and unfolds it on the kitchen counter. He thinks of her second essay—the flight from Algiers—and is kneed hard from behind by love: love for the morning thump of his neighbors through the muffling walls, love for his class's doomed zeal, love for the lying politicians above the page-one fold, and weirdly, most weirdly, love even for himself, as if he, too, were somehow worth his care.

He takes the coffee beans from the freezer, spoons them in the grinder, and churns. No evolutionary psychology will ever account for the pull of that smell.

He actually sits to eat, like it's some holiday. It is: Spontaneous Healing Day. He closes his eyes and holds a winter strawberry to the tip of his tongue. The fruit is spongy and sublime. The Arabica—as thick as his confusion—gingers as it hits the back of his throat. He can't imagine what Thassa's standing state of grace *feels like*; an hour of being her would blow him away. But this morning's gratuitous pleasure gives him an inkling. Liver means heart and heart means joy and she's stuck with the prophecy, and he is stuck with his gratitude for her.

He pictures the four of them—Candace, her Gabe, Russell, and his former student—on a makeshift outing to the Field Museum, sitting on hide beds around the fire in the massive Pawnee earth lodge, trading stories as winter locks in above the open chimney. They're up in the second balcony of Orchestra Hall, untouchable by anything but music. Or in the nosebleed heaven of Soldier Field, trying to explain to Thassa why steroid-laced men the size of *Arabian Nights* djinns are smashing into one another. They mill around in Maxwell Street's reborn flea market, combing through other people's castoffs, looking for buried treasure. And the unassailable Algerian turns every neighborhood into an A ticket.

Light streams into his studio from the eastern exposure. The breakfast dishes wash themselves, and still he's hungry. That's how surely this thing has come on.

By noon, he's buried again under other people's soul-crushing dangling participles and incoherent yearning. And yet, today, he's well. He himself may never be happy for more than a few island moments. But someone he knows is free, unsponsored, safe, well. He can stand near, catch the spillover. That's enough. Better than he ever expected. He wouldn't know what to do with more.

∞

John Thornell is evicted from his jail cell over his continued demands to be locked up. Mesquakie announces his withdrawal from college. It's not enough. Stone wants the man listed in a public roster of sex offenders, his hundreds of ink drawings defaced, and his journal burned.

∞

Russell schedules an impromptu writing exercise for the final night of class. Journal and Journey's last page. He carries the topic to school that evening on the train, as if it's a lightning bug in a jar with holes punched in the lid. *Write the journal entry for that future day you would most like to live.* The creature flashes when he shakes it.

But when he gets to Mesquakie, the final class is already under way. A reporter from the *Reader* is sitting in Russell's place with a flotilla of digital devices spread out on the table, conducting an interview. The journalist, Donna Washburn, has traced the attempted-rape story back to its guilty source. Russell fills with impotent rage. He wants to pitch the intruder out, break her voice recorder, and smash her PDA.

Instead, true to type, he stands feckless in the doorway. Who is he to fight the free spread of information, the public's right to know? Here is his syllabus, come to life: local detail, close observation, character, tension, inner values in collision — everything he's supposedly taught this semester, only real.

Thassa catches his eye in midreply. *Never mind; I know this. I can*

115

tell this. Stone has no doubt that she can acquit herself. It's the journalist he distrusts.

He takes a corner seat, watching his last lesson plan dissolve. Of course she's public domain. Nothing the race needs ever stays hidden. Artgrrl and Princess Heavy compete to tell their Thassa stories. Entitled, the reporter milks them. Even Stone gets grilled. But when he makes a move to break up the circus, the journalist asks Thassa, "This *hyperthymia.* So what exactly is that like?"

A murmur in Tamazight. "It's not like anything. It's absurd, this so-called condition. The news made it up."

"Okay, okay," Donna Washburn interrupts. "Just tell me, as simply as you can: What does it feel like, being you?"

Thassa lays her palms on the table, beseeching. "I'm telling you it's nothing. Everybody on earth has this symptom. They just don't know it!" At this, the whole class laughs.

"All right," the journalist says. "Let's leave that for now. Let's go back to your childhood. They killed your father . . . how?"

Russell cuts off the interview after half an hour. When the miffed Donna Washburn leaves, he looks down at his notes, the topic for the final impromptu. *That future day you would most like to live.* The topic is gibberish, nothing he'd be willing to write on, himself. *You know, Mister? You are a very unfair teacher.*

He assigns the topic. Each writes whatever sentences his or her temperament permits. "Write what you know," Harmon apes, as if it were possible to do anything else.

They do the assignment, then drag Stone to a makeshift end-of-year party, where they make him eat cheese fries and force him to listen again as they explain why blogs are better than print. Everyone wishes everyone else happy holidays, and wistful goodbyes proliferate, like a disease.

The last word belongs to next week's *Reader.* Underneath a photo of Thassadit Amzwar surrounded by admiring classmates is a half-page feature, part bio, part flubbed-rape account, part Maghreb travelogue, complete with quotes from a positive-psychology researcher at Northwestern about whether hyperthymia is real, all under the headline: SAVED BY JOY.

∞

A day after the piece appears, Russell Stone gets an e-mail from the department head, thanking him for his job this semester but saying Mesquakie won't be renewing his contract for spring.

∞

Russell is flipping numbly through von Graffenried's *Journal d'Al-gérie*—mass graves like potato fields, with plywood grave markers—when the phone rings. He checks the caller ID and it's neither his mother nor his brother. Which means it must be Misty from Mumbai or Brad from Bangalore, calling to ask a few simple questions about his personal satisfaction.

It's Thassa. From the South Loop. That she calls just when he needs to talk to her is hardly the one major coincidence that every long fiction is allowed. It's not even a minor one.

"Mister Stone," she says. "I need your help."

"Where are you?" he shouts. He's halfway down the stairs to the street before he hears the cranberry chuckle in her voice.

"No danger," she says. "I just need writing advice!"

It seems the *Reader* article has brought out the readers. Dozens of the terminally miserable have gotten her e-mail from the college directory server and are deluging her with intimate inquiries.

"Strange people with Hotmail accounts want me to make them happy. One woman wants to hire me as her personal trainer. She thinks her soul needs a professional workout. Twenty-three messages in two days. What should I tell them all?"

He tells her to throw the e-mails in the trash and empty it.

"I can't do that! That would be rude. I must write them *something*. Remember Mr. Harmon?"

"Thassa. Be careful. Don't tell these people anything about yourself."

"They don't want to know anything about *me*. They just want to know about themselves. They're so sure I have a secret. I could make up anything at all, and they would believe me."

"Don't encourage them. It'll just make things worse."

"Thank God I go back to Montreal tomorrow. Canadians are so much easier."

She asks about his holiday plans. He makes something up. By now I know this man: all the beautiful five-paragraph personal essays he composes for her and then redlines away, in two heartbeats. He doesn't tell her he won't be coming back to school in the spring. He just tells her to take care.

"You take care, too. Thank you for your class. I learned so much." He mumbles some meaningless reply, which makes her laugh. In return, she burbles out, "Happy New Year, Mister Stone! See you then?"

∞

He visits Candace Weld's office, without an appointment. "It's a total train wreck. Right out of my worst nightmares."

Candace studies the *Reader* article. She doesn't scold him now; she just reads with practiced steadiness.

"I should have thrown the journalist out the minute I got to class."

"She would have cornered Thassa afterward." There's something reconciled in her voice, the surrender to a development that psychology is powerless to deflect. "It's just a squib in a local freebie paper. They come and go by the thousands."

"She's getting dozens of e-mails from people who want to buy whatever she's taking."

Weld looks up from the paper. "Is she all right?"

"Of course she's all right. That's the problem. She's constitutionally incapable of being anything but all right."

"Are *you* all right?"

He snaps. "Didn't that Rogerian parroting go out in the eighties?"

She stays mild. His panic actually seems to fascinate her. "I'm sorry, I don't see . . ."

"How would you feel if total strangers started begging you all day long for magic mood bullets?"

She looks at him, lips twisted in amusement, until he realizes what he's just asked.

"Russell, this is one tough woman. She'll survive a little media. She's been through worse."

"She called me for help."

"Did she? Maybe she likes you."

"Don't be ridiculous. I'm not a grave . . . not a cradle robber, if that's what you're implying."

"She's nine years younger than you." Candace Weld has done the math. "Is that a cradle?"

"A dozen people a day are asking her to bless them. Yes, that makes me nervous."

The psychologist suggests several practical actions, starting with getting Thassa's e-mail address removed from the public directory. Just the sound of her voice calms him. He could grow dependent on her competence.

"Don't beat yourself up about this," she tells him.

"But that's my best skill." The air all around him is full of wireless gossipers and news surfers. "Is it too late for me to become a real patient of yours?"

"We don't call them patients," she says. "And yes. It's too late for that."

"I'm finished teaching. The college fired me." He feels nothing. He could be a moon of Pluto.

"Oh, Russell! I'm sorry. Why didn't you tell me before?"

His silence is textbook: *Show, don't tell.*

"That's not fair to you," she decides. "None of this is your doing."

"None of it would have happened if I hadn't said that damn word to the police."

"I'm sorry. This must be a real setback."

"I'm fine. Two jobs was more than I could handle anyway."

She's brutally comfortable with extended silence. After a bit, she asks, "So you're saying we're no longer colleagues?"

He hears. She's only six years older than he is. He has already done the math. Happy people have more friends than unhappy ones. Happy people tend to be in long-term relationships.

He feels like he's plunging. On the plummet down, he asks if he can make dinner for her, this Saturday, at his apartment. "I have one good recipe," he says. "Mushroom asparagus risotto."

She pauses long enough for him to think he's made an enormous miscalculation.

"I can get a sitter," she murmurs. "A really good grad student in child psych. She watches Gabe play video games all night, then writes up the child-machine interactions."

"I'm sorry. Bring him, of course."

"Are you sure? I will, then. You want the sitter, too?"

He just stares at her, slack-jawed, until she adds, "Joking."

∞

I'm caught like Buridan's ass, starving to death between allegory and realism, fact and fable, *creative* and nonfiction. I see now exactly who these people are and where they came from. But I can't quite make out what I'm to do with them.

I need to slow down, to describe Stone's terror of driving, his belief that he might be slated one day to hit a child. I have to mention Weld's aversion to security cameras, her thrice-weekly yoga class, or how she must feed mealworms to her son's horned toad when the boy forgets the living world. I need someone to transcribe for me the two lines of e-mail printout from Thassa's brother that she keeps rolled up in the hem of her shawl. But the three of them pull me along in their own rush to *arrive*, before all the world's books get rewritten.

I know the kind of novel I loved to read, back before fact and fable merged. I know what kind of story I'd make from this one, if I could: the kind that, from one word to the next, breaks free. The kind that invents itself out of meaningless detail and thin air. The kind in which there's no choice like chance.

∞

It would help tremendously if Stone could figure what the woman sees in him. She's masterfully self-controlled. Her work has her confronting every behavioral strategy and dodge that humans can indulge. Yet she indulges him.

He takes a break from food prep on Saturday afternoon to phone his brother. Robert might have made a great psychologist himself, were it not for the Asperger's.

Russell talks to his brother as freely as he ever has. "I can't tell if she actually enjoys my conversation or whether she's just lonely."

"You saying there's a difference?"

He hears Robert typing as he talks. "She must know I'm incapable of amusing anyone."

"Which is itself pretty damn entertaining."

"Maybe she's taken me on as a case after all."

A gap in the air. "Uhhn. You know . . . bro? You may want to work a little on that self-esteem thing."

"I can't imagine what's in it for her. All we ever talk about is Thassa."

More furtive mouse-clicking. "Hang . . . Who-sa? Oh, right. The smiley woman."

"Robert? Are you online? This is like talking to somebody in the middle of a gunfight."

"What? No. It's nothing. Just some chick in Romania I play cribbage with on weekends."

∞

All research gambles against time. Kurton calls it *hunting the mastodon*. An unruly band with sticks and stones stalks a creature larger than all of them combined. Hang back and lose the prey; rush too soon and get gored. Smart risks live to reproduce; poor ones die off. Thomas Kurton excels at research because his ancestors stalked well.

But for all his research skill, Kurton has never published a word without fear of prematurity. The same temperament that disposes him to skeptical curiosity leaves him forever holding out for more data. True, the road to discovery is paved with the graves of the hesitant. Yet better one of those modest headstones than the more spectacular memorials, those bubble-burst announcements like N-rays or cold fusion.

Back when Joseph Priestley defined research, the race went not to the swift but to the articulate. Ask Scheele or Lavoisier who really discovered oxygen. The clergyman-scientist could hold on to phlogiston for years, almost as a hobby, and still make his immortal contributions to human understanding through sheer eloquence.

But back then, no one could own scientific laws. Now you can. Metabolite has successfully sued another company for publishing the fact that vitamin B-12 deficiency correlates with elevated homocysteine, a risk for heart disease. Myriad can charge $2,600 for a questionable breast-cancer-gene screen, while shutting down labs that develop better alternatives.

Thomas Kurton survives in this world because he's good at knowing just when the eternally insufficient data must go public. But increasingly, the market is taking once-public facts private. Even colleagues in his own university department, funded by corporate grants, can no longer talk freely to one another.

Kurton doesn't particularly like the capitalization of life science. But life science doesn't particularly care about his private dislikes. Those who would keep growing must shed their legacy biases, the way that biology has shed everyone from Galen to Gajdusek. Someday microgreen machines will do to scarcity what Salk did to polio. Then the grants will exceed the applicants. Then we will defeat even competitive rivalry, and all this private profit-seeking will disappear into the eternal gift economy. Until then, Kurton hunts the mastodon as best he can.

But in recent months, some colleagues have wondered whether Kurton's sense of timing might be slipping. Truecyte has had a study in the pipeline for three years. Everyone down to the beaker washers knows this thing is coming. They've scanned the genes of hundreds of individuals, all of them falling along the high end of emotional health. Against these, they've compared the scans of hundreds more from deeper down that spectrum. Massive computational biology has identified a group of quantitative trait loci that associate strongly with performances on tests of emotional resilience.

DNA microarrays have already mapped these QTL more precisely, pinpointing them to much more closely spaced markers. Now the markers narrow down even further. The log of the odds scores show a high likelihood that a person's affective set point depends massively upon a certain network of genes involved in serotonin and dopamine synthesis and transport. The control regions for these genes are polymorphic, with several alleles each. And Truecyte's association studies identify those specific alleles that correlate with elevated well-being.

This network of genes seems to account for perhaps two-thirds or more of the heritability of emotional temperament. Various permutations of this gene network correlate with contentment, joy, and even, for want of a better term, exuberance. *Ex uberare*—the pouring forth of fruit.

The sample size is good, while the covariance and standard deviations satisfy almost everyone on the project. Researchers as levelheaded as Amar Patnaik and George Cheung voice the collective anxiety in multiple meetings: it's time to stake a claim. If they don't file something soon, some other group in Switzerland or Singapore is going to announce, with data a lot less firm than anything Kurton's group has already amassed.

But to everyone's dismay, Kurton remains averse to going public. His reluctance may be just legacy human nature: as stakes rise, even the fearless take cover. History is filled with scientists terrified of publishing big findings. Darwin himself tinkered with his theory for almost two decades before Alfred Wallace's letter forced his hand.

Some among the senior scientists close to Thomas wonder if his hesitation may even be sociological—just a fear of real-world consequences. From an unsympathetic distance, his reticence looks a lot like nostalgia. How else to explain his continued foot-drag, in the absence of solid objections? He has signed off on the statistical analysis. He's conceded the results of the index-test method for determining functional differences between the known allelic variations. Still Kurton waits. And he's begun to repeat with increasing, almost annoying frequency, "All good science pauses."

No one knows exactly what the chief's hesitation means. It may be good science; it may be loss of nerve. In practice, it means an extended delay in publishing that any day—given the rate of postgenomic discoveries being plucked daily from the air—could prove fatal. The mastodon will still kill you, whether you charge it or stand stock-still.

∞

Weld consulted with two colleagues first. She tried one of each: stringent Christa Kreuz and expansive Dennis Winfield, the counseling center's head. Christa was at her hardest-assed. "You're dating someone who works for the college?"

"He's not working for the college anymore. And I'm not exactly *dating* him."

"He got fired over this incident."

"He was temporary. They just didn't renew."

"It doesn't feel right, Candace. He comes to talk to you about this student, the student gets raped by another one of his students, and now . . . ?"

"She didn't get raped. She talked her way out."

"And now you want to sleep with the teacher."

"I don't want to sleep with him. I just enjoy his company."

"Why?"

Weld fell back on that old counseling trick: counting to five. "Because he's not fatuous and he's not banal. He feels things. He cares about something other than himself." She fights off a bizarre impulse to say: *He makes me smile.* "He thinks. That's hard to come by, these days."

"Have you thought about an epistolary relationship? And you might want to keep one copy of everything on file."

Nor did Dennis Winfield entirely let her off the hook. "In the best world, of course, I'd wish you something less problematical."

She'd seen it in Dennis's eye from time to time: in his best world, Dennis wouldn't be married, she wouldn't be working for him, and *he* would be her problem.

"It's not problematical, Dennis. It's just companionship."

"Does he get along with Gabe?"

"I've just met him. I only want to be sure I'm not breaking any rules."

"You're not breaking any rules. Technically. If you're sure that you've never had a professional relationship with him or the student . . ." He appraised her. "This is not about some kind of indirect therapy for either one of them, is it?"

She shook her head, exasperated.

"Good. Because you've had . . . We've been over this in the past. You are a wonderful woman, Candace. But you do need to protect yourself from your best intentions sometimes. Do be careful. Boundaries get blurry so fast."

She sat still for the justified lecture, and when Dennis encouraged her to come back and talk if she ever felt any uncertainty, she nodded and said she would.

∞

Candace Weld arrives right on time, Saturday night, an experimental tease in her tea-green eyes and a veil of light snow on her hair. She shows up with her chest-high son, who holds out one diffident paw to shake Russell's. The child has seen this drill before, and places no faith in the latest candidate. As soon as he rescues his hand from Russell's, he pulls a flashing, bleeping Game Boy back out of his pocket.

Stone ushers them in from the cold. She no longer looks that much like Grace. He was crazy ever to imagine a resemblance. Candace's features are more fluid and eager. Her eyes don't have Grace's webcam look. Her nose twitches like it's trying to sniff him. She hands him a nice Shiraz, then cups his elbow hello. With her other hand, she shakes a colorful sack of pungent Happy Meal. "For Gabe," she says.

"I'm carnivorous," the child at her side explains.

Russell slaps his forehead. "I should have asked."

The boy shrugs. "Many primates are. But those are cool pictures, anyway." He points to Stone's pastels. "Are they like dungeon creatures? Three stars, at least."

Russell takes a beat. "Thanks, I think."

Over the meal, he and Candace hunt for a conversation topic other than the only one they've ever talked about. Weld is oddly at ease in her awkwardness. She asks about Stone's magazine editing. He's too considerate to give her a real answer.

Finally, it's Stone and the boy who find a theme. Gabe regales his host with tales of an online world called Futopia. The boy raves about his life as a Ranger, discovering ancient artifacts and selling them for tons of gold in cities scattered around virgin continents. Stone marvels to see this sullen child bloom into a full-fledged raconteur, a Marco Polo who can't get enough of the questions Stone asks.

The mother is embarrassed for the first time all evening. "It's terrifying. Like there's a probe directly stimulating the pleasure centers of his brain. He gets ninety minutes a night. I know: it should be zero."

The kid is all over her in panic. "Mom, no! We've talked about this. It's *social*. It's completely social. There's almost no killing at all."

After dessert, when the talk runs out, Candace stands and starts stacking dishes. "Leave them," Russell says. "I'll get them after you go." But she insists on helping.

He fills the basin with hot water. She takes a dish towel and stands next to him, snatching dishes as he cleans them. It surprises him to discover how easy she is to be with—just company, just variation, a respite from his own inescapable self. Side by side, five inches from each other, in front of the double basin, he doesn't even have to look at her to find her painfully pleasing.

She grins, admiring his washing technique. "You've done this before, haven't you?"

Candace Weld is *flirting*. Russell would like to call it something else, but English won't cooperate. *Chapter four: in any closely observed scene, your key protagonists will have different action objectives, driven by different inner needs.*

The boy Gabe sits at the cleared table, flipping through a book that Stone has left out: *Emotional Chemistry: How the Brain Lifts and Lowers Us.*

"You're still researching?" she asks.

He twists the sponge into a drinking glass. "Did you know that most people say they are happier than average?"

"I'm not surprised," she says.

"You're not?"

"I'm not surprised that that's what most people *say*." She crosses to the cold window casement by the pantry and breathes on the glass. In the condensation, she draws two contentment graphs. The first is a steady, high, straight line. The second is a diagonal, starting at zero and maxing out at the end. She stands aside, a counselor pretending to be an actress playing a schoolteacher. "Which of these two is happier?"

By any measure that Stone can think of, it's the first.

"Now: which life do most people want to have?"

He stares at his choices. "Are you serious?"

She shrugs. "Number two is a better story. Most people are already pretty happy. What we really want is to be *happier*. And most people think they will be, in the future. Keeps us in the trenches, I guess."

She rubs her finger slowly across the chill glass, obliterating all graphs.

"Have you come across Norbert Schwarz's work? It's classic. Subjects fill in a questionnaire about life satisfaction. But the subject must go into the next room to make a copy of the questionnaire before filling it in. One group finds a dime sitting on the copy machine. Their lucky day. The control group finds nothing."

Stone grips a plate. "Don't tell me."

"I'm afraid I have to; it's science! The lucky group reports significantly higher satisfaction with their *entire life*."

He grins, shakes his head, and plunges his fists back in the hot water, now tepid to his accustomed hands.

"Don't take it so hard." She grazes his shoulder with her towel. "Works with a chocolate bar, too."

He lifts his hands from the water and presses his soapy palms to his cheeks. "We're pathetic."

"We're beautiful," she replies. "We just have no idea how we feel or what makes us feel that way!"

"So feeling good is really that cheap?"

"Not *cheap*." She traces out a quick hieroglyphic on the upper arm of his waffle shirt. "*Affordable*. And easier than we think."

Easy is exactly the problem. He turns and faces her, holds her eyes for the first time all evening. "And Thassa?"

"And Thassa." She gazes off into a ceiling corner full of cobwebs he missed in the afternoon's scrub-down. "She must carry around one hell of a chocolate bar."

At the evening's end, mother and son don coats, scarves, hats, and gloves. Outside, the snow is thin but gathering, a taste of things to come. The boy sticks out a king crab claw and shakes Russell's hand. He promises to show Stone his life in Futopia, anytime. Bundled, the mother turns to Stone, slips one padded arm around his middle, turns her head away, and pulls him into her. She lays her right ear on his clavicle and listens.

He plays dead. The one time Grace was this gentle was right before she left.

Dr. Weld breaks the embrace. "Merry Christmas," she says. She looks up at him, wincing. She waves an erasing mitten in the air. *Don't worry*, it says. *Means nothing. A dime's a dime. Grab it when you see it.*

∞

No one at Truecyte searches for the story. They come across it by data mining, scouring the Web with automated scripts and prospecting bots. The company's intelligent agents race from server to server at all hours, extracting patterns and converging on the next genetic trends before they've even materialized.

Nodes, clusters, trackbacks, memes . . . Truth follows bandwidth, as sure as use follows invention. By now, the idea is a commonplace: only that massively parallel computer, the entire human race, is powerful enough to interpret the traffic that it generates. No single expert can calculate the outcome of tomorrow's big game. But the averaged aggregate guess of hundreds of millions of amateurs can come as close as God.

In this way, a self-assembling network of page traffic presents itself daily to three graduate-student interns trained to prowl around each morning's tidal pools and pull out shiny things. If two out of the three of them tag the same story, it goes to Kurton's own news aggregator. And for an hour every morning before dawn, the inventor of rapid gene signature reading mulls over the day's trove of stories.

He consumes the feeds, looking for new upheaval, the same constant upheaval that has carried him this far. He still remembers the Boethius that his ex-wife made him read at Stanford a third of a century ago, insisting it would make him a better person: no one will ever be safe or well until Fortune upends him.

As Kurton reads, he drags various links into tree branches in his visual concept-mapper, trees that start out as bonsais but—tended and grafted and trained toward the light—grow into redwoods.

> People who read stories about *subjective well-being* also sub-scribe to posts about *affective set point*.
> People who subscribe to posts about *affective set point* are also interested in *genetic basis of happiness*.
> People who follow *genetic basis of happiness*
> comment and respond to/
> spend many page minutes with/
> rate highly/
> frequently link to
> one of several mutually quoting accounts of Kabylia's outpost in Chicago, stories that spread the keyword *hyperthymia* like a pheromone trail.

He reads the *Reader* story and feels the journalist's excitement. This Kabyle woman has grown up in a vicious free-for-all that makes the stoic Boethius look like a bed-wetting schoolboy. And despite the worst that environment can contribute, her body pumps out the stand-ing gladness that should be every human's birthright.

Hunch's role in science has never embarrassed Kurton. And he has a hunch that this woman may be the missing datum that True-cyte's three-year study needs. If she isn't, the study will only be strengthened by learning why. He checks with his schedule keeper, who tells him he'll be at the University of Chicago in the second week of January, for a debate with an Australian Nobelist in literature who believes that scientific investigation has killed the world's soul.

With six clicks, Kurton finds a contact for the immigrant student. He composes an e-mail, using a Tamazight greeting that he picked up on one of his trips to Morocco. He tells her about his work in under-standing what makes humans happy, and his hopes for using genetic information to heal the future. He describes how much his lab has already learned by exploring people like her, and he says how much she would contribute to the study. *Everyone alive would love to know a little more about how you tick!* He mentions that he's coming to

Chicago and asks if they might meet when he's in the city. He gives her five ways to contact him. And his e-mail software automatically appends, beneath the obligatory block of personal data, his signature quote:

> . . . *whatever was the beginning of this world, the end will be glorious and paradisiacal, beyond what our imaginations can now conceive.*
>
> —Joseph Priestley

PART THREE

WELL PAST CHANCE

For the point is this: not that myth refers us back to some original event which has been fancifully transcribed as it passed through the collective memory; but that it refers us forward to something that will happen, that must happen. Myth will become reality, however skeptical we might be.

—Julian Barnes, *A History of the World in 10½ Chapters*

And on a May night in the near future, Tonia Schiff will land at Tunis-Carthage International. Seen from the airport shuttle, the dense glow surprises her. So much flickering enterprise up so late, refining fresh surplus into new necessities. Tunis glitters as furtively as any of the earth's two-hundred-or-so-million-inhabitant cities. This one just happens to be four thousand years old.

The science-show host wakes up in the *Centre Ville*, feeling that she's landed by mistake in southern Italy. Only the palms along Avenue Mohammed V reassure Tonia. And these turn out to be just a holdover French colonial fantasy. For a day, she wanders at random. *The perfect day to play the tourist in one's own life.* She climbs up to the Belvedere, loses herself in the tight medina maze, strolls through the bey's palace. She stands overwhelmed in the heart of the suq, beyond the simplest bargaining.

A pair of guards turn her away at the entrance to the Grande Mosquée, on account of her clothes. She tells herself she'll try again later, more suitably dressed, but knows she won't.

The city's scent veers crazily from dawn to dusk. In the morning, fetid breezes blow over the dried salt lake, mixing with exhaust. Toward sundown, the flower vendors creep out to thread the cafés with jasmine garlands. A tiny white snail of a flower, whose scent is like falling down a bottomless well: solvent, secret, and as strange as sex, with final arrival lying just a few inches below reach . . . Tonia Schiff might have come to this place for that smell alone.

The next day will be clearer still. In midmorning, she'll make her way out to the marble carcass of Carthage. She winds up sitting at a stone table above the surf, aside the Chicago of the ancient world, scribbling production notes for her redemptive film now under way.

Salt spray from the Mediterranean curls her pages. Coastal sun douses her, in a country she was sure she'd never live long enough to see.

The sea air is heavenly. Even the smearing haze over the city is beautiful. At a nearby table, a family of six picnics. A sinuous voice dances out of their radio; a woman who sounds seven feet tall threads a melody around instruments Schiff can't even name. She won't be able to tell the key, the scale, the words, the age, or even the feelings at stake. Her ignorance verges on glorious.

She digs into her bag and pulls out a beaten-up copy of Frederick P. Harmon's *Make Your Writing Come Alive*. The book's spine was broken long before it came to Tonia. She lays the volume flat on the table, open to chapter two: "Vital Fiction." Ink fills the margins — words in three languages, sketches, diagrams, snaking arrows. Half the sentences are underlined in an elaborate, uncrackable color-code. The last paragraph on page 123 is double-underscored, in Berber red:

Here is the single most important secret of vivid writing: let your reader travel freely. No border checks, no customs declarations, no visa: let every reader reach the country of her innermost need.

In the margin, next to "travel freely," the Berber woman has written "scares some people." "Innermost" is circled. Above it, the words *"le plus profond"* lead to another phrase in a language Tonia Schiff won't be able to tell from random scratches in stone . . .

∞

Thassa reads Kurton's message on a computer in a Montreal Public Library branch six blocks from her aunt and uncle's council flat. She's still on winter vacation and looking for messages from someone else — an interest only now dawning on me. She has had scores of e-mails from strangers in the last week, but this one ranks with the strangest. She laughs at the would-be Berber greeting. She clicks on the link in Kurton's signature but can't make much of the site. She googles "how you tick," but ends up more in the dark than when she started.

She refuses to snub anyone, even obvious cranks. Many of the most interesting people in her life seemed like cranks, at first. She forwards the entire message to Chicago, adding a note of her own:

Chère Candace,

No foggy clue what this means. Yiii: it's sci-ence! So you know all about that, and you told me once if anything ever looks funny, just to ask your opinion.
Your opinion?
Je t'embrasse très fort.

T.

∞

Candace Weld's opinion was split at best. She read three print interviews with Thomas Kurton and listened to the man play himself on a podcast. She found him vaguely messianic, but neither the thuggish Edward Teller nor the grandiose Craig Venter that scared or envious reporters made him out to be. Weld knew plenty of researchers like Kurton. She'd gone to school with them, studied under them, competed with them for her own PhD. These men had simply accepted science's latest survival adaptation—salesmanship. Any funded researcher who condemned them was a hypocrite.

She looked up the full Priestley quote from Kurton's signature, finding ten different mutations that fanned across the Web in adaptive radiation. Thousands of people were out there, disseminating the clergyman-chemist's ecstatic vision. The coming paradise was fast becoming a start-up industry all its own:

> [N]ature, including both its materials, and its laws, will be more at our command; men will make their situation in this world abundantly more easy and comfortable; they will probably prolong their existence in it, and will grow daily more happy, each in himself, and more able (and, I believe, more disposed) to communicate happiness to others . . .

Part of Weld wanted this genomicist to see Thassa, to be there when the transhumanist met something that no amount of blood work, tissue samples, or gene sequencing would ever explain. Thassadit Amzwar's gift had little to do with molecules; on that, Candace was ready to bet her own well-being. The Kabyle had *found* something about how best to be alive. Mr. Omega Point could find the same, by meeting her.

Candace recalled Dennis Winfield's warning about boundaries, and she briefly considered consulting him. But Thassa had written her as a friend, not as a client. Candace wrote back on her Gmail account, not her college one. She told Thassa what she'd learned about the controversial scientist. Thassa should feel no obligation to meet the man, but if she wanted to, Candace would be happy to chaperone.

The reply came in, as good as predictable. *That's great. That's perfect. Can Mister Stone come, too?*

∞

Men will grow daily more happy, each in himself, and more able to communicate happiness to others. Schiff reads the words at the end of dozens of e-mails. She reads at night by the dim ceiling light in her hotel above the ficus trees on Avenue Habib Bourguiba. *Whatever the beginning of this world, the end will be glorious and paradisiacal. Beyond imagining . . .*

She carries the man's correspondence around the globe, along with a dossier of files stolen from the archives of *Over the Limit*. She searches her folders for that broad-based survey on America's attitudes toward genetic editing that will open her film in progress:

- Two-thirds of Americans would genetically intervene to keep their offspring disease free.
- Two-fifths would enhance their children, with the number rising every year.
- On average, American parents would give their child ninety-fourth percentile beauty and fifty-seventh percentile brains.

These data keep her awake, working in her narrow rented room as the scent of jasmine blows through her open window. When jet lag finally catches her, she curls up on the hard mattress and goes through the motions of sleep. All the while, on the insides of her eyelids, hopes rise, taboos fade, miracles get marked down, the impossible goes ordinary, chance becomes choice, and Scheherazade keeps whispering, "What is this tale, compared to the one I will tell you *tomorrow* night, if you but spare me and let me live?"

∞

A hurt message on Stone's answering machine: *Mister! I'm back. I went to your office hours, but they said you weren't with the college anymore. I sent you a mail, but it bounced. Can you just tell me you are okay?*

He writes back and says he's fine. He's returned to his real job. He wishes her well in the new semester. *I hope you keep up your journal.* He writes in a tone to preclude all reply, then checks his mail every fifteen minutes for the next ten hours.

Her answer is seven words: *Did they fire you because of me?*

No, he insists. That job was only temporary. He never expected to be renewed for spring. It's the first lie he can remember telling that wasn't prompted by real-time panic. He falls into the beginner's trap: too many explanations. *I have to focus my time and energies. I'm going to write a book.*

She replies immediately: *Mabrouk, mabrouk! Fantastic news. Maybe you can tell me all about it, the night of January 12? Candace and I are going to hear a mad scientist who wants to study me. Can you believe it?*

∞

Kurton is nursing the three-hundred-dollar shot of orange juice they serve in first class before takeoff when the flight attendant comes on the speakers like an old friend. *Good afternoon, ladies and gentlemen. Welcome to American flight 1803 from Boston to Chicago. If Chicago is not in your travel plans today, now might be a good time to deplane.*

He laughs out loud, which makes his seatmate stop thumbing her BlackBerry and look up in alarm. Kurton apologizes and turns back to his notes. He's working on his comments for the debate with the Australian Nobel novelist and searching for a good hook. As always, random assortment and selection hand him one. He scribbles onto his card stock with a fountain pen: *If the future is not your destination, now might be a good time to disembark.*

∞

They go down to Hyde Park together, Stone, Weld, and Thassadit. The event is billed as "a dialogue between the Two Cultures," but seems to be a cross between celebrity gawk and gladiatorial combat. Russell is a mess, and not just because each woman has a hold of an elbow and steers him in a different direction.

Candace needed days to talk him into coming. "You can't avoid her forever. She wants to see you."

In fact, he needs another look at her, now that the evening class is history. He's starting to think that he made her up, that she's just a good-natured kid he happened to meet in her first flush of college life in an exhilarating city. Even so, one small dose of her could take him through this winter's unusually rough patch and armor him for spring.

It's not Thassa he most dreads. It's the novelist. From their seats near the back of the auditorium, even before the writer steps onto the stage, Russell Stone eyes the exits. Years ago, in Tucson, he read one of the man's books, a stripped-down parable in the Eastern European style, set in no place or time, imbued with only the faintest outline of a plot and with no pretense of a psychological character study to carry it. But as young Stone homed in on the closing pages, fixed to the cadence of sentences almost biblical, his own life fell away, replaced by a glimpse of human collective desperation so rigorous that it left itself no place to land but in a futile embrace. Stone finished the last paragraph lying on his back on the quarry stone of his apartment floor, unable to raise himself or stop crying or do much of anything except lie there like a grazing animal struck by something massive and ruthless beyond comprehension. When at last he did stand up, startled by the sound of Grace letting herself in the front door, he hid the book behind a shelf of essays. He never mentioned reading it to Grace or anyone.

That was years ago, when he was Thassa's age. Since then, he's felt no need to read the man's six other books. And he's never again cracked the cover of the novel that so badly wrecked him, afraid of what he might discover. Last year, hearing that the novelist had taken a visiting position at Mr. Rockefeller's university, he stopped going to his favorite South Side bookstore, just to avoid an accidental sighting. He has avoided two previous, much-publicized public talks. Now he's condemned to sit in this overflowing auditorium and watch the man whose words transcended the human condition display all the tics of the weakest human. Stone cups his elbows to his ribs and swallows down a small, vague taste of complicit shame.

"Tell me about your book," Thassa whispers, as the crowd settles.

Candace leans forward. "You're writing a *book*?"

"It's a fiction," Stone says, and is rescued by a roomful of applause.

They come onstage together, the Nobel laureate, the genomicist, and the evening's moderator. Thassa, seated between her escorts, asks Candace, "Which one?" Weld indicates Kurton, who—as the pale laureate studies his shoes—shades his eyes from the stage lights and gazes out, searching the audience for something, perhaps even for Thassa herself.

The "debate" unnerves Russell, right out of the gate. The novelist reads stiffly from a prepared speech, voice shaking. Stone's man is the most painfully shy person who has ever been forced into a public spectacle. The writer's thought is so dense that every clause tries to circle back for another try before plunging on. For every point Russell grasps, three break away into the undergrowth. He wants to get down on hands and knees and crawl from the auditorium.

The novelist's argument is clear enough: genetic enhancement represents the end of human nature. Take control of fate, and you destroy everything that joins us to one another and dignifies life. A story with no end or impediment is no story at all. Replace limits with unbounded appetite, and everything meaningful turns into nightmare.

The quaking man sits down to damningly respectful applause. Stone steals a glance at Thassa; her hands fold in front of her mouth, like she's praying. She's off in a land he can't visit. The country of pure observation.

The geneticist follows. Even walking to the podium, Thomas Kurton is charming. His shoulders bob like a boy on his first day of summer camp. He opens with a quip. "Every divide between the Two Cultures is bridgeable, except this one: humanists write out their talks and scientists extemporize." Stone peeks at Weld; her knowing profile smile twists his stomach.

Kurton praises the long, mysterious journey of literature. "Imaginative writing has always been the engine of future fact." He thanks his opponent. "You've made a lot of good points that I'll have to think about." He concedes that genetic enhancement does force major reconsiderations, starting with the boundaries between justice and fate, the natural and the inevitable. "But so did the capture of fire and the invention of agriculture."

He invites a thought experiment. Suppose you want to have a baby, but you're at high risk for conveying cystic fibrosis. You go to the clinic, where the doctors, by screening your eggs, guarantee that your child will be born free of a hideous and fatal disease. "Not too many prospective parents will have a problem with that."

As the scientist speaks, the novelist stares down at the table in front of him, his head in his hands. Russell Stone wants to mercy-kill him.

Thomas Kurton sees only the audience. "Now suppose you come to the clinic already pregnant, and tests show cystic fibrosis in your fetus. Assuming that the doctors can bring a treatment risk down to acceptable levels . . ."

Russell glances at Candace, who winces back. He looks at Thassa. She holds up a tiny digital movie camera and pans it around the auditorium. At his glance, she grabs his arm and pulls his ear near her mouth. "Many beautiful faces in here tonight. I'm so glad we came!"

Her casual touch pumps his neck full of blood. Minutes pass before he can concentrate on Kurton again. The geneticist progresses to removing the disease gene from the germ line before the malicious message has a chance to get copied again.

Russell comes alert when Kurton invokes the uses of literature. "For most of human history, when existence was too short and bleak to mean anything, we needed stories to compensate. But now that we're on the verge of living the long, pain-reduced, and satisfying life that our brains deserve, it's time for art to lead us beyond noble stoicism."

In short: if it's getting too rich for you, get off the ride. The Nobel novelist looks like he wants to do just that. Kurton concedes that change is always upheaval. "But upheaval is opportunity's maiden name." He concludes by mentioning a construction sign he saw on the torn-up expressway coming in from O'Hare: *Inconvenience is temporary; improvement is permanent.* The hall laughs appreciatively, pretty much ready to play.

When the applause ends, the novelist begins the rebuttal. "I've used that same expressway myself, and it's true: improvement *has been* more or less permanent." It must be his timing, because only a few people in the hall chuckle. But the laureate now talks with a freedom that gives up on persuading anyone.

The novelist's metamorphosis baffles Kurton. He replies that anyone who prefers nasty, brutish, and short to glorious and paradisiacal may be suffering from depression. We've cured smallpox; we've done away with polio. "Of course we want to eliminate the toxic molecular sequences that predispose us to suffering, whether cystic fibrosis, Alzheimer's, or heart disease. And if we can prevent the harmful, why not promote the helpful?"

Bunkering down into his seat, Russell can't even begin to list the objections. He looks to Candace, but she stares straight ahead.

Right at the finish line, the novelist stumbles badly. Instead of pinning Pollyanna to the dissecting table, he capitulates. Enhance away, he says. Enhancement will mean nothing, in the long run. The remodeling of human nature will be as slapdash and flawed as its remodelers. We'll never *feel* enhanced. We'll always be banned from some further Eden. The misery business will remain a growth industry. When fiction goes real, reality will need a more resistant strain of fiction.

Uncertainty ripples through the house. The moderator, on orders from the co-sponsoring booksellers and café, chooses the unsettled moment to wrap things up. Democracy is thwarted; there is no Q and A.

Thassa is on her feet before her friends, camera in front of her, filming as the crowd drifts past. To those few who are old enough to resent someone recording them without asking, she just smiles and waves.

Russell is left alone with LPC Weld. "Well?" he asks. He doesn't have the heart to volunteer what he thinks.

"Well what? It's not a professional boxing match, you know."

He cocks an eyebrow. "And you're not a public relations manager."

She flares a little, then nods, embarrassed. "Right. Well. I'm afraid it was Optimism, by a technical knockout."

He wants to tally differently, but can't.

"Should we try to say hello?" she asks.

He points at the crowd mobbing Thomas Kurton and lifts his palms.

"You're right," she says. "Let's get out of here."

They find Thassa conversing with a couple who recognize her from the *Reader* story. The man asks, "Do your relatives in Canada have your same hypothermia?" The woman asks, "What kind of exercise do you do?"

Candace apologizes to the couple and leads a puzzled Thassa away by the arm. The woman calls after them. "What are your favorite dietary minerals?"

They press through the crowded foyer. Safely outside in the bone-crunching cold, Candace tests Thassa. "You still want to talk to him?"

Thassa stops on the salted sidewalk, clouds of breath condensing around her. "He's a funny man. We say: he knows how to make the donkey think it's choosing the rope."

Russell and Candace trade bewilderment.

Thassa takes their arms and starts forward again. "Yes, I'll meet him tomorrow, like he wants."

"He seems harmless enough." Candace checks with Russell, who is helpless even to nod.

"But the author!" Thassa exclaims. "He's the one I'd really like to meet. Did you read him ever, Russell?"

High up on the building's corner, a tiny white coffin of a security camera tracks them with its red cyclopean eye. The last five years of Russell's life could be reconstructed from archived videotape all over this city. He looks at the Algerian, his face a blank. "I don't think so."

"So many thoughts. I wonder if he might be ill? His sadness is so . . . steady. I would love to experiment emotionally on him."

Candace jerks to a stop. The arm-linked chain breaks. "You what?"

Thassa doesn't even blush. "Just once! Just for science."

∞

He has her with the belugas.

On the phone the next morning, Thomas Kurton tells Thassa Amzwar to pick a meeting spot anywhere in the city. She laughs at the blank check. This city has forests in the northwest big enough to get lost in. To the south, black neighborhoods the size of Constantine that white people never enter. Convention centers with the look of fifties science-fiction space colonies. Warehouse districts full of resale contraband peppered with refrigerated corpses. Cemeteries a hundred times the length of a soccer pitch, with gravestones in forty-one languages. There's Chinatown, Greek Town, Bucktown, Boystown, Little Italy, Little Seoul, little Mexico, little Palestine, little Assyria . . . Two Arab neighborhoods—the southwest Muslims and the northwest Christians—where people from a dozen countries congregate to eat, recite Arabic poetry, and mock one another's dialects.

She has my problem: too much possibility. A thousand parks, four hundred theaters, three dozen beaches, fifty colleges, fifteen bird sanctuaries, seven botanical gardens, two different zoos, and a glass-encased tropical jungle. Meet *anywhere?* The scientist doesn't realize the scale of the place.

She says to meet her in front of the fish temple.

So they meet at the Shedd Aquarium in the depths of winter, on a day pretending to June. For a week the earth has been so warm that even the bulbs in Grant Park are fooled into surfacing. All along the lakefront people stumble, light and jacketless, joking about the boon of planetary climate disaster. It's exactly the day on which to start the future's next blank page.

Kurton allots twenty minutes. He has read everything on the Net about Thassa Amzwar. He's gone through the *Reader* piece with a highlighter. If she's half what the accounts make her out to be, he's ready with a full invitation.

He spots her from a distance as his cab pulls up. She's standing at the foot of the aquarium steps, in full sun. She looks like a girl whose parents told her to stay put and wait for them, just before they were rounded up by the authorities.

He pays the cab and walks the final hundred yards, watching her chat up a ring of multiracial third graders. In a few sentences, she has the whole volatile class rapt, hypnotized as if by the best interactive television. Their faces are like Prize Day. Their teacher stands behind them, transfixed as well. Thassa Amzwar flips a hand back toward the Chicago cliffs: red and emerald, white and obsidian. The children look on, astonished by the city that springs up behind them.

She sweeps her hand across the panorama out beyond the match-stick marina, pointing to where an entire mirror city plunges into the surface of the lake. Her hands cup into a small open boat, which she floats out to the horizon, into the seaway, past Montreal, and over the swirling Atlantic. The third-grade field trip winds up on the shores of another country.

She catches sight of Kurton where he stands spying. She grins and waves. He crosses to her and takes her hand in his. She laughs and introduces him to the circle of kids, who glare at this party crasher. Their teacher leads them toward the buses and they drag themselves away, calling Thassa's name in singsong goodbye.

"What were you telling them?" he asks.

"We were just traveling." She looks back out over the curve of the lake, shaking her head. She's channeling Kateb Yacine: *If the sea were free, Algeria would be rich.*

He thanks her again for meeting. She shrugs. "Of course!" She says he looks kinder when he's not onstage.

"I think your debate partner was very upset, by the end. Maybe you should write him a letter."

He laughs. "Maybe I should!" He steals a look at his cell; he needs to be at O'Hare by one, for a flight to Minneapolis. And her tempo is clearly Sahara time. He waves toward a nearby bench. "Would you like to sit?"

She frowns. "I thought we could . . . ?" She glances at the octagonal Doric temple.

It takes him a moment. "Oh, of course. Have you ever been?"

Her face is like someone texting a lover. "Not today!"

As they stand in line for tickets, she confesses to coming almost every week. The simplest pleasure—watching fish glide by on the other side of murky-green glass—never goes stale and needs no escalation. She's jumped off the hedonic treadmill and *doesn't habituate.* Goose bumps run up Kurton's neck—piloerection, puffing up against danger—archaic reflex pirated by that spin-off of no known survival value: awe.

They circle the great central tank, Thassa studying the blue-spotted stingray and Kurton studying her. She holds the gaze of a leatherback; the creature is as transfixed by her as any scientist. Even her walk is eerie; she springs like she's on a smaller planet with weaker gravity.

They wander through the Caribbean and Amazon. They peer into the past of cichlid-mad Victoria, a lake on the brink of death. He understands: the aquarium is this woman's own test. She screens him first, before she'll let him draw a drop of blood. Two Hispanic schoolgirls tumble past them in front of the lungfish, each holding a sheet filled with furious check marks. The taller shouts at her rumpled sidekick, "Are you getting your theory yet?"

The meeting has already lasted longer than Kurton planned. They haven't even glanced at the consent paperwork. He should be anxious, but he's not. He has seen five previous cases of reputed hyperthymia without mania. This one is the first that might be real. Just being around her is a mild euphoric.

Half an hour in the woman's presence and Kurton makes a decision. Science is half hunch, and his funding is ample, anyway. This one needs more than DNA genotyping. She merits the full workup. He asks her, "How would you like to fly out to Boston for a weekend?" He lays it out: a full suite of psychological tests. Comprehensive biochemical analysis. Functional brain imaging. Salivary cortisol levels. Protein counts. Finally, genetic sequencing, beginning with three chromosomal areas of special interest . . .

"What are you looking for?" she asks.

He tells her about the hot sites already located: the dopamine receptor D_4 gene on chromosome 11, whose longer form correlates with extroversion and novelty-seeking. He describes the serotonin transporter gene on the long arm of chromosome 17, whose short allele associates with negative emotions.

"You want to see how long my genes are?"

"We're studying a genomic network that's involved in assembling the brain's emotional centers. A few variations seem to make a lot of difference. We'd like to see what varieties you have."

"Boston is by the ocean," she says.

"If you like this city," he promises, "you'll love Boston."

"Can I see where they made the tea party?"

He knows nothing at all about Algeria's war of independence. He has never even heard about the massacre at Sétif. "How do you know about that?"

"I did my homework! It's true, I would like to see this city of yours. But I don't like to miss classes."

Kurton says the visit can be as short as she likes.

She takes him down to the leafy sea dragons. The scientist has somehow missed these creatures' existence. He pushes his face up to the glass, boggled. They are, by any measure, beyond fiction, madder than anything out of Tolkien. A sea horse cousin, but gone Daliesque, the deformed things have flowing banners pasted all over them, from dappled branches down to frilly spines. The drapery looks like clunky high school theatrical costumes. Taxonomy's late-night brainstorming, gone unhinged.

The dragons float, propelled by tiny fins in their necks and tails. He stares into pure possibility, feeling how feeble imagination is, alongside evolution. He remembers *Life in a Coral Reef*, a book he wolfed down at age nine and came away from with a hunger he has yet to satisfy.

Thassa, on the far side of the tank, peeps through the creature foliage into Kurton's face. "What are those? Feet? Horns? Look: it's growing a tree out of the back of its head. Okay, Science. Please explain."

He starts with the standard model. The one you can find anywhere, aside from a quarter of American high schools. Start with a genetic template for making enzymes. Let chance make small errors copying the templates . . .

She waves her palm in the air. "That's no explanation."

He starts again, from the other end of the beautiful synthesis. Some slightly more seaweedy-looking sea horse has a slightly better chance . . .

"Yes. *Le camouflage*. That's always the reason. Hiding, and also advertising. Can nature say only two things? But look at the cost to these poor creatures. They struggle just to swim!"

"Whatever survives a little better"—Kurton drops into his media voice—"is a little more likely to—"

"Certainly," she replies. "Survival is always handy! But what are they surviving *better than?*"

Slightly better than something that's not quite a leafy sea dragon.

"You are the man who got cows to make medicines. If I come to Boston, can you give me one of those branches, growing out of the back of my head?"

"It might take a few tries."

She crouches down again, examining the implausible monster. "*Farhana? Hnnn? Tu es heureuse là-dedans, ma belle?* What do you think, Mr. Kurton? Can fish be happy the way we are happy?"

"No one knows—yet. But ask me again, in a few years."

An announcement comes over the building's speakers: a behavior display in the oceanarium will start in fifteen minutes. She shoots him a hopeful look. He checks his watch and decides that she's worth missing a plane for. Minneapolis can wait. For the first time in months, he's enjoying being in a place more than he'll enjoy leaving it.

The water-theater design is pure genius. The glass curtain arcing behind the huge tank vanishes, and the pool merges seamlessly with the endless lake beyond. The day is azure, and they could be sitting in a Carthaginian amphitheater on the shores of the Mediterranean. A creature breaks the surface, then another. Three sleek gray missiles clear the water and plunge in synchrony back in. The crowd gasps, music starts up, a human with a wireless headset and a fish bucket appears, and it's showtime.

Soon, pods of marine mammals are spinning, leaping, tail-dancing, squirting, and chattering—everything that the woman with the wireless headset asks them to do. It looks like mutually alien species breaking through into shared play.

No one is more pleased than this show's regular. She asks the scientist, "Do you think they truly understand her?"

"She's making little hand signals."

"Obviously! But this signal communicates, no?"

That's when he tells her. Only a handful of genes separate speaking primates from mute ones. When humans are born with one of these genes knocked out, they can't learn language. "Soon, we'll be able to fix or replace those genes. So . . . I don't know. If belugas are a kind of disabled intelligence, maybe we have a moral obligation to give them language genes, someday."

She grabs his elbow, thrilled. "Serious? *Serious?*"

And he knows, then, that she's coming to Boston.

They say goodbye where they met, out on the sun-coated steps. She stands peering at the rainbow skyline, enraptured again, as if she forgot these buildings existed while she was away, underwater. She promises to go over all the paperwork and call his secretary to make travel arrangements.

He offers a hand, which she squeezes. "*Houta alik,*" he says.

The words start her giggling.

"What? Did I say it wrong?"

She shakes her head, still laughing. "How do you know this?"

"I did my homework on you. At least I *thought* I did."

"No; I'm sorry. It's good. But do you know what it means?"

"I was *told* it meant good luck."

"Yes, sure. But really . . . ?" She jerks a thumb over her shoulder, backed toward the Doric temple. Her eyes light up with more pointless pleasure. Every novel is allowed one major coincidence and one minor one. "It means: A *fish on you.*"

∞

Stone succumbs and calls Candace. This must be three days before Thassa heads east. He should call Thassa herself, but that would involve courage. Instead, he abuses Weld. It's her *job* to calm neurotics. Everyone must suffer the penance of their abilities.

"You can't just let her go out there," he tells the psychologist.

"It's not my decision."

"One word from you and she'd return the tickets."

"Or one word from you," she counters.

"Me? What do I know about science? You're the authority."

"*Authority?*"

"This whole thing is bogus. Nothing as complicated as *feeling* can possibly reduce to genetics. You have to tell her that." Her silence rattles him. "Come on. You know this isn't good science. They can't possibly think they'll find anything."

"Are you worried they might?"

He reads to her from a ten-month-old article in *US News & World Report* calling Thomas Kurton the "Sergei Diaghilev of genomics."

She says something about science being self-correcting. If the man is bogus, he'll disappear. If not, others will validate his work. The discoverer doesn't matter; only the discovery does.

"You can't possibly believe that."

She asks, "Why does this upset you so much?"

He wants to say: *Please don't therapy me.* Instead, he manages, "It's exploitation. We're complicit. We've been given this amazing gift, and somebody wants to take it apart and look inside without voiding the warranty. She's not an object."

"No, you're right. She's a college kid who gets an all-expenses-paid vacation to Beantown. She can say no if she wants."

"All right. Fine. Just remind her she can refuse any test she doesn't want to take."

Candace says they've been over all the human subject protection guidelines. "Russell. She's fine. Anyone who survived a childhood in Algiers can survive a weekend in Boston."

∞

You know the story in Boston. You know what the lab will have to discover.

Thassa flies out. She lands on that Logan runway jutting out into Boston Harbor, thinking until the last second that the plane is going into the drink. She's prepared to die, but she's delighted when she doesn't.

148

Even as the plane touches down, it's snowing. The northern world is dark by early afternoon, and she finds the harborside dusk unbearably beautiful. They put her up in a hotel ten minutes from the lab. She's never stayed in a hotel before. She cries out at the spread of the Charles and laughs at the view of Beacon Hill climbing the far shore. She loves the town center, the jumbled harbor, the genteel circus of Downtown Crossing, the Freedom Trail's inscrutable red thread, the colonial churches with their thin white steeples fingering God. The whole city plays itself, as if a movie of the real place.

She gives all her money to street people. She listens to the buskers in the subway, staying for three full songs and applauding, solo, after each. She's a shameless tourist, keen for everything. She especially loves the graveyards—King's Chapel, the Granary, Copp's Hill. She gets no frisson from the names of the famous dead. Not even natives get that anymore. She just loves the slate tombstones, with their winged skulls and their quatrains of eternity, the patches of holy ground surrounded by amnesiac skyscrapers.

In Cambridge, near the lab, the streetlights carry banners celebrating the twenty-three human chromosomes. She succumbs fatalistically to the lab tests. If something interesting truly does coil up in her cells, someone will find it. If not Truecyte, then some other research group, private or public, will pinpoint whatever part of the secret of happiness lies hidden in the body. This decade or the next. The species will learn to read whatever is there to be read.

Her job, meanwhile, is to see the sights as best she can. Hit the Freedom Trail, before history catches up with it.

∞

Stone calls Candace on Thassa's second night out east. They compare the short e-mails each has received. Stone pillories her with questions. "What does she mean when she says, 'They took my DNA'?"

"That's nothing, Russell. Painless and noninvasive."

"But . . . they can do whatever they want with it?"

"Well, I can't think what they might do aside from study it."

"And when she writes, 'Everything is much more interesting than I thought . . .'?"

"I think it's safe to conclude that that's a good thing. Russell? Can I call you back in an hour, after Gabe goes down?"

She does. And whether it's the lateness of the hour, his Zen cupboard bedroom, the blackness cut by the single megaphone beam of streetlamp out his window, the shoehorn of phone pressed against his ear, the chill of his arms above the down comforter, or the sound of the woman's restorative voice, Stone feels it might be safe to conclude that Candace Weld is, herself, another good thing.

∞

A Truecyte geneticist named Dr. Julia Thorn takes Thassa's family history. Thassa gives what she can, although her knowledge of medical details is spotty at best. Dr. Thorn asks if they might test and take samples from her near kin. Thassa phones her aunt in Montreal, who declines on grounds of privacy. Her uncle in Paris refuses out of a deep-seated suspicion of all things biotechnological. Her brother, Mohand, is currently under house arrest in Algiers for participating in a march for Kabyle autonomy back in November.

Dr. Thorn can't help asking. The question isn't scientific; the answer nothing but anecdotal. "Are any of your relatives . . . like you?"

"They say I'm just like my mother's sister. Everyone always calls her the Sufi."

"Could we test her?"

"Oh, heaven no! She died in the Relizane massacres. With many others."

∞

Candace calls Russell at that same late hour each night Thassa is in Boston. Weld's field has known about the need for ritual almost as long as Stone's. And when the two of them go on talking three nights a week, even after Thassa returns to Chicago, this ritual becomes theirs:

The phone rings at 11:00 p.m., an hour after the cutoff set by every civilized rule for the day's last call. He picks up on the second ring and says "Hello?" as if it might be anyone from prank radio to Homeland Security. She tries for silly—*I was afraid you might say that* or *How does "hello" make you feel?*—and he'll smile in his street-lit room and say, "Hey." Then they'll be off and running, comparing notes about all old things under the sun.

Sometimes they talk for only ten minutes. Sometimes they go an hour. Thassa is no longer the sole focus of their investigation. Mostly they talk about humans, their infinite gullibility, and how you almost have to love them, just for the endless ways they're capable of being duped.

They become an ancient couple, and all their previous incarnations—Candace and her ex, Marty; Russell and his abortive Grace—become just experiments each tried once, failed hypotheses that now, at worst, provide good punch lines. They've both required some trial and error to hit on the obvious: talk beats passion, two out of three falls.

∞

Russell can't imagine Weld's motives, but he's deeply grateful for the distance. It helps him enormously, not to have to look at her. So long as her face doesn't set him off, he doesn't have to time-travel. All the real-world stresses that Stone can never handle in real time he can cope with like *this*—in words, revised together, stories at night that last only a few minutes and give him a day to prep for, in between.

He hears her doing chores as she talks. Picking up toys. Pulling dishes from the dishwasher. They are the sounds of the life he always thought might be his someday. The pleasures he has long found only in books.

∞

She asks him about the work in progress, the book that Thassa mentioned in Hyde Park. She's wanted to ask for weeks. Her waiting so long to raise the topic moves him.

"I lied," he says. "To keep Thassa from worrying about me. It's all in my head. There is no book. There's not even a nonbook."

"Do you wish there were?"

It no longer bothers him, the echo therapy. He knows now that it's just Candace, doing what she's trained to do. If she stopped doing it, she'd be someone else.

"I don't know. I've lost some basic human sympathy. I can see fantastic characters. Hear them perfectly. My head hurts sometimes, they're so close. I can see exactly what they're doing to themselves. But I get ill the minute I try to describe them."

"Use someone else," she whispers, as sexy as the dark. "Find a teller."

At the sound of her, his soul breaks out and tours. She's right. The city at this hour is packed with potential narrators. On a back street in

151

Wrigleyville, two of his former students are smoking salvia and filming each other traveling through the universe, for posting on YouTube. On Oak Street Beach, an old Polish civil servant with one and a quarter legs makes her annual February midnight plunge into the freezing lake, with her husband as lifeguard. In an invisible squat on the roof of the Aon Center, an illegal Tanzanian immigrant protects the whole town from destruction through the sheer force of his will. Any one of them could rescue Stone's fiction from crib death.

He does not tell her the real problem: fiction is obsolete. Engineering has lapped it.

What would his book be about, if it dared set foot in this world? She doesn't ask, and he doesn't say. It might be about the odds against ever feeling at home in the world again. About huge movements of capital that render self-realization quaint at best. About the catastrophe of collective wisdom getting what we want, at last.

∞

He gives up his secret to her: the three stories he published once, in another life. He tells her how badly he wishes he could unpublish them all.

She tells him that even God was appalled by His first draft. Candace's encouragement sounds exactly like the kind he once offered his students.

She says, "Are you in your bedroom?"

The question quickens him.

"Are you lying down? Do me a favor. Close your eyes and write a sentence in the air. Use your left hand. Just one sentence. A simple one."

He writes: *They sit and watch the Atlas go dark.*

"How does that feel?"

It feels strange. Almost alive.

"Does it make you want to know what happens next?"

"I'm afraid that *was* the next."

"Then write what happens just before."

He has no trouble writing, he tells her. It's the permanent public archive that terrifies him.

She says: Go to one of the free blog giveaway sites. Create an anonymous log-in, an altered ego. Just start watching, out loud, in words. Just say what has happened to you, in this life.

"I can't," he tells her. "That's the problem. It's not mine to tell."

Then change it all, slightly, so no one gets hurt. Set the tale in some imaginary landscape, some otherworldly Chicago of naked invention. Forget about scene or plot or dialogue. Engineer a style you yourself would never dream of using. Confess or lie, show or tell, over- or underwrite: it doesn't matter. Your words will be public again, and no one will even know they exist, except one or two accidental scavengers. And everything you write can alter in a heartbeat.

He does as commanded. It's almost a pleasure, two nights later, to describe how miserably the experiment fails.

"I just kept thinking, *We're overrun with this stuff. It's out of control. Kill yours before it multiplies.*"

"I see," she says. Wholly without judgment. He can hear her private diagnosis: patient has lost his nerve.

He closes his eyes and writes in the air. Left-handed, from Yacine's *Nedjma: Keep still or say the unspeakable.*

∞

Another night. Candace says, "Thassa called today."

"Did she?" The topic might be Chinese hydroelectric development.

"She was full of Boston stories."

"Was she?"

"She thinks she's upset you."

"Why would she think that?"

Candace won't play. She's trained not to. "You never answered her messages from the trip. She's afraid you're angry at her for going out."

He's not even sure what that might mean: Thassa *afraid.* She can't possibly be losing any sleep. He doesn't care who she gives her genome away to. He doesn't care what science might find out about her. He wants Truecyte to work out the precise biochemistry for every ridiculous bait-and-switch human emotion that people have ever taken seriously and then develop an antidote. Fifty years from tonight, between genetic intervention, rising consumer satisfaction, upgraded telecommunications, pharmacology, the solidifying hive mind, improved diet, exercise, and behavioral modification, anger will be less of a concern than ringworm.

"I'd be ridiculous to be angry at her," he says.

"You would be," the therapist agrees.

∞

Chance grows like a tumor in Stone. Ever since Thassa went to Boston, he's been plagued by the body's code, the twenty thousand genes hatching their million protein votes into his heart, lungs, and flooded brain. In the dark, safely on his end of the phone line, he asks the counselor, "How programmed are we?"

Candace will not fictionalize for him. The data keep accumulating: impulsivity, aggression, anxiety, self-destruction—all heritable. The genetic contribution to addictive behavior: 30 to 50 percent. Anorexia and bulimia: a 70 percent genetic component. "But still, the students who come to see me change. They can get better."

"From talking to you? Or from drugs?"

"From both. The point is, for better or worse, will and words make a difference."

"How much of a difference?"

For whatever reason, she humors his despair. "I don't know, Russell. How much is enough? Did I ever tell you about my tightrope lessons? For my final exam, I walked across a twelve-foot gap on a piece of hemp half the width of my foot. Twenty feet in the air. And I'm terrified of standing on a footstool. Turns out, you just take one baby step. Then another. I've seen it happen. Temperament can self-modify. People can get free, or at least a little freer. And then a little more."

"But not as free as we're bred to believe we are."

"Gosh, Russell. You make life sound like a sadistic experiment."

"Let's just say the grant proposal would never have passed *my* ethics board."

"Hope is useful, man. It keeps us moving."

"I see. Like a hamster wheel?"

He likes the sound of her midnight sigh.

∞

They talk nine times in two weeks. It's something out of the archaic novels he used to love: a prisoner who lives for the letters from a companion he's never met. An invalid obsessed with a vivid woman sealed in a century-and-a-half-old daguerreotype.

They keep deep down, amid the productive psychosis of the city. Neither one of them suggests that they get together for lunch or drinks or anything. They are each other's solitary reading. The world is graduating from face time to MySpace anyway. The two of them are simply a little ahead of the curve . . .

Stone puts it to himself: If the sound of Candace Weld's voice suffices for the night that needs getting through, why should he escalate? Who decided that words are just action's junior prom? He's richer with her now, in the tangled inventions of their nightly sentences, than they would be after three weeks stranded in sexual intimacy.

Not disabled: deliberate. He's read in his happiness books that deaf couples sometimes refuse medical intervention that might "cure" their offspring and banish them to the world of the hearing. Why should he be forced into the community of touch, when this is his real medium?

Candace's voice asks for nothing. He can't simply be imagining it: she's grateful, as well, for this reprieve from the short-range senses. Yes, their nightly calls may be all too much like how she makes her living. Yet *this*—the free trade of signs—is where she, too, would live.

∞

He likes when her midnight housekeeping stops, when the only background sound is Candace Weld lowering herself with contentment to a repose he can only imagine. *Make me a pallet on your floor.*

The question is whether affection can need no more than itself.

He stops being the one who says when their conversations end. She's the one who sends them off now. And that, too, becomes their ritual. "Well, Master Stone. Any further words for you tonight?"

And one night, to Russell Stone's quiet astonishment, he discovers: there might be.

∞

Kurton has held up the study for too long, waiting for an ideal subject who will solidify the correlation at the outer edges of their model. Then C3-16f comes to visit. Even before Thassa completes the routine tests, everyone on the project knows what they have: a candidate whose alleles confirm their extreme-end predictions. They measure the lengths of repeating segments in the promoter regions of her transporter genes, then map these variants onto a new data point, high up in the blank area of the graph pointed to by the rest of their data set.

And when they see how close she is to the existing straight line of their larger sample, even Thomas Kurton is ready to announce.

They pay the fee for fast-track peer review and—after filing all the appropriate patent papers—they publish in a respectable journal. From a holding pattern to a record finish. All viable labs have been bred for speed, and each generation, science gets better at hunting the mastodon. It's either that or go extinct.

∞

Time passes, as the novelist says. The single most useful trick of fiction for our repair and refreshment: the defeat of time. A century of family saga and a ride up an escalator can take the same number of pages. Fiction sets any conversion rate, then changes it in a syllable. The narrator's mother carries her child up the stairs and the reader follows, for days. But World War I passes in a paragraph. I needed 125 pages to get from Labor Day to Christmas vacation. In six more words, here's spring.

Weeks vanish, during which Stone achieves the moral equivalent of contentment. He works. One part per billion of the world's magazine prose gets detoxified. His days contain no agitations greater than spam. He returns all the happiness books to the public library, which makes him feel much better. In their place, he reads forty pages of gruesome details a day from a doorstop text about the French colonial enterprise *outre-mer*. And at intervals frequent enough to steady him and scarce enough to surprise, he has his nighttime lifelines with Candace—travelogues to anywhere.

But there comes a night, in late March, when Stone gets a different call. He can tell from the *hello*: Candace Weld has news she doesn't want to give. "Can you come for dinner tomorrow?" She adds a hurried truth-in-advertising, her voice unsure whether it will lure him or scare him away: "Thassa will be here."

"Is something wrong?"

"Not really *wrong*." She keeps her professional calm. "She has a piece she wants you to read."

"A piece? A story?"

"Maybe." Candace chuckles without mirth. "A preprint of an article from Kurton's lab. It's coming out next week, in something called *The Journal of Behavioral Genomics*."

"And she wants *me* to help her with it? *You're* the PhD."

"She says you're the best reader she's ever met."

He issues the appropriate cry of pain.

"It references her," Candace says.

"Jesus. Not by name?"

Weld cycles her breathing—*pūraka, kumbhaka, rechaka*. "Not exactly by name. Come have a look." And before he can beg her to fax him the article, she murmurs, "She'll be happy to see you."

Ah, but she's happy even when rebel groups shoot up her neighborhood.

He buses over to Edgewater the next night. The air is thick with supercooled rain that ices as it hits. It's six thirty, and the roads are already a hockey rink. He should have called Candace and canceled. The bus fishtails through the intersection at Western and smacks a Lincoln Town Car. Nobody's hurt, but the bus isn't going anywhere anytime soon. Russell gets out and slides the remaining half mile to Candace's apartment, slashed the whole way by tiny hypodermics of sleet.

Young Gabriel buzzes him through the foyer. The boy holds out one sullen hand for Russell to high-five. "Happy Persian New Year."

Stone's mouth is slow to thaw. "It's Persian New Year?"

"Well, I think it was like yesterday or something."

"How do you know that?"

"I don't," the boy confesses.

A high-pitched ululation, and Thassa comes flying at him from down the hall. "*Ween ghebtu, ya ustadh?* Russell, where have you been?" Her momentum rocks Stone. She squeezes his arms to his ribs. He reminds himself that she'd give the same greeting to a cashier just back from a week's vacation. She releases and inspects him more shyly. There's something different about her, some shadow of reserve: the article he's been summoned here to read.

Candace trails down the hall, smoothing her face and dusting off her flour-spattered teal shirt-dress. Her cheeks flush as she nears. "You're all ice!"

She strips him of coat and hat, shoes and socks. Over his objections, she pushes him down the hall and into a bathroom, instructing him to dry off his jeans with a blow dryer. She slips in a pair of men's heavy woolen socks, which just fit. Whose toe space is he taking?

He emerges into one of those casual, upholstered living rooms that experimenters strew with pillows and games and books, then watch from behind two-way mirrors as the inhabitants imitate their normal lives. His three hosts converge on him again, all talking at once. It's like he's been dropped down into a time-share burrow somewhere underneath the Shire. And for an instant he's stabbed by the feeling that the world might be far from over, that life might still have plans for him, that domesticity might yet survive the worst that knowledge can throw at it.

The preprint sits on a cleared edge of the cluttered coffee table, waiting for him. It looks like something that might come in a registered envelope: injunction, medical notification, summons. He glances at Candace. She's already read it, and her face shows.

"You promised," Gabe accosts him. "You said you would, back when I was at your house."

"Go," Candace instructs the mystified Stone. Discovery can wait. "We're busy in the kitchen anyway."

Thassa, too, shoos them off. "Don't worry. But get ready for the amazing!" It takes Stone a moment to realize: she means the meal. Only then does he smell the travelogue aromas issuing from down the hall.

"They're making something foreign," Gabe warns. "Zero stars." With the right male ally, he might be emboldened to make a break for it.

He pulls Stone into a back room that's a cross between a Hindu temple and NORAD's facility under Cheyenne Mountain. If some newly mutated virus were to decimate the race tomorrow, a fair chunk of civilization's id from the Paleolithic to the Nanotech Age could be re-created out of this room's strewn treasures. The overflowing dragon's hoard of Wi-Fi medieval castles, interstellar Monopoly sets, speech-recognizing ant colonies, and GPS-ready counterterrorist dolls seems to contain a total of three books. Stone picks up one: *Danny Dunn and the International Clone Cartel.* "Don't you read?"

Gabriel is already booting up Darth Sauron's Personal Quantum Rearrangement Center. "Uh . . . *ye*-ah? Like . . . *all the time*? Hey! Put that down and come over here."

Stone does as ordered. On the screen is something like the animated Saturday-morning adventures he and Robert used to watch back in the day, only sharper, richer, and much more deeply realized. Also, there's the little matter of Gabriel actually moving around in the animated universe and leaving behind footprints.

"I'm sorry about the quality," Gabe says, mostly to the screen. "The frame rates on this piece of junk are pretty much down the toilet. You should come see it on my dad's machine sometime."

"Sure," Russell says. What they move through on-screen is as smooth and textured as waking life.

"This is Chaoseeker. The character I was telling you about?"

Only then does Stone realize: they're in Futopia, the persistent, massively multiplayer world that Candace's son and millions of others around the globe find far more rewarding than anything the less persistent real world has to offer.

Gabe in Futopia looks much as he does in Edgewater, aside from the steroidal body mass and the wings. He circles in the air, a lazy spiral over a megalopolis that—unknown to either boy—is modeled on the most futuristic wards of Tokyo.

"Where do you want to go?" the flying child asks.

Omnipotence-induced nausea washes over Stone. He shrugs, paralyzed, but the angel doesn't wait for an answer. It peels over the cityscape, banking across a harbor filled with frenetic activity. Alter-Gabe heads over an ocean of deepening blues. Small craft toss on the stormy waters. The horizon offers a spectrum of available weather from sunburst to squalls.

The boy flies in a trance, beyond speech. They skim over monstrous islands, mashups of ancient cultural memories and historical nostalgia—medieval bestiaries, frontier romances, Victorian steampunk, and recombinant hybrids of everything from spell-casting spacemen to Panzer-driving elves.

Gabe mistakes his visitor's vertigo for thrill. "Can you believe my mother doesn't get this?"

"How big is this place?"

"Which? The *whole* . . . ? Endless! You can even create new lands, if you gather enough power."

Stone nods, for no one. When we run out of resources, we can always move here.

He breathes easier when the flying boy touches down in a desolate landscape. The coast, a plain of ocher rocks, a stone farmhouse. "One of my homes," Chaoseeker explains. The only moving things are birds and the occasional large mammals, off on the rim of olive-riddled mountains.

"Where are we?"

But the reward centers in the boy's brain spark so fiercely it degrades his power of speech. "I built this here . . . I'm a quest . . . There's a relic from the Old Ways I have to . . ."

He trots up into the foothills, ducking into hidden canyons, fending off the occasional assaults of hungry creatures under the remorseless sun. Now and then he finds a sparkling artifact, which he pockets. "We can trade this for great stuff, back in the village."

It's something out of colonialist fantasy literature. The boy's real jaw hangs panting and his eyes dart in heightened alert. Futopia taps into more of the child's legacy nervous system than Chicago ever will. Candace's boy is a junkie, addicted to something that can match any narcotic floating around the public school system.

Futopia spreads before Stone. He, too, might wander forever in mysterious mountains in search of hidden relics, driven by a pleasure as much in need of constant renewal as sex. After each momentary injection of success, always another goal. A little repeated exposure and Russell could easily become as enslaved as this child.

Years ago, in a different desert, under a rock face filled with petroglyphs, Grace cut him his first line of cocaine on a pocket mirror. It terrified him, but she offered up the rite in such innocence—an exploratory lark required of all aspiring writers—that he gave himself over to her and breathed in the dust. It did almost nothing. It made his two front teeth glow and numbed his gums. Yes, the afternoon was glorious; yes, he felt full and funny and grateful and even powerful. But that's what an afternoon with Grace always made him feel.

A week later, he asked, offhand, *How hard is it to get that stuff?* She laughed so long at his casual pretense that he realized: he would do this chemical never again, or he would do it forever. Something in his cells had come into life pre-addicted, as it had for his father and uncle and great-aunt and probably his brother. And the only cure for him was never to take the first taste.

"She hates this," the boy says. "She thinks it's fake. But it's no faker than her phone life."

Russell doesn't even want to ask. "Take me somewhere else," he tells Gabe.

"Wait! We're really close. Let's try over there."

There's no more talking to him. Stone leans back on his stool and watches his guide, the child of the future. Happy citizen of the place that cultural evolution has finally created to shelter the brain, after its long exile.

Just when Russell is about to flee, the door opens, framing Thassa against the blazing hallway. Two steps and she's kneeling between them, one arm around each of their shoulders. "Jibreel. Mister Stone. What are you men doing?"

Gabe says, "What did you call me?"

She studies the screen and her eyes narrow. "Hey! Where is that?"

"It's . . ." the smaller addict starts. "It's hard to, I can't really . . ."

"It's *Kabylie!*"

Gabriel snaps up, clutching the mouse. "No it's not."

"It is! That's Gouraya mountain, there. My grandfather came from not far away. Sidi Touati is just over *there*."

The boy's alarm confirms an invisible village just over the distant crest.

"Poor Algeria. Invaded by everyone."

Candace stands in the doorway, testing a smile. "What's going on?"

Thassa wheels toward her. "They're occupying my homeland. Again!"

"We aren't!" Gabe cries.

Thassa turns back to wag a finger at the plunderers, but Gabe's bewilderment is so complete that she hugs his head to her chest and coos a stream of Tamazight that seems to comfort him. "You want *Kabylie?* Come with me!"

The boy wants nothing but to be left alone to solitary marauding. But he follows the adults into the dining room and a table so generous that both males stop and stare. Thassa orbits the spread, naming everything. There's a small volcano of *couscous bel osbane*, pools of clabbered milk, a mountain lake of *shorba* with *frik* and coriander, stacked-up wedges of *brik* dripping with lemon. "And for dessert, if you are good . . ." She motions toward a mound of sacrificial almond cookies. "*Dziriettes*. 'Little Algerians.' "

Gabe stands stunned. "It's exactly what they eat . . ." He points back toward his remade shadow world.

Thassa grabs his head to her chest again. "Of course it is! Maybe you're a little Algerian, in your other life."

She sits next to the boy. All meal long she teaches him table words

161

in Arabic. He revels in the gutturals while his mother crows, astonished at his appetite.

∞

Checking out of her Centre Ville hotel, Tonia Schiff will ask the concierge how to catch the bus to El Kef. The concierge draws a map to the big station at Bab Alioua. Schiff will find the station without a problem—a cushy place, as world bus stations go. But something about Bab Alioua is a glimpse of things to come: a state-controlled, ad-libbed exercise in indirection and concealment. Take a number and pitch a tent.

She asks about the Kef bus at three guichets and gets five different answers. She boards the wrong bus but disembarks just before it takes off for the subterranean world of Tataouine. She gets sent to another waiting area, but a handmade Arabic sign on the door she's supposed to leave from announces a further unreadable change in plans. She asks around. And around. The bus threatens to leave. Then a semiofficial-looking man declares it's going to be badly delayed. When Schiff asks again half an hour later, she learns it left twenty minutes ago.

Tonia Schiff begins to think that her French—so secure her whole life—is nothing but a private hallucination. Finally, a kindly man with a flowing Old Testament beard takes pity on her. He tells Schiff that someone in her situation (one he doesn't bother spelling out) is better off getting to Kef by *louage*. He directs her to a nearby carrefour and tells her to ask for the *samsar*—the go-between—at the Café de l'Avenir.

The *samsar* can arrange everything. No worries. But the thing that takes the most arranging is how to divvy up Schiff's dinars between the potential driver, the samsar, and the *samsar's samsar*. A *louage* is coming soon, the man tells Tonia. But it's a crowded one, and yesterday, it overheated, two hours into the mountains. That *louage*, he ventures, is not the *louage* for her. One epic Arabic cell call later, he announces a much better one that he could probably get her into, if it's worth his while.

Schiff sits at a café table for a long time, in a mental fugue state straight out of postwar existentialist fiction. Waiting, she considers how much more fun it is to read such scenes than to live them. But the sun is mild, there is still coffee, and nothing on the horizon suggests that humanity can't hold out until she records her final interview with it.

Just as she begins to imagine that it might indeed be possible for even Sisyphus to be happy, a white Peugeot wagon with its rear-left quarter punched in pulls up to the terrace with four others already in it. Tonia hands over one final stack of dinars, gets in the front seat, and buckles in for the three-hour ride.

The *louage* passes through the salt flats west of the city, Tunis's only obvious shantytown. The driver catches Schiff looking and hints ominously that the slum owes its continued existence to World Bank master derivatives. The car bears south a little, then west again, through a plain that graduates—in another advance taste of things to come—imperceptibly from arable to arid.

Schiff's guidebook says to keep watch off the right side of the road, at about one hundred kilometers. The Peugeot crests a hill, and down a wide expanse spread the ruins of Dougga. Tonia cries out in admiration. One of the passengers—the one she has dubbed the Tunisian Robert De Niro—leans forward and says, "The best Roman town in North Africa. Edge of the empire."

The woman next to him objects with her whole body. Not Roman, she says. Numidian. Then Libyco-Punic.

Her other seatmate, who had spent the entire trip writing columns of figures into pocket ledgers, claims that the Numidians stole it from the Berbers. The driver plunges into the fray, and the debate turns violent in three languages, only one of which Tonia can follow. The argument over who built the city turns into a fight over who killed it— the Byzantines, the Vandals, the Ottomans, the French, or the UN World Heritage folks.

"No one killed it," the driver declares, in a voice suggesting that anyone who disagrees can walk the rest of the way to El Kef. "The land just dried up. The damn empire fell apart. What do you do about that?"

The whole *louage* falls silent for five kilometers.

In one of his long, Tom Swift monologues that began in self-replicating nucleotide sequences and ended up with human colonization of other star systems, Thomas Kurton once told Schiff how all the basic elements of survival—finding food, avoiding prey, selecting mates—depend on holding background noise steady enough to pick out foreground signals. We're tuned by a billion years of natural engineering to the flashing Now, designed to be dead blind to exactly the kind of huge, slow, incremental changes that will kill us. According to Kurton, the race had two choices: sit like the oblivious frog in the slowly warming pan until we cook, or take our natures into our own hands and sculpt out better angels.

The cab climbs the hairpin twists on the Grand Parcours Cinq, clawing its way up to Kef. As the massive Djebel Dyr plateau breaches the horizon, Tonia Schiff gets ill. She concentrates her willpower on surviving the last fifteen kilometers, but loses. The rattled driver makes an emergency stop, and Schiff finds a small pit in the yellow rocks just off the road to vomit in. When she comes back to the car, the passengers and driver are arguing about what made her sick.

On the ridge outside the city, Schiff gazes south toward the pre-Saharan steppe, even as the Sahara comes slowly northward, toward her.

∞

What does the foster family talk about, over the Maghrebi feast? Four feet from each other, Candace and Russell argue whether anonymous online user ratings for everything from holiday destinations to songbirds are a marvelous new form of cultural interaction (Weld) or the death of the private soul (Stone). Gabe gives the topic one star. When the heat of their hyperboles gets embarrassing, they switch to the recent unmasking of a literary hoax. It turns out that a troubled teenager's searing memoir—abuse, escape, horrific life on the streets—is really the work of a seasoned, middle-aged feature writer. Candace calls the whole episode fascinating contemporary ethnography. Stone wants the fraud to serve time. Thassa and Gabe just giggle, in bursts of street Arabic.

The food warms them all. But even with passionate debate, they finish the meal almost before they've started. The world's most ephemeral art form—even worse than magazine writing. What kind of life would let dinner pass in a tenth the time of its preparation? This kind. The kind we're built for.

Stone sits facing the coffee table. The article lies in wait for him, occupying one-quarter of his cerebrum all the way through the *dziriettes* and coffee. The report is to blame for Candace's distance all evening. Even Thassa's attentions to Gabe have seemed preoccupied.

Russell sits nibbling at his little Algerians, inside a familiar domestic scene that ought to know how badly the world has already doomed it. This craving for a shared meal uses him like a seed burr uses a trouser cuff. Stone has spent eight years getting free of exactly this need. Now he wants it back as badly as he's ever wanted anything.

All dinner long, wind shakes the building and sleet tattoos the windowpanes. An ice storm in late March: more freak weather becoming the norm. After dessert is over, the four of them stay huddled around the table, afraid to leave the one warm spot given them.

Gabe leaves first; he has a heat source elsewhere. He heads down the hall, off to a place whose payoff matrix is far more generous than this one's. Russell would follow, if Candace didn't chirp, "You read. We'll clean up."

When he objects to that division of labor, Thassa just laughs. "You want a typical Maghrebi meal? You have to exploit the women."

He sits down to study for his supper. The article is hard, harder than he feared. He's seen some of the vocabulary during his months with the happiness books, but every sentence here has something to defeat him: epistatic, allelic complementation, coefficient of relatedness, noncoding polymorphism, nucleus accumbens, dopaminergic and serotonergic pathways . . . He's waylaid in the dense hieroglyphics: 5-HTTLPR, QTL, VNTR, BDNF, monoamine oxidase, dihydroxyphenylalanine . . . He wants to stop after every clause and consult Candace. But he's the experimental control; his job is to say what this article will mean to the congenitally clueless.

So this is how the species ends. *Homo sapiens* has already divided, if not into Eloi and the Morlocks, then into demigods and dispossessed, those who can tame living chemistry and those who are mere downstream products. A tiny elite is assembling knowledge more magical than anything in Futopia, perfecting fantastic procedures, determining chemical sequences billions of units long, reading what these spell out, learning how a million proteins interact to assemble body and soul. Meanwhile, Stone and his 99.9 percent of the race can only sit by, helplessly illiterate, simply praying that the story will spare them.

Russell reads, the clink of dishes and soft words floating in from the next room. Apparently Kurton's group has found a network of several crucial genes that, rumor has it, help build the gates and portals that channel the brain's molecules of emotion. Control for any of them, and changes in the rest correlate with changes in sanguinity. The graphs are clean and the correlations strong. The variant combinations of these genes produce several clusters of data points along a spectrum running from darkness to bright. Tune each of the genes to the right flavor, and you have subject C3-16f, just now making her friend laugh over some silliness in the kitchen.

The article describes how psychological tests virtually predicted C3-16f's optimal allele assortment—the happiness jackpot. Russell sits back in the rickety recliner, the journal open on his lap. He himself imagined this development long ago, the first night of his writing class. From before she even arrived in this country, Thassadit Amzwar already belonged to these technicians, the child buyers, the purveyors of human improvement. Way back in chapter one, he predicted her ultimate capture by science before book's end.

He sits watching a skin of ice crystal culture itself across the living room's casements. The glass is almost covered, and the ice is thickening. When he looks up from this reverie, the women are standing next to him. They take the sofa, Candace gingerly and Thassa in a flop. The Algerian speaks first. "Nonsense, isn't it?"

Stone scans Candace, who clearly wants to believe the same thing.

"They make me sound like some kind of bio-factory for *ivresse*. I'm not like that, am I? That's just silly. Everyone can be as content as they like. It's *certainly* not predestiny."

Stone wills Candace to look at him. "Is the science any good?"

"Good science?" She's not the confident woman that he speaks to every other night, in the dark. He doesn't know the first thing about her, really. If she were the heroine of some hackneyed genre thing that he got it into his skull to write, he wouldn't even be able to jot down her main character traits. She seems experimental to him, curiously adrift in data. "I suppose we're already past worrying about that."

The words chill him. "What do you mean?"

Candace studies the ice-coated windows. "Every conclusion in the article could be discredited next month, and journalists will still be reporting it five years from now."

"But say they're right. It doesn't change anything in . . . real life, right? I mean, they guarantee confidentiality. No one can find out who . . . ?"

Candace, professional Candace, studies him, deciding whether jaw-dropping naïveté is genetic or environmental. It's not fair. He's the one who was against Thassa going to Boston. Candace thought they would find nothing.

He assumes a courage that he distinctly doesn't have. "Look. This isn't necessarily a crisis." He turns to Thassa. "If anyone does approach you about this . . . you don't have to say anything."

Russell glances to Candace for moral support. She looks back, crestfallen. Too late, he realizes: his job was not to reassure Thassa about her anonymity. His job was to prove that her friends won't change how they think of her. And in that, he has just failed spectacularly.

Thassa leans forward, indignant. "If anyone asks me? Of course I'll tell them! What do you think? If this is science, give me *vaudou. Le marabout!*"

As she speaks the word, the lights flicker and go black. Outside, the streetlamps, too, gutter and cut out. A howl comes from down the hall, then another yelp and a smack into a doorframe. A voice calls, "Mom!" Candace jumps up and blunders past the recliner, stumbling into the dark. Gabriel calls out again. "Mom, I didn't do anything! I was just playing, and suddenly everything . . ."

Mother finds child, and child finds hand-cranked flashlight where it lies hiding in the front closet. The four of them huddle in the front room, sure that the power will return any second. Out in the street, a few scattered lights still shine, but the ice coating the windows blunts them to streaks.

When darkness breaks the ten-minute mark, Thassa suggests an expedition. Candace acquiesces. Gabe is ecstatic as he dons his coat; for once, Edgewater can match Futopia for adventure. They pass through the blackened foyer, navigating by the anemic, hand-cranked light.

Out in the courtyard, the world has turned strange. The moon blazes crazily, and everything they look on—trees and bushes, the spiked iron fence, the funeral procession of parked cars—everything has gone diamond, encased in a quarter inch of ice.

Thassa goes down first. She hits the frictionless front stoop and her legs sweep out from under her. She lies on her back, cursing in Tamazight, then stops, amazed, gazing up into a sky sudden with black. All four look up on a scene that electric Chicago has obliterated for a hundred years.

The Algerian crawls up on her knees, giggling in pain and begging the others to take care. They latch onto one another, inching forward together, an eight-legged, skating thing way out of its biome.

Other such colonies edge through the shellacked neighborhood, waving their weak beams. A few cars still slalom down the glazed streets, no faster than the sliding pedestrians. Branches are down everywhere, sheared off of weakened trees by the weight of their sudden shells.

A group of explorers gather outside a house, pointing their flashlights where a branch bigger around than Stone has fallen onto coated power lines and draped them across the roof like a giant's aborted game of cat's cradle. Thassa and company slide up to the gathering, obeying some atavistic urge to band together as the world comes apart. Gabe gasps in awe at the destruction. A puffy Gore-Tex kid midway in age between Gabe and Russell chants, "Lines are down all over the place. It's like a war zone." He holds up his cell phone as his authority. "The whole Near North is without power!"

Everyone slides about, giddy with apocalypse. Strangers chatter together as if they're from the same close-knit tribe. Neighbors who've passed by anonymously every day for years now hug Gabe and pump Candace for her bio. No one knows anything about the ice storm, except for the weather bureau's complete failure to prepare anyone.

A young Indian woman consults Stone about canned food and bottled water when a shock crumples the air behind him. The group gasps, and Russell recoils in a hail of sparks. A power transformer comes unstapled from its pole and releases a fountain of fireworks over the group. Everyone shrieks backward, and a couple fall and smack the ice. The Indian woman is down and shouting.

Thassa skates to her side, helping her up and calming her down. Stone watches from his prone position. She's been through this before—ice storms in Montreal, explosions in Algiers. She helps the Indian woman away from the sparking transformer, soothing her. Then Thassa rejoins Candace and a frightened Gabe. She jokes and sings to the boy in sinuous Arabic. Before Stone's eyes his sunny former student turns into a genetic aberration, immune to disaster, a product of chemical reactions qualitatively different from his.

Even Candace, the eternal champion of nurture over nature, hovers near Thassa with newfound deference. Stone sees her hesitation, the slight bow of her head. Candace, too, can't help but marvel at that outlier data point, all by itself on the high end of Thomas Kurton's graph.

The group splits in two, those for camping around the sparking transformer and those for exploring further. Distant blocks still have light, but they're blinking out fast. Thassa leads her three down to Foster. The road is scattered with cars, some still creeping, but most left in crazy angles wherever they've slid to rest. The commercial strip on Clark through Andersonville is dim. Ice has them.

The air is chill, but not punishing. Not as bad as the February they've just come through. Colder air high above produces this super-cooled lacquer of instant ice that, but for a few degrees, would have washed away as March's final rain.

The foursome doubles back to the Red Line stop, to put Thassa on a train south. Thassa tows Gabe along by the back of her jacket, a compact droshky right out of Tolstoy. As the sleigh corners, the boy spins out, maniacal wonder in his eyes. The world is perverse and jagged after all. The boy absorbs this sudden wildness as if he'd willed it. He swings around and shoots Russell a crazed glance. The thrill goes right through Stone. He, too, the frozen boy in him, wants ice to be stronger than order.

They meet an elderly Asian in a parka coming out of the doors of the El stop. He waves both gloved hands: *Don't even try.* "No more train tonight. Everything stopped." He's wearing the dazed little grin of disaster.

They peek into the turnstiles, where a burly CTA official in a puffy coat turns them away.

"How long?" Stone asks. But the uniformed man just shrugs.

The four of them mill near the station doors, waiting for a second opinion. The trains are stilled. The network is breaking down. The city slips into dementia. Stone is primed by the article: signals, synapses, precursors and pathways, transporters and receptors. The urban web, too, has unthinkably more ways of wonking out than of working properly. What thought is Chicago seizing on now, as its cells misfire?

A young gay couple slides toward them from the east. "Forget about it," Gabe tells them. "They're not running."

"Get out! Are you serious?" They glance inside, but the CTA official nixes them. "Shit!" the smaller of the pair giggles, as if his music-player battery just went dead. "Plan B, come in. Where are you, Plan

B, over?" The couple skates off into blackness, singing, *I love to go a-wandering* . . .

Candace peers northbound down the tracks. They're as blank and silent as the afterlife. "Sleepover at my house," she announces. Her son cheers.

Stone's dread come to life. "I can walk home."

Candace groans. "Russell! I can*not* believe you just said that."

"Really. It's not that far."

"Don't be a nitwit."

Her son howls in pleasure at the slur. Thassa smiles, too. "You do say some funny things sometimes, Mister. Never mind. That's why we love you."

They creep back to Candace's through three lapidary blocks. The furnace is knocked out, but the apartment is still warm. The adults go about transforming the place into a candlelit séance. Candace gets her son in bed, with an extra blanket, although the odds of the boy sleeping anytime soon are what science might call nonexistent. Gabe whispers to her, like he's praying. "I'm scared, Mom. What's going to happen?"

She starts to reassure him. The night is not that cold; the power will be back soon.

"Not that! The whole computer shut off before I could save. I could be totally dead!"

She kisses his forehead in the dark. "You'll grow back." That's the beauty of the digital-replacement world. That's why everyone is moving there.

She comes back out to the living room, where Thassa and Russell are reviewing the article by the light of six votive candles. "You and I can share my bed," Candace says. Stone flinches, though she's pointing at Thassa. Candace smiles a little ruefully and adds, "The man gets the sofa."

Thassa stands and takes the article from Stone's hands. "Please stop reading, Russell. You'll hurt your eyes." She squeezes his shoulder, grabs two candles, and follows Candace down the hallway to the master bedroom, calling good night.

The sound of fumbling in a linen closet, and Candace comes back out, her arms full of flannel. Stone helps her tuck the sheets around the sofa cushions. His ribs clamp around his pounding heart.

His chemicals are idiots, unable to tell an empty symbol from a full one, suckered by nothing more meaningful than propinquity.

He drops his voice. "Is it true?" She looks at him, baffled. "The article?"

Candace stands, holding her neck. "I don't know. It sure sounds impressive." In the low light of all these candles, she's a La Tour. "Hang on. I'll get you some blankets." She heads back down the hall. Russell tags after her with a candle, pretending to be useful in this, at least.

She pauses before the linen-closet door. Signals race on the air. She feels the molding with one hand, then turns, the back of her pelvis pressing against the wall, bracing it. Her legs are slightly splayed. One hand drops and reads the stucco, while the other holds her auburn hair off her forehead. Russell comes to a stop in front of her. The flame of his votive casts a globe around them. She just studies him, her pupils dilated, her breath coming in surges. Waiting is her art; her medium, the confusion of others.

Wanting her has never been Stone's problem. She knows him exactly, his hopes and fears, his reach and shortfall, and still she stands there, holding her hair from her eyes, not quite daring him, just studying to see if he, too, might think that it's possible to double-cross nature, exploit the exploiter once, in this life.

He holds the candle to her cheek, leans forward, and puts his mouth on hers. Lowering a bucket to a well. He watches her close her eyes and thaw. His chemicals teach something that he long ago discounted.

A sigh comes from down the hall, the master bedroom door closes, and they both snap back to the business of blankets. "Here you are," she says, loading him. An inward smile tightens her lips. He doesn't know the word for it. *Wise.* "Call me if you need anything. You have my number, I think. Sleep well." And she walks down the hall, brisk and rhythmic, letting herself into the closed bedroom, from which emerges a brisk duet of laughter.

He goes about the apartment, putting out candles. For a minute, he's a surplice-covered twelve-year-old altar boy following the Benediction at St. John's Episcopal, Aurora. Amazingly, that ancient creature is still paddling around inside him like some coelacanth, protected by the rumor of its own extinction.

171

The apartment gathers in eerie silence—no compressor, no blower, no hum or ticking of any powered device. He gets in bed fully dressed. He falls asleep to a ridiculous sense of rightness, dopamine run pointlessly amok. And he does sleep, on his sofa-pillow bed, deeper than any reason. But he dreams himself into a Pynchon novel, with an international cartel trading in the arcane incunabula hidden in people's cells. His own sperm carries a sequence on the *Index Librorum Prohibitorum*, and he has to chase through several genomically controlled cities, looking for a doctor who will transfuse his gametes.

∞

He wakes early to the second day of spring. All the lights are on. He rises and makes the rounds, turning them all off. The devices all flash 12:00. He looks outside. The spell is broken. Sometime after midnight, the earth warmed ten degrees. The diamond crust has crumbled and liquefied. Neighbors are scraping off their cars and driving away. The disaster is over, before extracting any but the most token sacrifice. A shame.

Stone relieves his long-suffering bladder, splashes tepid water on his face, and bumbles in the kitchen to start the coffee. From the boy's room comes the click of keys. Voices muzzy with morning hum from down the hall. Steps falter; doors open and close. Communal return to consciousness: the routine that he's spent his whole life fleeing.

Candace emerges first. She's immaculate as ever, in tan blouse and creased gray slacks, but her face is somehow different. Pale and ever so slightly featureless. *Cosmetic-free.* She raises a thin eyebrow at him.

"Party's over? Back to the salt mines?"

He nods sympathetically and hands her a cup of coffee.

"Bless you. You're a secular saint." She sits wrapped around her stimulant, sufficient unto the day.

Before they're forced into the exigency of talk, Thassa shows. She's puffy, frazzled, and wobbly. Her eyes are still pinched shut. "Do *not* look at me. Not a happy sight!"

Her loginess is deeply comforting. She doesn't spring up full-blown with the sun. Science should test her now, put this bleary, sedated postadolescent into the data set, before she's had her morning tea.

Gabe comes out, more charged than the three adults combined.

"Everything's fine," he reassures Stone, chopping the air. "I only lost like a tenth of my Experience."

They share another meal, American style this time. They sit at the small round table over synchronized cereal. Why do we need to turn the most naked animal dependency aside from breathing into a religious ritual?

Everyone's already late. The whole city. The roads have mostly melted, and Candace decides to drive. Stone refuses a lift. All three beg him to get in the car, but he holds his ground. He looks at Thassa, heading off to a last week of normalcy before the subtlest biochemical assays ever discovered publicly declare her a freak of nature. Her face apologizes. *What else can I do?*

It's Chicago, morning rush hour. Crusts of ice fall from the blowing branches. Stone steps back, out of the range of anyone's embrace. The riders wave, the car pulls out, and he starts the long slog back home through the disenchanted world.

∞

"Give me your coffee cup," Thomas Kurton tells Schiff, who's caught by the second camera. "We can take a swab off that." It's a funny, telegenic moment. Director, camera operators, and sound tech share a look with Tonia, and they all wordlessly agree to a wrap.

But the minute the DV cameras turn off, Kurton does as threatened. He flings himself up off the porch rocker and into his utility room, where he retrieves a six-inch cotton swab. He tears the sterile packaging, dips into Tonia Schiff's coffee-cup backwash, and seals the swab in its plastic housing.

The gesture is weirdly intimate. "I now have your genetic profile. Your SNPs and indels—the variations in your genome of any significance. I can identify your ancestors—and your descendants. I can predict your health and development, and I can even speculate about your disposition. I can make a good bet of your likely age span and what you'll die of, if you don't get hit by a car first. Hide this away in the cooler for a few years, and I'll be able to do a whole lot more. Would you like a look? It's the closest thing to time travel you'll ever get."

The man has morphed into something out of Wagner. The whole crew regrets shutting down the cameras too soon. The future hits Tonia, and her stomach folds. She rearguards: "Am I *allowed* to look? Or is somebody like you going to sue me for infringement?"

"Good question. Let's say the law is in a period of adjustment at the moment."

She's not really listening. She has her eyes on the plastic tube and its contents, which he's waving around in the air like a conductor's baton. "I'm sorry. Could I just . . . ?"

He teases her for a second, the swab barely out of reach. "Sure. It's all yours." He turns to the mesmerized film crew. "Anyone want to wash the other cups?"

Schiff and Kurton are still disputing the phrase *the wisdom of repugnance* as the crew brings the gear down to the van. Tonia looks up to see her colleagues spinning their wheels, waiting for her. "Go on ahead. I'll meet you back at the B and B in Damariscotta."

The smirking crew pulls away in the van, but not before that punk Kenny Keyes gives her a little knowing finger salute off the side of his nose. She denies him the pleasure of a reaction.

She drifts alongside Kurton back up the driveway. They've talked to each other for weeks, on and off camera, testing each other's bright and dark places, familiar, now, as any two adversaries. She watches him stack empty flower pots. "People will be swabbing each other soon, won't they? Before you hire somebody. Before you *marry* somebody. Consent or not. We're going to be on file with hospitals, corporations, the government . . ."

"I believe that is already under way."

"It doesn't bother you, does it? How creepy society is going to get."

He shrugs his shoulders, like a sixteen-year-old answering the question *What the hell do you think you're doing?* "There was a time when income tax and government-issued IDs were unthinkably creepy. Technology changes what we think is intolerable."

She squirrels the line away for use in the interview's introduction.

He stares down through the thin line of pines across the road to the shimmering water, a *Boy's Book of Adventure* look. "Would you like to take a quick sail? We have a couple of hours before dusk."

His boat is a beautiful little gaff-rigged twelve-footer, cedar, oak, and Doug fir, from the sixties. He takes them down the inlet past the headlands, then hands her the rudder. Gulls gather on the rocky spit, like whispers. As the sky plushes out toward ginger and the waves quiet, he leans back against the front of the cockpit, toying with a cleat. They glide on no sound. She comes about, catches the wind, settles into the flow, and is filled with the most profound sense of aimlessness to be had anywhere.

"May I ask you something? Completely off the record."

He tilts his face back in a speckle of sun, eyes closed, smile compliant.

"How in God's name do your companies make a profit?"

He laughs so hard it folds him upright. "You're making a small assumption, there."

"Seriously. You must be bleeding money away into all these projects, some of which, if you'll pardon me, seem as flaky as pie crust. Okay: You have a couple of drug patents. You've licensed a pair of processes to larger pharmaceutical outfits. And you own the rights to two diagnostic screens. But all of that together can't possibly pay for even half the R and D—"

He juts out his iconoclastic chin. "You're right! It doesn't!"

She tacks again, taking a bead back up the inlet, toward his dock and home. "So how do you stay in business?"

He smiles more generously, unable to keep from admiring her. "You're not much of a businessman, are you?"

"Enough of one to know that credits are supposed to be greater than debits."

He waves away the nuisance technicalities. "Forget about bookkeeping. You can't bookkeep what's coming. In a few years, we're going to be biologically literate. We'll have figured out how to make cells do whatever chemistry we want. You think computer programming has changed the world? Wait till we start programming the genome."

"Thomas. Relax. We're done filming."

He turns toward starboard and pushes his curls back over the crown of his head. "I'm sorry if I sound like I'm still performing. But believe me. It's coming."

"Okay. So medicine keeps getting more complicated. I see the revenue potential there, down the line. But you can't run a business without products. What exactly are you selling?"

He gazes at her with the warmth caught so nakedly on film an hour earlier. "At the moment, Truecyte is in the business of selling the same product as most of the biotech sector: vaporware. But the venture capitalists know what's in the pipeline."

His voice drops to the hush of the wake against the hull. "The coming market is endless. Think about the five years just before the Internet. The five years just before the steam engine. Only those companies that free themselves of preconceptions will take advantage of the biggest structural change in society since . . ."

The simile eludes him, as irrelevant as bookkeeping. The sail starts to luff. She nudges the tiller and lets out the boom. Whatever Thomas Kurton's knowledge of the future, he's right, in any case, about *her*. For all her seasons *Over the Limit*, she's never really taken the flood of transcendental hype seriously. That's been her source of appeal: the clear-eyed, unflappable skeptic who simply wants to see the future's photo ID.

She brings the boat in line with his dock, now yawning up in front of them. Together she and Kurton furl the sail and drift into a light knock against the hanging tire bumpers. Kurton leaps onto the dock, ties down the prow and stern, and helps her over the gunwales.

On the dock, she says, "You really think we're going to get life to play by our rules?" The sun burnishes the water's surface. In a moment, the air and the pines on the crag behind them turn crazed orange.

He comes next to her and takes her forearm. She has predicted this, with no skill in futurism at all. She lets him. It feels lovely. In her experience, it has never *not* felt lovely, at first. Dopamine, serotonin, oxytocin. Does knowing the chemistry change anything? How long ago did she discover that *lovely* was a chemical trick?

"I'm telling you: Forget what you know. Free your mind. Use your *imagination*." His eyes fish for hers. No end of stories play in his. Microbes that live on dioxins and digest waste plastics. Fast-growing trees that sequester greenhouse gases. Human beings free from all congenital disease.

She looks away, back out over the water. "You're overselling again."

"It's not sales. It's just what happens next." His thumb strokes her wrist. He lets go of her arm. He shrugs again, and in that simple gesture suggests that all literature, all fiction, all prediction to date is nothing more than a preparatory sketch of the possibilities available to the human animal.

He detaches and wraps the tiller, tucks it under his arm, and climbs back up the boardwalk toward the house. She falls in at his side, the rhythm of this early evening remarkably familiar to her.

He thinks out loud. "Your show will run. Your gang will edit me into some sort of white-coated huckster too cheerily Faustian to hear how nutty he sounds. Good television, right?"

She asks him, with a scowl, not to pity himself or resent the millions of dollars in free advertising.

"You'll weave this whole story about a man and his company and its detractors and competitors. You'll construct this whole dramatic arc for Truecyte . . . Listen: Truecyte is nothing. Truecyte is irrelevant. Yes, we're in the spotlight at the moment. But you know how science works now. Several hundred thousand researchers, propelled along on collective will. None of us fast enough to keep up. We make this big announcement, this exciting but ambiguous finding, and within a few weeks, a dozen more start-ups are all breathing down our necks, threatening to beat us to this thing."

She can't keep irritation from flooding her voice. "What *thing*?"

He turns and points back out over the water, now a swirl of cinnamon. "Fifteen minutes ago, you were the queen of creation. Correct? I saw it in your face."

She blushes, some other flush of chemicals. But you can't have opinions about truth.

"If your alleles were a little different, you'd feel that way *most of the time*."

Her head shakes, all by itself. "And if I were William Gates the Third, I'd buy me a nice little inlet like this and a sloop to call my own."

He smiles as richly as she did fifteen minutes ago. "With the right genetic compliment, you wouldn't even need an inlet. You wouldn't need anything. Your enemies could be shelling you, and you'd still be filled with a confident desire to make something worthwhile of the day."

"And this is a good thing?"

They cross the coast road and head up the foot of his drive. She doesn't want to speak again, but she does. "This woman with all the right alleles: Does she even know she's that happy? If she's that lifted up all the time, does she even have a measure . . . ?"

"Oh, she goes up and down like anyone else. It's just that her envelope of high and low is considerably higher than ours."

Schiff pauses by her rented Camry. The crew is waiting for her in Damariscotta. She needs to rejoin them for dinner and postmortems.

They have to be at Logan first thing tomorrow. "That's my point. I'm happier than most people, but what good does that do me? She's happier than I am. If you moved us all up a notch, wouldn't we just acclimate and forget, like we do with everything else? Wouldn't ten just become the new seven?"

"I wondered about that, too, until I met this ten. And the weird thing is, her genome differs from yours by only a few small tweaks."

She sees it in Thomas Kurton's trusting, suppliant face: There's only one real resource. One fungible commodity that the future will trade in. "You're going to make us all happy. Is that the plan?"

His eyebrows crumple and his lips sour. She's hurt him, at least as much as he's capable of being hurt by anyone. He shrugs off her mockery. "A little more capable of being well in this world. But not if you don't want it, of course."

"You folks have finally found the formula for soma. Damn."

He breathes out a long-suffering sigh and leans against her car. "First, I really do hope that Aldous Huxley is burning in the pain-ennobling hell of his choice. That book is one of the most dangerous, hope-impeding, ideological rants ever written. Just because the author is stunted by some virtuous vision of embattled humanism, the rest of the race is supposed to keep suffering for all time?"

"I'm not sure that's exactly his—"

"Second, yes: our initial *products*, if you insist, will likely consist of pharmaceuticals. But not the shot-in-the-dark stuff that we dispense today. Drugs tailor-made to the genome of the recipient. Smart bullets, genetically personalized prescriptions, and the sooner we get there, the faster we can finally get medicine out of the dark ages. Once we understand the brain chemistry behind depression and elation . . ."

He catches himself this time. He nods, repentant, but the fingers of both hands flick rapidly against his thumbs. "I'm sorry. I'm an enthusiast. Guilty. What's your problem with that? I assume you have no moral qualms about curing depression? We're talking about substances that will be to today's serotonin reuptake inhibitors what fentanyl is to biting on a towel."

"Why do I have the funny feeling that genetically tailored pills are just the beginning?" She catches him appraising her hair with the gaze of a connoisseur. Her left hand sweeps up, brushes back her flowing bangs, and lets them fall again.

He copies her involuntarily. "Because you are America's most irreverent science television journalist." His voice can't help revering that *irreverent*.

"And all this public talk about life-span extension —"

"Oh, we're working on that, too. Quality *and* quantity. Listen. We're after the same thing humanity has been after since toolmaking."

"Except for the bit about rewriting the script?"

He looks genuinely puzzled. "We've been doing that all along, as well."

"And we're not allowed to stop until every appetite is satisfied and every itch is scratched."

The honest bafflement only grows. *What else would you suggest?* "Speaking of appetite satisfaction: stay for dinner."

She pushes off of the car and drifts toward the house before the invitation is out. "I don't know. What about this massive calorie-restriction diet you're on?"

"I make each one count."

∞

Back in a rocker on the wraparound porch, she calls Nicholas Garrett, in Damariscotta. "Boss? Listen. I'm going to be a little delayed. Go on and eat without me."

She can hear Keyes cackling in the background: *What did I tell you? A hundred bucks, suckers. Pay up.*

She tells Nick she won't be too late, but no need to wait up. Then she rings off, to her director's suppressed mirth. She sits in the rocker for a moment, examining herself. It's not even an effort, really. Not even a decision. Just large molecules, passing their oldest signals back and forth across the infinite synapse gap.

A noise comes from up in the woods. She can't tell if it's a mammal, bird, or something stranger. A throat considerably smaller than hers, but monstrous compared to the rest of creation, moans in spectral restlessness. She waits until the sound returns. It's a call from back long before contentment and agitation parted ways. She walks around the side of the porch to get a look. There's nothing to see but dark woods, the prison-bar stand of pines and spruce, the rising hillside, and needle-covered night.

I have no center. The thought wastes her. Not even a thought: just a fact the exact size of her body. She's disappeared into playing herself. She has no clue what her bliss is, and trying to follow it would lead worse than nowhere.

She walks back around the side door to the kitchen, where he's already started slicing a cornucopia of phytonutrients. "I'm sorry," she says. She doesn't even know what she's saying until she hears it announced. "I've got to get back."

"Really?" His disappointment is insultingly anemic. "Are you sure you wouldn't like to stay? You should stay. You should experiment. Almost sixty is the new forty."

She snickers, as she sometimes does during the show's more outrageous segments. "I can see that. You guys are all over these smart drugs already, aren't you?" He doesn't, she notices, deny it. "Unfortunately, almost forty is the new early retirement."

She walks back through the quarry-stone-and-cedar living room, past the shelf of pictures of the ex-wife and two kids, each already on their way to becoming multimillionaires. She grabs her bag and keeps walking. He follows her back out to the Camry. He doesn't try to touch her.

At the car, arm's distance, she tells him, "Thanks again for all the cooperation. This will be one of our better shows. You make fantastic television."

He stands there, open as ever, ready for the next big thing. His crinkled face would simply like to discover what drives her. Born researcher. He may not have the happiness gene, but he possesses an ebullience she finds more attractive than beauty.

"You should stay a little," he decides. "I'm telling you. You never know what might make you glad."

"True, that." She wants to beg him not to cure melancholy, not for another century or two, anyway. She hears the nocturnal creature call again, from up in the tomb of woods. She puts a hand on Kurton's shoulder, pecks his pursed lips, opens the car door, and is gone.

She's seven miles down the winding, dark road when story crashes over her like a whitecap. She pulls off in front of a trim saltbox store whose laddered signage reads:

GROCERIES
GIFTS
BAIT
UNITED STATES POST OFFICE

She fishes in her bag, finds the phone, and—something she never does—pulls back onto the road even while hitting the speed dial. Nicholas picks up. "Hey," she says. "It's me." Whoever that may be. "I'm on my way. Get your hundred dollars back from Pomade Boy. And listen. We need to do one more show on this. Exactly. You're a mind reader. I can't imagine she'll be too hard to hunt down."

She says goodbye and snaps the phone shut, feeling grim and purposeful and halfway to vague exuberance.

∞

Creative nonfiction comes down to this: science now holds routine press conferences. As the article hits print, Truecyte orchestrates their announcement about the network of genes that helps regulate the brain's set point for well-being. The few dozen science writers, photographers, lawyers, and investment researchers who show up for the Cambridge event know the drill. All the actors in the network adjusted to the fact ten years ago: genetics has become genomics. Science has long since passed beyond the realm of wonder into entrepreneurship. New biochemical properties mean new intellectual property. Nobody mobilizes this much apparatus or lays in that much catering unless they mean to recoup it many times, down the line.

The mobile crew of *Over the Limit* is there, of course. And if history ever needs it, they have forty-five minutes of raw video proving that Thomas Kurton is not the first to use the instantly notorious term. That honor belongs to a sixty-five-year-old geologist turned reporter for one of the last popular-science glossies not yet driven to extinction by the Net. It happens at around the thirty-eight-minute mark, after Kurton has talked through his slides, run his animations, and spoken about "a new era in our understanding of the foundations of emotion."

First, there's an erudite question from a wire-service newbie about the ways in which other flavors of 5-HT receptor genes might be implicated. A veteran public-radio reporter asks about the penetration: What percentage of people with these alleles will actually be extremely buoyant? Someone else wants to know what role micro- and macroenvironments play in getting these genes to express. Kurton just shrugs and admits that the hard questions are still at large.

Then the former geologist and soon-to-retire magazine writer uses the term that everyone else was going to report anyway. "Are you telling us that you've found the happiness gene?"

"No," Kurton says, the cameras catching his pained frown. "We're not saying that at all."

It's like Jesus commanding his apostles not to let on about the Lazarus thing.

"What exactly *are* you saying?" Something about the science writer's delivery makes the whole room laugh.

Kurton takes his time. "We're saying that we've measured a very strong correlation. People with this grouping of key gene variants will be far more likely to enjoy elevated affective set points than those who do not. All other things being equal."

All other things are never equal. But before anyone can point out that impossible catch, the éminence grise from the *Times* asks if the study has pharmaceutical or clinical implications. A grinning Kurton replies, "It might!" A sardonic chuckle issues from the audience, as they realize that's his final answer.

Schiff raises her hand. Kurton doesn't seem to recognize her as he takes her question. "Your hyperthymic subject . . . the one with the optimal combination? How many others like her would you say there are, walking around out there?"

Kurton can't suppress a covert grin. "We need more data on the frequency of alleles in different populations and the way they assort with regard to one another. Akiskal estimates that about one in a hundred people in the general population meet the research criteria for hyperthymia. If you forced me to guess right now, I'd say about one in ten thousand of *those* already fortunate subjects are also immune to unstable negative moods and intemperate behavior."

She does the math. "So roughly one in a million?"

His grin fades, unsure where she's going. "You could put it that way."

She means to ask: Why is the "optimal" configuration so damn rare? What doesn't natural selection like about it? Why should perfect bliss be hundreds of times less common than cystic fibrosis? But she misses her chance, and the rest of the conference plays out in variations on: *How soon can you make the rest of us feel a little better?*

∞

Even those journalists who use a question mark in their headlines barely disguise their excitement. Science has found a chief genetic contribution to bliss. Genomics now knows what combinations of inherited material help lower negative affect and raise positive. *Happiness gene identified?* Did you think it would evade detection forever?

The Alzheimer's gene, the alcoholism gene, the homosexuality gene, the aggression gene, the novelty gene, the fear gene, the stress gene, the xenophobia gene, the criminal-impulse gene, and the fidelity gene have all come and gone. By the time the happiness gene rolls around, even journalists should have long ago learned to hedge their bets. But traits are hard to shake, and writers have been waiting for this particular secret to come to market since Sumer.

The wire services each run their own account, reaching a whole rainbow of conclusions about what, if anything, the new findings mean. The 1,100-word *Science Times* article makes only five to seven errors, depending on who's counting. *Newsweek* puts the story on their cover: *Better than sex, stronger than money, more lasting than prestige . . . The secret of happiness? Be **Born Happy**.* Page 28 of the same issue is an ad for a drug company with a substantial financial interest in Truecyte.

Two of the big-four late-night comedians incorporate the story into their monologues:

> So science has finally discovered that happiness is mostly inherited. But just remember, these are the guys who discovered that *sterility* may be inherited . . . It's interesting that, for some reason, the happiness genes aren't particularly widespread. Not as widespread as, say, the obesity gene. Now the obesity gene: talk about *wide spread* . . .

The Truecyte announcement runs through the meme pool like a wave through a football stadium. Websites everywhere poll user responses; the story gets four stars for newsworthiness, four stars for importance, and five stars for entertainment value. By rough count, two-thirds of the commenting public believe that nature contributes more to happiness than nurture, up from 50 percent a year ago. Two in five believe that science will soon be able to manipulate the genetic component of happiness to our advantage. Most people believe that if Truecyte has done original work to make a useful discovery, they should be able to profit exclusively from it. Eleven percent of the general public thought the happiness gene had already been found.

The discovery hits at the perfect time. The war has spilled over into a third neighboring country, and fatalities are at a forty-five-month high. A new study from the Union of Concerned Scientists shows that global greenhouse-gas emissions may have been greatly underestimated. Scattered outbreaks of a new fatal flu strain come in from central Asia. Recent tests show heavy-metal contaminants increasing dramatically throughout the food chain. Two decades of Ponzi schemes have unraveled the global financial markets and erased trillions of dollars of imaginary wealth. A terrorist cell in Southern California is rounded up, halfway to constructing a dirty bomb.

And scientists discover the genetic cause of joy.

∞

In the final cut of "The Genie and the Genome," finished just after the first article comes out in *The Journal of Behavioral Genomics*, Kurton refers to her simply as "Jen." He describes how the group predicted her genomic signature, based solely on her psychological tests. He shows a color-enhanced animation of her fMRI:

> Coordinated activity in these areas associates with sustained positive emotions. Look at her baseline: it's a symphony.

His excitement ratchets up when talking about the process:

> You feed the amplified DNA fragments into this high-throughput optical reader . . . We can do a temperament analysis for under $1,000.

"Do you take Visa?" the off-camera host asks. His smile says: *Choose your payment method.*

He's guarded about the interconnected patents his data rely on, but more voluble about the countless interconnected enzyme factories that contribute to the brain's reward circuitry. He concedes the many genes that emotional well-being involves. Genes that control the pathways and synthesis of crucial neurotransmitters. Genes that assemble the machinery of neurotransmitter release and reuptake. Genes that wire together the centers of perception, memory, and emotion . . .

But after another splice, he's addressing an auditorium full of electrified people. Sixty percent of the room wants to sic the government regulators on him and the other forty are ready to send him to Stockholm. He's in front of a huge projected slide, twenty feet wide. As he paces in front of the image, waving and conducting, a graph dances across his body.

The cloud of scatterplots is a thin cigar tipped along a rising diagonal. The vertical axis aggregates selected indicators of subjective well-being. The horizontal axis aligns the alleles for genes whose precise identities Thomas Kurton and company now make public for the first time.

He doesn't have to draw the implied rising line. The line is *there*, running through the densest section of the cigar-shaped cloud. Data points fall all over the plane, but not randomly. The points rise as the number of repeated segments in certain gene polymorphisms changes. He focuses on a point high up to the far right, and calls it *Jen*.

Jump back to the smart house in Maine. Kurton's eyes shine for the show's host, or maybe its million viewers, live and on the Web.

> Think about falling in love. How vibrant and wise you feel. Everything full of meaningful secrets. Amazing things, just about to happen . . . Well, Jen and others up at the high end are like natural athletes of emotion. They fall in love with the entire world. And the world can't help reciprocating. Genes *plus* environment, in a positive-feedback loop . . .

Schiff lobs all the familiar criticisms at him, but he stays Zen.

> Sure, well-being is a quantitative trait. Yes, these genes interact with dozens of others, and with scores of other regulatory factors. We are devoting a whole lot of microarrays and computer cycles to untangling those interactions . . . *Of course* environment plays a role in their expression. But all these genes affect the way we

engage the environment in the first place. There's even some evidence that an adverse environment can *strengthen* the expression . . .

Off camera, Tonia asks:

But the more of these alleles I have, the greater my joie de vivre?

His face admits to complexities.

We don't even say that. We've simply noted a correlation . . .

Shot-reverse to Schiff, who is enjoying this ride. She herself is far too sunny for her own good. It hasn't yet dawned on her that this story might actually be nonfiction. She doesn't get that until a few hours after they stop filming. For the moment, she asks:

And you can look directly at my genes and tell me my alleles?

Kurton beams and says:

Give me your coffee cup. We can take a swab off that.

They cut the sequence into the piece's climax. The assembled show airs two weeks later.

PART FOUR

THE NEXT FIRST PAGE

... retain, O man! in all seasons a temperature of thine own.

—Herman Melville, *Moby-Dick*

Russell and Candace watch the recorded show together, in her apartment, on her tiny flat-panel television, after Gabe goes to bed. Neither has the nerve to watch the segment alone. Nor do they have the nerve to see each other again, without pretext.

They kiss each other experimentally on Stone's arrival, to Gabe's disgust. "What is this, France or something?" But Russell appeases the boy by spending a little while in Futopia with him, before lights-out for children and showtime for adults.

Then Russell and Candace settle in, deployed eighteen inches apart on her living room sofa. They kiss again, riskier, as the recording starts. "Thanks," Candace says. "Helps. Much better than a tranquilizer."

Stone almost jumps out of his skin. He has taken half a milligram of Ativan, from a little plastic bottle full of them borrowed from his brother, just before arriving.

The woman smoothes her hair and stares at the screen. Under her breath she tells herself, "Maybe just as habit-forming, Candace."

"It'll be fine," he says. He can't figure out what he's talking about. He finds her mouth again. A moment later, he's not sure if he really said anything at all.

Both of them are helpless and pounding by the time "The Genie and the Genome" starts. Each tries to concentrate, but they're throbbing in unison, audible to each other. They try to follow Kurton's argument, the one about our vast increase in the ability to improve people. The man seems somehow different from the person they saw onstage, the one who lured Thassa to Boston. "He *is* charming," Candace concedes, her hand tracing circles on Russell's thigh. "There's no arguing that."

Stone should say something. "There isn't?"

The show sweeps them headlong, rushed by CGI, rapid crosscuts, and a ruthless synth soundtrack. Everything about the show makes science as sexy as sports. Neither of them watches enough TV to be inoculated. The message floods them: strengthen, sharpen, enhance your chromosomes, be smarter, healthier, and truer. Thrive and be what you want, feeding every need. Live forever, suffused in joy.

Kurton mentions Thassa by pseudonym, near the show's end. He talks of her like some design template for the future. "We cured smallpox," he says. "We eradicated polio. We can hunt down and wipe out misery. There's no reason why every one of us can't be equals to our ideal." In the last lines of the profile, the scientist says, "I don't believe in God, but I do believe that it's humanity's job to bring God about."

By then, the two viewers are long gone, the television muted, Candace up and astride Russell, bobbing herself to a pulse they find together, Russell her fuse beneath her. They end up shattered, crumpled into each other, a double collapse, both so grateful to be back *here*, after so long away.

Then they're in her bed. The second time is slow. They turn each other all ways, tasting, playing, giving over—all either of them ever wanted. Whatever the first reason, there's no other point now than to fit together. It takes all his will not to tell her he loves her, over and over. And he would, if words weren't as hindering as fur on fish. But this is what he thinks, curled up safely into her amazing back, plummeting into sleep: *Thank you. Thank you for raising me from the dead.*

∞

They wake in light, to a disoriented Gabe calling, "Mom? Don't we need to get up? Mom? Why is the TV on?"

Candace springs up and startles when she sees Russell. She covers her mouth with her hand, half in this morning's start and half still in the ocean of last night. She kisses him, chastely now, her breath loamy and close, stale with slept-on bliss. Her neck and pits, too, smell fusty but familiar. Fitting. She grins and shies a finger to her lips. She shouts to the door, "Morning, sweetie. I'll be right out!" She pantomimes to Russell, *Wait here*, then laughs again at the idiot gesture. She tumbles into long johns and a sweatshirt and disappears.

So—a French farce: yet another story you know by heart. Only in this one, the other man is four feet tall.

Russell stretches out diagonally in her sheets, territory he has already marked. The sheets still hold her gamey scent. He has read how people choose their mates on smell and some sixth sense, a pheromone whiff off histocompatibility complexes other than their own, but recognized. He was doomed to end up here, in her bed, from the moment they sniffed each other.

For months he's watched the film in his head, sure that this inevitable collision would end in fumbling disaster. Sure he'd come away from a night with Candace condemned forever to the life of an impotent poet, without even the consolation of writing poems. Now all the focused force of dread vanishes in a rush of surprise fitness, leaving him vast amounts of surplus energy with which . . . to enjoy the woman again, at the earliest possible opportunity. All the best writing is rewriting.

He feels good. Contemptuously good. Every inscrutable thing that Thassa has ever said about how easy this state is to achieve now feels stunningly obvious. And yet this burst of happiness will be deducted from any remaining share owed to him in the afterlife.

Beyond the door, a mother makes right again the world of her child that has come apart a little in the night. Russell breathes in; only the memory of last night's television persists in rasping him. And even that burr is obscured by the side effects of the Ativan and the image of a woman lifting and lowering herself gratefully on him.

She lets herself back into the room, flushed. She leans against the door, a makeshift barricade. "I'm so sorry about this! I'll just get dressed and take him to school. Then I have to head in . . ."

"Sounds good. I'll just lie here like a satiated drone."

She grins, comes to the bed, and climbs all-fours on top of him. "You are wonderful. Simply wonderful."

She means someone else. Or some other word. But maybe he is, this morning. For this moment, anyway, full of something much like wonder.

He watches her stand in her closet and do a demure reverse striptease until she is Candace Weld again, pleated, rose-colored college psychologist. The moment she's dressed, they lose each other again. He pulls the covers over his thin chest. She looks everywhere but at him. "Stay as long as you like," she says. "You know where the coffee is. I'll check in with Thassa from work. See what she thought about the show."

"Good plan."

She crosses to him and kisses him on the forehead. He kisses her on the chin. In afterthought, she sits on the edge of the bed and rests her hand on his sternum. "I hope . . ."

"Yes," he says. "Me, too."

She goes to the door, touches her lips, sends his germs back to him on the carrier air. The door opens and she stumbles out into the hall, into a bolting ten-year-old.

∞

When Candace called, Thassa had already recovered from the show. She laughed at the scientific pseudonym that Dr. Kurton gave her. "He must have stolen it. From a film I showed him."

The Algerian seemed as resilient as her alleles made her. "It's not so bad as I feared. Kind of science fiction, right? Nothing to do with me, anyway. Now it's Jen's problem! Although, did you see that anime of my brain? My own brain, working. Very strange, that."

That night, at their usual time, Candace checked in with Russell. "How did she sound?" he asked.

The psychologist sighed. "Happy. As usual."

"I know the feeling. Except for the 'usual.' "

And the two of them went on to speak of more pressing things.

∞

The scientific community's reaction starts noisy and amps up fast. A madly democratic chorus weighs in on radio, television, and the Internet, and in newspapers and university lecture halls.

The press leaps on the usual expert witnesses. In the States, they swarm around Jonathan Dornan. Three internationally bestselling books explaining evolutionary genetics to the intelligent layperson make him the automatic go-to for anything spelled with the letters G, A, C, and T. Dr. Dornan gives a guardedly appreciative quote to the AP: "Ten thousand genes get expressed in the human brain. We understand fewer than one percent of them. This research begins to give us a handle on what happens in forming baseline temperament."

Others doubt the paper's details can be redeemed, let alone refined. In laboratories from Tübingen to Beijing, skeptical researchers object to the idea that anything so complex could derive from so small a number of genes.

Nobel laureate Anthony Blaze writes a much-reproduced *Guardian* op-ed:

> We must once and for all outgrow our obsolete ideas about heredity. Genes don't code for traits. They synthesize proteins. And single proteins can do incredibly different things, depending on where and when they're produced . . . We have no gambling gene, no intelligence gene, no gene for language or walking upright or even a single gene for curly hair, for that matter. We certainly possess no set of genes whose function is to make us happy.

This piece just feeds Truecyte's original firestorm. Geneticists on four continents caution about overstating the case for nurture. There's nothing magical about behavior or temperament. When the crucial genes are missing, no amount of outside stimuli can compensate. Maybe FOXP2 isn't a gene "for language," two German researchers point out in an *Economist* reply, but the lack of a good copy of it prevents the development of speech.

Other speakers come to Blaze's defense in dozens of international forums rushed together in the wake of the story. The Kurton-doubters concede that a single gene defect can knock out a complex behavior. But that doesn't mean complex behaviors derive from a single gene. One bad allele can cause depression. But a few good ones don't necessarily cause bliss.

Researchers whose greatest social stress consists of writing grant proposals slink out of their labs and into broadcast studios. They summarize the complex article using short, digestible sentences of simple words. On cue, across the big three monotheistic target markets, creationists flood the call-in lines, leading the discussions into threads more tangled than any enzyme pathway.

A hard-core genetic determinist from the University of Leiden, interviewed on BBC Four, points to the haunting twin studies: the more genes any two people share in common, the more likely they are to share dispositions, no matter how or where they're raised. A nurturist colleague from Hamburg refutes that "hardwire hype," suggesting that any individual's emotional highs and lows probably differ as much as any two people's baselines.

In the scattered sniping, both sides commit crimes of passion. A symposium at the University of Florida generates a complex exchange of ideas that culminates in face-slapping. An outspoken engineer from MIT who champions Kurton's paper as an important early step in the future structural improvement of humans receives death threats.

The most damning critique comes from the epigenetics community. A revolution is afoot, one that looks almost like retooled Lamarckism, calling into question the centrality of the gene and all the old dogma of fixed inheritance. The genome seethes with extragenetic inherited mechanisms, environmentally altered chemical switches. The gene-centric view looks increasingly like the domain of fifty-seven-year-olds still in the grip of obsolete paradigms. Nurture can directly affect germ cells. Old-style gene-association studies like Kurton's may be not even irrelevant. Temperament may be in the water, food, and air, as much as in the chromosomes . . .

For a few strange days, neither right-wing nor left-wing talk radio knows whether they should be for this discovery or against it. Both wings flap over the notorious footnote, Jen. Is she real, or just some kind of research artifact? Is she the poster child for the coming, new human? Or is she just some chick who's more chipper than she should be?

The consensus, if any, is vague. Most talking heads agree that the sculpting of affect is lifelong and fluid. But most also concede that people's bedrock emotional skills vary as greatly as their skills in math. For proof, witness the chaos of this public argument.

But in all the din, no one comes forward with any substantive criticism of the original paper's methodology. The statistics withstand scrutiny. Other studies will take years to confirm or contradict the outcome. The story could vanish in shame. It could be put to rest once and for all in a new definitive study. And still the genes of happiness will knock about in the collective marketplace for generations.

∞

Candace Weld did, at least, have the foresight to run one definitive experiment that spring. At the beginning of April, she entered into Google the quoted phrase "happiness gene." The search engine returned 727 hits, one-fifth of them false positives. She tried again near the beginning of May, when even the TiVo-and-leave-o people had gotten their first hive-mind vibe of Thomas Kurton. By then the hits had reached 162,315. Come June, she didn't have the nerve to try again. Nor did she have the need.

∞

In short, Truecyte's announcement produces the usual scientific free-for-all. No one is shocked but the general public. Science has never hidden the fact that truth is red in tooth and claw. Blood has flowed over the question of inherited temperament since Paleolithic humans started breeding dogs.

Usually the shouting takes place behind closed doors, out of earshot of the press. Few families bicker in public. The gap between any two scientists pales next to that between science and the science-hating public. But once betrayal is involved, all bets are off.

The betrayal in question splits along generational lines. In one corner, the old-style university geneticist, hands full of reagent, head full of a slowly accreting body of knowledge. In the other, the molecular engineer, hands on the computer simulations and head full of informatics, working for a start-up drug company that reduces even the research professor to a licensed client. Patience versus patents, say the old-style professors. Law versus awe, say the upstarts.

Like the worst of family fights, this one gets uglier as the stakes rise. But in the weeks following publication, Kurton sails above the fray. If he and Truecyte have indeed discovered deep foundations of human emotion, then they've just made themselves indispensable. And if they've moved a little too quickly or hopefully, the damage will be smaller than the potential gain. They're a private company after all, accountable to no one but their investors. Write off the loss, manage the resulting publicity, and stake a new claim.

The mastodon has evolved. It's a whole new elephant.

∞

Thassa's genome slips into the wild, joining the list of laboratory escapees from killer bees to SARS. A fifth of the popular articles about *The Journal of Behavioral Genomics* cite the footnote woman from the obscure ethnic population who has won the happiness triple crown. One million people hear Kurton marvel about "Jen." Ten million hear about her from that one million. And so the imaginary woman comes to life, growing from anonymous childhood to cult adolescence in about five days.

Of course, the bloggers get to her first. There's a funny piece on *Queen Elizabeast* (high authority ratings from all user indexes) called "No Cry, No Woman," suggesting that

> anybody who is that far above the human baseline—anyone whose brain scan looks like a symphony—probably should already be considered her own honorary species. If Jen truly is without sadness, then she's missing out on something profound, mysterious, and essentially human. That's my feeling, and I'll go on saying as much, at least until I get the Paxil tuned . . .

The piece gets a few dozen trackbacks and spawns four times as many uncredited imitations across sites large and small. The online magazine *Betatest* runs a longer, philosophical rumination, "Jen Mind, Beginner's Mind." It's a careful piece, distinguishing between destiny and predisposition. It paints a rich picture of positive psychology's current understanding of emotional set points. It surveys the huge body of research about environmental contributions to happiness and argues that from any point of view, we ought to be much more interested in the part of our mood that's under our control than in the part that's not. It concludes:

> Any contentment that Truecyte's mutant of happiness feels, the rest of us can also experience, much more meaningfully, because more intermittently, through daily effort.

The article gets e-mailed tens of thousands of times around the Net, and with every copy of the article comes a full-length color portrait of a woman in a pose suggesting euphoria. Her features have been Photoshopped out and replaced by the ubiquitous sunny smiley face.

Countless Internet top feeders follow the happiness-gene kerfuffle in detail. They browse to the *Behavioral Genomics* site and give up in frustration halfway through the abstract. They surf to the Truecyte home page and take the Flash guided tour. They add a few new key terms to their newsreaders, plunge into numerous user groups, or lurk invisibly around the corners of the crazier brawls. They post questions on various Answers Forums, asking whether Jen is for real or some kind of medical composite.

A Facebook user named OtherAngie confesses to being Jen. Her pokes explode, and within three days, her friend count skyrockets from 500 to 8,000+. Half the people leaving comments on her page dare her to prove the claim. She's holding her own, spinning out elaborate accounts of her irrepressible psychohistory and her recent discovery by science, when three other Facebook users announce that she's full of shit, because each of them happens to be Jen. Then a dozen people on MySpace jump the claim, and the game wipes out as fast as it started.

The tag phrase "u r so jen" disseminates through the mobile texting community. By the end of the month, the word graduates from adjective all the way to verb. I jen you not.

∞

Sometime near the invention of writing, a single mutation began making its way through the human gene pool. The variant may have arisen once, somewhere in the Middle East. Or it may have appeared independently in the Arabian Peninsula and somewhere in Sweden. Whatever else the gene variation does, it prevents the lactase enzyme from being shut off after weaning. Those with the variation enjoy a prolonged digestive infancy and can drink milk their whole life long.

When tribes began to keep domesticated cattle, the variant humans had a novel advantage: a food source the others couldn't digest. Some three hundred generations later, most adults of Northern European ancestry can consume milk with impunity, with the skill still spreading around the globe like a pandemic.

I want to know how long three hundred generations is, on an evolutionary scale. I want to know how fast lactose tolerance will move through the rest of the dairy-fed globe. I need to know how fast a tolerance for the lactose of human kindness might spread—how long it might take for the generosity haplotype to run through the race and fit us out with a new, stunning skill.

∞

Thassa gets wind of her anonymous renown. You'd have to be an off-the-grid Tuareg not to come across the happiness gene somewhere in some medium. And people who react to stories about the happiness gene also react to stories about the woman who has it in spades.

She follows the mounting Jen speculation on blogs across the Web. She even leaves comments here and there, saying that no such creature exists. In fact, Jen is more imaginary to her than Gabe Weld's little digital angel. If people want mystery and imagination and inexplicable temperament, they should just read Assia Djebar. The whole "genetically perfect happy woman" story will disappear as fast as last month's runaway curiosity—a young man from Maryland who can tell with 98 percent accuracy when any other human being is lying. And Jen will leave no more lasting a trace.

The doings of Thassa's alter ego are the least of her worries. The spring semester is nearing its climax, and she's struggling. The demands of the film curriculum and her own appetite leave her overstretched. She's taking Advanced Production; Culture, Race, and Media; History of Documentary; Location Sound Recording; and Ecology, the last of her general-education requirements. She's singing in the Balkan choir and trying to form a Maghrebi one. She's showing Kabyle films to the weekly CineClub, where she's already given elaborate presentations on Bouguermouh's *La Colline oubliée*, Meddour's *La Montagne de Baya*, and Hadjadj's *Machaho*. She's fallen in with bad mah-jongg influences. And she's started what can only be called a liaison.

It begins when Kiyoshi Sims, seated next to her in the media lab, shows her a transitions trick in the digital-video editing software. She, in turn, shows him how to sit for fifteen minutes in the school cafeteria without having a panic attack. Almost by chance, they develop a routine. He helps edit her semester studio project, a short composited sequence called *Come Spring*. And she slowly desensitizes him to going out deeper into public.

By late April, they've graduated to the point where he can sit with her in that famous blues club on South State on a Friday afternoon, long enough to eat something. They share fried catfish and okra with honey-mustard sauce and beers that neither of them touch, listening to the Delta twelve-bar keening over the sound system. Kiyoshi has grown so bold as to drum along on the tabletop. Now and then he even rips a little air-guitar lick, although his riffs are so discreet it's more like air ukulele. He stops when anyone nearby makes a sudden move.

They sit in the shallows of contentment, just about to wrap things up and return to their respective Friday-night film editing, when Sue Weston discovers them. Neither of them has seen Artgrrl for weeks. They share a minireunion, after which a terrified Kiyoshi slips away and barricades himself in the men's room.

Sue shoots Thassa an I'm-onto-you grin. Thassa braces, preparing an explanation of the Sims-Amzwar special relationship. Surely the art-school ecosystem is broad enough to permit such a symbiosis.

But Artgrrl blindsides her. "It's you, isn't it? The woman with the happiness genes. You're all over the Net. Jen is Miss Generosity."

Thassa flips a fork across the table, decidedly ungenerous. "Jen is a scientific hallucination."

Artgrrl steps back, her face crinkling. "Of course it's you!" She swallowed a little stimulant twenty minutes earlier, a prelude to Friday night, and it's juked her up a notch. "I can't believe nobody's made the connection. I mean, those other stories about you, last winter? The whole hyper thing . . . ?"

The Kabyle lowers her head and places her ear on the tabletop. "There is nothing special in my blood."

Weston sits down in Kiyoshi's abandoned chair and places a hand on her shoulder. "Maybe not. But what difference does that make? This whole Jen thing is on the verge of being, like, the *It* deal of the season, and it's not going to last much longer. You should go for this. Think of the eyeballs. You could post your films and get thousands . . . C'mon, girl. Fame is the new sex!"

Thassa lifts her head, a dry little glint. "Hey! What about the old sex, first?"

"Are you *for real*?"

"I can't help. I come from a repressive culture."

"Oh, my God." The American covers her gaping mouth. "They didn't . . . like, cut you or anything, over there?"

"Oh, not *that* repressive culture! I mean Quebec."

Sue's grin tries to steer into the skid.

Thassa touches two fingers to her elbow. "You shouldn't believe everything you think!"

The suckered American fingers her lips. "You lying little minx!" She steps back from the Algerian, approving. "You're messing with me." But before Sue can right herself, Kiyoshi returns, hoping to retrieve his computer bag and make a clean getaway before the human-contact thing gets out of hand. Sue reappraises the shrinking boy and giggles with new admiration.

Thassa follows Kiyoshi in escape. But before she can flee, Sue squeezes her goodbye, gauging her again with that gleam. *You can't hide from me*, the look says. *Have fun with Invisiboy, if you don't kill him first.*

∞

Later that night, Sue Weston logs in to her blog and posts her new entry: "Bird of Happiness, Tagged." She spells out the argument with a clarity that would make her onetime writing instructor proud. She links to last November's *StreetSharp* transcript, the *Reader* article, and all the noise of a few months before. Just the facts. Nonfiction, without the creative. Her own kind of science, with first prize for priority.

It's not like she's making facts public; the facts were never private to begin with. She's twenty-one, young enough to know that there is no more public or private. There are only slow facts and fast facts, linked and unlinked, and every two sequences of value will eventually be correlated. Someone will publish the connection in another few days anyway, if she doesn't. And why should someone else's blog get all the eyeballs?

∞

Schiff arrives in El Kef with her guts emptied and her brain in a similar state. She stands at the window of her hotel room in the Ville Nouvelle, above the Place de l'Indépendance, too light-headed to make out much more than the massive Byzantine fortress looming up out of a tumble of stone and whitewashed plaster. The streets of the medina twist down from the Casbah's foot. More town spills down the other slope, a jumble of white-and-tan blocks watched over by minarets and domes. The tip of a cellular radio tower peeks out above the fortress, puncturing Tonia's Orientalist fantasy. Coming here was mad. She's like a time traveler from the golden age of pulp science fiction, trying to change a future that has already happened.

Schiff stands motionless, looking, until a heavyset man with a paintbrush mustache comes out on a balcony across the Place and returns her inspection. She turns back into her stale room. The detailed discovery of the town will wait a day, until she can do it right.

As Thassa once told her, tomorrow will be there, as soon as you need it.

Schiff sheds her crumpled road clothes and takes a lukewarm shower in the tiny, open stall. Her head still spins from the *louage*, and she never wants to eat again. She wraps herself in a towel and stretches out on the bed. She finds her ratty pocket spiral notebook and writes: *We talk tomorrow*. For a moment, the whole expedition seems almost plausible. *If I can record ten minutes, I'll be happy*.

All the while, she pretends she isn't jonesing to discover whether the world as she knows it has continued to exist during her day away. At three minutes to the hour, she casually flips on the television (a broken remote left ceremoniously on the bedside table by the hotel staff) and trawls the channels like the worst of quidnuncs.

This two-star hotel in an outpost of forty thousand people in a remote western province of a little country wedged between the chaos of Algeria and the void of Libya pulls in more cosmopolitan broadcasts than she gets in New York. She pounces on the BBC like a starving person. The world is much as she left it. The day has gone like any other, held hostage by the past and doomed by coming appointments. In that closet hotel, each news story announces either imminent extinction or embryonic breakthrough. Hotel residents everywhere—any passenger in transit this night—must be forgiven for thinking that life will be solved at last, one way or the other, by the time they get home.

She flicks off the set and, in the highland silence of that molding room, opens her carry-on. She pulls out a plastic case packed with disks like makeup mirrors, each one storing hours of video. She's packed only three days of clothes, but more digital clips than she could watch in three weeks. The secret of happiness is meaningful work.

She flips through her archive, the clips she'll splice together to make her own real firstborn. In the middle of the stiff bed, surrounded by time capsules, she loads a short feature on the most notorious infant in living memory. The girl with that perfectly archaic middle name: Joy.

Whiplashing to think that the footage is three decades old. But the basic trope goes back millennia: a dangerous, destabilizing baby smuggled clandestinely into an unsuspecting world. The doctors don't even tell the prospective parents that their little girl will be the first of her kind. Tonia sits on the bed, watching the videotaped birth, a message posted forward to whatever people might inhabit the evolved future. The infant head crowns on Schiff's screen, and there is Louise Joy Brown, an impossibly slight five and three-quarters pounds, crying her lungs out in that first crisis, air.

The birth cries are nothing, compared to the ones they touch off. Perfectly moderate commentators face the camera and declare the doom of the human race. Almost ridiculous now, this dated hysteria. But almost right.

Schiff sits up in the bed and glances back out the window. A corsage of yellow lights now trace Kef's edges all the way up the jagged mountain. This town's basic cure for sterility may often still involve a prayer at the local *zaouia*. But then, so does New York's.

Tonia turns back to the warnings posted forward from a previous planet. Later technologies make that first artificial conception look like a Hail Mary play. Intrafallopian transfer, intracytoplasmic sperm injection: a dozen of her friends have shopped from that list. A few hundred thousand IVF babies make their way through this night, as dark swings around the globe. The process is nothing now, and the real show is only getting started. A new industry, following only voluntary guidelines, already screens embryos for hundreds of genetic diseases. And Tonia Schiff will bet her return ticket that some billionaire, somewhere, is already paying to have his offspring screened for good traits. The race will take to selling characteristics on websites, like downloadable songs, the day it becomes possible.

She ejects the disk and flips through the stack, looking for the second half of tonight's double feature. She has documentaries and biographies, old news clips on engineered bacteria, gene transfer, the world-famous photogenic sheep, xenotransplantation, embryos from skin DNA transplanted into eggs, embryos with two mothers and a father, and, from last week, the application for exclusive ownership of a wholly synthetic organism.

Apocalypse has become too commonplace to feel. Of the scribbling in books, there is no end. And all our writing will in time come alive.

She takes notes until she falls asleep. And falling asleep, she'll tell herself that she asks for almost nothing: one more documentary, one more interview, one more clandestine infant named Joy. But the rim of cliffs guarding this ancient town mock any theme she might care to film.

∞

Because Donna Washburn, the author of the *Reader* feature, googles her own name only once every two days, a full twenty-one hours pass before she sees herself mentioned in Sue Weston's blog. Immediately Washburn leaves a message on Thassa's voice mail, asking for confirmation. But Thassa doesn't reply by the time the next week's *Reader* is put to bed. So the paper runs an "unconfirmed rumor" squib. By the time the bit runs, it's redundant. Jen's secret identity has started to proliferate through the Web. Within a week, she's pretty much a publicly traded commodity.

Three weeks before final exams, and Thassadit Amzwar is working flat out on *Come Spring*, trying to get a rough cut done before semester's end. She hardly even notices the ripples. In this country, where continent-wide cultural transformations root, take over the biosphere, and go extinct several times in every twenty-four-hour news cycle, all she has to do is hunker down, finish the term, and wait until the public attention drifts back to celebrity divorces and custody fights, where it belongs.

The first assault is a simple repeat of last fall. She tries her best to answer the surge of e-mails. A few dozen fanboys and postpartum mothers write to ask, *Is Jen really you? How old were you when you first realized that your genes were making you joyous? Does it still work late at night in winter? Could we meet for coffee, for a chat, for just forty-five minutes? I could be there on Thursday. Minneapolis isn't all that far from Chicago . . .*

She's gentle with these people; it's not their fault they've been misled. After a few days, she reverts to a form letter. It breaks her heart, but she has no choice. She tries to add a personalized sentence at the end of every reply. When she begins to get replies to her replies, she grits her teeth and ignores them.

Then the phone starts ringing. It's *Self* magazine. Then *People*. Then *Psychology Today*. She gives a couple of phone interviews without even realizing she's doing so. She gives another one, just by trying to explain that she doesn't want to talk about what's not worth talking about. A journalist from the *Trib* begs her to come down to Rhapsody and just have a sandwich. She can hear in his voice that he's a fine man with a wife and children who only wants to do his job as best as he can; having a sandwich while explaining the massive misunderstanding can't do any more harm. When Thassa gets to Rhapsody, there's a photographer lying in wait alongside the journalist. And this photographer woman—a graduate of Mesquakie—is also just doing her job and living her art.

The interviewers keep asking her to describe exactly how it feels to be exuberant. She asks them, "You have never been?" Yes, they say, but . . . *all the time*? No, she says. Cheerful often. Exuberant sometimes, perhaps frequently, depending on the tally. Everyone alive should feel richly content, ridiculously ahead of the game, a million times luckier than the unborn. What more can she tell them?

They want to know whether she inherited her bliss, whether it comes from the environment, or whether she's simply willed herself to be happy. She tells them honestly: she hasn't a clue. They ask if other people in her family are as happy as she is. She says she'd never presume to say how happy anyone else might be.

After four days of the circus, she stops answering her phone. But it tears her up to hear the messages left on her voice mail. She can't listen to them and *not* call them back. At the same time, she'd dearly like to finish the semester without flunking out. The only answer is to cancel her phone service and start a new one.

This doesn't prevent total strangers who see the *Tribune* photo from stopping her in the street and greeting her warmly. But then, she used to stop total strangers in the street and greet them the same way. So it's a wash, and she meets some nice people as a result. Many people she meets tell her how exhilarating it is, just to talk to her. That feels like considerable evidence, to her unscientific mind, that the disease is more contagious than genetic. But no venture capitalists step forward to fund a double-blind controlled study.

∞

Where are Candace and Russell during all of this? They're slipping off to lunch like international pleasure smugglers. She's teaching him to cook. He's sketching her portrait. They're eating junk food on Navy Pier. They're listening to Scandinavian reggae at the Aragon. They watch a Chinese gangster film in a hole-in-the-wall Chinatown theater, without benefit of English subtitles. They take Gabe to the Living Toys of the Future exhibit at the Science and Industry.

On nights when Gabe is at his father's, they lie on Stone's narrow futon on the oak floor, reading out loud to each other. They do scenes from Shakespeare—Rosalind and Orlando in the Forest of Arden. Jessica and Lorenzo under the floor of heaven. On such a night as this, they might be anywhere.

They carry Thassa around between them, always, blessed by the girl who has brought them together. They see her in every passing curiosity, all the sharp, bright details that now fill their days, feeling a gratitude as obligatory as taxes and death. "We should call her tomorrow," Candace tells Russell, more than once, as they fall asleep holding each other.

∞

They draft an imaginary book together. The force with which Candace urges the idea on Russell overwhelms him. It doesn't feel like therapy at all. It feels like remodeling the house. It feels like gardening. It feels like having old friends over for dinner, only without having to clean up.

"Come on," she cajoles, nudging him with her hip and settling down next to him on his futon. She brandishes his canary-yellow legal pad. "Come on, Mr. Wordsmith. Our one good chance to have things our way. So what do you want to call this thing?"

He can't stop marveling at her. She's turned into a goofy twenty-year-old. A grin as infectious as any virus. "Don't we have to make a few choices first?"

"Like what?"

"Oh, I don't know. Like whether we're writing a novel, memoir, history, how-to, self-help, or cookbook?"

"Of course! You mean, like, facts or make-believe. Still a difference nowadays?"

For a while, anyway. Soon it will be all one thing or all the other, although Stone isn't willing yet to predict which.

Time to choose. "Make-believe," he declares.

"Great. That's the one where they can't sue you, right? So where do we start? We need a cast list. Dozens of three-dimensional, unforgettable characters who bleed when you cut them. People so real you can smell their toenails."

Unit two on his obsolete syllabus: mannerisms, traits, and core inner values.

"Do we really need characters?" he bleats. "I hate characters. It's such a cliché, *characters*."

"Okay, fine. No characters. That's new. That's fresh. I *like* it. So what's this thing about?"

∞

On the second Sunday after Easter, Mike Burns, one of the inner circle of younger, magnetic ministers at the two-hundred-acre campus of an interdenominational megachurch in South Barrington, preaches a sermon at the third of four mammoth weekend services on the theme: *Do we still enjoy God's most-favored-nation status?* The analysis is blunt—blunter than any recent balance sheet from Washington. Pastor Mike lists the symptoms of a national fall from grace. Drugs, promiscuity, and the occasional massacre plague the nation's schools. Whole communities are drowning in the Internet's cesspools. The Chinese economy is set to eat our lunch, along with most of our between-meal snacks. The banking industry has vanished into imagination and unemployment is booming. Violent crime and homosexuality are everywhere, and by any objective measure—standard of living, health care, and general quality of life—the whole country is scraping chassis.

At the climax of his daunting catalog, with a storyteller's timing, Pastor Mike shifts to a checklist of bounties remaining to those who have kept faith. Americans are still God's elect, the vicious envy of the rest of the world. Just as the lost could not abide Christ's serene power and had to put Him to death, so, too, do other clans, terrified by the freedom of America, long to harm it.

But who cares what the enemy wants? the preacher chants. *God wants your joyful noise. The best thing you can do for Him here on Earth is to parade His elation.* And in the closing minutes of his sermon—a commanding moment cut into the highlights reel for inclusion in the church's weekly videocast—Pastor Mike gives his flock a true-to-life parable:

"Now let me tell you about a young lady you may have heard about in the news, a girl from a persecuted minority family who somehow escaped from the fanatical, Islamo-sectarian hell of Arab Africa, a pilgrim soul who managed to make her way safely to college in one of the luckiest cities in the luckiest country on earth . . . Science gives this survivor's joy a medical name and tries to pretend that her perpetual bliss is nothing more than a random, chemical accident. My math—*my* science—works differently. Do you think it's just an accident that this woman, who has been through horrors that make our own safer souls shudder to imagine, that this recipient of God's unstoppable love just *happens to be* Christian? Do ya . . . ? Huh? Just *chance?*"

The laughter of the congregation plays loud and long, on desktop and handheld devices everywhere.

∞

Candace and Russell lie flank to cold flank, facing heaven, effigies on the lid of some Renaissance marble tomb.

"National novel-writing month coming up," she whispers. "Fifty thousand words in thirty days. Last year they had 95,000 entrants and 19,000 finishers. What do you think?"

"Excuse me for a moment," he tells her. "I have to go take my own life."

∞

Shortly after the megachurch posts Pastor Mike's sermon to their site, a member of its sprawling congregation shares the results of her research in the church's online forum: the street address of the pilgrim soul herself, should anyone wish to share with her their appreciation of God's blessing.

Response is swift and enthusiastic. Even faith enjoys economies of scale.

∞

Stone is sanguine enough these days to pick up the phone, even when he doesn't recognize a new number on his caller ID.

"Mister Stone! You have to help. They're after me!"

Her. The ground goes soft around him. "Who?"

"Very Christian people with too much free time. They're mailing me gifts. Bringing me things. They want to meet with me for prayer!"

She tells him about the sermon and its aftermath. Even now, she's more amused than panicked.

"You are the native," she says. "Tell me what am I to do with this."

He starts filing furious lawsuits, taking out restraining orders, threatening to prosecute everyone who mentions her name in public.

"Are you all right?" he asks, mimicking Candace's competence. "Is anyone harassing—"

"I'm perfectly fine. It's just embarrassing. They're sending me stickers and pins, pretty guitar-music discs, and crazy little Jesus trophies. One lady brought a whole nest of leftover chocolate Easter eggs in a little green-and-pink basket for my dorm room. I told her that chocolate eggs are a fertility ritual. At least that one didn't stay too long!"

"Wait." He feels as if a nearby gunshot has just dragged him up from the dead of sleep. "They're coming by your *place?*"

"Tell me how I'm supposed to stop them. Help me! I'm running out of tea and cakes. And you know, I have finals coming up. I need one hundred more hours to finish, and I have only sixty left."

"They're . . . What do they want from you?"

"Simple. They haunt me for being born a Christian. They want me to be their team . . . what do you call the funny little things . . . ?"

"Mascot."

"Exactly. I'm some kind of Jesus mascot. Or I'm going to cure their lives. Mister, it's pitiful. Some of them think I'm a messenger angel, sent down to earth with a secret message about the future. Tell them, Russell. I'm no fucking angel!"

The word stops him dead on the line. She doesn't swear. She must not know what she's saying. The French or Arab equivalents are just costume jewelry, and Tamazight can't even have a word that taboo. But, come to think of it, neither does English anymore: the word is fucking everywhere.

She breaks his silence. "Hey. You're not a Christian, are you? I'm sorry. I didn't mean to hurt."

He has dreamed of mailing her things himself—old folk mix tapes, guides for surviving America, essays that her essays reminded him of, dizzy little books of Hopkins and Blake. "No. I was born . . . My parents brought me up . . . It doesn't matter. I'm not really anything, really."

"Good. I'm nothing, either. I'm a Maghreb Algerian Kabyle Catholic Atheist French Canadian on a student visa. I can't help these people."

"We should ask Candace."

"I don't know, Russell. I love Candace. That's not the point. But Candace always tells me to do just what I think is right. She's a big one for self-discovery, that Candace. I'll simply pretend I already asked."

He could suggest other solutions. But he doesn't. He's weakened by his recent bout with joy. Joy does little to increase one's judgment. Happiness is not the condition you want to be in when you need to be at your most competent.

He asks if she has someplace in the city to hide out until finals. She can think of no place, and he doesn't offer any. He tells her to protect herself, to be gentle but firm about her time. The main thing is to get over the semester finish line and get back home.

"Home," she agrees. "That would be a beautiful place to get back to. One small problem, Mister. No trips home anytime soon. I'm enrolled in Summer One courses!"

They share an awkward pause. He thinks about offering her his place. But that's crazy. They both hold still. For a moment, it's so quiet I'm afraid they'll hear me listening in. Then she asks him how his book is going, and we're all safe again.

"Great." He laughs. "I have a coauthor. Friend of yours."

"Candace? Are you serious?" He can't read her, her nonnative register. But he can hear her doing the math. "You and Candace are together?"

As together as anything, he supposes. "Yes. Yes, we are." His answer surprises him more than her question.

"That's wonderful, Russell. I'm happy for you. I'm happy for Candace. You are great with Jibreel. And I'm happy for this book you're working on together. Now could you please tell me what it's about?"

He smiles at her petulance. Sunniest petulance ever. "It's an adventure story. It's about someone breaking out of prison."

"Really? You should talk to me. I have a cousin who broke out of prison. I can tell you stories."

Imagination dies of shame in the face of its blood relation.

"I miss you, Mister Stone. Miss how you are. We should go somewhere together, sometime. See some sights."

He has to remind himself. It doesn't mean anything. She would take even the Christians out sightseeing, if there weren't so many of them.

A buzzer rasps on her end. "Oh my God. More visitors. Wait a moment." She's off to the intercom and a short chat. She comes back laughing. "It's two sweet old women. I can see three more spinning around, down in the street. They want me to autograph some magazine clippings and talk about blessings."

"Tell them you're studying for exams."

"I give them ten minutes. Then I ask if they would like to sacrifice some goats together, out on the balcony. That sometimes speeds them up." She makes a kissing sound into the phone. "Thank you for everything, Russell. Love you. Bye!"

∞

This mutant Second City is home to a talk show. Lots of world cities and even some non-world ones have talk shows to call their own. The genre dates back to the book of Job, and it has spawned more variants than wolves have spawned dogs. But the world has seen no talk show like the one that has evolved in this particular Chicago.

It's less a show than a sovereign multinational charter. And its host is, by any measure, the most influential woman in the world. Her own story is a remarkable mix of motifs from American creative fiction, from Alger to Zelazny. Say only that she has grown from an impoverished, abused child into an adult who gives away more money than most industrialized nations. She has the power to create instant celebrities, sell hundreds of millions of books, make or break entire consumer industries, expose frauds, marshal mammoth relief efforts, and change the spoken language. All this by being tough, warm, vulnerable, and empathetic enough to get almost any other human being to disclose the most personal secrets on international television. If she didn't exist, allegory would have to invent her. Her name is O'Donough and she is the richest Irish American woman in history, but she, her show, her publishing house, and her chain of personal-overhaul boutiques are known the world over simply as *Oona*.

The guiding principle of her program—the one that has made Oona the most-watched human of the last two decades—is the belief that fortune lies not in our stars but in our changing selves. She has told several thousand guests that blaming any destiny—whether biological or environmental—just isn't going to cut it. Even in her own much-publicized battles with moods, mother, and metabolism, Oona has always insisted that anyone can escape any fate by a daily application of near-religious will. Every person has at least enough will on tap to overcome any statistically reasonable adversity and to become if not intercontinentally successful, then at least solvent.

So when the national media circulates the discovery of congenital happiness, it catches the attention of Oona's extensive stable of program developers. A predisposition to disposition: it's exactly the kind of fatalism the boss is determined not to be determined by. And nothing boosts the viewership like a good fight. When Oona's staff learn that the Happy Gene Woman lives in a dorm room in the South Loop not sixteen blocks from *The Oona Show*'s studio, it reads like fate.

∞

Thassa's name appeared in Weld's appointments calendar: a half-hour walk-in slot on the Thursday afternoon of finals week. The tidal bore of pre-finals desperation that surged annually through the counseling center had tapered off, and most of Candace's clients were crawling back home to piece themselves together over summer break. Weld hadn't spoken with Thassa for longer than she could count. She'd seen the swell of public nonsense, of course. But a student could face worse crises than a momentary deluge of anonymous love.

Yet there Thassa was, her 3:00 p.m. counseling appointment. Weld wondered how she could have let so many days pass without contact. In the seven years that Candace had worked at Mesquakie, she'd made three major miscalculations, one of them resulting in an attempted, thankfully inept suicide. Weld went into therapy herself after that, and Dennis Winfield and other colleagues helped restore her professional confidence. She learned a great deal from these slips, and she battled back from each one to become stronger at what she did and better at who she was. But every so many months a note or news or a surprise name on the appointments calendar grazed her, and she returned to that eroding state where everything was incomprehensible mistake and cascading consequence. The state in which many of her clients permanently resided.

Candace knew what she had to do: Listen carefully for any immediate danger. Sympathize with the disorienting stress Thassa must be under. Then suggest that Thassa make an appointment as soon as possible with one of the other counselors. Friendship and professionalism both demanded the switch.

The knock came promptly at three o'clock. Candace opened the door on the first student ever to enter her office and hug her. Thassa shook Weld's shoulders and kissed her on both cheeks. "So—you are still alive!"

"I'm sorry," Candace said. "Things have been so crazy lately, haven't they?"

"Total *folie*." Thassa's eyes could not stop moving. She glided around the office in her white muslin dress, inspecting the bookshelves, the Hopper print, and the photographs, as if this were the first she'd seen them. She settled into the leather chair, home at last.

Candace sat in the adjacent armchair, trying to place what was different about Thassa. Her aura had changed. She wasn't nervous: just the reverse. She radiated some intense urge toward stillness. Every conversational starter Candace could think of felt foolish.

"A colleague of mine showed me the *People* magazine piece."

Thassa shook her head to an inner rhythm and closed her eyes. "I can't even think of it, Candace. *C'est fou. C'est absolument fou.*"

"Are you . . . ? Is it wearing you down?"

The Kabyle looked off into a year's distance, at the distinct possibility that this might be the case. "These days have been so strange. A kind of funny hell. I never realized this before. I can make total strangers miserable, just by being well. I never thought this could happen, and I don't know what I am supposed to do with this."

"Is that what you came to talk about?"

Thassa's head jerked back, slapped. Candace heard the stupidity of her words. The two women blinked at each other for a raw instant. Thassa rallied first, covering for them both.

"Of course not! Do you think I would be that tedious, Candace? I made an appointment because you are too busy to see me anymore!"

They stumbled into a laugh. Then a little vanilla gossip. There was no other word for it, and although it felt mildly criminal to indulge, especially in her office, Candace proceeded to give the only other woman who would care a brief account of just what it felt like to be with Mr. Russell Stone.

The session timer chimed softly, much sooner than it should have. Thassa rose to go, Miss Generosity again, a perfect clone of the young woman whom Stone had introduced to Weld, as recently as last fall. The small damage from Weld's stupidity had healed. Candace would call her next week. They would do something together. Maybe a gallery opening. Maybe theater.

"By the way," the Kabyle said, her accent thickening, "I need to tell you. I'm going on *The Oona Show*."

Candace froze halfway to the door. Her face did a time-lapse Lon Chaney before settling on professional curiosity.

Thassa dropped her eyes and toyed with the inlaid Japanese pencil box on Candace's desk. "I know. You must think I've lost my mind. I was going to ask your opinion."

Seven years of psychological training, and Candace Weld had no reply. "Do you . . . *know* that show?"

"My God, Candace. What do you think? South Sea island people have Oona fan clubs."

"Have you thought about this? Do you really think . . . ?"

The younger woman reached out and touched two fingers to Candace's wrist, helping the patient through denial. "This is the right thing. The fastest way to make everything end. I made them ask Thomas Kurton, too. This way, I talk to that man face-to-face, in front of everyone. I only want my life back, Candace. This can clear up everything, once and forever."

Thassa left, but not before embracing Candace with such resigned encouragement that it scared the counselor. Thassa on the most-watched television show in history: Weld felt as if a Greek chorus had predicted that development all the way back at the start of Act 1.

A knock came five minutes too early to be the next student client. Before Weld could collect herself to answer, Christa Kreuz poked her head through the door. Her colleague's eyebrows struggled with the empirical evidence. "Excuse me. Was that who I think it was?"

∞

Complimentary tickets admit Stone and Weld to the most coveted studio-audience seats in the country. The gift is wasted on them—like a 1993 Petrus Bordeaux at a frat party. They aren't aware of the four-year waiting period. They know nothing about that famous pancreatic-cancer support group who banded together to request emergency tickets—the one thing the group all wanted to do while still together. They've never heard about the episode where Oona gave every person in the audience a fifty-inch television. They're just here to watch Thassa prove she's not a freak.

Russell is a mess. He's wrapped around Candace's upper arm like a blood-pressure cuff. He's way out behind hostile lines, in the core of an empire that would turn on him in an eyeblink if it knew his insur-

gent heart. He's clammy and numb, as if Colonel Mathieu has captured him in *The Battle of Algiers* and is about to hook him up to wet
electrodes.

"She'll be fine," Candace says, peeling his claw off of her arm and
taking it in her hand.

Of course, *she* will. He's never doubted that Thassa would be anything less.

The soundstage is a low-ceilinged box packed with raked theater
seats. It's filled with dolly-mounted cameras, floodlights, boom mics,
flat-screen monitors, and skeins of cabling as thick as anacondas. In a
glass-encased mezzanine, Stone can see banks of mixing boards—
a private space program or an underground command bunker. The
whole show is operated by tattooed, headset-wearing kids who look
like his former students. They probably *are* Mesquakie students, from
a few years ago at most.

The audience sits in a dark oubliette. In the center of the LED-
speckled blackness, bathed in grow lights so bright it hurts Stone's
eyes to look, sits a cozy living room ripped out of someone's mission-
style home: a flower show in the middle of an airplane hangar.

Five camera crews dolly around like crack artillery emplace-
ments. One of the squads is smaller, their gear more mobile. Russell
knows the woman standing next to the cameraman before he recognizes her. He looks away, somehow guilty.

Candace notices. "Is that who I think it is?"

"Who?" he says. But she's impossible to mistake: Thomas Kurton's
television interviewer. Popular science's most striking public face. The
woman who presided over their first moments of sexual exploration.

"What are they doing here?" Candace asks. "Didn't they film their
show already?"

Her question is lost in an audience swell. Someone walks out
onstage, but it's not Oona. It turns out to be the audience's personal
trainer. He starts with a few jokes that soon have the audience in the
aisles. Stone gets only half of them. He turns to Candace for explanation. She's pinching the bridge of her nose and smiling stoically. At
what, Stone can't say.

The trainer talks the audience through the next forty minutes. He
explains how important it is that everyone be themselves and respond
honestly to any meltdowns that Oona and her guests get into. Monitors spread throughout the room will give simple cues to help indicate

where laughter or surprise might be appropriate. "So let's try out a couple of responses, all right? I said, 'All right?' *I can't hear you . . .*"

The audience eats it up. Stone shoots a dazed look at the woman on his right. She's a kindly forty-year-old pukka elf who reminds him exactly of his sister, if he had a sister. She sneaks him a grin while shaking her head and applauding along with everyone. Stone starts to clap, too. He keeps his eyes on the trainer, afraid even to glance at Candace.

The personal trainer takes them through a gamut of responses. They get quite good at shared dismay, shock, and pleasure. When the audience is one finely tuned globe of communal good feeling, the trainer tells two more jokes and leaves to an ovation. Music starts up, brassy and buoyant. A voice comes out of nowhere and the audience starts pumping, even before Stone can check the monitors for a cue.

Oona skips into the glowing living room, warm and confident and a little abashed by the affection flowing from her hundreds of studio friends. Exhilaration courses over the rows of seats. When she steps to the front of the stage and smiles, Stone feels he's known this woman forever. She's someone he'd like to have as a friend-girl in an adjoining cubicle at *Becoming You*. She's the person his mother was, when his mother was young and still went out in public. He wants to reassure Oona, to thank her for her wry normality. She scares the hell out of him, and she hasn't even started talking.

Something pulls at his fingers. He looks down at Candace, who is trying to free her crushed hand from his grip.

Stop worrying, she mouths, over the applause. *It'll be fine.*

He's shot through with gratitude for this woman. He couldn't even sit in this place without her, let alone pretend that anything might be *fine*.

Oona waves her hands, helpless with pep. "Thank you, everybody. You're all simply amazing!"

The uproar crests again.

"Today on the show . . . Thank you! Today on the show . . ."

The word sends Stone into a fugue. They're on a *show*. Show, don't tell. All for show. If bad things come down while they're here, they can just return to the unshown.

". . . we're going to talk with several experts in different fields who'll tell us—ready for this?—the secret of happiness."

The audience erupts again, as if they already possess it.

"Yep. How about *that*? That's got to be worth your price of admission, right there!"

She makes several more promises, all in the voice of everyone's favorite high school English teacher. A great surge of appreciation ends in a sudden mood drop. Stone looks around, confused.

"Commercial break," Candace whispers.

Stone struggles with the idea. Out there, in the world, the show never wavers. In here, it ebbs and flows, like any bipolar creature.

In minutes, the thrill is back. Oona's first guest arrives with fanfare. He's a broadcast and Web psychologist whom everyone in the room friended long ago. His message: We're incapable of predicting what will make us happy. Consequently, it's best to stay loose and keep revising the plan. Socialize, volunteer, listen to music, and get out of the house. The man's witty pragmatism makes Russell want to bunker down with the shades pulled. Stone checks Candace. She screws up her mouth and sighs. The audience laughs and claps and resolves to forgive themselves more and live a little freer.

The broadcast psychologist and Oona debate about whether it's harder to be happy or to lose weight. They drop into another brief depressive interval, followed by a more manic return. Then Oona gets serious and asks her worldwide audience, "Could it be we're simply hardwired for happiness? Our next guest, a leading genomic researcher, believes he has the answer. Friends, please welcome Dr. Thomas Kurton."

Kurton's five minutes agitate even Candace. Every time the Donatello man speaks, she tugs at Stone's sleeve with silent objections. Kurton talks so rationally about dopamine receptors and inherited good cheer that the audience must see he's dangerous. But the monitors keep their counsel, and each guest is left alone to take her private cues directly from Oona's face.

And Oona's face harbors the wary hope coded into those humans who lie smack in the middle of the normal distribution curve. "So you can look at my DNA and tell me how upbeat I usually am, relative to the rest of humanity?"

Kurton grins into the studio lights. "We can make a reasonable guess at where, on the spectrum of human buoyancy, a given constellation of genetic variation will probably fall."

The broadcast psychologist tumbles forward in his chair and tries to interrupt. But Oona waves him down. "Hold on. And you can do this for . . . how much?"

Her half-guilty, half-greedy comic timing is perfect. The audience laughs, and Thomas Kurton laughs with them. "Gene sequencing is getting a hundred times cheaper and faster every year. Someday you'll be able to order behavioral-trait tests for less than you'd pay a psychological testing service. And the answers won't depend on self-reporting."

It hits Stone: the man can say anything at all. Sober measurement or wild prediction — it makes no difference. He's on the show. And the show, not the lab, is where the race will engineer its future.

The psychologist can contain himself no longer. "Is knowing my happiness quotient going to make me any happier?"

His timing is not as good as Oona's. She blows by him again, fascinated with Kurton. "Here's what I'm wondering. You see, I'm dating this guy? Yeah . . . Some of you may have read about that?"

The audience goes wild. Stone sees the future. The race is going to go down. But it will go down laughing. Oona blushes like only the Irish can. Along with 140 million other people, Stone wants to protect this woman from her own heart.

"So, yeah. I'm dating this guy, and I'm wondering if you can tell me whether he's really as cheerful, way deep down, as he seems to be right now?"

Kurton's smile isn't afraid to hint. Someday we'll all know more about one another than anyone knows about herself.

Oona passes the mic. One of the few men in the audience asks if constant happiness might actually be risky. The audience applauds. The radio psychologist nods and says that people who rate themselves as a ten are less productive than those who call themselves an eight. Kurton asks, "Is that such a bad thing?" The monitors murmur *HMM* . . . just before the audience does.

A pretty, terrified brunette not much older than Thassa asks how soon science will be able to turn sad genes into happy ones. Kurton grins and says he's never been very good at predicting the speed of science.

Then a slim, tall, poised woman nearing forty stands and addresses Kurton. "My husband and I are trying to have a child through in vitro fertilization." The audience falls quiet. "Genetic counselors say we can determine which of the fertilized embryos might have incurable monogenetic diseases. Can we now also tell which ones have the best chance of being happy?"

Oona's arms are all over the place. "Oh my God! Can you *do* that?"

It's not clear whether she means technically or legally. Kurton demurs, apologizing. And the audience murmurs something the monitors don't prompt.

A creature grips Stone's arm. He turns to Candace. Her face blanches. Her life's work is slipping away from her in an arms race of bliss. "They're buying it," she whispers. The wisdom of crowds has turned on her. All Stone can do is reach across his chest and touch one limp hand to her right shoulder. She grabs it in both of hers.

"Okay. Hold on!" Oona the sane and suspicious, Oona the level-headed avenging angel of common sense crosses her hands in a T. And *Yes*, my two throwback characters hope: she'll stop the madness now. The most influential woman in the world will buy humanity another twenty years of grace before the species splits into Ordinary and Enhanced. "So what's the catch? I mean: screening embryos? How much is something like that going to cost?"

An *Ah!* escapes the audience, then ripples through millions of people in seven time zones, at the speed of broadcast.

"Good question," Kurton says, rubbing his head. "My company is thinking hard about exactly that question."

"What do *you* think?" Oona asks, peering out into the black abyss of dollying machines. Stone thinks she's putting the matter up for public auction. But she narrows her gaze to the slender forty-year-old on the verge of in vitro. "How much would you pay to pick your child's profile?"

"I don't know," the woman says. "Parents already pay hundreds of thousands to give their children advantages."

Everyone talks at once. Oona takes forty seconds to reestablish order. She's dazed, like she doesn't believe any of this, and then like she does, like we've just set out from this world toward something glorious and paradisiacal. At last she falls back into her Everywoman look, still crash-tested but conditioned by a lifetime of biannual breakthroughs to believe that every story will still happen, in time. Through the corner of a mouth that can no longer tell which way to twist, she says, "You heard it here first, friends. The question is whether you're ready for it! Are we closing in at last on the thing we've been looking for from the beginning? More, after this."

∞

During the commercial break, a start-up down in New Mexico publishes an association study on predisposition to insomnia. An Illinois university lab secures more funding to study the suicide risks of three leading antidepressants. And a Bay Area biotech company prepares to announce a genetic test that will tell anyone their odds of developing bipolar disorder. "We're not claiming this is our ticket to Stockholm," the CEO tells his board. "We do, however, believe it offers people more value than any other diagnostic now on the market."

∞

While the cameras rest, Oona lets her guests debate, just to keep everyone happily on edge. Candace leans over to Stone in the dark. Her warm breath swirls in his ear. "Can we move to another planet?" He wants to tell her yes, anywhere. But multibillion-dollar deep-space probes have already laid claim to all the best reachable ones.

The audience starts to cheer before Stone realizes the real show has returned. "Welcome back," Oona says, perched on the arm of the emerald sofa. "Today we're all about the secret of happiness! And right now, I want you to meet a remarkable young woman you may have heard about. Until now, she's been known only by her pseudonym, Jen. She's the woman who our guest, Dr. Thomas Kurton, after a four-year study, says may just possess one of the best genetic signatures for personal well-being. How does it feel to be born with what the rest of us can only dream about? Let's find out. Friends, please welcome the woman with all the right happiness genes, Miss Thassadit Amzwar."

Thassa stumbles from the wings, squinting in the klieg lights' blaze. A gasp comes from the house: she's *foreign*. She's wearing a pair of tight green straight-leg jeans and a puffy white Berber blouse embroidered with rainbow around the collar and wrists. She has on every piece of good-luck silver Russell has ever seen her wear. Those onstage clap along with the audience. Thassa sits on the sofa, leaning forward, legs together, peering out into the blackness. She spots her friends and waves. When the clapping quiets, she says, "Why are you all cheering? I haven't said anything yet!"

Stone presses his eyes and Candace starts to cry. Everyone around them breaks out in a new, delighted ovation.

∞

Nine minutes of television—a broadcast eternity. Watching the scene unfold over the shoulder of her own show's cameraman, Tonia Schiff couldn't help feeling, *I've seen this film before.* She could have written the spectacle's script herself. Thassadit Amzwar came out onstage to a rock anthem, as if some trained seal of elation. The ingenue sat down, surrounded by her examiners, before an audience cranked up on a network high, teetering between the two primal feeding frenzies of hope and doubt. And as in every version of this movie that Schiff had ever seen, some well-meaning but helpless figure lurked on the boundaries of the audience, filled with shameful complicity. At least she was off camera this time.

The Algerian woman sat in the eye of the churning show, far away in an impenetrable place, pulling an imaginary shawl over her shoulders. Schiff marveled at the self-possession, freakish for a woman of any age, let alone twenty-three. In another era, Thassadit Amzwar might have been celebrated as a mystic. The famous host dangled questions in front of her like twine before a cat.

O: Would you call yourself one of the happiest people ever born?
TA: Of course not! Why would I call myself that?
O: You know what I'm asking.
TA: I feel very well. Very happy to be alive.
O: And you feel like that . . . all the time?
TA: Naturally, no. I'm often sleeping.
O: How much of your personal happiness is in your genes?
TA: Ask this man. He knows everything about genes.
O: We've asked him already. What do you think?
TA: How can I know, Oona? What does it even mean? One hundred percent? Fifty? Zero?

Confusion gathered in the room behind Schiff, the buzz of a stirred hive. Even the prompting monitors were perplexed. Schiff made Keyes pan around the restive room.

O: *Were you born happy? Were you a happy baby?*
TA: *Listen. I was thinking. Maybe happiness is like a virus. Maybe it's one of those bugs that sits for a long time, so we don't even know that we are infected. A virus can even change your genes, can't it?*

Here the woman appealed to the scientist, who smiled so broadly that anyone just tuning in would have thought that he was the one guilty of inherited pleasure. Keyes caught both faces in close-up at just the right moment. He also managed to catch, in the iconic host's reaction, the first awareness that she faced a guest rebellion.

O: *Okay, let me ask it this way. Were your parents happy?*
TA: *My parents? My parents lived through war their whole lives. They never knew their own language. Everyone was their enemy, and then they died. How happy are most Americans?*

The Americans in this room were less than pleased. Many of them looked ready to demand an emotional refund. Someone had misled the general public. The woman with the perfect genetic temperament wasn't even amusing. This woman was *testy*. And the audience had been set up for some elaborate practical joke.

The famous host made further jabs, increasingly desperate. She shifted to Kurton, asking him to talk about Miss Amzwar's neurotransmitter levels and her fMRI. Miss Amzwar interrupted. *Why are you looking for our spirits in molecules? Very old wine in new bottles!*

Her exasperation turned contagious. The program headed toward precisely the kind of disaster that kept audiences addicted to live broadcasts.

O: *Sister, if you're telling us that you're as miserable as the rest of us, why did you come on this show?*

The audience exploded into cheers and catcalls. The despondent Jen bent her neck oddly away from the camera, as if someone had her soul pinched between his thumb and forefinger and was twisting it. Her face clouded, and she sank into a darkness that bordered on bitter. Schiff felt the woman drift to the brink of a public breakdown. Yet even the descent seemed a work of art—repugnance as robustly enjoyed as any mood.

Keyes's camera, along with the four *Oona Show* units, nailed what happened next. With another shoulder twist, the Algerian shook off temptation and passed into a state more solid than anger. She rose up on the couch and surveyed the room. Something large hijacked her irritation, some uncontainable affection for everything that grew from twenty-three chromosomes. Her enzymes aligned, she began to speak, and in one surge her easy tide lifted all the boats.

Digital clips of her outbreak hit the Web for worldwide consumption as early as that evening. They multiplied for days after the air date. And by the following week, the YouTube imitations began to appear. The otherworldly glow of the soliloquy came less from Thassa Amzwar's words than from her posture, the quiet knowledge that poured out of the woman, despite her best efforts. And this was the aura that teenage girls everywhere attempted to copy, in an epidemic of two-minute DV viruses that broke out on machines across all the advanced countries.

Later, Schiff spent hours hunting down the proliferating performances, which had by then become one of the most popular amateur theatricals on the Net.

"Oona, listen," a pretty Vancouver Eurasian lip-synchs, in her own shot-perfect re-creation of the segment. "I promise you: This is easy. Nothing is more obvious."

A stocky blond high school junior wearing a Berber blouse in her Orlando bedroom recites for the lens, "People think they need to be healed, but the truth is much more beautiful."

Atlanta: "Even a minute is more than we deserve." Spokane, Allentown: "No one should be anything but dead." San Diego, Concord, Moline: "Instead, we get honey out of rocks. Miracles from nothing."

"It's easy," all the Thassa Amzwars across the globe swear to anyone who'll listen. "We don't need to get better. We're already us. And everything that is, is ours."

∞

Stone and Weld snatch her from the clamoring studio audience and whisk her off to a hidden soft-serve ice cream dive somewhere west of

Greek Town. Neither of Thassa's foster guardians has the courage to ask anything but whether she's all right.

Her all-rightness extends to being ravenous. She wolfs down nine hundred calories while wondering out loud, "What exactly is my crime, do you think? I simply enjoy this world. Why do they treat me as some kind of threat to civilization?" She says nothing about her teetering in front of the camera, that brittle moment when she seemed half in love with nihilism. But she confesses to thinking she'd never escape the post-show crush alive.

When she comes up for air two waffle cones later, she mentions, a little embarrassed, her pre-show meeting with Tonia Schiff. "You remember her? The funny narrator from the genomes program? Of course you do!"

Stone and Weld nod, red.

"She wants to make another film. The other side of this so-called destiny story. She thinks there's much more to tell about my . . . feeling well. She thinks I'm being made into some kind of prophecy. She wants to help, I think."

Stone checks with Candace, who chooses this precise moment to clam up. He sees in her face exactly how it is: too scrupulous to give the advice she wants to, too committed to trust to intervene. He pleads with her: *Don't leave me here alone.* But Candace's eyes blink with a first little ten-dollar dose of fear.

"Do you think that's a good idea?" he asks Thassa. If Weld won't be herself, he'll have to be her. "With all this exposure right now . . ."

Thassa pets his shoulder with her paper cup. "You're right, Russell. Of course you are. But this is the woman who I want to be when I grow up. She can teach me a lot about film. Maybe more than school can."

With a glance, she implores Candace. All the psychologist can do is raise an eyebrow.

Methodically, Thassa shreds her napkin. She murmurs a few Tamazight words of encouragement to herself. "It's a funny thing. I'm Kabyle. We're supposed to be so private by nature. Ach—*nature*! It's meaningless, isn't it? I know what you think. But maybe another show can finish all this nonsense. Jen must disappear. Maybe Miss Schiff can help kill her."

She looks to her friends for their approval. She's forgotten, in the moment's stress, how no one needs to decide more than God. And God decides at just that minute to send through the door of the ice cream joint a pair of retired women who instantly recognize the foreign creature they just saw on television an hour ago. It takes the trio twenty minutes to escape from Thassa's admirers.

They say goodbye to one another back in the South Loop. Thassa is restless again, her eyes casting in all directions for the sequel that might extricate her. They drop her off at her dorm, where a cluster of superchurch Christians and Mesquakie *Oona Show* fans already gather for autographs. Thassa goes stoically to her fate. "Russell, Candace: you are wonderful. Let's meet again, on a calmer day."

∞

They watch the recorded show again that night, in Edgewater. Gabe watches with them. The boy is so excited he almost levitates. "We *know* her, Mom. She's my *friend*. This is like . . . six stars. Seven!" He's a little upset by that moment when Thassa threatens to implode. But he knows how a good ending needs a brush with disaster in order for it to mean anything. When the strong finish comes, it's like he's willed it into being.

On his way off to bed, the happy boy asks Russell, "You staying over again tonight? Whatever. My dad says he's cool with it."

In bed, Russell and Candace reprise the argument they've been rehearsing all day. "The stress is getting to her," he says. A second look at the show convinces him. "I've never seen her like that. She was this close to losing it."

Candace, meanwhile, has recovered. Her own little worm of fear has put out wings and become some beautiful gadfly. "Russell. It's over. She won't have to do it again. So she hit a shaky patch. Rough edges, same as anyone. I don't think she was in real trouble, even for a minute. Look how she ended!"

But all he can think about are those thirty seconds when Miss Generosity lay pinned under a boulder as heavy as any that has ever crushed him. He sees something new in her, something better than he ever expected.

"Leave it," the woman in bed next to him says. "Stop worrying. She was fine."

He rolls over and straddles her. He presses his body down across her length, cupping her shoulders, pressing his mouth between her breasts. How wrong can this counselor be? The girl wasn't fine, not by a long shot. She was susceptible. Desperate. Magnificent. *Exhilarating.*

∞

The note from Dennis Winfield reached Weld two days later. A note, not a visit: trouble. Weld knew what it had to be about. The only mystery was why it took so long in coming. Perhaps the counseling center needed time to make an airtight case.

At least Dennis showed the decency to reprimand her privately before convening the whole tribunal. She could work with Dennis one-on-one. He had a thing about her. She didn't even need to play him; he played himself, whenever the two of them sat in a room together.

She came to his office at the appointed time, all sails trim and ready to navigate any accusation.

Dennis opened conventionally enough. "You're in a relationship with this man? Sleeping together?" He sounded more than professionally hurt.

Weld reminded Dennis that she'd consulted him. Both he and Christa Kreuz had green-lighted her dating Russell Stone.

"We did not give you license to violate ethics."

She fell back in her chair. "Violate . . . ?" Dennis fended off her glance with his chin. She no longer recognized him. She tried to slow her heartbeat and take stock. "I have never violated professional ethics in my life."

She'd blurred a boundary once or twice. Let clients need her more than was good. But that was early on, before she graduated from her own temperamental weaknesses. "How dare you, Dennis. I've done nothing that you and your morals policewoman didn't sign off on. Just what are you accusing me of?"

"Inappropriate emotional intimacy with a client."

She jerked forward, indignant. "He's *not* a client. We've been all over this—"

"Not your boyfriend," Dennis said. "Your boyfriend's girlfriend."

Candace slumped back into her chair. Panic plumed through her chest. Someone held her head underwater. Even before Dennis

225

spelled out the accusation, she saw it, complete. And indisputable. She sobered horribly, like she'd been on a jag with some wild, five-minute party drug and she was just now coming to, witnessing her sluttish behavior from a distance.

"She isn't a client," Weld said, pathetic even to herself.

"She's a student at this college. She was in your office for an appointment last week."

"That wasn't an appointment," Candace bleated. "That was . . ." But all she could think to say was *personal*.

"You're in a severely impaired position here." Dennis examined a legal tablet full of evidence.

Candace looked away to the window, into the dappled sunlight of the west. No objection possible. How had she managed to hide the truth from herself for so many months? It had all seemed genuine, legitimate. In truth, she'd backslid massively into her own worst trait, sought the love and approval of someone she should never have been more than professionally considerate to. She'd fancied herself the girl's big sister, her guide and protector. What had she been, really? Her flatterer. *Impaired.* Years' worth of self-correcting effort, and Weld had gone nowhere. Her character had her chained, forever complicit.

"Dennis?" she said, finding his eyes. "Yes. You're right. I need to go back into counseling."

He kept his gaze on his legal pad. "You need more than that. This is license-threatening stuff. This student is on national television, on the edge of emotional disaster, and she's sleeping over at your house? She's your *pal*? And all the while you're dispensing advice like some kind of fairy godmother, setting her up with private research outfits . . ."

Candace Weld sat and watched as the future stripped her of meaningful work. Everything she'd struggled to become would be held against her. She cast about for *prāṇāyāma*, but her lungs were crushed. She dropped her head, cupped her hands around her engorged throat, and dissolved in tears.

Dennis studied his notes, pretending composure. "You will go into therapy," he said. "Christa will get you referred."

She almost stood up then and walked out of the office. Only the mortgage prevented her.

"And of course you'll have no contact with Thassadit Amzwar." He pronounced the name like something from Iowa. "If she approaches you for advice of any kind, you will refer her to Christa and curtail any further interaction."

Neither bearable nor possible. She fully granted the wrongness of her action and the validity of every reprimand that Dennis threw at her. But she did not merit punitive action. Not reprimand for what she'd fought so hard to correct.

"And my relationship?"

Dennis looked at her at last, his eyes narrowed in what any student of human psychology could only call disgust. "That's between you and him. You think he's willing to give her up for you?"

∞

I always knew I'd lose my nerve in the end. Kurton set free by his data; Thassa turning brittle; Stone an easy mark in the crosshairs of love. Now Candace, on the auction block. A part of me wanted to love this woman since she was no more than the sketchiest invention. I thought she would be my mainstay, and now she's breaking. I don't have the heart to learn her choice.

All I want is for my friends to survive the story intact. All the story wants is to wreck anything solid in them. No one would write a word, if he remembered how much fiction eventually comes true.

∞

The genomicist, too, has a rough night. I've said so little about him that you may not care. That's more cowardice on my part. In the absence of detail, you've been seeing him as an uncle, an old biology teacher, some more solid scientist you recently came across in another book or film. You might feel anything toward him—curiosity, hatred, attraction. The world's two camps of readers, split by inborn temperament, need two inimical things, and each has long ago decided to love or loathe this man according to those needs.

But feel this much, anyway:

Thomas arrives back in Logan on the flight from Chicago, mystified as to why Thassa Amzwar would lash out at him on national TV. The audience outcry also baffles him. He's satisfied enough with his own performance: hopeful but accurate. He's confident that public controversy can't hurt science. Nothing, really, can hurt science. All the Luddites in the country turning out with torches and pitchforks would succeed only in sending research abroad. Everything discoverable will be discovered; he'd bet his lab on that. And every truth that research turns up simply becomes more environment, part of survival's calculus, no less than air, food, climate, or water.

Yet this backlash takes him on the chin, as bad as the first fray he landed in, back at the Cardinal Hayes High School science fair. He understands the tribal fear and self-protection behind this aggression. But his work aims only to relieve ill health, free people from the body's caprice, and crack open the prison of inherited fate.

He strolls through the mobbed baggage claim with his single carry-on. The airport loop is a snarl of shuttles, taxis, and cars. The matter transporter will not come a day too soon. Two people on the Blue Line back into the city think they recognize him from *The Oona Show*. But they decide no; the founder of seven biotech companies, adviser to six scientific journals, and discoverer of the major genetic contribution to human well-being can't possibly be riding the subway.

He gets out at Government Center and walks to his brownstone on Beacon Street; walking reduces the risk of many major disease predispositions. It's late afternoon, and the streets fill with the change of shifts. Vendors, Bible-waving preachers, one-man bands, and stump speakers cluster at the foot of the hill beneath the State House, as crowds pour down the subway steps at Park Street. He cuts across the lustrous Common, exhilarated by the human pageant. Fifty yards away from his front door, he sees that his first-floor bay window has been smashed. He trots the rest of the way, saving a few seconds by rushing to a crime committed hours earlier.

He finds a paver pulled up from the sidewalk sitting in his living room. He turns it over in his trembling hands, looking for the attached note. There is no attached note. He sits down, light-headed, confused. Why send someone a message, if there's no message?

He knows the message. *Are we not men? Leave us the hell alone.* He sits for a few minutes, afraid to call the police. He shuts off the light, to hide his silhouette. After a while, he goes down into the cellar and brings up a piece of pressboard large enough to cover the broken window. He tacks it into place, a barrier, at least. Then he leaves a voice mail with his handyman.

He makes himself a blueberry soy shake, which calms him a little. He goes online to see what kind of hate-mongering the show produced. Reaction is all over the map, from morose to ecstatic. But he sees no violent threats, at first glance. He logs off the browser and occupies himself with the surge of waiting correspondence. But he works at no more than half efficiency. He recoils at every floorboard creek, waiting for the follow-up message. After an hour of twitching, rather than continue to spin out, he decides to drive up to Maine.

It's late already, but a night drive will clear his head. He throws his still-packed bag into the Insight, the most fuel-efficient vehicle ever sold on the mass market. He'd have bought it for the engineering achievement alone. Only innovation, now, will buy the race enough time to work its next escape.

He drives for hours, into the night. He keeps himself awake listening to an audiobook of *The Plague*, the novel that defeated him at Stanford, when his ex-wife made him read it. *You want to devote your life to life science? Read this first.*

He's gone back to Camus after talking with Thassa about the man. She filled him in on all the context he missed when reading the work in his twenties. She quoted the author's notorious declaration, at the height of the savage war: *If I have to choose between justice and my mother, I would choose my mother.* Kurton's justice is the freedom of research, rapidly decamping to the western Pacific Rim. His mother has been in a home in Westchester County for the last four years, ever since her defective APOE allele caught up with her. The choice would still not be easy, but it would be clear.

As a young man, Thomas never thought to wonder why Camus's Oran had so few named Arabs in it. Thassa set him straight on that as well. *I do love him,* the Algerian said. *He was both beautiful and humane. But also as blind as anyone with his background.* Thomas finds him blindly humane, too, as he drives up to Maine in the dark. But the problem is not with the enlightened *pied-noir*. The problem is with the craft of fiction.

The whole grandiose idea that life's meaning plays out in individual negotiations makes the scientist wince. Intimate consciousness, domestic tranquility, self-making: Kurton considers them all blatant distractions from the true explosion in human capability. Fiction seems at best willfully naïve. Too many soul-searchers wandering head-down through too many self-created crises, while all about them, the race is changing the universe. That much is clear to Kurton, as he slips off the interstate and onto the winding, coastal Route 1.

Worse, fiction's perpetual mistaking of correlation for causation drives Kurton nuts. Even Camus can't help deploying bits of his characters' histories as if they explained all subsequent behaviors and beliefs. The trick smacks of an environmental determinism more reductive than anything that has ever come out of Kurton's labs. *My upbringing made me do it . . .*

Kurton knows never to give his own biographical details to any reporter, or if he has to, to make them up. That's what the brain-body loop does, anyway: it's not the traumas Thomas remembers that shape Thomas—not so long as Thomas shapes the traumas Thomas remembers. He has never tried to hide his background; it's just irrelevant. Kurton's discoveries are only interesting if someone with completely different needs can reproduce them. The double-blind study frees human history from the trap of bias and sets it loose in a place beyond personality.

He wants to live long enough to witness a new, post-genomic fiction, one that grasps the interpenetrating loops of inheritance and upbringing so tangled that every cause is some other cause's effect. One that, through a kind of collaborative writing, shakes free of the prejudices of any individual maker. For now, fiction remains at best a scattershot mood-regulating concoction—a powerful if erratic cocktail like Ritalin for ADHD, or benzodiazepines for the sociophobe. In time, like every other human creation, it will be replaced by better, more precise molecular fine-tuning.

The Plague ends about half an hour outside of East Boothbay. The road by then is black and barely two car widths. Through the speakers scattered around the capsule of Kurton's car, the narrator speaks those words that so puzzled Thomas as a grad student:

> He knew what those jubilant crowds did not know but could have learned from books: that the plague bacillus never dies or disappears for good; that it can lie dormant for years and years in furniture and linen-chests; that it bides its time in bedrooms, cellars, trunks, and bookshelves; and that perhaps the day would come when, for the bane and the enlightening of men, it would rouse up its rats again and send them forth to die in a happy city.

He parks his car halfway up the driveway and stands for a while on the sloping hill, looking down toward his dock. He scouts the sheltered cove just to the left of the dock, where once again tonight, from the dark water (although not so dark that day as now), his eleven-year-old brother Brad emerges, bathed in a magic blue light, an electro-static globe that jerks him about like a livid puppet before kicking him up limp, forever, onto the pebbled beach. Brad, so skeptical and taci-turn that even a sky full of thunderheads could not rouse him from the water. And Tommy, empirical Tommy, long out of the water and halfway up to the house, and life . . .

Upstairs in what was for decades his parents' old bayside bed-room, the smell of cedar and musty quilts sends Kurton instantly to sleep.

∞

He wakes refreshed but a little hangdog that something so small as a paving brick could send him so far for safety. Over a breakfast of half a scoop of steel-cut oats, he checks his BlackBerry feeds. His aggregator for the name Amzwar produces so much junk he is forced to skim. He's stopped by an item that has already started to multiply and mutate. Several print and Web journalists are reporting an offer by a midsized Bay Area biotech firm of $14,000 for ten of the Algerian woman's eggs.

He looks up from the device in disbelief. Down the hill on the rock-scattered coast, a stand of spruce bends out over the contesting water, as they have for longer than people have been here to see them.

∞

Twice more in the days after the broadcast, Stone tries to get Candace to talk about Thassa's on-air transformation into Joan of Arc. He watches the segment again online. Candace does, too, or he doesn't know her from Eve. But each time he brings up the performance, Candace—by taint or training one shade saner than Russell—shunts him onto healthier topics.

But now he's okay with her dodge. Okay with everything; not even her growing yogic retreat bothers him. These last three nights, his appetite for her has been embarrassing. He's taken her above, behind, in front, below. And she lets him. She's been painfully beautiful, in the wake of Oona. She has been his keel, since even before they were lovers. She helps him see himself, helps him have a say over who he wants to be. Whatever the world insists on dragging them into, he is with her, and her bubble of self-possession is big enough for three.

He, Candace, and Gabe sit at her kitchen playing Yahtzee. She's given the boy unlimited gaming time, so long as the game has physical bits and he's playing with real, present humans. Russell is on a literal roll, pushing his luck far beyond what the dice should allow and getting away with it. He hits number after number, as if controlling the pips telekinetically. His odds-defying streak sends the boy into thrilled fits. "You're cheating! Mom, tell him to stop!" When the game ends, they leave Gabe sitting at the kitchen table, still rolling the dice, trying to crack the secret of Stone's spectacular run.

In her bed, Candace is sapphire, something he does not know in her. She runs her hands all over him, hunting from a distance for a key she has misplaced. After much searching, her need is answered. They lie together, emptied out. She curls away from him, tucks her backside into his belly, but holds on tight to his encircling arm. In the still room, she says, *I love you.* It's simple discovery, all surprise forbearance, like she's just been assigned a difficult but necessary journey.

Her head nods a minute confirmation on the pillow next to him. He fills with a certainty such as he has only felt twice in his life. The thought rushes him. Whatever this brings, he wants it. "That sounds very good to me," he whispers to her spine. "Can we put that in our book?"

She clasps his arm tighter: a given. The scene has already been written. He watches her fall from confirmation into sleep, by intervals too small to change anything. There is no fear; there is no elation. Only the fact of this shared day.

He watches her asleep. What could he say about her face, emptied of look, that would make it live for someone a hundred years from now? Or a hundred hundred. A sleeping face forgets every waking technology; sleep at 2020 should be intelligible to the Neolithic. Her eyes start to twitch a little, and then her lips. He could make her say anything at all, in her sleep, in their growing, coauthored volume.

She starts to snore. Small, seersucker, Laura Ashley snores. If he was fighting his love for her at all up until this moment, he now loses. The snores crescendo, and although he holds perfectly still in his joy, her own sound rouses her. She wakes confused, defensive. "I wasn't!" she says, still asleep. She opens her eyes, turns to look at him. "Was I?"

"Hey," he tells her, nuzzling her downy neck. "Let's get engaged, or something."

She sits up and inspects the room, puzzled. Someone has rearranged all its furniture in her sleep. "Russell? I have to tell you something. We can't see Thassa anymore."

∞

The footage of Thassa on *The Oona Show* made an eerie art film in its own right: her far-focusing eyes, the ecstatic fear, the angelic irritation shaking free of all human markets. Schiff couldn't get enough. She studied the shots of the genetically blessed woman, already splicing them into a much larger script: a single forty-two-minute hour about how the eons-long pursuit of happiness was at last cutting to the chase.

She and the *Over the Limit* crew worked from a rough outline: nine minutes on the chemical bases of moods; eight on neurogenetics; eleven on hyperthymia and its now famous mascot, Thassa Amzwar; and ten on the coming ability to manipulate genetic disposition. That left four minutes for transitions and Schiff's interludes. She'd already done two interviews with key researchers in the biology of contentment. The show interns were busy raiding the archive for usable footage, while the art team set to work on fantastic animation.

The day after *The Oona Show*, Schiff and Garrett arrived to film Thassa in her dorm. The building had thinned out for the summer break, but a cluster of Jen-spotters loitered in the entrance. They clamored around Garrett's tripods and lights, bugging him for information. A sallow ectomorph asked Schiff to sign his iPod with a Sharpie. One woman of about thirty, puffy and near tears, tried to force her way into the building alongside them, saying it was absolutely essential that she talk to the happiness girl right away. The lobby security guard turned her away, not for the first time.

Upstairs, in Thassa's narrow, film-filled efficiency, they found a woman far from ecstatic. She sat holding her elbows on a small, three-colored kilim that stretched across the room. Garrett barely had space to mount the camera and lights, unfurl the reflectors, and still get both women into the shot. As he started filming, Thassa wrapped herself in stoicism. Schiff, stripped of sass, transformed into some kind of acolyte. She asked Thassa about her upbringing. Garrett, nonplussed, kept shooting. But when the two women began to talk about Kabylia,

Thassa relaxed and showed the first sparks of a spirit that might be worth filming, let alone engineering.

Schiff asked, "Do Algerians trust happiness?" Garrett almost knocked the tripod over. But Thassa fielded the question on the fly. "We say, *Ki nchouf ham el nass nansa hami*: 'When I see someone else's desolation, I forget mine.' Every Algerian knows that every other Algerian has seen great miseries. And that is . . . *consolation*? Do any of my countrymen hope that science will discover a solution to the sorrow of history? Please! How can even Americans believe this?"

Instead of volleying, as she usually would have, Schiff gave one of the lamest follow-ups Garrett ever heard her deliver. "What makes you happy?"

Before Garrett could stop shooting, the Algerian woman smiled for the first time all interview. She lifted one thin, brown finger, and pointed at him. "That. Oh my God! If I could do what this man does, all day long? That would be a life. I love to look at the world through a viewfinder. I just love it. The worst things about life are beautiful on film."

Garrett killed the camera and asked to talk to Schiff out in the hall. He started in before she could defend. "You aren't exactly advancing the frontiers of science here."

Schiff leveled him with her unnerving hazel eyes. "Not my job, Nick."

"No? What exactly is your job? I thought it was to give me something engrossing to—"

"We're telling this woman's story."

The words slowed him. But only a little. "You're supposed to interview hyperthymia, not befriend it. This woman is not exactly a bottomless wellspring of cheer."

"We're supposed to film whatever is really there."

"Oh, shit. Don't get righteous on me. Not the time for philosophy, Ton. We're on a deadline here."

"This girl is not what Kurton says she is. I just think our viewers want to see—"

"Our viewers want science. It's a *science* show."

A voice called from inside the apartment. "Everything okay out there?"

When they slunk back into the room, they found Thassa filming

Garrett's camcorder and lighting gear with her own MiniDV. "Some-one wants to pay for my eggs," she told them. She lifted up her camera coolly and filmed their faces as understanding spread across them: Her *eggs*. *Her* eggs.

Garrett asked her to repeat the fact on film. Thassa laughed him off. "Interviews must be spontaneous. You can't tell your subjects what to say. That's what they teach in film school, *en tout cas*."

∞

Russell Stone lies in his beloved's bed, stilled by her bombshell. I step through his possible choices. Every combination of heritage and upbringing dooms him to keep pulling at the sheets and smiling. "What do you mean?"

Candace tells him, in mature phrases, the law as laid down to her. She explains what her job dictates. She lays it out the way she might tell a client that he needs to undergo certain stringent therapies. She goes down the list of Russell's possible objections, addressing each one sensitively.

"You can't be saying this," he says. "She's a *friend*, isn't she?"

She nods her head, helpful. "I suppose that's the point. By any responsible standard of behavior, I should never have become Thassa's friend in the first place."

He isn't getting this. "Are you just worried about your job? Because, Jesus: the whole country's a nut case. It's a buyer's market for what you do. You could work anywhere."

She explains about personnel files, letters of reference, and all the realities of adult life for which he's never had much innate aptitude.

"I see," he says. He sees nothing, except the accusation that he doesn't make.

She trembles and tears up. But her shoulders and torso remain strangely marble. He puts his arm around her and pulls her flush to him. He murmurs up near her ear. "Don't worry," he tells her. "It's all right. Sleep. You need to work tomorrow. We'll talk about it in daylight."

In daylight, they say nothing. She gets Gabe off to school while Stone is still clearing his head and trying to decide if she really said, in the middle of the night, what she really said. His best response is the billion-year-old, time-tested method of freezing up. If he does nothing, the whole thing may pass overhead without incident. So he keeps still and waits, like the rodent in a raptor's shadow with whom he shares so many genes.

∞

He doesn't have the luxury of waiting long. Three days later, he gets an e-mail from Princess Heavy Hullinger. Half a year ago, he shared a weird intimacy with this woman three nights a week. Now her name in his Inbox seems like a fable. The note is a cruel slash at all the writing conventions he once urged on the woman:

> hi there, u know there bidding on her genes now? the bid is up to 19K; no u dont and maybe dont care since u havent been in touch but shes getting a bit sick of everything coming down on her at the moment. dont worry were taking care of her, someone has to. I know shed like to hear something so if u have any teachery advice (;)) just e me, im sure shell appreciate.

The note wraps him in a gray cocoon. All of Charlotte's pieces for him were just exercises in deceit. This is how the woman really writes. Writing has become some mutant thing that will eat him alive and shit him into fertilizer.

He calls Thassa. There's no answer and no voice mail. He hops on the Red Line and rides down to Roosevelt. It takes a fiscal quarter. He jogs to her dorm building, the pedestrian streams cursing as he wades through them. He turns the corner at Eighth Street and stops.

A knot of people flock the entrance to her building. It's some kind of ad-hoc Flag Day. A woman with her hands and face painted cerulean sports a hand-lettered poster mounted on her head: *No Jenetic Jimmying*. A younger female, perhaps her daughter, painted to match, wears a sandwich board that reads *Sad and Proud*. A man struggles to remove the helmet of his cartoony hazmat suit. Three college kids in matching *Gee, I'm a GMO* T-shirts exchange raucous laughter. Policemen make two others take down a first-story banner with the two-foot-high words *Bio-Value-Add Me*. A short, hoary black woman—eighty years old if she's a day—jabs her finger at a white gnome a decade her senior, who holds a limp megaphone at his thigh.

Even as the police try to break up the geriatric scuffle, the woman keeps shouting, "Where the hell is the law in all of this?"

Around the edges, the parade trickles out. But the core of the spectacle holds steady, and other bystanders stop to watch. A woman Stone's age toting a stack of pamphlets mistakes his expression for disappointment. "You just missed the *StreetSharp News*. They sent two vans. They pulled out about fifteen minutes ago." She hands him a pamphlet; it's about how virtually anyone can atomize their egos, dissolve the boundary between their cells and the rest of creation, and tap into the nirvana that spiritual leaders have known about for millennia, all with little medical intervention to speak of. She smiles, like she wants to be his friend.

"Is she here?" Stone asks, his voice veering.

"Who?"

Helpless, he points upward, toward the plate glass of Thassa's apartment.

"You mean *her*?" The pamphlet woman laughs, like he's making a joke she doesn't quite understand yet. "Nobody has seen her for days. That guy says she was at the window on Thursday night. But he's probably lying."

Russell Stone clamps both sides of his forehead. "How long have you been here?"

The pamphlet woman seems ready to help, if only she could follow him. "Me? Here? You mean, all together?"

He pauses in the doorway of the music shop where he once hid out from Thassa's gaze. For the first time in his life, he wishes he had a cell phone. He jogs to the Roosevelt stop, waits for a train, and rides it back up to Logan Square. He calls her latest number, which he's surprised to find he has memorized. No one answers, of course, and there is no voice mail.

∞

Schiff called Thomas Kurton from the concourse at O'Hare. Garrett sat in the scoop chair next to her, eavesdropping.

"I figured I'd hear from you," Kurton said, before she could identify herself. "Did you call to gloat?"

"Is it true?" she asked.

"I'm wondering if I'm really your best go-to person for that question."

"Someone is trying to auction her gametes? I thought it was illegal to bid on body parts."

He chuckled without mirth. "Thousands of coeds are paying their way through school by 'donating.' It's a bazaar, online. One hundred and fifty ads a day on Craigslist. The question is: What's a fair market price, for someone with her genetic profile?"

"What's the going rate?"

"Up to $10,000, if you're 1300 or higher on the SAT."

Lots more, apparently, for off-the-chart scores in well-being.

"But are these bids coming from commercial scientists, or just . . ."

"Just rich, infertile couples running their own experiments?"

She could hear the water kneading the rocks and the wind slipping through the evergreens.

"I can think of no use of her sex cells that is both scientifically legitimate and legal. This year, that is. But put them in the freezer for a while—"

"Where are you?" she asked. If he were within shooting distance of LaGuardia, they could get him in front of a camera that evening, while this wistful, penitent mood still ran him. Science. Real science.

"Front porch. I've been holing up here all week. I answered when I saw it was you. Tell me, Tonia. Should I have predicted this?"

She was merciful and did not quote back any of a dozen incriminating things he'd said to her on camera. She only wished she had a recorder running now.

He said, "You know, I'm sorry if this complicates the woman's life. But choices are coming that we all simply have to hammer out."

Paradise, his voice maintained, was still just down the road. And to bring it about, even suffering was a civic duty.

Then Thomas Kurton's tone turned, tilted by some small change in the quality of light. "I heard from a colleague at MIT who has been looking over her fMRIs. He thinks there might be something distinctive about the way her hemispheres are communicating. It might help explain . . ."

Tonia Schiff gestured madly in the air to Garrett—a computer, a pad of paper, a wiretap, anything. "I don't understand. Something structural, or just something she's learned to . . . ?"

Kurton started to come alive again. "That's not entirely clear. A good team needs to take a closer look."

Say that the six thousand years of writing are a six-hundred-page novel, suitable for getting you through the longest captive flight. Romance, mystery, thriller: a little something for everyone. At a decade a page, it's a slow starter. Only belatedly does the opening hook—secret marks that hurl meaning magically through time and space—reveal itself to be a Trojan horse. By page 200, memory is embalmed beyond recognition, lamented only when anyone still notices it's gone. If a thing isn't written down, you can forget about it. The rest is history.

The plot starts to pick up on page 350. After a ridiculously long exposition, the development section starts at last. Characters emerge, cities clashing in the freshness of youth, driven by the varied needs of their patron gods. Wars spread and trade expands. The characters harden and age. They join together into sprawling clans. Freed from the present, papyrus starts to spawn new subplots. By page 400, the basic conflict becomes clear: preservers against revisers, sufficers against maximizers, those who think the book is coming apart versus those who think it's coming together.

There are a few longueurs for some readers in the middle two-thirds. But this is when the story is at its most desperate: when techne and sophia are still kin, when the distant climax is still ambiguous, the outcome a dead heat between salvation and ruin.

Page 575 starts a series of quick reveals (although each one fore-shadowed, early on). Every discovery triggers two more. The cast of characters explodes, as do the sudden reverses. The book makes one of those massive finish-line sprints—twenty-five pages to wrap up all the lingering plot points and force a denouement. The last chapter is filled with deus ex machinas, and on the very final page, the very last paragraph, the characters throw off the limits of the Story So Far and complete their revolt. The ultimate sentence is a direct quote— "Author, we're outta here"—the happy ending of the race's own making.

∞

Russell and Candace are clearing the table for Gabe's choice of evening off-line methadone—Monsters and Mutants: Personal Edition—when she arrives. They all know it's her, just from the rhythm of the buzzer. Candace implores Russell with a look, as if they might pretend that no one's home. But all the lights are on, jazz piano trickles out through the windows, and where else would they be, on a work night, after dinner?

Gabe bounds up and presses the intercom. A homunculus voice comes through the tiny speaker, "Jibreel, Jibreel. *As-Salaamu 'Alaykum.*"

The boy practically shouts back "*Wa 'Alaykum As-Salaam,*" and buzzes her in, in triumph. He's scolding the woman by the time she reaches the top of the stairs. "I thought you decided we were scum or something."

Her hands run through the boy's hair, and he abides them. Her limbs move through a thicker liquid than air. "Jibreel, life has been teaching me."

Stone holds back in the dining room, trying not to look relieved. He stands between the two women, hands in pockets, facing neither.

"Are you all right?" It must be all right to ask. An awful freedom infuses him, like that day at sixteen when he came home and told both parents he was agnostic. His father went to his grave neither forgiving nor believing him.

Thassa's eyes close and her chin rises and falls. Her face is primal acquiescence. "I am," she says, with a peace bordering on irony. She opens her eyes and fixes Candace, timidly. "I'm so sorry to stop in. I am living without a plan these days. My friends are . . . moving me around the city."

She steps forward and kisses both adults, four face-sides in all. Candace is hospitality itself. She gestures for Thassa to sit, which the Algerian does, as if the tiny dining room is sanctuary.

"Tea?" Candace offers. "Something herbal?" It scares Stone, how easy she is. "Gabe, if you want to put in ten minutes on the machine, you can."

Pleasure ambushes the boy from all sides. "Can she come?"

"Maybe in a little bit, bird."

Thassa nods, and he speeds off in a rapture. As soon as he disappears, the Kabyle announces, "I think I must sell these eggs of mine."

She takes the couple's shock for disapproval.

"Don't hate me. The top offering is now $32,000, American. I know: this is insanity. But I could give half to my brother. Five times what he earns in one year! He could quit his killing job and find a good one. And half for my uncle and aunt, to pay on my student loans."

"You can't," Stone says. He recoils at his own voice.

"Apparently you can, in this country. Our friend Sue Weston has done it twice, up in Evanston."

"No," Stone says. "I mean, you can't do it to yourself."

The woman turns to him, pleading. She claps the table with one palm. "Russell, what is the difference? You told me yourself you don't believe my genes are the key to anything. So if some crazy person wants to pay for hallucinations, is it my job to stop them? The more they pay for this, the happier it will make them. And that is the product they want to buy, anyway!"

The argument repels him. He can't believe she's making it. "You can't sell your own offspring."

Her face crumples in pure bewilderment. "My *what*? You say these eggs . . . ? So you do think these genes are the secret real me!"

Thassa turns to Candace. Stone is mortified to see his girlfriend stand motionless between the table and wall, clutching her elbows. Then Weld comes out of her clinical coma and sits down across from Thassa. A dozen years of classes, research, and professional training have all prepared the counselor for this moment. Candace speaks, and for a moment, her voice drives all the madness from the room.

She explains her compromised position, the protocols of her profession, and the decision her superiors have taken on her behalf. It stuns Stone: the woman is a model of maturity, matter-of-fact, even-keeled. For a moment he thinks: Yes, this is what they should have done months ago. Just the sound of Candace's voice shows the way back to port.

She stands, goes into her study, and returns with a glossy pamphlet. "This explains everything you need to know about the consultation facilities available to you. Here are the numbers of people you can call. This woman is very good; she can refer you to a reproductive medical counselor."

"But I want to talk to *you*, Candace."

Candace nods, in complete agreement. "I can't help you anymore, sweetie."

The Algerian sits blinking as at the news of some FIS attack. "Candace? You're sending me away?"

Weld touches her arm, rubs it. Open and honest. "You know how I will always feel about you."

The words explain everything. The words are gibberish. Thassa looks to Stone to interpret. Stone stares at the pamphlet in her hands, unable to remember even what he's doing there.

Thassa looks back and forth between them, insight blossoming. "If this is what you've chosen, Candace, I'm sure it's the right thing. I'm sure it's best. But I think I should go now."

She backs toward the door. Candace steps forward to embrace her, but Thassa holds up one palm. She's down the stairs at a trot before either adult can say anything.

Candace sits, passing her quaking fingers over her eyes. Stone takes awhile to realize that she's crying, those blank tears that might as easily have been made by biking into a cold wind. He wants to step forward and place his arm on her frozen shoulders. He wants to chase down the stairs and find Thassa, tell her that nothing is as it seems. Candace rises and begins putting away dinner dishes. Stone is still standing on his tiny, germ-free island when Gabe comes back into the room.

The boy is crushed. "She left? Where'd she go? She said she was going to play. She lied!"

Stone looks to Candace, who pauses in her chores. Her voice comes out more trebly than her child's: "I think it went pretty well. How about you?"

PART FIVE

NO MORE THAN GOD

No hay extensión como la que vivimos.
(No place is bigger than where we live.)

—Pablo Neruda, "Soneto XCII," *Cien sonetos de amor*

She'll rise early, before the sun, and for a moment won't know where she is. She won't even be sure of *who*. Then the hotel room, her notebook, her computer, the view of a mountain town from a window in western Tunisia, and Tonia Schiff will rematerialize.

The hotel breakfast: a coffee the consistency of clay slip, a baguette, and jam made from a biblical-tasting fruit she can't identify. After breakfast, Schiff wanders out into a day that's like a thousand-watt bulb mounted inside an inverted cobalt bowl. She carries a tiny digital video camera. It's not her first instrument of choice, but it's light, practical, and sharp enough to give an authentic vérité edge to the pilgrimage. She films everything she sees. She remembers Thassa's pronouncement: all existence becomes a prize again, through a viewfinder.

She climbs and plunges down the steep streets, through a suq that has seen better centuries, the best of the morning's produce already gone, the knickknacks tawdry, the vendors calling to her to free up her purse a little for once in her life. She navigates by guidebook up to the Casbah, just to shoot the town's panorama. There she prowls around La Basilique, documenting the building's changes in ownership: fourth-century grain storage turned Byzantine church turned mosque, recently returned to a Roman ruin. History is just fluctuations in appetite. Technology changes nothing. Someone, somewhere, sometime will auction off every inclination. When we tire of happiness, someone will make a market in useful despair.

She films the tiny courtyard, lingering on the Latin tablets and tomb inscriptions. She tries to decipher the inflections and conjugations, the ordered grammar of a dead language she learned in a Brussels high school, forgot all up and down the Atlantic seaboard, and revives now in this flyspeck town on the edge of the old empire, as vendors in the nearby streets call out fruit and vegetable names in Arabic. No place like home. Glued to one pillar is a worn poster for a local band, Rien à Dyr.

Tonia will spend an hour in the church, until an attendant asks her to stop filming. When she rolls out again, the comic-book sky will have tilted toward turquoise. She tracks through the half-excavated Roman baths alongside the spring that has kept the town alive for millennia. She strolls back to the esplanade—pristine, wide, and beautiful—through the heart of the old town that Bourguiba bulldozed in the sixties, in a ruthless improvement to touristic spec. Even this, she preserves in digital video.

On toward noon, she turns down a side alley and is stunned to find herself back near her hotel. She has gotten so twisted around in the maze of streets that for a minute, she can't shake the feeling that there are two hotels, twin squares absolutely identical, parallel universes occupying identical colonial quartiers on opposite ends of the same hillside town.

She runs back up to her room and gets the two books that she has toted with her all the way from the States. She slips them into her shoulder bag. Her cheap attempt at emotional blackmail: gifts from the irrecoverable past. Secrets of the personal genome.

She debates whether to risk bringing the video camera. She has promised no film, no recording of any kind—absolute concessions required to get the interview at all. But she has banked this whole visit on a change of heart, a softening, once they begin to talk. She has come all this way, at greater expense than the project's budget allows, in the hopes that she can elicit what no one in two years has been able to obtain. But any chance she has will vanish, if she angers her subject. Fortunately, the camera is no bigger than a family Bible. She drops it into her bag alongside the two books, where it discreetly disappears. She locks her room and trots down two flights of stairs, back into the blazing day.

She wanted to meet in Algiers, of course. Better yet, Bône, Sétif—anyplace in Kabylia. But two months ago, an unnamed terrorist group attached a bomb to the undercarriage of a personnel carrier near the Hassi Messaoud oil field in east-central Algeria, killing nineteen people and wounding twelve. The attack would have been routine, in a country that suffers such strikes as often as North America suffers sports championships. But among the dead this time were three U.S. "advisers," all of them in uniform.

Schiff didn't even know her country had military personnel in Algeria. Nor did most of the world, gauging from the fallout on six continents. The State Department immediately issued a travel ban, and the chance of a visa vanished into fiction. A town just over the Tunisian border is as close as she will get—a compromise solution with narrative possibilities all its own.

Schiff will find herself sitting in the designated café, forty-five minutes early. She has no trouble finding the place. *The Café de la Liberté, just behind the Association de Sauvegarde de la Médina.* She has checked it on maps for a week. She made sure it was truly there, earlier that morning. *You're a Western woman; no one will trouble you.*

She has been denied further phone contact on the thinnest of fatalisms. "I will be there, Ms. Schiff. And if I'm not, a phone won't help. We both just have to trust." Schiff sits nursing what is surely the worst tea she has ever encountered anywhere in the world, served in a beautiful enameled glass. The liquid has been repeatedly boiled down to something the consistency and sweetness of a hot Popsicle, served with a jaunty sprig of mint on top. She wants to film it, but she's afraid to take the DV camera out of the bag. Every ten minutes a waiter turns up to scowl at her for being a single woman sitting in a café, for thinking taboo thoughts, and for not making any more headway on the innocuous beverage. But Tonia has bought her right to sit in silence, and no one shoos her away.

She sits and does what she's done now for three days: reads Thassa's beaten-up copy of *Make Your Writing Come Alive*. At 12:48 local time, she opens it and points to a passage at random, divining by scripture. Harmon says:

Everywhere in the world, for almost all of human history, most people would have mocked the thought that a person might beat fate.

Several lifetimes later, at 12:53, she goes to the well again:

Some characters seem to be born with a blazing red X on their forehead.

The author seems to be getting shrewder, the longer that Schiff spends away from home. At 12:57, Harmon decides:

> The great paradox of existence may be that only the dead certainty of losing everything makes anything at all worth keeping.

She can't decide whether this is profound or portentous common-place. All she knows is that the author isn't helping her nerves. She periscopes the streets, jerking in recognition at every moving figure of approximately the right size and age. She goes on checking her watch every forty seconds until five minutes after the appointed hour. The whole idea is absurd: two people on opposite sides of the planet arranging to meet at a café on the edge of nowhere, at exactly 1:00 p.m. local time on a Thursday afternoon at the end of the age of chance.

The midday muezzins sing longingly to her, promises scattered evenly around the horizon. Long after all the root causes of such needs have been found and addressed, people will still answer the nomadic call to prayer. For centuries after the transgenics have pulled up stakes and gone elsewhere, many will still seek the cure this world cannot give.

At exactly 1:20, Schiff comes to the conclusion that she's been stood up. She has blown a week out of her life, spent $3,000, and jour-neyed 5,000 miles just to sit in a café and sip the most cloying tea known to mankind. Her film will never get made. No chance to redeem herself. The race will blunder into the age of choice without so much as a proxy vote from her.

She'll flip open Harmon again, but she won't like the passage she lands on. She'll try again, and once more after that—as many times as I say—until she hits upon a divination destined for her:

> A great amount of ink has been spilled in the belief that when every other peace fails us, we still have words.

She'll look up from the page, trying to decide if the words give her any consolation to write home about. And there, working toward her down the sloping street, still two hundred meters away, will be the leisurely, reconciled, unmistakable silhouette of the figure she has come halfway around the world to learn from.

∞

Kurton descends from his coastal cabin and returns to work. His first public act is an injunction against the Houston clinic that wins the bidding for a dozen of Thassa's sex cells. News of a deal has spread like a contagion from biotech newsletters to tacky bio sites: the happiness woman has signed away her eggs for $32,000.

Kurton files to stop the deal. His argument is simple, and similar to those upheld for decades in America's courts. Whatever they mean to use the eggs for, this clinic is buying a genome whose increased bio-value results directly from the association studies performed by Truecyte. Truecyte's intellectual efforts have established a correlation, and the company has filed for the appropriate patents. So if this fertility clinic means to profit from the probability of increased emotional health inherent in Thassadit Amzwar's genome, then they owe Truecyte a licensing fee.

Journalists of every stripe converge on Kurton, and he talks to all of them. "We've done the research," he tells a prominent op-ed commentator, for a wire-syndicated piece called "Fixing the Price of Delight": "And we've determined $800 million to be a fair pro rata evaluation of the accumulated future benefits of our finding, as enjoyed by all its direct descendants into the indefinite future . . ."

In short, a nuisance suit, but one whose motives baffle all commentators. Thomas Kurton, who has long taken a beating for hustling humanity into the consumer-genomics era, is now hammered in scores of blogs for gratuitously impeding a free-market transaction and asserting ownership over a woman's genes.

Several posses of self-deputizing reporters descend on the Houston clinic for comment. Dr. Sidney Green, the facility's director, declares that his staff will carry on with their collection of the woman's gametes unless restrained by a court of law.

As the public furor spins out, the wheels of justice fail to find traction. Legal analysts split between those who see this case as no different from a routine egg donation and those who feel that denying Truecyte compensation would reverse three decades of intellectual-property rulings. Uphold the claim, and everyone might soon be paying licensing fees to procreate. Throw it out, and billions of dollars of bio-economic property rights will go up in pollen dust.

An Episcopalian priest turned bioethicist who teaches at Illinois Institute of Technology goes on Chicago talk radio to try to slow down "this terrible and dehumanizing drift toward the trade in human traits." He points out that successful donation can happen fairly efficiently these days, and if the extracted things get fertilized and turned into embryos soon after collection, no amount of law short of slaughter of the innocents will be able to reverse that step. But the judge in the Truecyte filing refuses to be hurried.

The alarmed congressman from Illinois's Seventh Congressional District makes a speech on Capitol Hill. It's really just a long-planned attack on the use of paid studies in the pharmaceutical industry. But the congressman works in a reference to the "joy genome" controversy in his home district, playing to his constituency while insisting on the need to rein in the bio-economy.

In all the noise, Jen falls badly in the eyes of those millions who so recently took her to their hearts. As far as the vocal majority is concerned, she's become something sinister. Sure, lots of people take money for their potential offspring, but few agree to take *so much*. How could this shining woman, the standard-bearer of bodily happiness, put such a price tag on her gift? She should place it in the public domain.

Thassa's egg contract makes her fair game for every kind of Web-disinhibited public attack. She turns pariah in several demographic sectors, especially among the adoring teenage girls who aped her *Oona* appearance just a few news cycles ago. A West Coast techno band writes her into a biting song, which ultimately goes on to make ten times more money than Houston wants to pay Thassa for her eggs.

Pastor Mike Burns, from the South Barrington megachurch, preaches a much e-mailed sermon in which he distances himself from his earlier proclamations about Thassadit Amzwar. "God may send us many messages, but we make our own errors in translation. Thank God He's always ready to forgive!"

A great national debate ensues on whether feeling happy is the same as being happy, and over the ways in which earned happiness differs from happiness purchased by one's parents at birth. This debate plays out on sitcoms everywhere.

The Economist runs an experimental, Java-based decision market program that allows people to bid on the actual price—somewhere between $32,000 and $800 million—that a tenfold increase in the odds of inheriting an unshakably happy disposition should fetch on the open market. The running average closes in asymptotically on $740,000, which is, coincidentally, close to the lifetime cost of chronic, nonresponsive bipolar disorder.

A giant international reality-show production company called Endemic successfully markets the idea of a sudden-death competition pitting gangs of potential sperm donors against one another for the honor of fertilizing a single woman, who must eliminate them on the basis of their genotypes until only one remains. The company tells the skeptical press that the concept was in development long before Thassa's egg auction went public.

Three writers from National Lampoon, Inc. (AMEX: NLN) start a humor site called killthesmileyarabchick.com. It spawns several more violent imitations.

Throughout, Thomas Kurton goes on giving his careful, scientific opinion on every question that anyone places in front of him. He does one final television interview with Tonia Schiff, for her genomic-happiness episode. They sit on a bench in the Boston Common, twenty yards from where Ralph Waldo Emerson turned into a transparent eyeball and saw all the currents of the Universal Being circulating through him. On film, Kurton struggles to remain game, but he comes across as stoic at best.

> I frankly don't understand most of this reaction. Mass psychology is too hard for me. Genomics is trivial, compared to sociology.

Tonia Schiff seems almost indignant. She asks whether Truecyte can honestly demand a licensing fee on an unmodified human genome. He replies:

> We're licensing the laborious and expensive discovery that a particular combination of alleles increases the probability of a particularly desirable health benefit. If you want to keep encouraging innovation, you have to reward that.

She asks him why Truecyte, a for-profit venture, has undercut their own business interests by demanding a fee that no potential client could pay. He replies that many human institutions have paid much larger sums for much smaller return. She can't flush him out of hiding. When she goads him into predicting how large the genomic-happiness industry might be in ten years, he responds with all the resignation of a Tibetan monk.

> If a reasonably alert person wants to be exhilarated, she just has to read a little evolution. Think of it: a Jupiter flyby, emerging out of nothing. A few slavish chemicals producing damn near omnipotent brains . . . That discovery is better than any drug, any luxury commodity, or any religion. Science should be enough to make any person endlessly well. Why do we need happiness when we can have knowing?

When she suggests that very few people are temperamentally capable of sharing his vision, he bites out his words.

> Listen: Six hundred generations ago, we were scratching on the walls of caves. Now we're sequencing genomes. Three billion years of accident is about to become something truly meaningful. If that doesn't inspire us, we don't deserve to survive ourselves.

When the camera stops, journalist and subject say goodbye without so much as shaking hands.

∞

Saint Augustine, the old Berber, once wrote, *Factus est Deus homo ut homo fieret Deus*: God became man so that man might become God. He also said, even more popularly, *Dilige et quod vis fac*: Love, and do as you wish. But that was before our abilities so far outstripped our love.

∞

Oona decides on a follow-up show long before the demands for one start swelling. Dr. Sidney Green, afraid of the legal repercussions of anything he might say in public, hedges until his accountants run spreadsheets on all the possible scenarios and his lawyers devise an unbeatable game plan. Thomas Kurton is ready in a heartbeat for a second chance.

But when Oona's people try to contact Thassadit Amzwar, they discover what the wired world has known for two days: Jen has gone missing. She can't be raised by any medium. A continuous vigil outside her Mesquakie dorm attests that nothing remotely resembling a five-foot-one North African woman has come anywhere near the building. The bandwidth swarms with so many flavors of rumor that the police begin to make inquiries. The school has no idea of her whereabouts. Kurton swears he's had no communication with her since their joint TV appearance. No one comes forward with any further information.

The police find the record of the now ancient attempted rape. They contact her erstwhile teacher, who, like the law-abiding, civilization-committed idiot he is, surrenders the e-mail from Charlotte Hullinger. Princess Heavy, savvier child of the future age, lies through her teeth to the authorities. She admits that a few of Thassa's friends were, for a while, moving her around from apartment to apartment. But Charlotte claims that no one has seen or heard from Thassa for weeks.

The truth is, the genetic destiny of the race is holed up in Adam Tovar's vacant apartment in Pilsen. Adam is off cruising with Somali pirate friends that he has stayed in touch with since their brief introduction the summer before. Thassa stays in the two-room apartment all day long, afraid of stepping out and being recognized. The apartment is a sweatbox, but the heat pleases Thassa, triggering primal memories.

For hours, she points her camera out Adam's fifth-story window, toward Eighteenth Street, filming the Mexican shoppers passing in front of the once Bohemian and Polish neo-baroque buildings. Then she loads her clips into the editing software on her notebook, using her graphics tablet to paint over and animate them. As imprisonments go, this one is omnipotent. Sometimes she uses Adam's Internet connection to go online and see what the world is saying about her. She finds the website that says she should be killed. She begins to see why some people might want that.

At night she has her books. She memorizes long Tamazight lyric poems from out of her beloved leather-bound anthology. These she performs out loud, in the apartment's front room, as if for a gathered audience. In bed, she makes herself drowsy by reading Frederick P. Harmon. She falls asleep thinking of all the ways that a creative narrator might rescue her from nonfiction. She's sustained only by knowing that the public must eventually grow bored, forget about her, and go on to the next story.

Her friends bring her food, supplies, and DVDs. Sue, Charlotte, and even Mason take their turns in the rotation. Roberto drives her to the North Side facility that monitors her for the Houston clinic.

From Invisiboy Sims, she asks more heroic services. She has been fine injecting herself with the first round of fertility hormones. But now the follow-up must be administered via a vastly larger needle. "I just can't anymore," she tells Kiyoshi. "I need your help."

He tries to negotiate. He asks if he can just jab her through her skirt. It's not possible, she tells the terrified apprentice. "You have to swab the area first."

∞

In a Midtown production studio, the *Over the Limit* crew gathered in a screening room to watch the rough first pass of the episode called "The Cooking of Joy." A stiff dose of hormonal excitement passed through the assembled group, the anticipation that always came with a hot episode. Nothing in all of life could match work that tapped into the moment.

Schiff slipped into a second-row seat next to Kenny Keyes and Nick Garrett, just behind Pete Vitale, the segment's director. Keyes and Garrett brayed at each other, even louder than usual. "You know," Keyes said, "if I die just before all this crap gets implemented, I'm going to be supremely pissed. Can you imagine? Being the last generation to suffer from stupid, pointless misery."

"Christ," Garrett said. "One hundred and fifty billion people just like you have lived and died. You've had it better than any of them."

"I see," Kenny answered bitterly. "So you're one of those glass 99 percent full guys?"

As the lights dimmed, Schiff looked around the room at the full crew—twenty-five men and seven women—a ratio as bad as that of the fields they filmed. The double-X chromosome and scientific aptitude: yet one more hot-button issue of scriptedness that no one would ever be able to think clearly about. It struck Schiff that she'd never get to do a show on the topic. Such issues were, for any foreseeable future, over the limits of acceptable science entertainment.

Tonia always enjoyed the episodes before the music got added—a last chance to grasp the ideas without her viscera being manipulated by sound. But nothing ever protected her from the vague disgust of watching herself play herself on the screen. She did not slink like that; she did not purr like that; she was not that soul of cool, remote hip.

Tonia the viewer battened down to weather this episode's intro. Schiff the on-screen host said, *Why is it that some human beings seem to be born with an extra dose of delight in life?* The off-screen Tonia twisted in her seat. She'd thought it the most simpleminded of all the intros they had filmed; she couldn't believe that Vitale had settled on it. *Some people just seem to shoot straight toward joy, the way an airport dog heads for backpacks full of contraband.*

From there, Schiff's voice-over plunged into the biological basis of bliss. A stunning, swooshy CGI sequence zoomed into the eyes of a deliriously happy woman, tunneling through her optic nerve and into her brain. The view tunneled down by several orders of magnitude, landing in the nucleus of one of her nerve cells. There, in spectacular 3-D, the histone-wound coils of her DNA unzipped and bared their template surfaces to complementary strings of mRNA, which slipped into the ribosomes to be read by fleets of tRNA, each one porting its specified amino acid into the growing folds of a catalytic protein.

The molecular flyby gave Tonia vertigo. She watched the newly minted protein machines spin off the assembly line. As the sequence zoomed out, these catalysts began clamping and unzipping more DNA, igniting new genes, clipping and tamping together more RNA messages. Pulling back steadily by powers of ten, the sequence revealed the feedback loops of transmitters, receptors, and synapses that aggregated in ever-higher networks of neuronal chorus.

Just as Tonia forgot that she was inside an artist's rendering, the animation zoomed out in a whoosh until it snaked back through the eyes of the deliriously happy woman, whose molecules had engineered her into something like the velvet rapture of orgasm.

The on-screen Schiff reappeared and said something clever that the off-screen Tonia tried not to hear. And before Tonia could follow the jump, her filmic alter ego was telling the story of twin boys, one raised in Minneapolis and the other in L.A. The two brothers never met until they were thirty-five, at which point they discovered that they shared a list of identical happiness triggers that included juggling, harmonica music, cedar trees, and the actress Felicity Kendal.

"Amazing," Kenny Keyes said, shaking his head in awe. "That's just killer."

The on-screen Schiff said, *Some researchers believe that the genetic contribution to our gladness thermostat may be as high as 80 percent.*

The off-screen Tonia raised her hand. "Hang on a sec." The film kept rolling. "Something's been cut here. That whole segment about how quickly the hedonic set-point correlation falls off for fraternal twins."

Pete Vitale nodded, on top of the objection. "We were getting several people saying it was complicated. Confusing."

"But it's important," Schiff insisted. "We don't want viewers to think that happiness is hereditary like height is."

"What is it with you and height?" Kenny asked.

Vitale surveyed the group, even as they kept watching the segment. "Show of hands? Those for restoring the complications? Right. We run as is."

By then the show had progressed to interviews with a neuroscientist, a positive psychologist, and Thomas Kurton. Talk of genes involved in extroversion, anxiety, and congeniality led to speculation about the "gladness thermostat." Various predictions about gene-tailored happiness drugs seemed as groundless to Tonia as they had during filming.

By the time the scene with Thassadit Amzwar unfolded, Tonia felt ill. All their clips of the manhandled, displaced Berber had been edited to eliminate any cloud or edge. The woman's increasingly tumbled landscape had been cropped to just the smooth vistas. "This isn't right," Schiff said, without turning around. "We're not doing justice to her. We have to use some of the rockier stuff, too."

"We're trying to tell a story here," Garrett said.

"A story? You mean a fib?" But Schiff's on-screen voice-over drowned Tonia out. *The day may come,* hostess Schiff said, *when we will choose our children as carefully as we now choose our mates. We may select our natures the way we screen for a career.* All the larger, qualifying, problematical follow-up had been clipped away.

The show ended with a rapid-fire, crosscut auction—various people saying how much they would pay for an imperturbably luminous outlook on life. The last face in the accelerating cavalcade was Thomas Kurton's, repeating, *Listen.* The shot pulled back to reveal the man speaking on Schiff's two-inch phone screen. The show host watched as the genomicist intoned again, *Six hundred generations ago, we were scratching on the walls of caves. Now we're sequencing genomes.*

In the last shot, Schiff looked up from the minuscule screen, smiled her crooked smile, and asked the camera, *If we accomplished all of that as frightened, negatively biased, misery-prone creatures, what might we accomplish when genomics takes us . . . over our inborn limits?*

In the cut to black, the few dozen people in the room began to applaud. Pete Vitale craned around from the row in front of Tonia and scanned the reactions. "Yeah? Pretty clean? No major surgery?" He stood and stretched, beaming. "All right. Thanks, all. Off to finishing. Remember: meeting on the transcranial-stimulation script at three. And everyone back here for the cyberwar brainstorming on Friday."

"Pete," Tonia said, and felt herself falling. "Pete. We have some *major* problems here."

The crew kept filing out. Tonia herself barely registered her own objection. Vitale turned to look, sidesaddling away from her.

Tonia tried smiling. "You do realize this is total shit?"

The director stopped and turned, along with Garrett and Keyes.

"The way this has been cut, we are just fanning the unsubstantiated hype. If even one-tenth of this should turn out to be real, then we ought . . . Don't you think we should at least mention the challenges? We're still a science show, right? Don't you think we should restore some of those scenes with all the objecting researchers?"

The cluster of rearguard crew paused in the double doors of the theater at the scent of drama. "Tonia," Garrett said, somewhere between peremptory and resigned.

"We've got Kurton himself having all those second thoughts. And that poor girl—she was ragged, Pete. This whole carnival is making her wretched. You've cut the interview to make her look—"

"It's done, Ton. You heard everyone sign off."

She saw, in clean animation, the assembly lines inside her cells thrown into wartime production. Even as it rose up in her throat, she wanted to know what *caused* this bile. These men she hated? But she'd hated them for years. Her public smackdown and humiliation of a few minutes ago? She wasn't so vain. Some early parental moral inculcation that she'd managed to resist for decades? Late-onset honesty or scruples or guilt or any of a dozen other predispositions lurking inside her haplotype, just waiting like a heart attack or cancer to be pushed over a threshold and expressed full-blown? Why get righteous *now*?

Runaway branching feedback—who knew how? Everything, she decided: everything is caused by nothing short of everything else.

What she found so amusing about the unfolding scene was how well all the performers already knew it, even before she spoke her lines. They'd seen it too often to count, in every packaged narrative they'd ever consumed. They had her revolt pegged, long before she herself had seen it coming. The room filled with a deep, almost respectful compliance, everyone ready to play the parts that had been scored for each of them so long ago.

Pete Vitale asked, from a great way off, "You have problems with this work?"

"Tonia, don't," Garrett warned again.

"It's cool," Kenny said. "Let her blow. She can't be the only one of us who never uncorks."

But even the coffee-bearers and copyboys standing in the doorway already knew this story.

Schiff gave in to the warm, predestined familiarity of it all. "I'm sorry. I'm sorry to be so predict . . . We don't have to labor this. I can just cut to the credits here." She turned and walked up the aisle and through the knot in the doorway, which parted, fascinated, for her.

Behind her, Garrett told Vitale, "You better go save your nest egg."

Vitale called out, "Tonia, come on. Come back. We can recut anything you want."

"Hey: bye-bye, baby," Kenny said. "Who needs her? Bring on the clones." And the last thing she heard as she slipped from the screening room was Keyes asking, "Bitch thinks her face can't be replaced?"

∞

For three crosstown blocks, Tonia Schiff hammers herself for her own long complicity. Five seasons perfecting a voguey pose in the face of anything iridescent. But the future has been feeding on her all along, as sure as any bloodsucker. As sure as she and her collaborators have fed on that ragged woman.

Every twelfth person she passes almost recognizes her. I glimpse her at last, skirting along at a panicked if aimless trot, reflected in five long panes of department-store glass. She glimpses herself—all she has ever tried for, the thing she's wanted to be from birth. Blameless observer. But the blameless can't afford to look. Just looking is already the worst kind of guilt.

She comes up for air again in Times Square. Genes loose, tearing everywhere, splash their riot messages across a horizon of hundred-foot flashing screens. The future floods her with messages. She stops for the light at Eighth, and for a long sixty seconds, she wants to be more than dead.

Chance tries to hand her something, a film she can just dimly begin to see. I want to heckle her, from years away: *Look harder . . .*

She turns uptown. For the next six blocks, she starts to make out the shape of her reparation. She'll assemble the simplest of documentaries, a look at life about to be born. A simple take on things to come, the past's only shot at payback . . . Production should be no problem. Schiff has a track record, fame; funding is hers for the asking.

By the time she hits the park, she's committed. She has a name already: "The Child of Choice." She heads through the Merchants' Gate and cuts up toward the Reservoir, already filming in her head. And a hundred steps into that town-sized open-air ark, she feels suddenly, inexplicably well, ridiculously healthy. She'd almost say free, if she didn't know better.

∞

The long-deliberating judge in *Truecyte v. Future Families Fertility Center, Houston* at last concludes that the fair market value of Thassa's eggs in no way depends upon the discovered association patented by Thomas Kurton, et al. Truecyte is entitled to a reasonable licensing fee for any novel tests or products resulting from their discovery, but they cannot profit from any transactions involving an unaltered, preexisting genome.

The decision is a blow to Truecyte, one that might never have happened without Kurton's provocation. Yet the judgment rocks the biotech industry, shocking the experts in intellectual property law as well as that small fraction of the general public who are still following the case. It calls into question the whole idea of ownable bio-value. Some talking heads declare it the fast track to the future. More say that the choke of potential profit will kill innovation.

Future Families declares it a forward-looking guarantee of social progress. Truecyte instantly files an appeal. Pundits both paid and self-employed conclude that the decision can't possibly stand.

But for now—*this* now—Thassa Amzwar is free to donate her eggs for more money than her brother could earn in years.

∞

Days pass in a short forever. Stone and Weld go on seeing each other. They spend three nights out of seven together. They cook, revising favorite recipes. They talk less and watch more family television. They watch several incredibly dramatic historical re-creations. They watch documentaries about forms of life that should never have survived into the present. Gabe no longer considers either of them a Yahtzee challenge, and he tries to train them in Liar's Dice.

Candace starts Stone on little projects. She teaches him yoga and brings him to the gym for a session on the balance beam. They no longer play the novel-writing game. She no longer brings up work, psychology, will, North Africa, science, French, Arabic, or the future. He is just as careful never to say a thing that could be mistaken for second-guessing.

Their days are stable and respectful, and they could go on un-changed until Stone dies and his genome disappears peacefully from the face of the earth. But when he's home alone, he scours the Web for news. It doesn't feel traitorous. He can't endanger Candace just by looking. His searches turn up hearsay enough to make him all flavors of crazy.

He wakes up in hot darkness, from a vile dream. He was some-thing medical, in a surgical gown, maybe an anesthesiologist, watch-ing while the patient woke up in the middle of having a gelatinous internal organ removed with a coal scoop. He shudders awake, then in-stantly suppresses any movement, lest he wake Candace.

But Candace isn't there. He's in his own bed, his own apartment, by himself. He has confused the chill of solitude with the other kind, again. It's 1:30, but it takes him three entire lifetimes between then and 2:45 before he admits there will be no more sleeping tonight.

He tries reading, old guilty pleasures—love poetry, nineteenth-century behemoth novels, clever contemporary metafiction—but nothing speeds the clock or makes him the least bit drowsy. He's done with breakfast by five. At 8:00 a.m., he starts wandering around the apartment with the phone in his hands. At 9:01, he calls in late to work. Immediately after, he dials Charlotte Hullinger. He gets her voice mail. He hangs up and goes down his old class roster, landing on Sue Weston.

Artgrrl picks up with a sleepy "Hey." He starts to identify himself, but she cuts him off. "I know who it is, Teacherman." Her voice is odd, almost flirtatious. She says, "We were wondering how long it would take you to check in."

"Where is she?" he asks, too quickly.

"Southwest side? She's fine. She's like a week or two away from delivering the goods. Only . . ."

He hears her teeter, trying to decide. Decide if the thing is worth mentioning. Decide if he can be trusted. A twenty-one-year-old, experimenting with wisdom.

"I think the shots are changing her. They can do that, you know. She's different."

Shots. Changing. He's back in the depravity of his dream. "What do you mean, different?"

"Those hormones have her on a roller coaster. I actually saw her cry. She's just like anybody, now."

He wants to ask if he can see her, but he can't. Can't do that to Candace. Can't bear to hear Sue Weston tell him, *She doesn't want that.*

"Give her my best," he tells his former student.

Artgrrl asks, "How good is that?" He doesn't wield the grade book anymore. He never really did.

∞

He creeps to work and spends nine hours making bad prose worse. He calls Candace in the afternoon and asks if they might see each other later, although they aren't scheduled until tomorrow. She's characteristically supportive, and he's at her place before she gets home. He waits on her doorstep; he's still not comfortable with letting himself in.

She greets him with a kiss, apologizing. "I don't have much for

261

dinner. Gabe is at his father's." Stone wonders why people can never call their former spouses by name. He suggests they go out, to a Lebanese place four blocks away. Lebanon: far enough for mutual comfort. Candace perks up at the idea, a chance holiday.

He tells her over the *mezze*. He's been debating all day whether to say anything. But withholding finally seems the bigger betrayal. He says, "I heard from one of my students today." Is it possible for anyone to go through forty-eight hours without inviting someone else to buy a lie? "She was very concerned about Thassa."

Candace folds her arms on the table in front of her. She looks up, bright, game. But she's not about to volunteer a thing.

"She thinks the hormone treatment for the . . . the donation thing might be making Thassa emotionally unstable." He lets the statement hang just long enough for the two of them to die a few times. "Can they do that?"

Her smile doesn't waver, per se. It just turns inward, chastising itself for the foolishness of hope. Of course they had to arrive here, eventually. What self-respecting author would let them escape alive? Weld spreads her palms out flat on the tabletop. "I suppose they can, Russell. It's not really my line. You might see what you find on the Web."

He throws his knife down on his plate. A dime-sized chip shoots off the edge, narrowly skirting her eye. She cries out and shields her face. She drops her hands into her lap, looks down, and composes herself, yoga-style.

He wants to apologize, but his body won't let him. A censorious waiter comes by to swap out the broken plate. They sit silently while order is restored. Then she's all decorum again. It relieves and maddens him, how quickly she recovers.

"Russell, don't hate me. I've worked so hard on this. Since I was two years old I've been a helper. Total facilitator. Absolutely codependent. My first marriage?" She hears the adjective, and flushes a little. But practice powers through embarrassment. "All my life I've defined myself by what I can do for others. I've finally found a way to do that legitimately, without slighting myself or anyone else, with the help of a whole lot of other people to keep me honest. Don't make me backslide. You know I love you."

"Me?" he intones dully. "What about her?"

Her head tilts. "Thassa? *Of course* I love her. What do you think? The whole world loves her. That's the problem here."

Some primal mucus thing seizes his brain, and he can't even have thoughts, let alone speak them.

"Russell. She's beyond my help now. Letting her go is my gift to her. Honoring the work that I've done on myself. Trusting her. Not interfering."

"Your gift? Your *gift* to her?"

"And to myself. To my real clients. The ones I can keep helping, if I can keep this job."

"What if they tell you to stop seeing me? What if I still taught at that hellhole?"

She reaches across the table to stay his buzzing hand. Or contain it, before it throws something else. "You don't. And they won't. Truth is? Thassa doesn't need us. She has more inner strength than any person her age I've ever met. The public is already sick of her. When this is done, she can go back to living her own rich life."

But the truth is in her voice as clear as if she spoke it: Not at Mesquakie. Not in Chicago. Not in this country. He takes his hand away from her and applies it industriously to removing the condensation from his water glass. "It doesn't sicken you, what's happening? This psychosis over the . . . eggs?"

She nods, infinitely patient. She closes her eyes in admission. Her understanding disgusts him. "I hate that this is happening. It makes me very sad. I hate myself for not fighting it. But this is the life I have to live in."

The words sound to Stone like some kind of pop-psych Serenity Prayer. Yet screaming at her would be insane. Everything he values — even his bedrock fidelity — is as arbitrary as any sequence of nucleotides. How valuable can fidelity be, anyway, if it isn't viable? Candace is more fit for the future than he will ever be. She must be right about all of this. About everything except the only thing: Thassa does need them.

After dinner, they walk ad hoc back toward her apartment. Candace chatters about a beautiful book she's reading, in which a contemporary man falls in love with a nineteenth-century woman on the basis of the comments she has scrawled in the margins of several books. Stone freezes at the top of her street.

"You know, I should probably go home."

Something spasms across her face and is gone in a heartbeat.

"I'm about three weeks behind at the magazine. Also, I didn't sleep that well last night."

She's nodding sympathetically before he even finishes explaining. "Of course, of course. I didn't think I'd see you until . . . What a treat!" She kisses him full on and squeezes his ribs until he gasps. He smiles apologetically, breaks free, waves, then turns back toward the El stop.

But he doesn't go straight to the train. Instead, he wanders down Ridge until he finds a pharmacy. He's nervous going in, ready for someone to stop him and check his motives. He wants to call his brother, Robert, for advice, but of course the only good pay phone is a dead pay phone. He tells himself that if any twelve-year-old in America can do this, so can he. He goes to the sleep-aid aisle and focuses, until he finds a package with a bright-red starburst reading, "Most powerful help with insomnia available without a prescription!" Active ingredient, doxylamine. The high school cashier can't sell the person in front of Stone a bottle of beer, but she can sell Stone the sedative.

"Hi!" She greets Russell hugely. "Are you a member of our Rewards Program?"

He blinks. "You're going to reward me for taking these?"

"You don't have to take them." Her laugh turns timid. "You just have to pay for them."

"And my reward?"

She looks at him the way she might regard a mid-season-replacement show destined to be canceled itself after two episodes. "You get to buy more of them, for less."

He has what he's sure is a billion-dollar idea: a single punch card valid at all the outlets owned by the top multinationals, from maternity hospitals to mortuaries. A huge lump of cash—percentage of your gross lifetime payout—handed back at the finish line.

"I try not to store up my rewards in this world," he tells the cashier.

He's still feeling guilty about the crack long after he gets home. It's the most aggressive thing he's said to any stranger in years.

∞

He's so fatigued he's sure he'll be all right without the doxylamine. In fact, he does fall asleep, but wakes several pages later, in what he thinks must be the middle of the night. It's 10:18. He tosses for a while, until he's sure he has exhausted the possibilities of stoicism. He gets up and takes exactly 50 percent of the recommended dose. He does that three more times, at twenty-minute intervals, until consciousness is just some dim glint in the proto-eye of some bony fish in him, evolving on the cold sea floor of the Carboniferous.

The tear of a fire alarm rips him awake. It's still just half past ten, and his brain works for many cycles before it latches onto the concept of *morning*. His room blazes with sunlight. The fire alarm is his phone. He wonders whatever possessed him to keep the phone by the bed.

He's an hour and a half late for work. The phone must be his old relay-race buddy from high school, the owner of *Becoming You*, calling to fire him. If he ignores the call and gets to the office before the phone stops ringing, he might still be able to save himself.

When his brain consolidates a bit more, it occurs to him that for the last three years he's worked at home twice a week at his discretion. But the thought gives him little peace, and he doesn't understand why, until he realizes the phone is still nagging him.

He picks up and says something with approximately two syllables. The voice on the other end cries out, "Mister! I'm so glad you're alive."

The sound of her voice retrieves his dream: a paragraph in an essay that Thassa had written for him had gotten loose and was infecting all kinds of other printed material with sentences that no one had composed.

"It's you," he says stupidly, himself again.

"Russell. I'm so happy to hear you. Please tell me you don't hate me."

"I don't hate you," he says. Even to himself, he sounds robotic.

"And Candace? Have I made permanent damage with her?"

A voice in his head that sounds like Candace says, *You know I can't speak for her; you'll have to talk to Candace.* But out loud he reverts: "Candace loves you. She told me, just yesterday."

"*Al-hamdulillah.* Thank God!" And the voice at the other end crumples off into a grateful silence. After a bit, she rallies. "Then why won't she talk to me, Russell? Everything has become such an ocean."

Everything has always been mostly ocean. It strikes Stone that a constitutionally happy person in this country is like a New World native at the first touch of smallpox. No antibodies.

"Russell, the news has found me. Another story started spreading this morning. A worse one is going to come out, very soon."

He tries to remember Candace's assurances from the night before. Something about bored people going on to the next thing. Apparently, Candace Weld, LCP, is as deluded by need as anyone.

He hears the frail voice say, "Did you know that total strangers want me dead?" The frailty flashes out in anger. "Russell, I'm fed up with this."

She is entitled.

"Do you remember you once told me, if I had any problems, just ask?"

"Anything," he says, underlining his own word and flanking it with red-pen question marks.

"Are you very busy in your life at the moment?"

He's forgotten exactly what subassembly of the collective human project he is responsible for, or when exactly it might be due. "No," he tells her. "Not very busy . . . at the moment."

"Can you take me home?"

"To Kabylia?" he asks, incredulous.

The word tears a laugh from her. "Not that one. Too far, that one."

She wants him to drive her to Canada.

"I'm so sorry to ask, Russell. But if I don't escape this soon, I'll go mad. You're the only one left who can help. I will pay for the essence and expenses, of course."

When he doesn't answer, her voice grows frantic. "You could be back home again in three or four days."

The word baffles him beyond words. Not *home*; that one has at least some journalistic meaning. But *back* isn't even fiction.

∞

He has never been to Canada.

He hasn't gone on a road trip with anyone since he and Grace visited the Grand Canyon.

He has never missed two days of work in a row.

He has never gone behind the back of anyone he loves.

He has never in his life done anything that anyone else could possibly construe as resolute.

He has, for most of his existence, dismissed the idea that he might author his own life.

He has become an accessory to her destiny, drive or not.

He does have a driver's license and a major credit card.

He has never felt so daunted by his own breathing.

∞

He calls Robert, who talks him through the steps of renting a car. His brother is shocked to hear his plans. "Are you sure? *Canada*, man? It's a parallel universe up there. The queen on the dollar bills. The guaranteed health care. You are aware of the whole French thing?"

Russell rushes to reassure his brother.

"Chill, Roscoe. It's called irony. Supposed to be our generation's native idiom."

There's something weirdly chipper about Robert. Stone asks if he's feeling all right.

"Me? I feel like a million bucks. In 1960 dollars. Don't hate me, bro, but I'm in good shape these days. Law of averages, I guess. If the docs keep waving their arms around at random, eventually they flick on the light switch by mistake."

For a few sentences, Robert becomes a salesman for the American Mental Health Industry.

"Go ahead and do this trip, Roscoe. Niagara Falls with this chick. Whatever. And when the honeymoon is over, we'll get you in to talk to my mechanic. He's got the whole Stone pharmacogenetic profile worked out already."

Russell promises to be in touch as soon as he reaches Montreal or runs into trouble, whichever comes first. "Incidentally," he adds, "you don't have to mention this trip to Mom."

"Of course not. Canada? The matriarch would have a coronary. She still thinks the Blue Jays are a terrorist sleeper cell."

∞

Russell slinks through Pilsen the next morning, scanning the rows of russet apartments in a clownish, chartreuse PT Cruiser. In this part of Chicago, such a car is begging to be rammed. People eye his vehicle as he cowers at the red lights. Every one of them knows he is about to make off with his former student.

Only the implausible staginess of the scene protects Stone. He knows this story: a modernist classic. He's overly familiar with the book, and he's even seen both movie adaptations. If this were his actual life, he would never in a million years be caught dead re-creating it.

He finds a spot just half a block down from the designated building. He stands in the brick foyer and buzzes. A suspicious "Yes?" cuts through the intercom. He says, "Hello?" He can't say her name, or his.

"Yes," she announces. "I'm coming right there." Her once idiomatic English has spent too many weeks immobile in a plaster cast.

He waits furtively in the vestibule until the elevator rattles to ground and a strange figure peeks around the corner. She steps into the lobby carrying two shoulder bags as large as she is. She's wearing sunglasses, a dun-colored scarf, and drab olive sweats designed to be invisible. But there's something else wrong, something he can't make out until she comes through the foyer door and sweeps him up in a desperate, luggage-crushing hug: her hair has been cut harshly and dyed reddish brown.

"My God," he says. "What happened?"

She grabs his arm and tugs him out to the street. "Come on, Mister. We're gone."

He takes the bags and they fumble to the car. He can't stop looking at the transformation. She shifts the sunglasses and pulls the scarf tighter around her face. "Please don't, Russell. You're making me very sad." She perks up a little when she sees the car. "It's fantastic! Totally absurd. Some kind of film *accessoire*." She beams at him, convinced that he's the right man for this job. He puts her bags in back with his, and she climbs into the shotgun seat like they're off on a family outing.

He steers by trial and error out to the southbound Dan Ryan. Beyond that, improvisation. He has picked up a map at the rental agency: everything from Chicago to Nova Scotia on one double-spread sheet. He just assumed Thassa would know the route, but she's hopeless as a navigator. She shrugs at the lack of correspondence between the squiggly green interstate on the page and anything observable in the real world. "This map is total fantasy. Someone just invented it!"

He sees an exit ramp that says Indiana and heads toward it. Chapters later, they're still stopped in a bumper-to-bumper bottleneck somewhere this side of Gary. Thassa fishes across the radio dial, but every station only leaves her more agitated. She knows how to be a refugee, but not a renegade.

She shuts off the radio and turns to him. "Tell me about your childhood, Russell. Did you ever run away from home before?"

The journey of a single mile begins with a thousand regrets.

∞

Man goes fugitive with ambiguous woman: the oldest story in the book. I've written that one myself, hundreds of times, in my sleep. And every time, the story wanted to break away, lose itself, escape altogether its birthright *plot* . . .

∞

On the day that Russell and Thassa make their break for the north, Thomas Kurton walks into a special meeting of the Truecyte board of directors.

He knows these men and women. He handpicked them: good scientists and skillful executives all. But he has small patience for even regular meetings, let alone the extra sessions. The whole purpose of incorporating is to let business free up science to do science. It's not really Kurton's job to keep teaching the adolescent enterprise new ways to stay solvent; that's what the MBAs are for. He does not really care if Truecyte manages to stay in business or not: the point is to discover if it can.

Every company Kurton has founded is a creature let loose in the world. Together, they're part of a longitudinal experiment in determining which forms of human desire are evolutionarily viable. Still, he shows up for the latest Truecyte fire drill, sips at the herbal tea, nibbles at the spreads of fruit, and jokes with his fellow board members, all the while prepared to supply his own blunt opinions about any course corrections the collective organism needs to make.

Peter Weschler, CFO, starts the formal meeting. He calls for two quick presentations—mind-numbing slides by the inner circle meant to reassure the inner circle that the company is fundamentally fit, with no Mendelian diseases. Truecyte has two new products in the pipeline and a small library of licensable processes that may prove instrumental to future genetic research.

But the venture capitalists have threatened to pull the plug and write off Truecyte's rising flood of red. "I'll put it simply," Weschler says. "Two of the top three stakeholders want to know what in hell is going on."

All eyes at the long glass conference table flicker deniably toward Thomas Kurton, who takes some time to realize that he's being reprimanded. When he does come alive, he's sardonic in his own defense. "You know, if this association study has survived the scrutiny of hundreds of hostile competitors over the last few months, it should survive the scrutiny of friendly investors."

"No one is challenging the study," Weschler says.

"It's impeccable science," Thomas says.

Zhang Jung Li, the CEO, says, "This is not really about scientific practice qua science."

"We had to push *you* to get the study out," Weschler reminds Thomas.

Kurton simply can't imagine what the investors have a right to fuss about. Research has tied a genomic network to a high-level behavioral trait. How can such a finding be anything but a gold mine?

"They want," the steady proteomics researcher George Cheung growls, "an explanation of all the recent questionable business decisions and publicity."

Calm falls over Kurton. "I don't see how they can hold us accountable for the media fallout . . ."

Weschler flips through a yellow legal pad. It looks to me, from my distance, weirdly like the pad Stone used to prepare his first day of class. "They want to know why you grandstanded for an $800 million licensing fee and came up empty-handed. They want to know how getting humiliated in court fits into the company business model."

Kurton nods appreciatively. It's the first interesting question posed by the VCs since founding. He himself, after several days of reflection, still has no good public explanation for his action aside from sentimentality.

"I see," he says. "And they won't be satisfied until heads roll."

He means it poetically. But no one at the table speaks a word.

The silence replicates until even Kurton can't fail to read it. "You're not . . . Are you asking me to resign?"

He looks around the table, enlightened at last. If only these hired assassins were bolder, could plunge the knife in with less sheepish chagrin, he might take some pleasure in this scene. He glares at them, grinning: Run your damn cost-benefit analyses. Side with the smart money. But do not apologize for surviving.

No one says anything for way too long. Finally, Zhang Jung Li speaks. "Realistically put, Thomas, we have to get back to more practical research."

What does nature call this? Cannibalism? Parricide? Fatal parasitism? Thomas fights down the urge to say anything; the entire spectrum of available responses feels puerile. He can't keep from smiling; the drama just seems so absurdly conventional, like one of those cheap paperback genres: death by robot insurrection or unstoppable nanotech gray goo. *His* company, straight out of his own . . . what? Loins? Frontal lobes? His own company is transcending him.

He wants to dismiss the lot, as summarily as he appointed them. But his every possible defense is forestalled. He himself saw to that, when he set up the company bylaws. Has made sure that the group desire would not be crippled by his own.

His feet and hands go cold. He's not what he was. He has let some strange idealism blind him. He hasn't even the strength to play himself anymore. The alpha researcher in him falters, and with the stumble comes an almost instant drop in serotonin. So long as he produced the prizes, so long as he was *profitable*, the tribe let him mate with everything in sight. Now, at the first sign of weakness, they launch this inevitable takedown . . .

He remembers the thousand beautiful implications of his association study, and a parent's panic seizes him. The genetic screen for well-being will be shelved in favor of more practical, portable projects. The real work—overcoming the limits of our archaic design—will be crushed underneath this creature that cares less about the nature of things than about feeding and shitting and reproducing and expanding its range.

All life long, he has believed in the one nonarbitrary enterprise, fairer than any politics, truer than any religion, deeper than any artwork: measurement. Double-blind, randomize, and test again: something will circulate, something cold and real and beyond mere desire. Something that can put us inside the atom, outside the solar system. Something that can come to change even its own enabling code . . .

The method is life's magnificence, our one external court of appeal. Koch, Reed, Pasteur—the pantheon of heroes stenciled onto his boyhood ceiling—could have been other names. Often, they *were* other names, not always recorded. Individuals will come and go; the method will leverage them, or find new bodies. Truth can escape all local frailties.

Or so he has always thought. Now, way too late for an intelligent man, he sees: Crucial facts might easily go missing. To be discovered, it hardly suffices that a thing be true.

Yet the beauty of the method is its utter indifference. All life long, Kurton has predicted the upgrade of human life by its evolutionary heirs. It remains the species' unique destiny to preside over the design of its own obsolescence. Thomas's one job now is to show how peacefully a good transhumanist can die.

"I understand," he tells the board, only two of whom meet his eye. And weirdly, he does. He stands, makes the rounds, shakes the hands of his executioners. But already he's working again. For the last several months, since the study was published, he has had in the back of his mind the idea for another project, a whole new experiment for releasing the happiness-gene complex back into the wild and studying it in situ. But the idea is far too rich for any institutional backing. Now he has the time, the liberty, the isolation to run that test. The final freedom of the exiled mind. Every event—especially extinction—can turn to endless new forms most beautiful.

∞

And by a minor coincidence I don't know how to handle any other way, Candace Weld reads the *Time* article about *Truecyte v. Future Families*, late that afternoon. No one has told Weld that she can't read about Thassa in her off hours. She wants to call Russell, just to talk about the decision. She hasn't heard from him since he bolted from her front stoop.

By ring four, she wonders if he's ducking her. His silence has been too long to be anything but choice. By the seventh ring, she's gripping the phone and mouthing, *Pick up, damn it.* Of course he has no voice mail.

She squeezes the Off button and cradles the phone. She spends forty-five minutes cleaning up after Gabe, her time-honored method for regaining emotional control. When she finishes, she goes online and binges horribly, like she hasn't in months. She searches the news pages of the top three engines, sorting by time. She combs the blogs for every occurrence and permutation of "Thassa Amzwar." It stuns her, how much poisonous shit is milling around out there, toxic bacteria doubling and redoubling, dividing and mutating on no food supply whatsoever.

But after ten minutes of scouring, she discovers: there *is* food. A whole, steaming barnyard full of it. An energy source big enough that even the moribund print media start to tap into it. Four Mesquakie art students have announced that the Algerian woman is missing from the apartment where they've been hiding her. And they claim she has been lured away by her former writing teacher.

I watch to see how Candace Weld can respond to this news. But she herself is paralyzed with looking.

∞

For a long time, Chicago refuses to disappear behind them. The city sprawls for a hundred miles, its hinterland industries like freight strewn from a cargo plane. Only the sun proves that the car isn't stuck in an enormous loop.

Just beyond South Bend, Stone has an epiphany. He knows why he could never in his life or anytime thereafter write fiction: he's crushed under the unbearable burden of a plot. He could never survive the responsibility of making something happen. Plot is preposterous: event following event in a chain of clean causes, rising action building to inevitable climax and resolving into meaning. Who could be suckered by that? The classic tension graph is a vicious lie, the negation of a mature grasp of reality. Story is antilife, the brain protecting itself from its only possible finale.

Right around Elkhart, Russell concludes that truth laughs at narrative design. Realism—the whole threadbare patch job of consoling conventions—is like one of those painkillers that gets you addicted without helping anything. In reality, a million things happen all at once for no good reason, until some idiot texting on his cell plows into you on the expressway in northern Indiana. The End. Not exactly *The Great Gatsby*. Sales: zip. Critical reception: total bewilderment. A failed avant-garde experiment. Not even a decent allegory. Even the cutout bin doesn't want it.

Stone shares none of these literary insights with his former pupil. In fact, he studiously avoids talking about anything substantive whatsoever. He just drives as best he can, while Thassa rides shotgun and flips nervously across the AM spectrum. Love Radio and Hate Radio: both only succeed in further agitating her. Every one hundred seconds, she cranes around to look through the back window of the PT Cruiser, as if the assembled posse of human history were coming down the interstate after them, to take tissue samples.

Stone's covert glances suffice to confirm: she has lost her repertoire for defeating anxiety. But then, she has never really had such repertoire. She never needed any; she didn't know what anxiety was. She sits quietly, trying to smile, smoothing her chopped hair. On the outskirts of Toledo, listening to a call-in show on the possibility of opening up a second Security Front, she says, "Tell me the craziness is over, Russell."

He tells her.

She doesn't need to stop to stretch or relieve herself. She needs nothing to eat or drink. She wants only to keep driving. When they do stop for gas outside Sandusky, she won't take more than three steps away from the car.

Stone buys a real map and studies it. He discovers that they should have headed north out of the city toward Flint, to cross over the border at Port Huron. They could still double back, swing up to Detroit and cross to Windsor. But he decides it's too late to do anything but follow the long skirt south of the lakes, toward the crossings another few hundred miles to the east.

He apologizes for lengthening the trip. She pats his shoulder and lays her cheek against it. "Everything is fine," she tells him. "Don't worry. I don't care, if only we're getting closer."

She'll be better when they're farther down the road. She's had more practice at being well than anyone Stone has ever known. If she can't find her center once they're free and clear, then humans have no center honest enough to be worth finding.

Somewhere still in Ohio the radio becomes too much, and Thassa sends the voices into limbo. Silence then is glorious, keeping them alert and safe for a good thirty-five minutes. After another half an hour, even silence adds to the weight of breathing.

Beyond the expressway shoulder, distant descendants of Burma-Shave signs flick past. Thassa reads them out loud, for no reason except to speed another fifteen seconds. "Terrorists love," she murmurs above the wheel noise. "Gun control. An unarmed public. Is their goal."

Her sunglasses rest on top of the unnervingly cropped dyed hair. The scarf is shed, nowhere. She holds her camera on her lap, often lifting and pointing it over the dash or through the passenger window. If she's really filming, all she's getting is desolate Midwest motion blur. She reads through the viewfinder, chasing the tiny white signs with her lens. "Tested in peace. Proven in war. Guns in the home. Even the score."

She reads aloud at odd intervals, for more than an hour. "Two million dead in Darfur Sudan," she tells him. "And it all started with a gun ban."

She looks at him for explanations. He offers none. She says, to the window, "I see why Dr. Kurton wants to upgrade people."

∞

He says, "Tell me about your brother." The question surprises them both. Her vision dimples, and she's off, remembering stories she hasn't told anyone in years. Mohand organizing a World Cup in the streets around the Parc de la Louisiane with boys from eleven different countries. His thinking that Quebec winters weren't fit even for animals. Wanting to become the premier Amazigh Canadian hip-hop artist, practicing for hours in the council apartment's bathroom, driving their aunt and uncle mad. How he planned to make a living as a male model, and how he spent five months' savings on a portfolio of publicity shots that came to nothing. How he blamed all the troubles in his life on having to learn his native language after he already spoke two others. How he left Montreal and returned to Algiers just to prove that his mind hadn't been permanently colonized by two hundred years of nightmare.

Russell needs to know: *Have you told him what's happening to you?* But he doesn't ask. It's enough for now that her tales of Mohand return Thassa a little to herself.

Miles down the road, she takes off her seat belt, ignoring the car's bleating protests. She spins around up on her knees, nestles into the seat back, and films the interstate disappearing behind them. She speaks to the vanishing landscape. "How can I thank you, Mister? You saved me. You were the only one I could call. I was letting them kill me a little, back there."

"I did nothing. I just love you." His militant demurral pops out of him before he hears it. Blood runs uphill into his face, and he wants to red-pen his whole existence.

She swings back down onto the seat, facing him. Weight lifts off her, and for a moment, she's invulnerable again, converting all the world's madness into grateful play. She clasps his right thigh near the knee and shakes it, making him accelerate. "Don't you think I know this thing, Russell Stone? You are a very amusing fellow, sometimes."

It takes another twenty miles for his pulse to return to base rate. She stays aloft for the whole stretch, scribbling into an art notebook, smiling to herself. "Always keep a journal of your day. You never know when you might experience something you want to remember!" How she can work without carsickness is a mystery as profound as the rest of her physiology.

In the jutting nub of Pennsylvania, Thassa pulls a phone from her purse and calls her aunt. Stone can decode nothing except the other-worldly, musical cadence, the switches from French to Arabic. She's relating some story with no emotional tie whatsoever to the nightmare she has just escaped. Stone listens, grateful for every note that sounds like the woman who sat in his classroom last fall, reminding the entire roster that only a fool tries to decide more than God.

If she mentions an estimated arrival in Montreal, it must be on some scale of mountain time that Stone has never experienced. She hangs up without any explanation aside from "Good food waiting for us at home, Mister."

They pass billboards for everything—clothing outlets, telcom packages, medical supplies, fast food and faster drink, starter homes, recreational vehicles, casinos, lottery tickets, psychological counseling, secret surefire investments, teen abstinence, sex-toy warehouses, partnering websites, and cutting-edge prophecy services.

"Give in to the Present," Thassa reads.

"What?" he snaps.

She flinches, then giggles. "It's just a sign, Russell. 'Give in to the Pleasant. Pleasant taste of . . .' "

"Oh," he says. "Of course."

"Avoid hell," she says, her affect falling again. "Repent. Trust Jesus now. Next exit sixty miles."

Somewhere between Fredonia and Angola, New York—in short, smack in the middle of implausible invention—they stop to get more gas. She's edgy again, in the parking lot of the service station. She dons the sunglasses and head scarf before she gets out of the car, as if disguise is just common sense. Maybe she's right. Proliferating pictures of the bliss mutant long ago stole her freedom of movement.

The nineteen-year-old behind the cash register does gawk at her, but only, Stone hopes, the way any young American heterosexual hormonal firestorm from upstate New York would gawk at a twenty-three-year-old Berber in a drab olive sweat suit and bad hair dye.

The map suggests they shoot north at Syracuse and cross at a place called Thousand Islands. Thassa measures the distance with a barrette and calculates the remaining travel time on her fingers. They're halfway home, and if they push, they could pull into Montreal before sunrise. She breathes easier, seeing how close they are to the border. But even an Algerian—especially an Algerian—ought to know this genre.

They pass through archaic resort towns, famous ghost wrecks of American industrial history, collapsed utopian and religious communities. They talk about everything now—her parents' infatuated anger toward the French, his long fascination with the Unabomber, the mythic origin of the Kabyles, a fantastic Egyptian film he saw eleven years ago and has never since been able to identify, an old family car that he and his brother once wrecked, the varied agendas of the world's great cities, the odds of humanity soon cooking to death, a thrush that once threw itself at her bedroom window at ten-second intervals for the better part of two days.

The camera is long since packed away. Thassa needs to keep talking now, about anything at all, so long as it dates back before the last three months. She's like some infected farm animal, brought low by something it can't even imagine. Microbes without borders. Her system struggles to reject this invasion, as it would any alien tissue. His job is to keep talking, to hold up his end of the trivia as if everything will come right again, if they only imagine.

Even now, just riding alongside her helps him recognize himself. If he could drive with her in this car until he learned the habit by heart, the certainty of who he is, equal to the brief, scattered days he's been given . . .

She means more to him now, stunned, than she did when she rode the world.

Pointless tenderness, evolution's ultimate trick. The product of a handful of genes, hitting on strategies to keep themselves in play. A force three billion years in the making, coughing up a thing ridiculously makeshift and erratic, more wasteful than the peacock's tail. Stone tags along behind a caravan of SUVs, tooling north. Maybe even love is just a minor node in a vast network pushing toward new and unimaginable exploits . . .

Candace should be with them. She loves this woman as much as anyone.

∞

In the neck of upstate New York, Thassa falls asleep. She goes slack in her seat, slumping onto Stone's shoulder. There's a burr that sounds like a problem with the engine. Then he places it: she's humming in her sleep. A simple, repetitive tune built on no scale Stone recognizes. He thinks he hears her chant the word *vava* . . . When she wakes ten minutes later, he doesn't ask her what song she was dreaming, and she doesn't volunteer.

They track north along the edge of Lake Ontario. Late afternoon is done and evening layers in. The sun falters, and they've been driving so long that the highway starts to float. They pass through an enfilade of pines flanking the road. They roll down the windows. The dry, cool air plays on their skin and their hearts crack open.

The day is late, and they know each other now in the way that only two people stuck together in a car forever can. "You know," he tells her, his eyes three hundred yards down the road, "it's funny. I think about that old woman all the time. I go through long stretches where I think about her almost every day."

"What old woman, Russell?"

He's shocked that she can't read his mind. "The one you wrote about for your first paper. The one who took forever to climb a few stairs of the Cultural Center."

He feels her studying his profile. She asks, "Why do you think about her?"

He's wondered about this, too, almost as long as he's wondered about the woman. He can't say why, but he can say something. "You did, in two pages, without effort, what I've wanted to do my whole life. You took the simplest, most ordinary thing—something I've rushed past a thousand times a day—and lifted . . . You made her next step the only thing in existence worth worrying about. I think about the woman, whether she's still alive, what she's doing right now, whether she could still make it up those stairs, nine months later."

"No," Thassa says. "She can't."

He turns to look at her. The car hits the right shoulder rumble strip, and he jerks it back into the lane.

"There is no woman," Thassa says.

"I don't . . . There's *what*?"

"You said creative."

He keeps his eye on the median, watching his past revise. "You're saying you made her up?"

She waves to a tinted-window minivan passing them. "I assembled from some separate parts. Things I've seen."

"But the real . . ." He has to stop talking. They pass a mile and a half in silence. She studies the thickets of pine. He does the two breathing exercises that Candace taught him.

A lentil-sized thought at the base of his brain swells to a chickpea. "Your father," he asks, as calm as midnight. "How did he die?"

"You read about it," she answers, just as calmly.

"Yes. I did."

"He was shot," Thassa says. "In the civil war."

"By someone else?" Those two finch-eyed holes in the man's skull . . .

She doesn't confirm. Or deny.

He thinks: the depression gene, just waiting for the right environment to flower. But his own native spinelessness overcomes Stone, and question time is over. They drive for a long time, through no more than a hair's breath, on the map. The flanking pines and spruce fall away to a sunny clearing. He asks, "Has this ever happened to you before?"

She smiles at him, an echo of her smile on the first day of class. "*This?*" That radiance again, hounded by the hungry, clutched by the desperate, reduced by the scientific, dissected by the newshounds, stoned by the religious, bid on by the entrepreneurs, denounced by the disappointed. "*This?* Antecedent, Mister Stone!"

For a moment, he sees her on the night of the ice storm. But he wipes away that memory, a nuisance spiderweb. "Is this the first time you've ever felt yourself coming apart?"

She puts her sunglasses back on. Her fingers rake shaky lines through her colored hair. "Is that what's happening to me?"

∞

They're saved from themselves by the sealike St. Lawrence. They glimpse the islands multiplying on that broad boundary, wooded, still, and sovereign. The spread of highway collapses into a clogged line of vehicles waiting to pass the border check. Under her breath, Thassa half chants a thanksgiving that Stone can't make out.

It dawns on Russell that he's about to cross a national border with an Algerian. The press has been diligent these days with rumors and counter-rumors, factions linked to Al Qaeda, an entity that is itself either a finely tuned worldwide network or a fake post-office box. Stone never even noticed the reports until this woman dragged him into the world. In a minute he'll have to convince an official that he and this woman aren't sworn to the destruction of any major Christian industrial democracies. With luck, the official might be an Oona fan.

The four lanes of traffic lengthen to a dozen vehicles deep. New cars arrive faster than the old ones clear. A jitter on the newswires, maybe, or Canadian retaliation for some American slight. Every third car is routed off to a holding area and searched. If everyone came out of their protective shells to mill around in political confusion, this would be one of those great scenes of collective meltdown from contemporary developing-world fiction.

They pull up to the border guard, whose day has clearly been longer than their own. But Thassa's bright "Hello, *bonjour!*" softens him some. She hands over her Canadian passport, and Stone surrenders his driver's license.

The guard hands back Russell's license. "Passport, please."

Stone laughs, then doesn't. "I'm sorry. I'm an American. We don't . . ."

The guard does his own deep-breathing exercise. He's more or less ready for the system of nation-states to break down, and Stone, the millionth ignorant prince he's had to deal with on this matter, has been put on earth merely to mortify him. "The rules have changed, sir. You can still get *into* Canada with a driver's license. But you need a passport to get back into the States."

"What's happened? Has something happened?"

The man looks at Stone as if he's dropped down from another planet. "Read much?"

"You're kidding. So everybody's a suspect now?"

One glance from the border officer indicates that if Stone speaks another word he will be strip-searched until his skin comes off. Only Thassa's apologetic smile pacifies the official. He gives the American another chance. "You wouldn't happen to be carrying a birth certificate?"

Stone has no option but to proceed to the holding area. He and Thassa get out of the car and review their choices. But choice is exactly what they don't have. Thassa calls her aunt; no one in Montreal can drive the two hundred and fifty kilometers until tomorrow morning. She's ready to sit in the border detention holding center until then.

She sits on a plastic scoop chair inside the grim concrete room, alongside a platoon of the equally lost, under the eyes of two watchful police. She starts to get the shakes. Her hands are like broom bristles, sweeping the air. "Russell, I'm so sorry. I'm making your life miserable."

"You aren't," he says, confirming with lameness.

"I'm making millions of people miserable. Russell? I can't seem to stop that." She curls both arms across her narrow chest and cups her shoulder blades. "Kill the smiling Arab bitch. Dot com."

He takes her by the elbow. "Come on. It's nothing. We'll turn around and find a place for the night. I'll bring you back tomorrow. Your uncle can come down and take you home. Everything will be fine."

"Fine?" she asks. "You think this is still possible?"

"I'm sure," he says. And they walk back to the car.

The motels near the border are full. They find a place on a winding state highway about six miles off the interstate, nestled into the side of a wooded hill. It's a *motor lodge*, one of those wormholes back into the sixties, a place right out of Stone's parents' Ektachrome slides, from when his folks were young and in love and still vacationing, before the kids came along and soured that show.

An elderly desk clerk with a growth the size of a honeydew melon coming out of his neck is using a magnifier to read an enormous volume of Boccaccio illustrated by Rockwell Kent. He's surprised by customers and irritated by the interruption. He holds up the magnifying glass as if to fry them.

"Yes? Can I help you?"

Thassa pushes forward and slips off her sunglasses. "Do you have room for us tonight?"

The man glances down at an ancient ledger grid, the day's blocks more or less empty. "Double?"

Stone freezes. He's on the South Rim, unable to say just how many rooms they need.

"Yes, please," Thassa says, pleading with Stone by clasping his wrist bone. *Do not abandon me tonight.*

The clerk looks up, scrutinizing them. Stone thinks he's going to demand a marriage license. "Queen or two twins?"

Thassa stumbles on the idiom and Stone blurts out, "Two twins, thanks."

They sign in and get a dense metal key. On their way out of the lobby to the room, the desk clerk calls after them, *"Ahlan wa Sahlan."*

I look it up, two years later. It means, *Welcome. You're with kin.*

Thassa stops, slapped by the words. She starts to tear up. *"Yaïchek,"* she calls back, shaky with gratitude. *"Shukran, shukran."*

∞

The room spins and shakes as Stone lies on his bed. Pine trees still whip by in his peripheral vision. His blood sugar is all over the place, casualty of the long road fast followed by a fried-dinner binge. The dingy room, filled with a stale stink when they first checked in, now smells fine, either because they've opened the windows or because he's habituated.

She's in the bathroom, under the shower for close to thirty minutes. At dinner, she was listless. He wants to knock on the door to makes sure she's all right. He's thinking: *Her beautiful essays for me were lies.*

All right: not lies. Invention. What did that make them? Less beautiful? More suspect? Unfair, misleading, personal . . .

Performance, in place of the real. Devices, in place of facts. The events she described were all fabricated from whole cloth. Not what happened: what could have happened. What might have.

Her father was shot, but maybe not by someone else.

Then, a thought that sits him up in bed. Those essays are not her only fiction. She has been authoring something else. How high is her real emotional set point, by nature? How happy is she, *really*? All of that testing, out in Boston, the psychological measurements so carefully correlated with the rigorous gene sequencing: nothing but self-reportage. Even science asked her to tell them a story.

Maybe she has faked a good half of her bliss.

And now, when he most needs time to think, to process the causal chains rippling through his head, she chooses that moment to come out of the bathroom at last. She's in a loose, rose-colored shift that falls to her knees, a towel wrapped around her head. She tries to beam at him, as if she were the same content creature she ever was. Only now, the act exhausts her.

She sits on the end of her own bed, loosens the towel from her head, and squeezes clumps of hair in the roll of terry cloth. "You know, Mister Stone, if this were Algeria, my brother and uncle would have to come here tomorrow morning and kill us both."

A forced laugh escapes her. She tilts her head and begins running a hairbrush through her now red tangles. Her hand moves slowly, as if combing oatmeal. He can see the outline of her tiny breasts through the billow of her shift and looks away.

He thinks of anything but her, listens to anything but that brush wicking through her ruined hair.

She stops dead still. "What is that beeping?"

"What beeping?" he echoes. He sits up, and his bed rustles.

"Shh. Listen. There. That."

He titters, in case she's joking. She isn't. "That? That's a *bird*, Thassa."

Her words come out flushed and wild. "A bird? Oh my God, Russell, you're right. It's a bird. A bird, beeping." Something small hits the floor with a soft thud. The hairbrush. And something larger falls back on the squeaking bed: Thassadit Amzwar. These sounds are followed by another one, even stranger. It starts as almost a whistle, then a low wail turning terrified. Weeks of bombardment, and she breaks.

She tries to turn the keening into words. "Something's happening to me, Russell. I have to get out of this place."

He does not move. He feels himself go weirdly calm. "Tomorrow," he promises. "It will be okay. You'll feel stronger. You should call your uncle now."

"I can't. I just . . . can't." The words are clayey, distorted through a horrible mouth that can't hold its shape.

"That's fine," he tells her. "We'll do it in a little while."

She's hyperventilating. Long, muffled sobs rise up in her. "I'm sorry," she keeps repeating. "I'm sorry. I'm so sorry." And then, would-be businesslike, "I dropped my hairbrush."

She tries to move her arm, to sit up. He recognizes the complete debilitation—the outermost promontory of an outcrop he's visited. If the hairbrush were God's magic talisman for returning the world to Eden, she would not be able to sit up and take it. She's defeated by the future, and a few shots of follicle stimulating hormone.

He raises himself upright but can't move either. He, too, is paralyzed, by a realization all his own. Maybe she doesn't have hyperthymia after all. Maybe it's the other, wilder ride, there all along and undiagnosed, hidden by a mighty effort of will. Only: what is will but what the body allows? If she has been acting up until now, she's an actress of unthinkable natural gifts.

The dread that grips him lasts only half a minute, wiped away by surprise relief. Their problem is over. Her haplotype has no bio-value whatsoever. She's just another garden-variety mood-swinger. The world will finally leave the woman in peace. When this news gets out, it will delay genetic improvement by years. The race will be thrown back on inescapable, everyday, ordinary, glorious, redeeming moodiness.

"Russell? Are they going to come after us?"

"No," he tells her. Something lifts him up bodily, from the inside out. *Happiness.* "No one even knows we're here."

Her torso goes limp and drops back. She can't have plunged often into this abyss. There's too much shock in the fall.

He crosses to her and takes her hand. She reaches up and clamps his forearm like a tourniquet. She fixes her eyes on him. "Stone. *Hajarī.* Am I something you might want? Would you like to just hold me for a little and see what happens?"

The sick thought comes to him before he can stop it: one little relentless sperm hitting home, and the $32,000 harvesting problem would be moot. But the problem is solved already. The minute the public learns just what her genes dispose her toward, the market for her eggs will burst as spectacularly as any speculative bubble.

He sits her up and puts his arm around her shoulder. She turns and grapples herself to his chest. He can feel through her shift the full, bony column of her. Desperate warmth, mistakable for anything. Holding her is like coming home. Returning to the soul's first neighborhood.

"Thassa. You aren't well. We have to take care of you. You'll be back in Montreal tomorrow, and you can start to get better. We just need to ride out tonight. Nothing can hurt you; I'm here."

One of a hundred things he's learned from her. *Assume a virtue, if you have it not.* A little creativity with the facts. Lie, if it keeps you alive.

She grabs on to him like she'll take him down with her. After a while, she breathes a little easier. Her head on his chest nods in agreement. "Yes," she says. "You are right." She pushes away and smooths her face with both palms. "I'll be better soon. I'm a little better already, in fact." She bends down and retrieves her hairbrush. She brings it back into the bathroom. She goes about the room straightening things, although there's nothing to straighten.

The film speed gradually returns to normal. Her simple, wishful recovery floors him. It always takes him days to pick himself up again. Is that kind of force willable, or was she born with *that* as well?

A sound rises like the patience of the sea. He thinks he hears surf. He does, and only on the third breaking wave does he place it: her ringtone. She freezes, as if the device can't hurt her if she doesn't reveal her whereabouts.

"You should answer," he says. "It could be Montreal."

She goes to her bag and extracts the phone. She reads the ID and cries out. "It's Candace."

Russell cringes. His fingers ask for time, recalculating the need to answer.

Thassa monotones, "She wants to tell me to die in hell."

He tries to object, but bungles it. The two of them sit and listen to the surf die out.

For a long time in the close room, he's as crippled as she is. Then he masters himself, on nothing but silent words.

"Can I borrow that?" he asks. She nods, but hasn't the strength to hand him the phone. He has to stand, take it from her lap, and step outside.

∞

The world outside their rented casket floors him. Night is deep and crackling. The air smells of sap, as it must have smelled for millions of years before the first flicker of awareness. He walks down the deserted road, away from the motel's throb, across a grassy slope and into something that might have been a pasture once. He climbs up along a fence under a stand of trees.

Life is beeping everywhere, past naming.

He walks until his pretense of courage feels almost believable. Then he opens the phone, looks at the lit dial, and calls back Candace's number. Nothing happens until he presses a little green receiver icon, a silhouette of a species recently driven extinct by just this kind of device. At the press of that key, all his hopes and fears fly up into geosynchronous orbit and back down again, a lifetime and a few hundred miles to the west.

A woman he once knew picks up and says, "Hello?" Her voice peeks out over sandbags.

"Candace."

"Russell," she says, and the word splits through the middle.

"Listen," he blurts. "This isn't what you think."

"Russell." She's not exactly crying. But the sounds can't find traction in her throat. "It doesn't matter what I think." She talks fast, before he can embarrass himself further. "Where are you? What are you *doing*?"

He falters, but he tells her. There is trust, or there is nothing.

"Yes," she says. "Okay. I figured you'd be together. You're all over the news. The two of you. Your students are saying you've abducted her. She's wanted for questioning. And you're the most famous kidnapping suspect since the guy who stole the Lindbergh baby."

He looks up into the bones of an enormous conifer. For a while, he wonders if he might not reply at all. "She called me," he says. "She asked for my help." He can't even comprehend the public charges. He only needs to explain himself to his mate. "I'm trying to take her home."

"Russell." The name comes sharp and pointed, like a command. "Do you think I didn't figure that?"

Light bobs over the hill to the west. A lone car slips down the road, some Jurassic creature. He draws closer to the fence and crouches in the dark.

"I told them as much," Candace says. "I made a statement."

He can't follow her. "I don't . . . You mean you talked to reporters? About . . . What about your job?"

At last the psychologist chuckles. "Job?"

The thing that clamps his throat must have some use. He just can't imagine what. He sits down on the damp ground. All he can say is, "Thank you."

"Any time," she says. "What else is Welfare for? Besides: I'm getting as famous as the two of you. Up there every hour, on the hour. Not the most flattering clip of me, however. A little puffy-looking."

"Fuck," he whispers. Not a word either heredity or environment allows him. "Don't people have anything real to concern themselves with?"

"Russell, the police are out looking for you. People are phoning in tips. A manhunt. *Headline News* is calling it 'The Pursuit of Happiness.' "

"They'll get us tomorrow," he says. "When I take her back to the border. They'll have our names in the database." It would have happened today, if he'd given them a passport to process. The police will take them both into custody, until all the stories get ironed out. Thassa will be dragged back into the inferno. She'll never get home.

"She's in very bad shape," he says. "I don't know what to do."

"I could come. I could be there by this time tomorrow. It might help." When the two of them get arrested and held for questioning.

Russell leans against his fence post, underneath the trees and turning stars. This is the woman who once counseled him, in the dark: *Close your eyes and write a sentence in the air. Use your left hand. Just one sentence. A simple one.* They silent each other. The stars wheel in place above him. And at the center of the innermost circle, he imagines himself signing the air: *You're already here.*

∞

When he gets back to the room, the TV is blaring. A man wearing a paratrooper baseball cap is carrying on about a dog who took a bullet for him. Thassa is asleep, curled up on her bed. He cuts the volume slowly, then shuts the set off. He lies faceup on his own bed, reading palmistry in the ceiling cracks. He'll tell her tomorrow, at breakfast, if the manhunt doesn't beat him to it. There's been a slight change in plans. No need to call Montreal anymore, he supposes. It would only trade one anxiety for another.

He turns on his side and watches her sleep, across the gap of beds. Her chest moves so slightly that he must almost supply the motion himself. Even now, she amazes him, how she can find such peace, in the middle of her magnetic storm. It seems to Stone, in this moment, a greater gift: not something given; something made.

Today she felt what he has felt, one day out of every thirty. And she'll feel worse tomorrow. She must live now with everyone, in turbulent smashed hope. Despair: the mother of science, father of art, discarder of hypotheses, a thing that wants only to eliminate itself from the pool.

But even now, if given the choice, he'd spare her. He watches the flimsy engine of her lungs, holding out against the whole weight of atmosphere. It doesn't matter what Stone wants, what he believes. The genes of discontentment are loose, and painting the universe. Life's job is to get out of their way.

He gets up, empties his pockets onto the writing desk, slips off his shoes, pulls a long T-shirt out of his bag, and heads into the bathroom. His Dopp kit sits by the side of the sink, wide open. He steps on a small, hard nub: a pill lodges in the sole of his foot. He looks down and sees three others on the floor. One more on the sink counter, next to the open empty containers. Robert's Ativan. Russell's doxylamine. Old Darvons from a wisdom-tooth extraction he was saving for a rainy day. Every remedy his kit has to offer.

He slams back into the other room and crouches at her bedside. He grasps her shoulder and shakes, first briskly, then with real force. She's pliant, but makes no motion of her own. He shouts at her; the rage comes so easily. Her face stays composed, beatific. He tries to stand her upright and walk her on his arm. She will not stiffen into life.

He holds his ear up to her rib cage, his left eye crushed to her right breast. He's sure there's something; there must be something, however far away. Tide in a lake. Her surf ringtone, at the bottom of a deep well.

He holds his finger underneath her nose: the vacuum of deep space.

He scrambles to his feet and heads for the door, the phone, the bathroom faucet, all at once. He hears a voice tell him that he needs to get her to throw up. He can't figure out how he's supposed to do that. He sits down on the floor, shaking, clouded, and adrift. And in that instant of annihilation, art at last overtakes him, and he writes.

He can rescind this. He works his way back to the bed, pauses his hand under her nose again: the slightest, world-battering typhoon.

He hacks a path to the phone on the dresser. He flips it open and dials Emergency. He hears a woman on the other end, trying to slow him and get details. He doesn't have details. The woman asks for an address; he has to scramble outside to read the name of the motel off the marquee. The nurse walks Stone through the steps of clearing the victim's air passages, checking to see if she's vomited up into her trachea. The nurse gives him a few simple commands to perform, which Stone confuses as soon as he hangs up.

He settles in to wait for the paramedics. He sponges Thassa and slaps her, trying to keep her as alert as possible. Once, briefly, her muscles take on a little tension, and he manages to walk her for six steps around the bed before dropping her back down onto it. He goes to the door of the room twenty times, looking for anything faintly resembling flashing lights. All he sees is a laughing couple in their late twenties, vivid as newlyweds, out in the parking lot photographing each other as they make comic faces.

He roots through her bag, looking for contact information, next of kin. A number, a datum, a molecule that will make sense. Some antidote. Something he can act on. The bag has nothing. A packet of sunflower seeds. Keys. A Handycam. The book of Tamazight poems he once saw her press to a window, its sentences filled with petroglyphs from another planet. Her copy of the text from his godforsaken class. No sane reason in the world for Harmon to be here, unless she meant it as his goodbye gift.

No cashier's check for $32,000. No journal. Not a scribbled word.

In the infinite wait, he replays everything. All day long he saw her drowning. Yet he turned his back on her for who knows how long, to make his call. Left her alone in a fetid room with cable TV and all the toxins of the dial. Abandoned her to twenty-four-hour headlines, "The Pursuit of Happiness." She had no antibodies for the dark. No practiced resistance.

He watches her, stretched out peacefully on her bed—almost a sane escape. He bargains, ready to accept anything in science's arsenal. Cloning. Genetic editing. Yes to it all. Anything but this. He prays to something he doesn't believe in, begging that she might already have visited a Chicago clinic and harvested.

He can do nothing for her but revise. And he has time to rework entire world anthologies. In the scene he keeps returning to, all the principals assemble in her hospital room. Aunt and uncle, brother, scientists, legal counsel. The group comes to a decision: posthumous reproduction. Try the whole experiment again, in vivo.

He promises God that if she lives, he'll become another person.

A noise pounds on the air. It descends on the room, slicing and beating. The pulsed assault homes in on Stone until he grasps: the ambulance is airborne.

By the time the helicopter lands in a bare corner of the parking lot, every soul in the remote motel turns out to spectate. The newly-wed couple, now vaguely criminal. An elderly pair in crumpled bathrobes. A four-year-old trying to break from his mother's clutches toward the swinging blades. The motel manager, his finger in a beaten-up volume, his glasses dangling from a lanyard around his neck as he gazes out on the fulfillment of old prophecies.

The paramedics climb from the craft. Stone is out his door, both hands waving. They blow past him in a few steps, a minor obstacle. Everything is uniforms, straps, chrome, electronics, pumps and masks, clipboards and signatures and flashing protocols. Unthinkable capital, thrown at saving a single life.

And as the two med techs strap Thassa into the mobile sling bed, her eyes open. The world gives her nothing to focus on. Her gaze swims at random through the atmosphere, before snagging on Stone. It locks there, even as her bearers port her out the motel room door. Her eyes say, *Why is this happening?* They say, *Forgive me.* They say, *Stone*: Hajari: *Please come with.*

He stands in the parking lot in the cluster of onlookers, watching the helicopter lift back into the air. The metal insect shrinks away until it is nothing but strobing lights against the seamless night, the blink of an awful species that will succeed ours.

∞

The figure strolls down the hill, growing. But for a long time, Tonia Schiff will be unable to tell anything. Mood, health, mental state: impossible to determine. Not until the figure reaches the café will Tonia even be sure it's Thassadit Amzwar.

Greatly changed, of course. How could she not be? She descends deliberately—sure-footed mountain Kabyle. Her head cranes, measuring the shops and crowds and markets all around her. At home in the chaos of this day: that's how Schiff will describe it in her film.

She's in a loose yellow blouse over a long jade skirt. Her hair is scarved; she looks like a fifties fashion photographer stepping from a top-down Chevy. When she comes within singing distance of the table, her face breaks camouflage. But her smile checks now, to see who might be watching. "Miss Schiff. Tonia. Imagine seeing you again. Imagine!"

They hug, as if they've known each other forever. As if they ever knew each other. The waiter descends on them as soon as Thassa sits. He starts in French, but she switches him to Arabic. They talk, an end-of-term quiz that becomes a game show that mutates to a sass match that ends in the waiter's departure in grinning salute.

Schiff sits back, at sea. "What was all that?"

Can there be more amused embarrassment? "Getting coffee. Welcome to the Maghreb."

Maybe Schiff will almost understand: the smaller the transaction, the longer the needed parley. I slow her down, let her come into her film the back way, through the suq of endless negotiation.

Tonia switches to French. The whole point of giving her a Brussels childhood. She asks how things stand, back over the border.

The spirit lifts her hands to her shoulders, searching for words large enough to say what is happening again, *chez nous.* "It's Algeria. When we hit bottom, we keep digging."

But the journalist deserves a more detailed answer, and the Algerian gives her one. She lists the week's death count, says where the attacks occurred, guesses how long the bedlam will likely last this time. She has no hope that her country will escape its inheritance anytime soon. The future has no cure.

"It's nice to escape for a little," Thassa says. "Sane here, in this country." She points to the west. "How long do you suppose that imaginary line through those mountains will make any difference?"

She's a different person in French—broader and more nimble. The ecstasy is gone now, the untouchable buoyancy muted. What's left to take its place can at best be called ease. Yet something in her still seems to Schiff ready to go as exuberant as ever, later in this life. Or early in the next.

Thassa asks about Schiff's trip, but she doesn't quite hear the reply. She's looking across the dusty street, at a shirtless boy sitting on a three-legged stool talking to a yellow bird he pins gently between two fingers.

"How are my friends?" she asks. The words are so mild they hardly seem a question.

It strikes Schiff that she could say anything at all. "They're well, I think."

"Mister Stone? Candace? Did they get married?"

"I think they will."

"Good." Thassa nods to herself. "They must get married. Helping to raise Jibreel could cure Russell."

Schiff follows the other's gaze across the street: an empty stool on a sun-splashed sidewalk. She turns back to Thassa and tells her why she's come.

She tries to describe her film in progress. She starts with the funding, as if the signed donors and secured grants prove the project's pedigree. But as she gives her sales talk, running through the storyboards, she's crushed once again by the gap between bright seed and brute germination.

That gap will kill her, but there's nowhere else to live. She muddles on, hoping that a few choice words might animate the limp thing. Her goal is simple, when it comes down to it: a film about what happens next. The coming age of molecular control, "The Child of Choice" . . .

As Schiff talks, the Algerian comes alive. Play comes back into that face, the kind of light that only art releases. Now Thassa is all questions: How are you shooting it? What gear will you use? Where did you find the archival material? How about hand-drawn compositing?

For a moment, Schiff thinks her pitch might be easier than she ever dreamed. Then Thassa stops cold, on some future memory.

"But why are you making this?"

Schiff reddens and looks about the café for the waiter to rescue her. The one question she prepped for, and still she's worthless. How can she name her late-onset need? "I thought I might figure that out as I go."

Thassa laughs again, tomorrow's child. "Of course. How else?" She looks up at the mountains, resigned to desire. "Of course you must put me in your film. You have my permission. My blessing. Whatever you came to get from me."

Schiff takes the calculated gamble. Her downside risk is next to nothing now. She feels under her chair for her shoulder bag. She reaches in and pulls out the digital-video camera.

The Amzwar smile breaks free, matching North Africa's noon. "Oh, Miss Schiff! You know that's not possible anymore." She's in no way reluctant. In fact, her face is willing, if only film could still record her.

Schiff has long expected the answer, but still she deflates: condemned to nonfiction, no creation allowed. But not quite surrendering yet, she says, "Let me show you something." She flips open the camera's viewer and rewinds several weeks, finding the shot she's after. She hands the device to Thassa.

On the tiny screen, a brown infant girl in a lime jumper takes three speedy all-fours strides, then hoists herself vertical on the leg of a coffee table. She swells with her dazzling triumph over gravity. She squeals in ecstasy and cuts loose, releasing the table leg to tear across the open frontier of carpet. Two steps in, she slams into nothing, comes to a splendidly unplanned stop, and drops seat-first to earth. She sits, stunned by the setback, on the threshold of howling. Instead, she breaks out into gales of untouchable laughter. Her head swivels around the room, already planning her next bone-jarring break into unknown regions.

Thassa studies the shot, her face up close to the three-inch screen. "Mine?" she asks.

Schiff considers the question. Who is anyone's? But even her long pause is already an answer.

The infant scoots off again for another go at the table leg, the world's greatest amusement ride. The camera bobs up for a moment, to shoot the reaction of three adults, laughing in reflected joy. One of the faces is familiar—a Donatello still successfully refuting his sixty years. Thassa's brows pinch in comprehension. She grasps the experiment and nods.

"Are there others? Brothers and sisters?"

"Soon."

"Her father? Her . . . birth mother?"

"No one you know."

Feelings fight for Thassa's face. Anxiety. Bliss. Other related strains. She switches off the device and sets it down.

"Did they rewrite?"

The journalist in Schiff wants to say: Does it matter if they did, this time? They will, in one or another test market, in some country, somewhere, soon. That's a story no story can deflect. Schiff says nothing at all. Chooses to.

"Is she happy?"

At last an easy one. Schiff grins in pain. "Yes." Happy as any new toddler, up on two legs for the first time.

And how long might that last? That question, too, is part of the privately funded study.

Schiff makes to retrieve the camera, but Thassa grabs it back. "One more look? If you don't have to rush anywhere?" She peeks again. Life is out of the crib, and will not be held back by anything so crude as accident.

Thassa keeps rewinding the shot, looking for some denouement. And how does she feel, in the teeth of the evidence? I can't yet see. I look closer, the whole point of having been out anywhere tonight. I look, and try to decide no more than God.

I watch her fondle the camera for a moment, then slide it back across the table to the filmmaker. Just down the hill, back toward the market, a vendor sings out a marvelous sinew of melody. Another, younger voice mimics him, a whole step higher. The song is a sales pitch, something perishable, yogurt or fruit or fresh bread that will keep only until today's end. The contest of tenors crescendos and ascends. The dozen patrons of the café share stoic grins. Thassa pushes back her hair and shakes her head.

"Make your film. Tell everything. Tell them my genes had no cure that this place couldn't break."

They sit in silence for a long time. But the reporter has one more bribe. "Listen! I brought you some things." She dives back in the bag and fetches two small books. She hands them across to the apparition, a last temptation from life and the living.

Thassa takes them, and now her face full-flowers into that girl I first saw one night in a tired classroom in a city on the shores of a sea-sized inland lake. She takes the book of Tamazight poems and opens it on a surge of memory. Her lips tighten on the surprise twist of plot. "Perfect. Bless you. I will take this with me."

She looks past the open page to see the other volume. *"Non. C'est pas vrai!"* She knows this book. *Make Your Writing Come Alive.* She reaches out with her left hand, afraid to touch the thing. She flips the pages at random. Ink annotations fill the margins—eager notes and glosses that now seem like the black box of a plane shot out of the sky.

She looks up, her eyes sparking. All might still be well. *Yes* may yet have the last word, even from across this uncrossable chasm.

"It's not mine," she says. "Give it to Russell. He will need this."

I will need much more. Endless, what I'll need. But I'll take what I'm given, and go from there.

She slips the book back across the space between them. But just as Schiff takes it, the text disappears. Neither woman, I guess, will even flinch. The next to vanish off the table will be the camera, then the poems, leaving only their two half-finished teas, a condiments rack, and a menu.

As the two look on, the menu's French fades. The Arabic follows it into white. So, too, do the sounds from the air around the café, until the only language running through the nearby streets is the one that existed in these parts long before the arrival of writing.

Then the menus and the tea and the condiments dematerialize. Then the filmmaker's bag. Then the filmmaker herself vanishes back into documentary, banished to nonfiction.

And I'm here again, across from the daughter of happiness, as I never will be again, in anything but story. The two of us sit sampling the afternoon's slow changes, this sun under which there can be nothing new. She's still alive, my invented friend, and I can read her, still uncrushed by the collective need for happier endings. All writing is rewriting.

The air here is tinged with new scents, or old ones I'd forgotten. These smells are the reason I've traveled out here, alone. And I am, for once, ready to try on anything the story might permit. What else can I do for her, except defy my type? Happiness, the scientist says, is not a reward for virtue. Happiness *is* the virtue.

She looks across at me. She always knew it would end like this, that I would follow her into this next new place. She smiles and shakes her head, as if to claim once more that fate has no power over anything crucial. Which it never really does, if I could just remember. What we have been is as nothing; what we will be is ever beyond us. But what kind of story would ever end with *us*?

The time for deciding is after you're dead. I have no choice; delight pours out of me. "How *are* you?" I ask. "How do you *feel?*" She answers in all kinds of generous ways. And for a little while, before this small shared joy, too, disappears back into fact, we sit and watch the Atlas go dark.